BLACK MEETS WHITE

Down the numberless alleyways that crossed Wreck City like burst capillaries, Iridium stopped walking and turned around. "You can come out, you know. That Shadow-walking trick hasn't fooled me since we were fourteen years old."

Still the bricks behind her stayed quiet and empty.

"Jet, get your ass out here. I read *The Art of War* in the same unit you did. This is not dampening my morale, or whatever it is you're hoping to accomplish with the Big Scary Shadow Puppet routine."

"You cheated in that unit," Jet said, finally letting herself separate from the shadow of a computerized Dumpster that bore the grinning face of Green Thumb, super-shill for Chicago Consolidated Hauling. The fact that a plant controller was posing for a major polluter made Iridium smile.

"Honey, I cheated at a lot of things. Sun Tzu doesn't actually have a problem with cheating."

Jet flexed her hands. "I do."

"Is that some elective I missed out on?" Iridium muttered. "'How to Sound Like a Cheesy Action Vid'?"

"I didn't come here to talk."

Iridium felt a pang in the air, like a stray draft of cold wind had come off Lake Michigan. Just a moment before they wrapped around her ankles, she saw the shadows running off Jet's form, crawling toward her feet. Creepers, manifestations of Jet's power. Alive.

"Imagine that," said Iridium, creating a strobe that hung in the air above the pair, arcing and spitting. Jet hissed as her goggles irised from the sudden burst of light. With her black cowl, skinsuit, and leather belt and gauntlets, she looked more like a nightmare than anything Iridium saw when she shut her eyes.

Seeing the shadows crawl back to their mistress, Iridium pushed the strobe closer.

"Any other day, I'd love to stay and continue our witty repartee, but right now I've got places to go and corporate slimewads to rob, so I'll be jetting. No pun intended..."

BLACK AND WHITE

JACKIE KESSLER
CAITLIN KITTREDGE

BALLANTINE BOOKS
NEW YORK

FICTION

A Spectra Trade Paperback Original

Copyright © 2009 by Jacqueline H. Kessler and Caitlin Kittredge

Published in the United States by Spectra, an imprint of The Random House Publishing Group, a division of Random House, Inc., New York.

Spectra and the portrayal of a boxed "s" are trademarks of Random House, Inc.

ISBN 978-0-553-38631-8

Cover design: James S. Warren
Cover illustration: Juda Tverski

Printed in the United States of America

www.ballantinebooks.com

BVG 2 4 6 8 9 7 5 3 1

Book design by Steve Kennedy

The authors dedicate this book to the incredible comic book writers and artists who gave us super-heroes . . . and who took them the next step and made them human.

Acknowledgments

JACKIE SAYS...

A standing ovation to Miriam Kriss, the best damn literary agent in the world, and to Anne Groell, editor extraordinaire—thank you! To Caitlin, who constantly amazes me—and hey, who knew this would be so much fun? To Margo Lipschultz, who made this all possible. Hats off to Backspace! To Neil Gaiman, who gave me the dream of writing. As always, to Heather Brewer, the most awesome crit partner ever, and to Renee Barr, who believed from the start. To my mom and dad, who gave me *X-Men* #94–100 in mint condition for my bat mitzvah present. To my boys, Ryan and Mason—I can't wait until you're old enough to read comics with me! And to my husband, Brett, forever and always.

CAITLIN SAYS...

As always, thanks to my dedicated and infinitely patient literary agent, Rachel Vater, and to Anne Groell, our editor, for taking a chance on superheroes. To Jackie, my funny and fearless coauthor, and to everyone who helped make *Black and White* possible: Richelle, Mark, Cherie, Kat, Warren Ellis for making me want to write a new and disturbing twist on superpowered families, and most of all my parents, Pam and Hal, who never thought it was strange that I kept three thousand comic books in my closet as a kid.

BLACK
AND
WHITE

PROLOGUE:

Propaganda

[Fragment, recovered from Icarus Fertility Clinic fire, Newark, New Jersey]

patient and spouse/signatory hereby absolve Icarus Biological, Dr. Matthew Icarus, and all partners, primaries, or surrogates, from any lawsuit involving:

A) Wrongful death
B) Infertility resulting from clinical procedure
C) Birth defects in fetuses resulting from clinical procedures
D) Early-onset child illnesses and disorders
E) Aberrations in fetuses conceived with Icarus Method

Patient and spouse/signatory acknowledge that they are participating in a clinical trial of experimental fertility procedures. (SEE ATTACHED WAIVER.)

New York Times, December 12, 1991

LAWSUITS, VANDALISM PLAGUE "MIRACLE" FERTILITY SPECIALIST

Dr. Matthew Icarus announced today that he would be suspending operations at his Newark, NJ, clinic indefinitely. Icarus first came to prominence as the pioneer of the Icarus Method, an experiment designed to stimulate fertility in women and allow them to conceive naturally. After a fire at his clinic last month and numerous lawsuits from parents of babies conceived with the Icarus Method (a disproportionate number of whom were born with birth defects suspected to be the result of Icarus's gene therapy), the doctor is attending court today in New Jersey under a cloud of suspicion and dissension from both the pro-life and pro-choice sectors. New Jersey State Police spokesmen stated that they expect a large number of protesters and family members of the affected babies to be present. Icarus Biological was bought last year by Corp-Co and has been trading at

[article truncated]

LOS ANGELES POLICE DEPARTMENT

Subject: MacArthur Park "supergang"—all patrol
            officers required to wear body armor
            while on duty

Body: Because of the unprovoked attack on city
            personnel of May 23, 2007, the
            Commissioner has issued a directive that
            all patrol personnel assigned to the
            MacArthur Park area must wear full
            tactical gear while on duty. Assault
            rifles will be issued to patrol officers
            in the following sectors: Homicide,
            Warrants, School Outreach, and Gang Unit.

Attached, please see the report generated for the May 23
incident by Sergeant Hector Ramirez.

Officer Delgado and I were called to the west side of
the park at 10:30 p.m. to investigate a disturbance. We
were confronted by four youths wearing colors and signs
associated with the SkullXBones, a white/Asian mixed
gang. One youth, who identified himself as Kyle
Bradford, became hostile when Officer Delgado attempted
to search him and emitted what Delgado and I concur was
a beam of high-intensity light, which caused facial
burns on Officer Delgado and temporary blindness to
myself. The three other youths had fled the scene when I
recovered my vision, and subject Bradford continued to
taunt me by emitting light flashes and obscenities until
I lost him in a foot pursuit at the park's entrance.

[report becomes illegible]

Stockholder's report for Corp-Co, Fourth Quarter 2018

As our fiscal year draws to a close it gives me great pleasure to announce our dissolution of Icarus Biologicals. The properties Icarus formerly controlled now fall directly under the umbrella of Corp-Co's biological sciences division.

These assets include:
- Neuroscience and patented behavior therapies
- Living biological assets (as stated under the Human Scientific Carrier Asset Act of 2010)
- Experimental therapeutic drug treatments

Our new human assets will be present at the Corp-Co stockholder's meeting in one week's time. We extend the invitation to every one of our shareholders to be introduced to these "extra" humans, and hear Corp-Co's CEO, Sebastian Lister, outline our plans for Corp-Co's future.

Up in the sky!
Could it be . . .?
MEET A SUPERHERO!

**SATURDAY, JUNE 5,
AT KNOXVILLE FAIRGROUNDS COMPLEX!**

SEE **CAPTAIN COLOSSAL**

AND THE **FIREBOLT!**

**LIVE!
IN PERSON!
FRESH FROM THEIR VICTORY AGAINST
DOCTOR HYPNOTIC!**

**AUTOGRAPHS FROM 2 – 4, DIGISNAPS e5 APIECE
DEMONSTRATION OF POWERS AT 4:30
*BE THE FIRST TO MEET THE
ORIGINAL EXTRAHUMAN HEROES!***

Sponsored by CORP-Co Extrahuman Support Division

NOW

CHAPTER 1

IRIDIUM

The thing people seem all too happy to forget is that where there be superheroes, there also be supervillans. It makes one wonder: If the heroes went away, would the villains follow?

Lynda Kidder, "Origins, Part Five,"
New Chicago Tribune, April 23, 2112

Heroes always need someone to play the villain. Iridium saw the truth in this when a hero tried to slip up and coldcock her on the back of the head.

She spun around and blasted him with a strobe—nothing crippling, strictly visible spectrum, but the hero landed on his ass and started yelling. Probably "Ahhh, my eyes, my eyes!" That one was the most common.

"That was sloppy," Iridium tsked. "Where's your mentor? Did he go get a latte and leave you all alone?"

By her feet, a bank guard whimpered under his gag. "Shut it," said Iridium. "It's not like you won't get a fat settlement in the lawsuit that you're going to file against the bank for hazardous working conditions. Right?"

The guard considered this for a minute, shrugged as

much as he could with Iridium's disposable handcuffs around his wrists, and nodded.

Iridium turned her attention back to the vault, watching the hero stagger to his feet out of the corner of her eye. He was wearing a purple-and-black skinsuit—that alone pegged him as an amateur. No one in their right minds stuck with the skinsuits after they graduated from the Academy.

Well, except one, and *her* picture was splashed on every piece of extrahuman propaganda in Wreck City—or, if you had to get official and euphemistic about it, *Reclaimed Grid 16, for the City of New Chicago*—so the junior hero could be forgiven for thinking that skinsuits were the thing.

"Turn and face me! You're under arrest," the hero shouted.

Iridium continued her contemplation of the vault. A triple-retinal lock. A backup deadfall-bolt system. Two and a half inches of tilithium steel with iocore tumblers. "I'm just gonna have to melt it," she said, more to herself than the hero.

He took out the silver baton he'd first tried to hit her with, and some kind of Energy power turned it blue and crackling with electricity. "Last chance, bitch!"

Iridium let one black eyebrow slide up. " 'Bitch'? Don't you feel that's uncalled for? All I did was strobe you in self-defense."

"You almost burned my damned eyes out of my head!" He was edging up on her slowly, in some kind of textbook combat stance they must have started teaching after Iridium's time at the Academy. It made the hero resemble a colorful, deranged crab. Aside from the skinskuit, his costume had a purple face shield and bulbous black goggles that did a poor job of hiding big, scared eyes.

"Now, see, that's the thing," said Iridium. "In my day, they taught us not to swear."

The hero struck with the baton and Iridium sidestepped,

then put a foot into his side, just below his last rib. There was a *crack* like a twig being stepped on. Oops. So maybe not exactly *below* it.

"They also taught us to guard our offhand side," said Iridium, standing over the groaning hero. "Who the hell trained you? They should have their mentor merit badge revoked."

"I . . ."

"Look, kid. What's your name?"

"Blackwasp," he managed.

"Ouch. Sue whoever stuck you with that one. My point is, Blackwasp, that to survive as a goody-goody, you need to learn when you're outclassed." She turned her gaze back to the safe, *pushed* with the part of her mind that saw in spectrums, and felt the light concentrate on the surface of the door, blossoming like a small sun. The tilithium began to hiss as it peeled slowly away from the tumblers.

"I'll always be better than a rabid . . . freak . . . like you," Blackwasp gritted. He was pale with pain, but he wasn't fading. She had to give the kid credit—he had more balls than most Corp rentboys.

Iridium favored him with a close-lipped smile. "Maybe so, Blackwasp, but today, I'm the one walking out of here with e75,000 in digichips, and you're the one who's on the floor with a silly look on his face."

"Never . . . defeat me . . ."

Iridium strobed Blackwasp hard enough to knock him out, then stepped through the dripping hole in the vault and collected the cases of chips from their gleaming mount next to the long boxes of cash. As she left, she leaned down and gave Blackwasp a kiss on the cheek. "Better luck next time, kid."

Her lips left a faint imprint, like a sunburn.

CHAPTER 2

JET

Of course, the best thing about superheroes is that they're real. We get to see them, hear them, cheer for them. If they were in a zoo, we could even pet them and feed them.

Lynda Kidder, "Origins, Part Twelve,"
New Chicago Tribune, June 11, 2112

If she had to smile for another minute, her cheeks would fall off.

Jet wouldn't dream of complaining, though; she never questioned orders, and Ops had told her in no uncertain terms that Jet was to publicly accept the Humanitarian Award in all good cheer. No assigned Runner would take her place; no official Corp or Academy member would appear on her behalf. So Jet increased the wattage of her smile, dazzling the crowd with her pearly whites.

And told herself that she absolutely would not vomit. Light, she hated these public engagements.

Outside of New Chicago City Hall, thousands of spectators roared their approval, cheering loud and proud for their favorite heroine. Beneath her cowl, Jet stood tall and breathed heavily through her wide grin. Give her a villain or a terrorist over public speaking any day. Would it be too much for her to hope for an Everyman protest? Probably.

She smiled, big and false, and prayed the ordeal would be over soon.

Next to her onstage, the mayor beamed as the crowd applauded. He'd overdone it with the cologne, which he tended to do whenever he anticipated a crush of people. Jet had noticed that about Mayor Lee long ago, just like she'd noticed that these sorts of events happened only during election years. She fought the urge to wave away the overly musky smell. *Seduction,* she thought ruefully. *Lady Killer's cologne.* Jet wondered if the mayor had actually believed it when the charismatic hero had announced to the world at large that *Every lady killer knows it's all about the seduction.* Stupid tagline, in Jet's opinion, but the cologne sold like crazy. Superheroes and celebrities: the best assets when it came to selling products.

In her left ear, her comlink hummed. Meteorite's low, husky voice said, "Babe, would it kill you to smile like you mean it?"

It just might, Jet thought, stretching her mouth impossibly wide.

Meteorite chuckled. "I said 'smile,' not 'set your mouth in a rictus of horror.'"

Jet ground her teeth. Light knew, she depended on her comlink; the white noise it filtered into her ear was as necessary to her as breathing, and getting immediate feedback from Ops at the Academy was fabulous when she was on the hunt—there was nothing like having electronic eyes and ears to do her scouting for her and scan any opponents for weapons and tech. But at times like this, when the comlink was all about the PR—especially when someone as media-savvy as Meteorite was pulling a shift—Jet was tempted to yank the thing from her ear and stomp on it until it bled wires.

Keeping her lips frozen in a grin, Jet whispered, "I'm trying."

"Try harder. You look like you're constipated."

Right, she thought. Smile for the vids, wave happily at all the civilians, act like you want to be on display at City Hall like some fashion model instead of out there, fighting crime. Making a difference.

Jet exhaled her frustration and smiled. The sponsor was always right—especially in her case, when the sponsor was the City of New Chicago. The mayor's voice boomed as he extolled the virtues of the extrahumans in general and Jet in particular, and how proud he was to be the mayor of the city that housed the Squadron, UCSA Division. Yet even as the crowd before Jet proclaimed its undying love, behind her on the platform, the uniformed officers of the New Chicago Police Department radiated their hatred. The space between Jet's shoulder blades itched, as if one of the officers were taking aim. As always, she tried not to dwell on how the police loathed her, pretended it didn't sting.

Her comlink hummed. "Come on, babe. Think happy thoughts. They gave you flowers."

"They were lovely," Jet whispered, not moving her lips.

"Any phone numbers tucked between the petals this time?"

"A few."

"Poor Jet." Meteorite laughed. "Burdened by her adoring fans."

It did sound foolish that way. But Meteorite didn't understand; the former Weather power had been grounded in Ops for three years. She'd forgotten how maddening it was to be tied up at some so-called goodwill event when everyone knew it was just political maneuvering.

Not that Jet was complaining. Jet never complained. Duty first, always. And when her duty happened to be smiling for the cameras and making a public speech, then that was what she did. Even when it was a monumental waste of her time. And made her sick to her stomach. The mayor pumped her hand and thanked her loudly as he grinned at the cameras.

"Lee's in fine form today," Meteorite said. "I figure he'll run out of breath in about forty minutes, but Two-Tone here thinks he's good for at least an hour. It's an election year and all."

Jet bit back a groan as the mayor prattled on and on about her good deeds while he himself managed to take the credit for cleaning up New Chicago. Fine by her. She'd be happy to shout out that all her successes were part of the mayor's grand plan, if only she wouldn't have to do any more of these ceremonies. Beneath her leather gauntlets, her palms began to sweat.

"Not to worry," Meteorite said. "Even if he runs long, you'll have plenty of time to make your three o'clock with Rabbi Cohn."

Jet whispered, "On Third Street?"

"No, that's Reverend Cohen, at the Templeton Church on Third. Jews for Jesus sect. I'm talking about Rabbi Cohn, of the Third Temple. He's on Lakeside Drive."

"Ah. Right."

"Cohn's a good spot. According to Two-Tone, today's sermon will be all about how humans and extrahumans are all children of God. Or Gods, I suppose, depending on the affiliation."

Good. Cohn wouldn't be openly hostile. Most of the religious leaders were at least tolerant of extrahumans and the Squadron. Some were ardent fans. Others . . . were not.

"And at four thirty, you have that thing with Jack Goldwater."

"Light," Jet muttered. The only thing worse than public speaking was talk-show appearances. "Can't Steele take that one?"

"Sorry, babe. She's in the Canadian States for the next few days, helping the Dudley Do-Rights. Besides, Goldwater wanted you specifically to go head-to-head with Frank Wurtham."

Damn it to Darkness. "You didn't tell me the chairman of the Everyman Society was going to be on the Goldwater show with me."

"I just did. Play nice with the fanatic, Jetster. The vids will be recording. Just let Wurtham be all insane and bug-eyed and ranting about humans first. You be the demure superheroine who modestly saved New Chicago no less than two times this calendar year alone. Oh," Meteorite added, "PR says no cowl for the show. Too intimidating. You're to appear with your hood back, hair gleaming. Ponytail or braid; your choice. Light makeup—nothing sluttish. And no perfume, so be sure to catch a shower before you go."

Jet hated election years.

"On to happier news," Meteorite said, sounding perky enough to set Jet's internal radar beeping. "You've got yourself a new Runner, effective immediately."

"Oh?"

"Yeah. Smile and nod; Lee's talking about the reclaiming of New Chicago. Be all supportive."

Jet nodded in response. The vids whirled; lights flashed. She whispered, "What happened to Cathy?"

"Her PTO kicked in this morning. Vacationing in the Adirondacks for a month. So it's a new gopher for you, fresh out of the lottery." A pause, then Meteorite purred, "And he's a cutie, I must say. Even Two-Tone agrees, and he doesn't play for that team."

Straining to keep her lips from moving, Jet said, "You met him?"

"Two-Tone? I've done more than that with him."

Through clenched teeth, Jet whispered, "No, the Runner. You met him?"

"Babe, I meet all of them." Jet could practically hear the woman's grin. "I think you're going to like this one."

"I liked Cathy."

"Not *this* way, you didn't."

Oh boy.

The mayor droned on, oblivious to her nearly silent conversation. In the audience, the civilians cheered on cue. It was a spectacle sure to make the headlines for the next two days; Lee must be almost fevered with the thought of deliriously happy constituents. Jet whispered, "Aren't you supposed to be keeping me informed instead of setting me up?"

"Far as I'm concerned, Jetster, it's the same thing. When's the last time you got laid?"

Jet choked, which she quickly covered with a dainty cough into her gauntlet. Mouth hidden behind her hand, she hissed, "That's none of your business!"

"Like I thought. Forever and a day. You need to loosen up, babe. Or get yourself someone to loosen you up. If not the new Runner, then I highly recommend Two-Tone. And I'm not just saying that because he's right next to me."

Terrific, Jet thought, checking herself from rolling her eyes. Between Meteorite, the mayor, and the carefully screened civilians in attendance, it was practically a Jet lovefest—which made someone who strongly preferred to blend with the shadows exceptionally uncomfortable. At least this time no one was showering her in chocolates or throwing men's underwear. Or, Light help her, women's underwear.

Mayor Lee boomed on, calling Jet New Chicago's "Lady of Shadows." Behind her, Jet distinctly heard one of the cops snort.

"My goodness," Meteorite said brightly. "I think you just lost a member of your fan club."

Just a little longer, Jet told herself as she smiled, smiled, smiled. Soon the mayor would finish, and Jet would gratefully accept his gift and murmur her thank-yous, and make a very fast acceptance speech. Then on to the religious and television stops of her daily circuit. And then, finally, she could get out on the streets and actually do her job. Off camera.

"Hang on," Meteorite said. "Data coming in." The Ops voice clicked off, filling Jet's ear with the white noise of a waterfall.

Jet smiled and waited, hoping that the data would be something big enough to pull her out before she had to launch into a speech that she really, *really* didn't want to give. Maybe an armed robbery, or a fire...

The earpiece hummed, and Meteorite said, "New marching orders, babe. We spotted her."

Jet's heartbeat quickened. "*Her?* You're sure?"

"Positive. It's her energy signature. Whatever she's been using to block it these past few months must've sprung a leak. You'll have to ask her when you find her."

"Where?"

Ops gave her the coordinates. "And Jet?" Meteorite said, all traces of playfulness gone. "Corp'll be all over us if she pulls another vanishing act. Don't let her get away again."

"Oh, I won't," Jet said, her voice dark and full of promise. No, there was no way that she'd let *her* slip away. Again. After five years of cat and mouse, Jet was done playing.

"I'll reschedule Cohn for tomorrow, but you have to make the Goldwater spot."

"Understood."

"Now make with the apologies to the mayor and get your ass in gear."

Jet cleared her throat, then interrupted Mayor Lee. "Thank you, Mr. Mayor. It's a real honor to be receiving this award today."

Lee stared at her, his mouth working as if it dearly wanted to keep speaking, his eyes betraying his irritation. The audience hushed, waited in rapt attention as their savior stood on the Mount.

She smiled at the people of New Chicago, and this time,

it felt right on her face. "And thank you all. Your support means more than I could ever say." Flicking her wrist, she summoned a floater of Shadow. "But now I must go."

"But..." The mayor spluttered, caught between indignation and professional courtesy. "We haven't even given you the award yet!"

"I'm sorry, sir, but duty calls. A villain is at large, and I must rein her in." Stepping onto the smoky black circle, she commanded it to rise. Her cape billowed around her as she hovered over the crowd, giving them one last look. The vids clicked and whirred, and the spectators cheered as Jet waved.

"Enough posing," Ops said. "Time to go kick some rabid ass."

"Oh, yeah," Jet said, and her smile pulled into something feral. "She'll never know what hit her."

And Jet rocketed away.

CHAPTER 3

IRIDIUM

Down the numberless alleyways that crossed Wreck City like burst capillaries, Iridium stopped walking and turned around. "You can come out, you know. That Shadow-walking trick hasn't fooled me since we were fourteen years old."

Iridium waited, patiently. *She* was so goddamn paranoid. Probably expected a lasgrid cage, or a net with pointy sticks attached. "Anytime now," Iridium coaxed.

Yet the bricks behind her, bars and brights of light and dark, stayed quiet, still, and empty.

Iridium set down the metal case of digichips and rolled her eyes. "For Christo's sake, Jet. Get your ass out here. I read *Art of War* in the same unit you did. This is not dampening my morale, or whatever it is you're hoping to accomplish with the big, scary Shadow puppet routine."

"You cheated in that unit," Jet said, finally letting herself separate from the shadow of a computerized Dumpster that bore the grinning face of Green Thumb, supershill for Chicago Consolidated Hauling. The fact that a plant-controller was posing for a major polluter made Iridium smile.

"Honey, I cheated at a lot of things," she told Jet. "Sun Tzu doesn't actually have a problem with cheating."

Jet flexed her hands so the night-colored leather gauntlets casing them creaked. "I do."

"Jehovah," Iridium muttered. "Is that some elective I missed out on? 'How to Sound Like a Cheesy Action Vid'?"

"I didn't come here to talk."

Iridium felt a pang in the air, like a stray draft of cold wind had come off Lake Michigan. Just a moment before they wrapped around her ankles, she saw the shadows running off Jet's form, crawling toward her feet. Creepers, manifestations of Jet's power. Alive.

"Imagine that," said Iridium, creating a strobe that hung in the air above the pair, arcing and spitting. Jet hissed as her goggles irised from the sudden burst of light. With her cowl, skinsuit, and leather belt and gauntlets, she looked more like a nightmare than anything Iridium saw when she shut her eyes.

Seeing the shadows crawl back to their mistress, Iridium pushed the strobe closer. "Any other day, I'd love to stay and continue our witty repartee, but right now I've got places to go and corporate slimewads to rob, so I'll be jetting. No pun intended."

"You stay where you are!" Jet shouted. "You can't get past me, Iridium, no matter how much your ego likes to think so!"

"Christo, *shut up!*" Jet couldn't just speak; it was always a Superman with her. A platitude, pat and rehearsed. She might as well have been one of the 'bots the Academy kept around to wax floors and wash dishes. She was wired into Corp, as much as all of their machines. "You make me sick, Jet," Iridium said. "You can either get in my way and be burned by my strobe—*careful,*" she snapped when Jet tried to bat the ball of ever-brightening light away, "that's over a thousand BTUs of heat! Or you can slither away into the dark. As usual."

Jet held her ground.

Iridium took another step forward and felt a droplet of sweat slide down her spine underneath her unikilt. *Just the light heat,* she lied to herself. *Don't worry about it.* "You forget that I *know* you, Jet." She pushed at the strobe, making it fly at the cowled woman.

Jet dove to the side at the last second and landed in a heap of garbage, clawing at her face as her goggles overloaded from the brilliance.

Iridium went to Jet, leaned down, and ripped off Jet's earpiece, crushing the squawk of her operator's voice beneath her bootheel. "You scare easy," Iridium hissed into Jet's ear. "You always have."

She turned her back on Jet, got the digichip case, and walked away at a measured pace, into the ruins of Wreck City, feeling only a slight prick of guilt for what she'd said.

CHAPTER 4

JET

Out of all the various Powers represented in the Academy—and, of course, the Squadron itself—the most enigmatic one is Shadow.

Lynda Kidder, "Origins, Part Six,"
New Chicago Tribune, April 30, 2112

No, no, no, no, no...

Jet took a shuddering breath, told herself not to panic. So what that she didn't have Ops or the white noise to ground her? Within minutes, a Runner would arrive with another earpiece, and probably with backup, just in case.

Plenty of time.

Trembling from rage and adrenaline, Jet called out, "Iridium, stop in the name of the law!"

Of course, the woman kept on walking. No, strolling, as if she had all the time in the world.

Scrambling to her feet, Jet cursed herself for three kinds of fool. This was all her fault; she never should have led with the creepers to restrain Iri. Even knowing what the woman had become over the past five years, Jet had still attempted to intimidate her with subtlety instead of bludgeoning her with power.

And she'd hoped that maybe some of the old Iri was still there, inside that rabid shell. "I said stop!"

Iridium kept on strolling. And . . . now she was whistling a jaunty tune. Acting for all the world as if Jet were insignificant.

She thought she heard laughter, dark and syrupy thick.

Over the thumping of her heartbeat, her blood pounding in her ears, Jet shouted, "Don't you walk away from me!"

If Iridium heard her, she didn't deign to show it.

Jet's thoughts blackened with fury. How dare she act as if Jet was irrelevant? As if she wasn't a threat?

She'd show her a threat.

Snarling, Jet leveled a blast of Shadow at Iridium's receding back—nothing subtle this time. She meant to take her down, no matter what.

Iridium turned, then yelped as she dove out of the way, her metal case clanging to the pavement. The ebony bolt rocketed past her, and Jet had to force it to dissipate before it hit streetside. She grunted as the Shadow faded to nothing but gray motes in the afternoon sun, and felt a headache pound behind her eyes. Dissipation always drained her. Maybe Iri wouldn't remember that; it had been five years.

Iridium had landed on her palms, then used the movement to somersault gracefully onto her feet. Now she stood proudly in the middle of the alley, arms out, looking for all the world like an acrobat in her white unikilt.

Still agile as a freaking cat, Jet thought, feeling clumsy and reeking of garbage. Ignoring the way her head throbbed, she aimed directly at Iridium's smirking mouth.

"Hitting me from behind?" Iri chuffed laughter. "Isn't that against the rules?"

"I gave you fair warning," Jet said, approaching slowly. She'd distract her with talk—just enough for Jet to get her strength back. And then she'd blanket her. It would be fast and cold, and Iri would be out before she knew what had hit her. "Maybe you should get your hearing checked."

"Right, this is the part where you try to distract me." Iridium shook her head and sighed. "Christo, could you be any more by the book?"

"Sure. I could launch into all the codes you've violated in the past five years." Jet stepped forward, her hand pointed at Iri's head. "I could list all your crimes. But then we'd be here for days."

"You think of that comeback all by yourself, or did Ops feed you that line too? Oh, wait—you don't have Ops in your ear right now, do you?"

Just beyond the steady ache of her head, Jet heard whispers amid the laughter. She grimaced; it was too soon. No more time for banter, or games. With her free hand, she reached into one of her belt pouches to take out a pair of stun-cuffs. "Raise them."

Iridium put her hands up in a "don't-shoot" gesture, but Jet wasn't completely stupid; she felt the change in the temperature around her, the slight shift in heat. Iri was getting ready to strobe her.

She glared at Iridium, debated whether she should raise graymatter to whip up a Shadowshield against the coming attack, or just blanket Iri now. She wasn't back up to full power, but maybe—

hit her hurt her do it now do it

Shut up! Jet's outstretched arm shook, and she hoped that Iri hadn't seen her flinch. *Just shut up!*

do it do it make her scream make her bleed

Sweat beaded on her brow. Light, she needed her comlink. She had to drown out the voices—

"Still overthinking it, aren't you?" Iridium's voice forced Jet to focus on the other woman: Iri was grinning, and she'd lowered her hands. "Some things never change. Poor Jet."

"Shut up!"

"Maybe you're scared of little old me." Iridium took a step forward—to attack? No, she was walking toward the discarded box, no doubt filled with digichips or plasigold. She winked at Jet, as if she was in on a secret. "Maybe you're just jumping at shadows."

Jet gasped. Iri knew.

No, impossible. Iri didn't know about the voices. Only one other person did. Iri *couldn't* know.

do it do it now do it NOW do it

The Shadow laughed . . . and Jet smiled.

"Scared?" Jet said, voice flat. "Me? You don't know anything about fear. Or jumping at shadows." The power poured out of her—oh, so fluid and electric, like shocks of pleasure dancing along her limbs—and wrapped Iridium in a blanket of night. "I'll teach you to be afraid of the dark."

She watched Iri double over. Grinned as Iri started to scream.

sweet screams sweet sounds suck out the light the life

"No!" Iri's voice was muffled in the Shadow, desperate. "Jet . . . Joannie, stop! *Stop!*"

Jet blinked, then gasped when she saw the cocooned form bent on the floor of the alley, struggling.

Oh Light . . . Iri?

Joannie!

Jet ripped away the blanket, barely feeling the wave of dizziness hit her as Shadow evaporated. On the ground, Iri crouched, head down, her body wracked with shivers, her arms wrapped around herself.

Biting back a cry, Jet stumbled to her side, put her hand on the woman's shoulder to offer comfort. "Iri? Callie? Are you okay?"

The punch landed squarely in Jet's gut, stealing her breath. She doubled over, and a right hook to her jaw knocked her flat. Sprawled on the ground, she wheezed in garbage-tainted air.

Iridium sniffed. "Sucker."

Jet couldn't even lift her head to glare. She hurt all over—she'd dissipated too much Shadow instead of absorbing it back. Tiny tremors wracked her limbs, like fog-inspired DTs. Lying there, she heard Iri's booted footfalls as she walked past Jet, heard Iri scoop up the metal box.

Damn it—get up!

"If you're going to play with the bad girls," Iri said lightly, "you have to stop being one of the good guys."

By the time Jet pulled herself to her feet, Iridium was long gone.

Jet bent over, her hands on her thighs, concentrating on taking deep breaths. Forget how Iri had gotten away, again; forget the voices licking at her mind. Just ride out the pain and wait for the Runner to show up with the new earpiece . . .

"My, my. Lookee here."

Jet forced her head up to see a group of seven toughs decked out in their street leathers and chains.

"Boys," their leader said, "I think we're going to have us a bit of fun."

CHAPTER 5

IRIDIUM

As reassuring as it is to know that the Squadron is committed to protecting us regular folk, we all know that even the best of heroes can go bad. To say nothing, of course, about the worst of heroes, or the myriad of those in between.

Lynda Kidder, "Flight of the Blackbird,"
New Chicago Tribune, July 2, 2112

The gates of Blackbird Prison weren't steel and barred, like in the old days. They weren't forbidding or stern or even particularly noteworthy to anyone passing by on the motorway above; but just the same, Iridium felt fingers of nerves all up and down her spine when the force fields parted to let her through. This was where she belonged—at least, according to Corp-Co.

Calista Bradford. Life without parole. The sentence felt like a small stone in the back of Iridium's throat, every time the gates parted and she walked through a free woman.

Blackbird Prison was where supervillains were punished for daring to step off the party line. Lord Chaos, the Exterminator, Terror Man.

She'd be inside, too, in shackles, if Jet had been just a little sharper in the alley...

No.

Iridium breathed slow and easy, through the nose, just like combat training taught. Keep it slow, keep it calm, keep your head. One of the few useful tenets of life at the Academy. She'd come here dozens of times. They hadn't caught her yet.

"Identification, miss," said the guard at the entrance desk. He was enclosed in a rippling blue-purple fortress of magnetic force; the only other furniture in his personal enclosure was a serenely glowing data terminal. Behind him, an enormous bank of five hundred vid screens flickered and twitched, time codes ticking away in the corners. Each of Blackbird Prison's inmates, the rabids of New Chicago and Mid-America—on display for the public to gawk at, if they chose—with the time left on their sentences delineated at the corner of the screen. On many displays, it simply read LIFE.

Someone in the tour group that had come through the doors behind Iridium snapped a picture of the screens. "This way to the costume gallery," said the guide. "Much of the rabid—or supervillain, as they prefer—garb in these cases was preserved just as the Illinois prison system received it from the Corp's capturing hero: laser-burned, bloodstained, and tattered. Please refrain from using vidlights, as the materials might become discolored..."

"Bloody tours," said the guard. "Up to three times a week, now. Corp's raking in every E of that money. But does our funding for these freaks increase? You better believe it doesn't."

Iridium presented her Medico Society ID to the guard, which featured her blond, smiling, and bespectacled. The name on the ID claimed she was Dr. Teschi Sampson, who was ten years older than Iridium really was and lived in a part of New Chicago with no guards on the windows and a new floatcar in every driveway.

If Iridium thought about it, she would have hated Teschi Sampson. But she never gave the fake psychiatrist any real thought; the ID allowed Iri access to Blackbird. That was all.

"Right," said the guard. He had a Welsh accent and red hair that stood out in all directions. "On you go."

"Thank you," Iridium purred. Dr. Sampson was an incurable flirt, and Iridium was all too happy to play the role to its fullest.

Another guard, this one in full riot gear, buzzed her through a series of gates to the high-security wing. Finally, they entered a plain meeting room, with light-plast, prefab table and chairs that couldn't be used as weapons, and an enormous old-style clock on the wall. He motioned to the seats, and curtly said, "Wait."

After three minutes by the clock, a buzzer sounded and a robot voice announced, "Inmate walking. Number 342785, Bradford, Lester Daedalus, formerly known as Arclight."

Iridium grimaced. They always broadcast his villain name, but never his old designation as Luster, from when he was a hero. Wouldn't do to confuse the citizens—Luster saved lives, had fought the Ominous Eight to a standstill, had been New Chicago's sponsored hero. Arclight was the boogeyman, what Corp would make sure Lester was remembered as.

It was hot in the room, and her head itched. Even with a scalp meld, wigs were uncomfortable, and the bright purple contacts that were Dr. Sampson's eyes made her own blue eyes sting.

Never mind that the ugly off-the-rack blue power suit was ill-fitting and made her look twenty pounds heavier in her ass and hips than she actually was. Sweat started to trickle under her collar as the clock went *tick, tick, tick*.

Sometimes, she wished for nothing more than Ice

powers, like Snowman or Frostbite. They'd never have to suffer inside a crappy off-the-rack costume.

The door to the interview room buzzed, then slid back to reveal two guards and a much taller, thinner man with a full shock of black hair, and hollow cheeks made knife-edged by black stubble.

Lester Bradford shuffled in, his force shackles partly accounting for his hunched, shambling posture, and the good old-fashioned Halcyon in his system for the rest. Sedatives were standard issue for rabids, especially ones who had been involved in violent captures, like Lester. In his more jovial moments, he claimed that Owl Girl had to wear long-sleeved uniforms to this day to hide her burn scars.

"Thank you," said Iridium in the crisp doctoral tone that she'd perfected. "Please kill the surveillance on your way out. Confidentiality still has a place in this prison, I hope?"

"Yes, Doctor," said the guard with a sigh. "No one is going to listen in on your precious rabids."

The door hissed shut and locked.

Iridium silently counted to thirty as she and Arclight sat, waiting. Thirty seconds was as long as Corp and the police could legally surveil a patient in a closed session.

"Blimey, girl," said Lester when time had ticked over. "You look terrible as a blonde." He had resolutely kept his accent, even though overseas students at the Academy were encouraged to take dialect coaching to make themselves more brandable in America.

"You say that every time, Dad," said Iridium with a roll of her eyes. She stripped off the fake glasses and tossed them on the table. "What in Christo's name is the deal with that gigantic clock? It's creepy. Like some old Terry Gilliam thing."

"Warden Post's latest idea, to remind us all of our sins and the time we've yet to serve."

"Warden Post and his wacky schemes," said Iridium

with a mock laugh. "How much more off his nut can that man go?"

"Having your mind raped by the Invader during a prison break does strange things to a man," said Lester, scratching his chin. "Poor Bob's never been quite the same."

"Did he ever find out it was you who replaced the Invader's sedative IV with saline?"

Lester's eyes sparkled. "I'm still breathing."

"Good point," said Iridium. "You look good, Dad. Well fed." He didn't look anything of the sort, but she figured that if she said something enough, it might eventually turn out true. That, or she might suddenly sprout wings like an Air power and be able to leave New Chicago behind for good.

Christo, now *that* was a dream.

"You look like you've been dragged through the river by your bloody hair," said Lester. "The polluted bits."

"I wouldn't have any hair left if that were the case," said Iridium. "Or skin." She made a few shorthand chicken scratches on her data tablet for appearance's sake when she was searched at the end of the session.

"If I wanted logic, I'd put in for a real psychiatrist," said Lester. "What happened, girl?"

"I don't wanna talk about it."

Her father glared at her. "Well, tough, because you're going to." He sat back and crossed his arms.

"I hate that," said Iridium.

"What?"

"How even in prison, shackled to a chair, with your powers inhibited, you manage to be such a *dad*. It's maddening!"

Lester smiled, showing a flash of very white teeth. "It's a gift, Callie girl. One that you're going to have to learn if you ever want to do more than hit-and-run robberies on rich, complacent civilian types."

"Watch it, old man. You're not so feeble that I can't smack you in the head."

"Backbone, on the other hand, isn't something you lack," said Lester. "I wasn't an utter washout as a father, eh? Now tell me what happened to make you so damned twitchy."

"I had a run-in with *her*," Iridium muttered. "She got the drop on me."

"Hitting from behind," Lester mused. "Our girl has come a long way. Whatever did you do to draw her ire?"

"I stole digichips."

"Mercantile?"

"Bank vault," said Iridium, feeling a trace of a grin rise to her face.

Lester returned it with his own ghostly expression. "That's my girl."

"It's for the data outlets in Wreck City," said Iridium. "Those systems are fifty years old with no upgrades. The more information that gets to the people about the Corp, the less of a stranglehold they'll have on this city."

"You sound like me, in my young and foolish days," Lester muttered. "Information only goes so far, Callie. People need to be shown. They're content to believe lies."

"You sound like that's a bad thing," Iridium said. "Being like you, I mean."

"Sooner or later, if you really want to spread the word on Corp, you're going to have to take action," said Lester.

"People aren't stupid," Iridium argued. "They're capable of recognizing the hypocrisy and the lies. I did."

"Most people didn't have the luxury of seeing their father hauled away in chains for having the temerity to question Corp. Lead by example, Callie, not by preaching." Lester sighed. "I just wish you'd learn that there's a difference between being a rabid and being Robin Hood."

"Seemed to work okay for you."

"Until I landed in here," Lester said grimly. "The goodness of your heart will get you killed, Callie. Take it from me. Toughen up."

Iridium fell silent. She *had* let Jet get the drop on her. She'd been cocky. Arrogance was death—one of the few good lessons the Academy had instilled, whether it meant to or not.

"What's wrong?" Lester said. "I know that look."

"I run and run," Iridium said finally, "and I feel like I do it in one spot. She knew *exactly* where to find me, Daddy. She just coiled up that cold power of hers, and she would have killed me. I have no doubt the Academy authorized *that*." She made herself remember the fear in Jet's eyes when she'd taken away her earpiece, but it didn't warm her like it should have. "She was ready to kill me," Iridium repeated.

"It happens," said Lester, "when two soldiers find themselves on opposite sides of a war that they used to fight together. Are you sayin' you *wouldn't* kill her?"

Iridium looked up at the clock. Their session had just under a minute left. "This isn't supposed to be a war."

"But it is, girl. It is a war, and right now you're on the losing side. Figure out how you're gonna change that. Or before too long, you'll be Inmate Number 501."

Iridium bristled. "I'll never let them get me. I'll die first." She'd known since the day she lost her hero status and gone on the run that she'd rather go to a graveyard than to prison under the thumb of Corp. She wouldn't give Jet the satisfaction. "Tell me what to do, Dad. You fought them. You stood up to Commander Courage and the Prestidigitator. Owl Girl. Velocity. All of those fossils from the glory days." She reached across the table and gripped Lester's hand as the guard's footsteps drew closer in the hall. "You want me to learn what it is to be rabid? Fine. Tell me what to do to hurt Corp. *Really* hurt them."

"Enough with this rob-from-the-rich bollocks," said

Lester. "I've got a bloke. He can help us hit them so hard and fast, they'll still be teaching units about you in fifty years."

"I want to do it," Iridium said. "Today made me certain. Jet's forgotten everything that may have been between us. She's just another drone, and next time I'm pretty sure she'll kill me." Admitting that Jet might be better at *anything* caused a distinct twinge, but Iridium could still feel the shadows feeding on her, taking out everything inside her and leaving a husk...

"You'll have to fight dirty, Callie," said Lester, as the latches on the door hissed open. "Dirty and mean. There can be no quarter with Corp. Make no mistake about that."

CHAPTER 6

JET

Sometimes, it seems unfair that an extrahuman would take on mere mortal criminals. What chance does a standard human, a normal, have against someone who can fly, or can bend steel, or can dazzle you with light? But then again, as many extrahumans would tell us, life isn't fair.

—Lynda Kidder, "Origins, Part Eight," *New Chicago Tribune*, May 14, 2112

You have *got* to be kidding me," Jet muttered. It figured. The way her day was going, she was about to get mugged.

As the street tough approached, cracking his knuckles and grinning like a shark, Jet blew out a cleansing breath. If he was more than sixteen, she'd eat her goggles.

Which Iridium had shorted out.

She grimaced at the thought. Ops was going to rip her a new orifice for letting Iri get away. Because no matter how Jet tried to rationalize her reactions, that was exactly what had happened. She'd had the woman trapped, and she'd gotten sucker punched when she thought Iri had been hurt.

screaming she was screaming so sweet so succulent so

Shut up.

She clenched her gloved fist. Compassion was death. Next time, she wouldn't hold back. Iridium was rabid, pure and simple. Like her father.

The voices giggled, agreed that next time things would be different indeed.

Jet bit back a hiss. She needed the white noise of her comlink. Where in the Dark was her Runner?

"Looks like we've got us a winged hero," the gangbanger said, all teeth. "You lost, hero?"

Jet stood tall. Never mind her aching jaw and sore body; never mind the whispers that had nearly driven her to do something inexcusable to a woman who'd once been her friend. She was in control.

In the next two seconds—as the teen took two more steps forward—Jet directed herself through the ABC exercise taught to all second-year Academy students, from Introduction to Peacekeeping: analyze, battlescan, confront.

Analyze.

Seven toughs, dressed in black leather dusters, black work boots, black fingerless gloves. Faces studded with silver rings in intricate patterns. Clothes and jewelry marked them as Grendels, the gang that lorded it over New Chicago from Grids 3–6, the northern boundary of what the street-savvy residents referred to as Wreck City. Grendels were troublemakers, mostly; into vandalism, petty theft, carjackings. Assault. Some links to the Undergoths and other seedier elements of the city's Rat Network that ran the black and gray markets. But for the most part, Grendels were all bark, no bite.

Battlescan.

They'd moved into a phalanx stance, blocking the alley. Body language and open coats suggested concealed weapons. Leader at point, hands dangling at his sides. Still grinning, his lips and nostrils were littered with silver hoops. Seven against one—either intimidation or lack of honor. None of them had the obvious signs of a junk freak—no tremor in the limbs, no red-tinged eyes.

Confront.

Forcing a thin-lipped smile, Jet said, "Thank you for your concern, citizen. I'm fine."

"We can see that, baby," a second kid said, almost swimming in his leather jacket. "You're *so* fine."

"Absolutely luscious," said the leader.

From one of the others: "Must be hot under that cape, 'cause I'm sweating just looking at her." Various snorts and chortles accompanied the statement like a laugh track.

Jet felt her cheeks heat. Her face was hidden by her cowl, so she didn't have to worry about revealing her embarrassment. Professional, polite, powerful—the three *P*s of being an extrahuman civil servant. Voice crisp, she replied, "Thank you."

"No, thank *you*, hero." This from the leader, still the grinning shark. "Me, I'm glad you're here. I've got to make me a citizen's arrest."

"Oh?" She considered him in his blacks and heavily ringed face. He leered at her, all but undressed her with his eyes. But no matter how loud his bark, he was just an average human—no powers of which to speak.

In other words, not a threat. She said, "Whom do you wish to arrest?"

"You."

That took her aback. "On what grounds?"

"The things you're doing to that bodysuit have *got* to be illegal." Shark wolf-whistled and slobbered as his friends high-fived and made kissy noises. And one of them pumped his crotch, miming sex.

Fighting back the urge to roll her eyes, Jet's smile stretched painfully thin; her cheeks were still sore from all the fake smiles for the holovids before, and her jaw throbbed from where Iridium had punched her.

She got away, Jet thought. *Again.*

"What do you say, hero? Want to get down and dirty, Grendel-style?"

Jet prayed that her Runner would show up in the next thirty seconds, because otherwise she might let out some of her frustration on these kids. And not the frustration the gangbanger was implying, either.

"I'll even let you be on top. I know you heroes like that sort of shit."

She clenched her fists. Once she had her new comlink in place and Ops back in her ear, she could fly and scan the rooftops. Iri could still be in the area; it might not be too late to rectify her mistake. "I'm flattered," she said to the teen, "but now I must be off. A villain is on the loose, and I must stop her before she hurts someone. Good day."

She turned away, already concentrating to summon a floater to whisk her into the air for her to better see the Runner—who should have been here by now—but a fierce tug on her cap spun her around . . . and into Shark's arms.

"No, Luscious," he purred, his hands gripping her biceps tightly, "it's going to be a *great* day."

Stupid kid. "Unhand me."

"I don't think so." He grinned hugely, revealing smoker's teeth and halitosis that would fell a rhino. "I don't think you want to be heroing off just yet. I don't think you've had a good time in ages."

Planting her feet for leverage, Jet said, "Actually, you just don't think." Then she slammed her forehead into his ringed nose.

He screeched and let her go to cover his face. An uppercut to his chin knocked him back. He fell against the alley wall and slid to the ground, hands still over his nose, blood gushing between his fingers.

There was the sound of metal behind her.

She spun to see three of the six Grendels holding naked blades—Hogans, she thought; what were they doing with

Hogans?—and two sporting plasguns. One had morning stars poised and ready to throw.

It looked like she'd get to release some of her frustration, after all.

A flicker of Shadow was enough to clog the barrels of the guns; a bit more concentration to ring the edges of the throwing stars and dull the blades into a child's toy. All in less than a second; their weapons were rendered useless before the toughs even blinked.

The three with knives closed in, their blades shining, their eyes bright with the thought of violence. Jet let them come. The first one charged, swinging widely. She caught his knife arm and used his momentum to flip him over while knocking the weapon out of his grip. The kid landed hard on his back, his head connecting solidly with the pavement. He stayed down and didn't move.

Before the thud finished echoing, his buddy struck, aiming to gut her. She easily spun out of his reach, then grabbed his wrist and karate-chopped his forearm. He squawked and dropped the Hogan. Jet grabbed his shoulders and rammed her knee into his belly, and he doubled over with a sad grunt. She sensed more than heard another gangbanger moving in, so she gripped the doubled-over kid and, using just a whiff of Shadow to float him, she pivoted fast, slamming him into another Grendel. The two boys collapsed to the ground, groaning, their knives gleaming on the dirty ground of the alley.

Four down.

The remaining three circled her, the two with their plasguns still not realizing their weapons were little more than paperweights. The Grendel with the morning stars must have seen his damaged blades, because the only weapons he held were his hands—but based on his stance, he'd had some formal training.

One of the gunmen pulled the trigger, and kept pulling

even after the dull *click*. The other followed suit. Then as one, they dropped the guns and charged her, one on her left, one on her right. Too easy. She leapt into the air, springing high thanks to a thin coil of Shadow—and the two teens slammed into each other, full tilt. Down they went. She landed on her feet, almost as gracefully as Iridium had before.

The last gang member motioned with his arms, made a "come-on" gesture. Instead, Jet blanketed him in Shadow. The thick bands of blackness swathed him completely, kept holding him even when his struggles ceased. After a full minute, she called the blanket back into herself and absorbed it—no more dissipation today; she was beyond her limit—and as she shivered from the cold merging with her body, the kid crashed to the ground, his skin pale, his breathing slow and steady in a Shadow-induced sleep.

Breathing hard, Jet scanned the litter of bodies. The seven Grendels on the ground were battered, and some were bloody, but none of them tried to attack her. Actually, most looked like they were unconscious.

Nodding, she blew out a tired sigh. She was done here; all that was left was to call in an ambulance to take the gang away, and file her report with the local authorities. And then get Corp PR in the loop to take it from there.

Someone clapped.

She whirled around, already calling up her power to raise a graymatter shield and let a blackball fly, but froze when she saw the civilian leaning against the alley wall, grinning like he'd just seen a terrific show and was applauding the players.

"Man," he said, "that was terrific! I've never seen you work up close before, just on the vids and in the crowds. You took them down without breaking a sweat."

Not exactly true, but she wasn't about to correct him. "Thank you," she said, remembering to smile as she let her power settle down. Her left shoulder twinged sharply; her weak spot, acting up again. "But you really shouldn't have approached until it was safe."

The dark-haired man laughed—oh, Jet liked that deep, musical sound. A sexy sound. He said, "I wasn't worried. After all, you were right here. What could possibly be bad about that?"

She felt herself blush from the roots of her hair down to her toes. No matter; he couldn't see her face clearly. "What brought you into the alley before it was secure?"

"You did." He held up a metal communications device that winked in the sunlight. "Ops sent me. I'm your new Runner."

Jet's tight smile melted into a genuine grin. About freaking time. She forced herself not to rip the comlink from his hand and stuff it into her ear. *Professional. Polite. Powerful.* A breath later, she said, "I'm really glad to meet you."

"The feeling's mutual. I'm Bruce Hunter. And I'm a huge fan."

Still blushing like a schoolgirl, Jet took the comlink. As her gloved fingers brushed against his bare ones, she could have sworn she felt a tingle, like a hum of energy that danced over her body.

Nonsense; Runners were strictly normals. The feeling had to be all in her imagination.

If only the way her body was tingling was also just her imagination. Ignoring the warmth spreading through her, she said, "Thank you, Mr. Hunter. I appreciate you coming so soon."

His blue eyes twinkled, and Jet noticed he had a dimple in his right cheek. "Please, call me Bruce. 'Mister Hunter' makes me feel old."

"You can't be more than twenty," she said, then bit her tongue when she realized she'd said the thought aloud.

What on earth was wrong with her? First she'd let Iridium escape, and now she was practically flirting with a Runner?

Chuckling, he said, "Actually, twenty-three."

A year older than she was. Jet felt the heat travel through her torso, making her stomach flutter and her breasts...

Oh, Light.

She shrugged her shoulders so that her cape shrouded her entire body. Her body hidden, she returned his smile, was fascinated by how his eyes seemed almost electric.

After a moment, he cleared his throat, and that was when it dawned on her that she'd been staring like a lovestruck teenager. She smiled broader so that she wouldn't groan.

If Bruce saw her distress, he was too much of a gentleman to mention it. Instead, he said, "Want me to call these guys in for you, save you the hassle with the cops? I'm sure you've got places to be."

She almost sighed with relief. "That would be terrific. You sure you don't mind?"

"Hey, I'm here to make your life easier."

That sounded incredibly nice. None of her other Runners had ever gone out of their way to do something without being asked; most, she thought, were afraid of her. Even the beloved Lady of Shadows was, after all, a Shadow power. Pushing that sour thought aside, she said, "Well, it's a pleasure to meet you, Bruce."

"Same here. I'll see you tonight, then?"

Her eyes bugged before she schooled her face to impassivity. "Oh?"

He smiled again, and Jet found herself enjoying how his blue eyes seemed to ripple with mirth. "Um, to bring you dinner? Unless you'll be on a mission tonight...?"

"Oh...right." Of course he'd be bringing her dinner; that was part of what Runners did. They made sure that the extrahumans didn't have to waste any of their limited downtime by mingling with civilians to do mundane things, like order food. Or pay for it. "I'll be home this evening. If there's any change in my plans, I'll let Ops know."

Eyes twinkling, he said, "See you tonight at the Complex."

She was in the air before she realized that she'd summoned a Shadow floater to fly her away. *Bruce,* she thought, his name reverberating in her mind. *Bruce. Bruce. Bruce.*

It was five minutes before she remembered to put the comlink in her ear.

THEN

YEAR 1

CHAPTER 7

IRIDIUM

No student shall willfully or knowingly defy Corp's conduct code, and no student shall willfully or knowingly engage in behavior detrimental to Corp's approved marketing plan for their Heroic Identity...

Corp Extrahuman Academy Handbook,
Chapter 3, "Branding"

Hey." The boy standing in rank behind Iridium poked her on the shoulder. "Hey, you wanna have some fun?"

Iridium turned around and gave the boy a glare that would melt through securiplast. "Get lost."

"What's your handle?" he whispered.

At the front of the Academy auditorium, the Superintendent was droning through student orientation. "As members of the Academy, you are not children any longer. You will be held to a higher standard of decorum..." He paused to glance around the room, managing to meet every child's eyes. Behind him, the row of twelve proctors stood in their costumes, or plain black jumpsuits if they were retired from active heroic service, silent and immobile as temple pillars. Eviscerator, Night, Celestina...Iridium couldn't be bothered to remember the rest.

"You will become the finest of a new generation," said the Superintendent. "Powerful, brave, compassionate, and heroic. Make no mistake."

"Hey, I'm talking to you!" the boy hissed. "What's your handle?"

Iridium stared resolutely ahead, watching the Superintendent's Adam's apple bob up and down under his too-thin, too-pale skin. Not that she had any interest in what he was saying, but she wasn't about to get busted out on her first day. She could just hear her old Primary School proctor's voice. *Even rabid dogs have more self-control than you, Iridium...*

"Bitch," the boy muttered. "Think you're so great? Well, my name's Hornblower, and you just pissed me off."

Iridium rotated on her heel to face him. The boy was big and blond, and looked like he should be in the sponsorship draft rather than here with children. He had bright, birdlike blue eyes under a prominent brow that made him look like a pit dog about to bite Iridium's head off.

She didn't let the boy see he'd bothered her, or scared her. *Never show weakness. Never show fear. Never let anyone smell your blood.* That was her father's voice.

"My name's Iridium," she hissed at the jerk. "And my *real* name is Callie. Callie *Bradford*. You got anything else stupid to say, wasteoid?"

"Shh!" another trainee admonished from farther down the line.

The Superintendent was still talking, and now he was using holoslides. The Academy's grid lit up, along with the forbidden hallways of the Mental power's wing as well as the situation complex, where junior heroes went to train for field duty.

"The situation levels are strictly off-limits to all students under the age of fifteen," the Superintendent said. "And only those with the proper clearance are allowed to access the Mental wing. Any students discovered outside the designated Academy areas will be disciplined immediately and may be expelled. Your complete rulebook is downloading to your wristlets. You will be required to read this document before a comprehension test tomorrow morning."

Iridium didn't take her eyes off the blond boy.

Hornblower had gone pale, and he looked at his polished boots rather than meeting Iridium's gaze.

She smiled. "That's what I thought, *bitch.*"

"This concludes your orientation," said the Superintendent. "Your room assignments will be transmitted to your data wristlets. You will report to your rooms for attendance-taking immediately."

Iridium's wristlet beeped in concert with every other student's, and the room code D38 flashed on her readout, along with directions to the girls' dormitories.

When she turned to march out of the gym in lockstep with the other students, Hornblower caught her hard in the ribs with his elbow. "I'm gonna see you again," he said as he walked past.

Iridium watched the back of his crew-cut blond head bob away. "Bet your ass," she muttered.

The girl who had shushed her before *tsked.* "Heroes don't swear, Iridium."

"Shut your fat mouth, Dawnlighter."

Dawnlighter lifted her nose into the air and pointedly looked away as the column of girls broke off from the line of boys and marched under the arch of the Girls' wing.

The door to room D38 was closed, and Iridium held out her data wristlet to the lock for a scan. Her wristlet was made out of iridescent white plastic, inset with a small datascreen and chip like the badge she'd worn around her neck in Primary School. The small, fully black circle branded against the white shine designated her as a Light power. The Academy was very big on branding. Yellow for Earth powers. Blue for Water powers. So original.

The latches flipped back after the Corp's central Ops computer scanned and logged Iridium's entry, and the door opened with a hiss like that of an isolation chamber.

"Hi," said Iridium to the room's other occupant.

The girl was sitting on the edge of her twin bed, twisting the fringe of the white coverlet between her fingers. Short honey blond hair masked a heart-shaped face that stared fixedly at her knees.

Iridium stepped in and squinted. Every light in the place, including the floor panels that usually only turned on during drills and emergencies, was lit. The girl's things were already occupying one half of the dresser and closet space, as well as half the small bathroom shelf over the sink and the steam shower. She didn't have much. No play clothes; just black or gray Academy jumpsuits and one formal white unikilt. No books, no vid console, nothing to suggest to Iridium that anyone had cared about her roommate, wherever she'd come from.

Then again, all of the girl's things *were* painfully organized, so maybe she did have a fussy mother or Support tender somewhere telling her to sit up straight and eat her vegetables.

"Please don't turn any of the lights off," said the girl when Iridium started to wave her hand in front of the sensor panel. "I need the lights."

"Huh," said Iridium. She bent over at the waist and looked at the seated girl from below. She recognized the thin, serious face from somewhere, from a class in Primary School or one of the many self-defense and theory units they all had to study the summer before their work at the Academy began. After a minute she said, "Jet."

The girl flinched at the name. "Iridium," she muttered.

"You can call me Callie, if my handle bothers you."

Iridium didn't know why she had the sudden urge to be nice. She wasn't nice. The other extrahuman kids at the Academy stayed *away* from her because of that. But Jet was so small, almost pathetic. Kids like Dawnlighter and Hornblower were going to eat her alive. *I just feel sorry for her, that's all,* Iridium told herself firmly.

"I hear your dad's rabid," said Jet, fingers still braiding and unbraiding the fringe.

On second thought, screw being nice.

"I hear yours went nuts," said Iridium without missing a beat.

Jet's hands stopped moving. After a moment, she curled on her side and faced the wall. She stayed that way until the dinner bell sounded over the comm.

"Tonight's menu is casserole with a vegetable side dish," said the Superintendent's prerecorded voice. "Your three-deefilm will be *Once a Hero,* the biography of Captain Colossal, showing in the recreation block at nineteen hundred hours."

Iridium stopped unpacking the things the Support staff had dropped off from her old room, in the compartment she shared with her foster mother, Abbie. Abbie was Support, too, but she was nice and occasionally let Iridium go to the roof of Housing and practice her strobes—which was strictly against the rules.

She'd never see Abbie again, now that she was a full-time student of the Academy. It didn't bother her, exactly, but she did feel distinctly unwelcome. And she'd only been there a few hours.

Iridium realized that Jet hadn't even had a foster parent to take the place of her mother and father. She'd been raised with all of the other orphaned extrahumans on the Orphanage level, which Abbie and the other adults talked about when they thought Iridium was studying or listening to her digipod.

Jet hadn't moved when the comm rang.

Iridium bit her lip, her stomach and her reputation fighting with the pity that Jet's hunched figure stirred within her.

Rough as it was dealing with whispers and stares, with other kids like Hornblower trying to beat her up until she'd learned to fight back hard enough to make all but the toughest bullies too scared to try, it must be harder living as the daughter of a crazy ex-hero.

Iridium tried to listen to her father, even if Arclight had been in Blackbird Prison for five and a half years. *Friends are a luxury people like us cannot afford, Callie.*

Did she really want to go through five years of Academy without anyone to keep her company but the net and the music on her digipod?

Not really.

"Listen," she said to Jet. "You want me to bring you some gingerbread from the cafeteria?"

"No food in the rooms," Jet said softly.

Iridium approached the bed. "I won't tell if you won't."

"I'm not hungry."

Iridium sighed, then sat down on the bed. "Jet, this is none of my business, 'kay? But if you don't go out there now, then jerks like Hornblower are gonna be talking about you for the rest of the year."

"I don't care what Hornblower says."

"Hornblower's fifth-generation hero. His dad is on the front of that stupid cereal we eat every morning. *Everyone* in our class cares what he says."

Jet's shoulder blades hunched together like a faulty doll. "You don't."

Iridium felt the venom creep from her chest into her voice. "With my family, believe me . . . I've heard it all before."

"If I go out there," Jet said, "Dawnlighter and the other girls are going to say things about me."

"I'll make you a deal, 'kay? Anyone starts talking shit, I'll punch them in the face."

Jet rolled over and sat up, facing Iridium. "But you'll get into trouble and stuff."

"My dad's rabid, like you said." Iridium shrugged. "What have I got to lose?"

CHAPTER 8

JET

Of all the forms our abilities take, from Fire to Mental to Shadow, each has had its share of misunderstandings and each has had its notorious disasters...

Dr. Lyle Lee (formerly known as Firebolt), from
Within: Theories of Extrahuman Power

She's just a dirty Shadow," the girl laughed, pointing at her. "No mistaking that wristlet."

Jet swallowed, darted a nervous glance at the inky band around her left wrist. The color branded her as if it were a mark on her skin. Black meant she worked with the shadows, bent them to her will. And everyone knew what *that* ultimately meant: She would go insane. Eventually. She could still hear her father screeching her name before they took him away.

A hand on Jet's shoulder, then Iridium's loud voice: "You're so concerned about dirt, Dawnie, go take a bath."

The tall redhead blinked at Iridium, then scowled as her friends laughed behind their hands. There were a lot of girls clustered around them; sweet Jehovah, it seemed like the entire Academy was in line for the cafeteria. Jet's mind whirled as she assessed the laughing girls crowded in front of her. About ten of them, already cliquing. They'd worked fast on this first day of the Academy—and Dawnlighter had already grasped the reins.

Jet glanced around, tried to find an adult for help. Where was the Superintendent? Or the proctors? Or any of the instructors? Weren't they supposed to have the students eat in shifts, to avoid having so many kids with powers in one place at one time? This had to be against the rules, or an oversight . . .

The girl cast a long look at Iridium, who was standing next to Jet as if the two of them had been paired. Ridiculous, Jet thought; pairings didn't happen until Third Year. Besides, why would any Lighter want to be partnered with a Shadow? Jet's lips quirked as she thought of how funny that would be—so very black and white. Dark and light. Yin and yang.

After sizing them up, the red-haired girl sniffed, "That's Dawn*lighter*."

"And *there's* a handle to be proud of," Iridium said. Jet didn't see her face, but based on the sound of her voice, Iridium was rolling her eyes. "So original, they should have called you Original Girl."

Around them, a gossip of teens said "Oooh." Jet fought an insane urge to giggle.

Dawnlighter smiled—it was a cold movement of her lips, and it would have looked at home on the face of Maleficent or Vixen or any of the other Code Red villain-esses. "I'd tell you what they call mutts like you, with a rabid dad and no mom, but heroes don't swear."

Iridium's hand bit into Jet's shoulder. "Hey, bitch, I dare you to come here and say that to my face."

Dawnlighter smirked. "What, you didn't hear me the first time? Maybe you should be Deaf Girl."

Iridium took a step forward, but Jet pulled her new roommate back. "Stop that," she hissed. "You'll get written up!"

"Who cares about that? I'm not going to let her talk trash about me or my dad."

"What are you going to do," Dawnlighter said, "hit me? They'll put you down like the dog you are."

"Rabid," another girl said.

"Just like the dad," said a third.

Iridium shrugged off Jet's hand and took a step forward. "If they're going to put me down, it'll be worth it if I re-arrange your face first."

Dawnlighter blanched, then darted her gaze as if seeking the nearest exit. "If you touch me, you'll be sorry."

"I'm already sorry we're breathing the same air."

Another "Oooh" from the posse—and Jet noticed at least two other girls muffling giggles.

"Just like a mutt," Dawnlighter sniffed, obviously trying to act nonchalant and failing rather spectacularly; Jet noticed the sweat beading on the other girl's brow, the slight tremor to her pouty lips before she clenched her jaw. "Growling big, acting like she'll bite. Some hero you'll be, Mutt."

Iridium cocked her fist back.

Jet flinched, expecting the fight and the repercussions... and that was when the plastiflor bulbs overhead exploded.

The girls squealed as shattered plastic splattered them, and their cries were echoed by others in line as every bulb in the hallway outside the cafeteria shattered one by one.

In the darkness, Jet covered her mouth with both hands to keep from screaming. *We're in the hall,* she thought desperately, *we're in the hall and we're safe and there are no voices here no voices it's safe it's safe—*

A globe of white light cut through the blackness. Jet almost trembled in relief as she stepped closer to the ball of light emanating from Iridium's hand.

"Freaking brilliant," one of the other girls said with a snort. "Now the proctors'll be on all our asses."

Another girl hissed, "Way to go, Mutt."

"It wasn't me," Iridium said, startled. "I was going to punch out Dawnie's teeth. Had to be another Lighter."

All the girls glared at Dawnlighter, who squawked, "It wasn't me—she's lying!"

Iridium rolled her eyes. "As if I'd bother lying about someone as lame as you."

"Why, you little—"

"What is going on here?"

The proctor's voice cut through the volley of threats, and all the girls hushed. The darkness seemed to creep forward until it became man-shaped, but maybe that was just the backup track lighting kicking in along the edges of the hallway, banishing the shadows.

One student whispered a prayer, the sound startlingly loud.

Jet's eyes widened as she gazed upon Night—other than her, the only Shadow power at the Academy—who was lancing each of the students with his dark gaze. A black cowl obscured his face; the matching cape draped from his shoulders like a king's mantle. The little she could see of the skinsuit beneath was even darker, shadows swallowed by a black hole. Around him, the very air seemed to still, as if it, too, was in awe of this one man who could repel light with a thought.

Part of Jet wanted to throw herself at his feet and beg for mercy. And part of her wanted to kiss those feet and worship him.

Hero worship, she thought wildly. She bit her lip to keep from giggling.

When he glanced her way, Jet gleeped, and stared down at her boots.

"Someone answer me." Night's voice was very low, and very cold.

No one said a thing. Maybe they were afraid of risking the ire of a proctor on First Night, or maybe they were uneasy about angering a full-grown Shadow.

Because everyone knew what happened when a Shadow power got angry.

Once again, Jet thought of her father, screaming her name as they'd come to take him away before he could hurt anyone else.

Well, Jet was a Shadow power too.

She cleared her throat and forced herself to speak. She couldn't bring herself to meet Night's eyes, but she did manage to look at where she assumed his chin was. "Well, sir"—but Jehovah, her voice was a barely controlled scream—"we were waiting in line to enter the cafeteria. When Dawnlighter started to harass me, Iridium stood up to her. They exchanged words, and Dawnlighter got very angry. Then the lights exploded."

Modified truth; every heroine's secret weapon. And she hadn't even learned that in class.

The look of pure hatred Dawnlighter shot her should have flayed all the skin from her bones.

Jet smiled at her. She tried to make it sweet, but it felt sickly. "What? Heroes tell the truth. Don't they?"

She felt Night's gaze heavy upon her. Summoning all of her courage, she looked into his eyes—for exactly a half second before she quickly stared back at her boots.

Night said, "Is this true, Dawnlighter?"

A long pause, filled with the sound of someone swallowing. Finally, the girl replied, "Sir, it's true that Iridium started mouthing off to me." She must have remembered that her posse was there, because her next words came faster, louder. "Iridium started the whole thing. Jet's just saying it's my fault because she and Iridium are roommates."

"I see." Night turned to face Iridium. "And you, Iridium? What do you have to say?"

Jet risked a glance at her roommate, who smiled—sweetly, Jet noticed; she had to learn how to pull that off. Looking right at Night, she said, "Sir, when Dawnlighter referred to Jet as a 'dirty Shadow,' I had to let her know that sort of language is inappropriate for heroes."

Night's eyes narrowed, and he whirled on Dawnlighter. "You will come with me. You, too, Iridium. We're going to find the Soothsayer to determine the truth of your words." He paused, and the air vibrated with menace. "I sincerely hope for your sake, Dawnlighter, that Iridium was lying."

Jet watched all the color drain from Dawnlighter's face. The girl whispered, "Yes, sir."

The two girls followed Night—but Iridium glanced back over her shoulder and winked at Jet.

Jet's lips twitched into a startled smile, one that she quickly forced down. So what that Iridium had stood by her side, or that she had gotten in trouble because of Jet? The girl probably would have done the same for anyone who'd gotten picked on. That was what heroes did: They defended the weak.

But if Jet dared hope that the two of them would ever go from roommates to friends, she was kidding herself.

CHAPTER 9

IRIDIUM

*I never met a supervillain who wouldn't be better off
with a superhero's boot planted on his neck.*

**Road Rage, in an interview given after his
defeat of Lava Man to Channel 1 in New Chicago**

Iridium knew she had a problem when their self-defense
instructor paired them off and she found herself face-to-
face with Hornblower. Or, as Iridium and Jet had privately
come to call him in the weeks since the Academy had been
in session, the Boy Moron.

From the other end of the line, Jet gave her a sympathetic glance. She'd gotten the skinny kid who controlled
plants and sort of looked like a spindly tree himself.
"Lucky," Iridium muttered to herself.

"Listen up!" their defense instructor bellowed. He was
the size of a small mountain, but Iridium decided he would
have been a lot scarier without the cyber leg and a metal
pin in the arm on the same side. "My name is Erik Taft, but
you will call me Lancer! I am here to teach you that all of

your powers and your so-called skills are nothing next to a gangster with a plasgun. Or a junkfreak with a Talon cutter. Or anyone, anywhere, who takes advantage of a moment of inattention from you!"

Iridium saw Jet wince. She wanted to tell her that Lancer was just trying to scare them, that her dad said he was a washout who'd gotten dropped by a gangbanger because he was busy posing for a reporter. But she couldn't, so she stuck her tongue out at Hornblower instead.

"I'm gonna rip you apart," he hissed.

"I'm soooo scared," Iridium responded, flipping a finger at him.

"Two volunteers!" Lancer bellowed. "My nephew and his skinny partner. Front and center!"

Iridium was genuinely startled when Hornblower grabbed her by the sleeve of her uniform and jerked her to the mat at the head of the class. "You're the coach's nephew?" she said.

"The three Taft brothers are the triple terror of criminals everywhere," Lancer rumbled, like two avalanches colliding.

"I heard one of you was a dud," said Iridium. "No powers," she elucidated, when Lancer turned the color of tomato sauce.

"Little lady," he said, "assume the defensive position." He clapped his nephew on the shoulder. "Hornblower, why don't you demonstrate that move we practiced at home for the class?"

"Sir?" Jet stuck up her hand. "Shouldn't the partners be equal in size for an effective demonstration of the technique?"

"What's your name?" Lancer snapped.

"Jet, sir."

"Jet, shut your Shadow mouth and let the class move along," Lancer bellowed. "When I want any of your snot-nosed opinions, I'll ask for them! Is that clear?"

"Yes, Lancer, sir," the class chorused.

Then, without waiting for a signal, Hornblower lunged at Iridium. He was twice her size, and he moved fast for a stocky kid.

Iridium didn't bother trying to use any of the physical techniques she and Abbie had practiced. She stuck out her hand, called her power, and strobed Hornblower in the face.

He fell to the ground, screaming and clawing at his skin as he rolled back and forth.

Lancer grabbed Iridium by the back of her collar. "What in Christo's name was that?"

"He attacked me," said Iridium calmly. "I defended myself. Was that not the point of this lesson?"

"You take a good look at this girl," Lancer said loudly. "She is *not* a team player. The hero in this room who gets paired with her come Third Year is as unfortunate as my poor...underpowered...brother, Boxer. You mark my words."

To Iridium he hissed, "Get your ass moving. You're going to the Superintendent's office."

As she was dragged off the mat by her uniform, Hornblower moaned, "I'm gonna get you back for this, Iridium! I swear." His face was lobster-colored from sunburn, and his eyes were watering.

"Next time you try and threaten me, don't cry like a little girl," said Iridium. "It cheapens the moment."

"Move!" Lancer shouted, dragging her out of the classroom. Iridium saluted to the students at large and was gratified when she saw Jet smile.

CHAPTER 10

JET

Dreams are just that—dreams—until coupled with the skills and training that we are gifted with at the Academy. You should each and every one of you be thanking your proctors and Corp for the ability to protect and serve that they have given you. I know I am, because my dream to serve a greater good is finally reality.

Celestina's valedictorian address, Class of 2099

Jet didn't know she was screaming. Well, she didn't know she was screaming in real life. In her dream, oh yeah, she was shrieking for all she was worth.

"Joannie," the black thing that had once been her father said, "come out and give your papa a kiss."

Jet...no, Joannie, she was Joannie, she was five and could barely make Shadow puppets on the walls...whimpered and shrank back to the farthest corner of her closet.

Outside the door, her father giggled. It was a wet, burbling sound that made Joannie think of the water in the big plastic jug whenever she pressed the button to fill her cup. *Glug glug* went the water; *glug glug* went Papa as he hiccuped laughter. "Joannie," he said, stretching her name into something terrifying. "Don't you love your papa?"

Yes. But her real papa wouldn't be scaring her like this. Her real papa wouldn't have wrapped Mama in a black blanket and squeezed her until there was only a spill of bright, wet red on the ground and an empty thing that used to smile and laugh and call her "My precious Jet."

"Go away," she whispered to the monster that was her father.

"Joannnnnieeeee . . ."

"Go away!"

"You broke the rules, Joannie."

She shivered, cradled her arms around her legs and rocked, wishing the floor would swallow her up. He was going to hurt her. He was going to rip open the door and grab her and shake her and squeeze her, no matter how much she cried for him to stop.

Stop, her mama had screamed. *For the love of Jehovah, stop!*

But he hadn't, not even when Mama had used his private just-between-Blackout-and-Angelica names. *George,* her mama had shrieked, *please! Stop!*

And then came the crunching sounds, like leaves in the autumn, caught underfoot.

"You're a bad girl, Joannie. You broke the rules, didn't you?"

She swallowed, felt hot stabs of guilt and shame in her belly and her heart.

"Come out, girl, and take your punishment like a good Squadron soldier. I won't hurt you."

She covered her ears, thinking, *Liar, liar, pants on fire . . .*

The closet doorknob rattled. "Time to come out. Give Papa a hug."

Like the way he'd hugged Mama, just before. Papa had wrapped bands of blackness around Angelica and squeezed. Maybe her mama had thought he was joking at first, and that was why she hadn't fought until it was too late. Maybe, even as the inky strips had squeezed Angelica like a hungry snake, maybe she thought he was just kidding, playing Bad Guys the way they did with Joannie. Because Angelica didn't cry at first, not even when the black bands squeezed too much—she'd waited, with a patient smile, as if she knew that Blackout would stop and everything would be okay, because he would never hurt her, not really . . .

At least, that was what Joannie thought her mama had been thinking. That was what it had looked like to Joannie, who'd been standing in the kitchen, sneaking a third cookie before dinner. Sneaking, like a thief. Taking something that she knew she wasn't supposed to have.

Papa had seen the crumbs on the floor. And that was when he'd gone all scary Shadow and had started yelling at her. And when Angelica tried to calm him down with her Light touch, like how she'd do for Joannie when Joannie was a baby and crying when the things in the dark whispered to her, that was when Blackout let the shadows out and made them hug Mama.

Wrapping her arms around her legs, keening softly, Joannie understood, deep in her soul, that this was all her fault. If she hadn't been sneaking, stealing, this wouldn't have happened.

"Joannie, are you going to make me come in there?"

She swallowed, said nothing.

"Here I come, Joannie. Here . . . I . . . come!"

That was what he'd said to her after he'd dropped Mama to the ground—empty, misshapen, broken. Bleeding. Joannie didn't even really see Angelica's body—she was too busy scrambling for the Panic Button next to the comlink on the wall. She skidded in a pool of thick, red wetness and banged her small fist against the big red button—the one thing she was told never, ever to do unless someone was hurt because the button was a Serious Thing, and if she did it just for fun, she'd get into so much trouble that she'd never sit down for a whole week.

Remember, Angelica had told her from the time she was little, *no touching the Panic Button unless it's an Emergency.* She'd taught Joannie that "Emergency" meant they needed the heroes to come, fast.

She really needed the heroes to come, right now, and make everything okay. Make her papa not a monster and make her mama well again. Make her stop being so scared.

So she'd hit the button and run into her room and slammed the door, and she'd run into the closet and slammed that door, too, and she'd scampered to the very back and had hidden in the darkness, waiting for the nightmare to end.

There, in the darkness, with her mother's blood staining the bottoms of her bare feet, the voices started to whisper to her.

lost so lost little girl lost little lamb

They sounded like part of the closet itself, like the walls had peeled away and stretched long and thin like rolls of paper and had crumpled into words pasted on the thick air. She pressed her hands against her ears and tried to listen only to the sounds of her heart thumping madly in her chest, of her ragged breaths, tried to convince herself that she was really very brave and not at all scared because she was supposed to grow up to be a hero . . .

. . . and then her father had found her.

"Here . . . I . . . come!"

The door ripped open, and Joannie screamed and screamed and screamed . . .

. . . and her father's hand clamped onto her shoulder and she screamed louder, so loud that she almost didn't hear Iridium's panicked voice: "Jet! Wake up! It's a nightmare, Jet. Listen to me—it's a nightmare! Joannie, wake up!"

Jet stared owlishly at the girl on her bed, blinked as she took in the clear blue eyes, the thick black hair, the worried set of the mouth. Recognition dawned, pushed through the fog of her dream. "Iri?"

"Yeah."

She exhaled, slowly, and when she mopped her sweat-slick bangs away from her eyes, her hand trembled. As she took another shaky breath, she noticed that the room had every light panel on. "Where..." Her throat was raw, and she swallowed, tried to work some moisture into it before she spoke again. "Where're my goggles?"

Iridium bent down, grabbed something from the carpet. "You mean these?" She dangled the ruined optiframes from a finger. "Looks like you tore them off in your sleep."

"Oh." Biting her lip, Jet felt her heart sink into her stomach. Without the special lenses, how would she shut out the darkness at night?

Iridium placed the goggles on Jet's nightstand, right next to her clock. "Um. Until you get them fixed, you can, you know, keep the lights on overnight." She sounded caught between worry and embarrassment.

"But..." Jet frowned, said, "but that'll interfere with your sleep. And it's against code."

"Don't worry about me—I'm happy in the light." Iridium grinned wickedly. "And as for code, what the proctors don't know won't hurt us."

"But it's breaking the rules."

Her father's voice, smoky with insanity: *You broke the rules.*

If Iridium noticed how the blood had drained from her face, she ignored it, instead stabbing a finger at Jet. "You want to sleep in the dark?"

She wrapped her arms around herself, shivered. Her voice a whisper, she said, "No."

"Then let me do this for you, and don't bitch about it." Iridium blew out a frustrated breath. "Christo, I try to do something nice, and I get 'code' shoved in my face."

"Sorry."

Iridium blinked at her, then sighed. "No, I'm being bitchy. Happens when my sleep gets interrupted with the screaming meemies. So. You want to talk about it?"

Remembering her mother's bloody, broken form, her father's capering glee, Jet shook her head.

"Well. Okay." Iridium got up and headed to her own bed. "You change your mind, you know where I am."

"Thanks," Jet mumbled, lying back and surrounding herself in the thick comforter. "You sure you're okay with the lights like this?"

"Jehovah!" Iridium spat. "Don't push your luck. Bad enough that I'm nice to you. People hear about this, and my rep's ruined for sure."

"Sorry . . ."

"Christo, Joan, I'm joking."

Jet shivered. She wanted to tell Iri not to call her that—it was against code to refer to each other by anything other than their designations. And she still heard the echoes of her father's voice, whispering her name. But she held her tongue.

"Listen," Iridium said, "my dad once told me something when I was little, and it's helped me whenever I get nervous."

Jet rolled onto her side to look at her roommate. Iri, nervous? Unheard of. "Really? What was it?"

"A quote, from a long-dead president. 'The only thing we have to fear is fear itself.' "

What utter nonsense. "And that helps?"

Iridium shrugged. "Yeah. It reminds me that whatever's scaring the piss out of me is also scaring everyone around me, even if they're not showing it. So all I have to do is not show it. So I don't. Next thing I know, I'm really not afraid anymore."

Spoken like someone who didn't learn the hard way that you really should be afraid of the dark. But still, maybe she had a point. "So a nightmare's just a nightmare, and let it go?"

Iridium beamed. "Look who took a crash course in psychology. That's exactly what I mean."

"Thanks." Jet smiled, faintly, not because she felt better but because Iri expected it.

"Stick with me, kid," Iridium said, rolling over. "I'll get you through this hellhole of an Academy."

"You really think it's that bad?"

"Nah. But I'm not convinced it's all that good. 'Night."

This time, Jet smiled for real. "Lancer."

She and Iridium laughed at the old joke, then Jet settled back and eventually fell asleep, feeling safe in the light... and in the company of a friend.

NOW

CHAPTER 11

JET

Where do the heroes unwind when they're done heroing? Do they go home to their spouses, kiss their children, and have a warm dinner? Or are they alone, in a forgotten part of town, desperate for downtime in a place that isn't filled with people begging them to come help or to get their autograph?

Lynda Kidder, "Origins, Part Three,"
New Chicago Tribune, April 9, 2112

Jet coasted over New Chicago. Beneath her, the city ebbed and flowed: pedestrians on the walkways, scurrying like crabs; groundcars skimming the roads, leaving trails of exhaust in their wake; hovers cutting through the air currents. Buildings stretched up regally, their chrome-and-glass sides gleaming like sunlight on the water, dazzling the eyes, mesmerizing and exquisite. Usually, Jet enjoyed her patrols, even the quick ones she grabbed when she was on her way back to the Squadron Complex. From up high on a floater of Shadow, it was impossible to see the urban decay scarring the face of the city—the Everyman posters speckling the cityscape like a pox, or the filth of the lawless, marking their territory with debris and crime. Above New Chicago, there were no police emanating resentment, no blistering looks from citizens wrapped in anti-Squadron propaganda. Soaring above meant escaping the troubles below.

But today, there was no solace as winds kissed Jet's face. Her lips pressed together thinly as she once again replayed how she had screwed up. Light, Meteorite had been livid with her.

"I should kick you," Meteorite had shouted. "Kick you hard in the ass!"

"There's no need—"

"Of *course* there's a need! Where's your brain? Christo, Jet, how could you let her get away?"

"It's not like I gave her a free pass," Jet had seethed, more angry with herself than with Ops—and she counted her blessings that it was Meteorite on shift. At least she got along well enough with the onetime Weather power; if it had been Frostbite, Jet would have been filing reports for the foreseeable future . . . and probably would have had to explain herself to the executive committee of Corp. She'd sooner repeat all of her five years at the Academy, twice, before having to explain herself to the EC. They made the Everyman Society look positively docile. "I fought hard, did my best!"

"Sure you did. And in the process, you let a rabid escape. A rabid who's won over the minds of the police and Wreck City."

"New Chicago," Jet said with a sniff. "Grid Sixteen."

Meteorite waved a hand dismissively. "You and I both know the truth, babe, no matter how politically correct you try to be. It's Wreck City, and it belongs to Iridium."

"You're overreacting. She pulls small-time crimes, corporate jobs. Nothing belongs to her, not unless she steals it."

"You don't listen to the street, do you?" Meteorite's ice-gray eyes regarded her, scanned her face to see her reaction. "Maybe she pulls small-time heists directly, but she's got her fingers in all the action. The gangbangers all answer to her. The cops look the other way. She runs New Chicago, Grid Sixteen, in everything but name."

"Iri isn't into power games. She wouldn't do that."

"You have no idea what *Iri* would or would not do." Meteorite glared at her, and Jet thought she saw storms swirling in the former hero's eyes. "Don't tell me you still think you can turn her?"

"It's never too late. With rehabilitation and constant support, Iri would be fine."

"Therapy?" Meteorite said, arching an eyebrow.

"No!" Jet took a deep breath and shoved aside her anger from the suggestion. "Standard rehab, with a counselor. She could be a hero again. I know her. She's a good person."

"Tell that to Paul Collins." Meteorite snorted. "Iridium is rabid."

"Even rabids can be turned. Look at Doctor Fantasy, at Thunderstruck. Textbook cases of how the system works."

"Iridium would never submit to incarceration, let alone rehab."

"Her father did. She would."

A very, very long pause, filled with unspoken accusation. Finally, Meteorite said, "It's all moot until you bring her in, babe. And Jehovah knows when we'll get another fix on her. Don't suppose you managed to pop a trace on her when she wasn't looking?"

Jet felt her cheeks heat. "No."

"Freaking terrific. Get out of here, Jet. Fast, before I decide to keep you here to file your report directly to the EC." Meteorite turned away, adding, "And you smell like a garbage heap. Grab a shower before you go on Goldwater's show."

Jet replied through clenched teeth: "Already on my to-do list, remember? Along with light makeup and no perfume."

Blinking, Jet realized that as she'd lost herself to the memory of Ops tearing her a new one, she'd flown on autopilot to the Squadron Complex. *Terrific,* she thought angrily. *Get your mind out of the past.*

But a rebellious part of her mind whispered: *What about the good part? Meeting the new Runner was worth all the angst from Ops and the fight with the Grendels.*

But it hadn't been worth losing Iridium. Again.

Hands balled into fists, Jet landed in front of the Complex's security gate. She walked up to the guard book, passing her own image on the way: a holo of New Chicago's own Lady of Shadows, standing proudly, with the words DUTY FIRST above her and PROTECTED BY THE SQUADRON below, complete with the Squadron starburst. Not many people bothered to read the small note at the bottom: THE SQUADRON IS THE EXTRAHUMAN DIVISION OF CORP-CO.

The guard tapped something on a keyboard. "Go ahead, ma'am."

Jet's lips quirked into a brief smile. *Ma'am* never ceased to make her feel like she should have gray hair. Then again, she was feeling so beat-up and exhausted that a little old lady could probably have knocked her flat. "Thank you, Ryan."

She stepped up to the register and opened her eyes wide. She barely felt the beam bisecting her gaze; after all this time, the retinal scan was as much a part of her daily routine as brushing her teeth or her thousand morning sit-ups.

"All set, ma'am." Ryan smiled, perfectly perfunctory, and waved her through. "Have a nice afternoon."

"You, too, Ryan."

She headed toward the elevator bank. The lobby was empty, which wasn't really a surprise; two o'clock was between shifts. Plenty of time to get ready for the thrice-damned *Jack Goldwater Show.*

She replayed the conversation with Meteorite as she waited for an elevator, and again as she rode up to the twenty-ninth floor. By the time she was standing outside her apartment, she was feeling exhausted, wrung out. And ashamed of her momentary weakness.

A hero always had to be on guard. Especially with former friends.

Next time, she told herself as she stripped off her gauntlet. *Next time.*

She waved her palm in front of the door sensor. It hummed in recognition, then the door slid open. Massaging her sweaty hand, Jet stepped inside, and light slowly illuminated the apartment. She paused just beyond the threshold, waiting, as always, for the lights to finish brightening to their fullest before she pulled back her cowl and unpinned her cape. The lights would stay on as long as she remained inside, even when she slept.

Jet knew what lurked in the dark. And she preferred not to meet it in the safety of her own home.

She hung up her hooded cape on a hook by the door, then stripped off her other glove and put both on the small table there. Next came the boots, made of the same thick leather as the gauntlets; she unzipped them and pulled her stockinged feet free. *Whoa—time for a new deodorizer in the boots.* Or maybe she should leave off the antisweat pads and let her stinky feet take out all criminals unfortunate enough to be downwind.

Her lips twitched in a sudden smile. *Code name: Body Odor.*

Placing the boots neatly beneath the table, she removed the thick, pouched belt from her waist and looped it in a tight circle before setting it down on top of her gauntlets. Then she let out a tired sigh. Maybe other heroes felt lighter when they removed their official accoutrements of office. But standing in nothing but the shiny skinsuit, swathed from chin to toe in inky black, Jet felt naked. Exposed.

Sweeping her glance over her living room, she paused at the cushioned glider-rocker tucked in the corner, next to the window that showed the hazy New Chicago skyline and, most important, next to her overstuffed bookcase. She knew it was eccentric, but she preferred the old-fashioned paper books to reading electronically. Something about the feel of the book in her hands, of the smell of the paper, gave her comfort. Most of the novels crammed on the shelves were romances. Maybe it was trite, but Jet loved to read books that guaranteed a happily-ever-after.

Real life so rarely ended well; it was nice to lose herself in a fantasy of happiness, even if it was just in the well-worn pages of a book.

Tonight she'd read one of the historicals from the early twenty-first century. Those always made her smile. Assuming she didn't have a mission, of course. Or another beat on Iridium.

Unzipping her costume, she padded over to her vidphone. Two messages. She'd forgotten to set visual for messaging, so she was stuck with voice only. Light, she was tired.

"Hey, Jet. It's Bruce. Looking forward to dinner later."

Warmth tingled in her belly as she replayed the quick message. None of the other Runners had ever confirmed that she'd be home, or had bothered to leave messages. Then again, none of the other Runners had been sexy, dark-haired men who made her skin feel electric . . .

"Hello, Jet. I hear you've had an interesting day."

The second speaker's voice both sent ice up her spine and, incongruously, made her relax. Then again, Night always sounded cold, even when he was laughing—like now, with his low chuckle.

"Interesting in the Chinese sense, of course. When you get in, call me."

No mention of whether he was calling as her former mentor or as an ex-officio member of the Corp EC. As the Academy representative, Night was in the loop on all things extrahuman. Including, apparently, her screwup with Iridium.

She blew out a frustrated sigh. Iri had caught her completely off guard. Twice. There was a time when she'd known exactly what Iri was capable of.

You have no idea what Iri *would or would not do,* Meteorite's voice chided.

Maybe. And maybe Iridium was really nothing more than a rabid extrahuman, and she'd have to be put away or put down.

But it had been Jet who'd nearly killed her former friend earlier today, not the other way around. She shivered, remembered the whisper of the Shadow voices goading her on. All it took was a squeeze...

Enough, she told herself angrily. She'd stopped herself from going too far. Iridium was fine.

She tapped her comlink.

"Ops," a voice responded—not Meteorite. Another woman she couldn't place.

"This is Jet. When my Runner comes with dinner, please ensure he also brings me a new set of optiframes. Alpha-issue."

"Processing. One moment."

As she waited for the request to clear, she turned on the white-noise machine—one of three in the apartment—next to the vidphone and selected the NIGHTTIME SERENADE setting. The sounds of crickets and peepers croaked from the hidden speakers throughout her small apartment, as if this particular Complex were in a rural part of Montana instead of sequestered in New Chicago. The white noise was in place.

"One pair of optiframe goggles, Alpha-issue. Approved."

"Thank you," she murmured. "Jet signing off." She disconnected Ops with a tap of her finger. Taking off her comlink, she deposited the earpiece in a cradle beneath the vidphone so that it could recharge.

She erased both messages, then debated whether she should call Night now and get her scolding out of the way, wait until after a shower, or do it after she did her duty on the Goldwater show. She wrinkled her nose. Smelling like a garbage barge wasn't exactly a morale boost. Decided. First get clean, then do the Goldwater show. After that, she'd return Night's call.

Walking into the bathroom, she peeled off her skinsuit—one of ten she owned. She briefly considered sending the suit to the Academy cleaners directly instead of having Bruce handle it. And then she laughed quietly as she realized she didn't want him to do her dirty laundry.

Foolishness, she told herself. *He's your Runner. He's supposed to do the dirty work.*

But stripping off her sports bra and underwear, she fretted over the thought of his seeing her private clothes. Her dirty, sweaty, plain-cotton underthings.

Now she was being ridiculous.

Getting the water pressure and temperature in the shower just so, she wondered if the heroes and villains in the sexier outfits also wore sexy underwear. Actually, based on some of the outfits she'd seen over the years, she was sure that some of them went commando.

Ick.

She unwound her blond braids and shook out her sweat-damp hair, then dropped the elastic bands into a drawer beneath the sink. And then she stepped into the streaming water.

Usually her showers were perfunctory, a necessity. Not today. Instead, she took her time, allowing herself to enjoy the hot water thrumming on her bruised skin, the feeling of the soap as she scrubbed away her sweat and mistakes. It was as if the heat seared away her worries and melted her unease. The shampoo smelled of berries and coconut. She lathered and rinsed twice. She felt vaguely guilty for taking so long, but she had enough time before she had to get ready for the talk show. Ironically, going after Iridium (and losing her, again, argh), getting waylaid by Grendels, and reporting to Ops had gotten her home faster than if she'd have stayed to receive Lee's award.

She'd probably still be sweating onstage even now, if not for Iridium. The thought almost made her laugh.

When she was finished, she wrapped her hair into a towel and her body in a warm bathrobe. Her left shoulder throbbed, and her jaw ached from Iri's punch. *Phantom pains,* she told herself. Feeling fuzzy-headed from the long, hot shower, she went into her bedroom and sat in front of the vanity table she almost never used. Standard issue in Squadron quarters; sponsors expected their heroes to look glamorous. Jet's cowl usually allowed her to get away without makeup. With a sigh, she pulled out her cosmetics bag and rummaged through it for her eyeliner. The things she did to be a hero.

You're the big damn hero around here, Jet, Iri whispered in her mind. *But you know that I know you.*

Jet knew her too. Knew her from when they were young.

Young, but not innocent. Not even back then, when they were twelve. Life had already been hard for both of them by that time.

But some of it had been good too. It was almost ten years to the day that she and Iri had met at the Academy. Jet had been sullen; Iri had been loud.

A sad smile flitted across Jet's lips as she remembered Iri offering to punch anyone in the face who gave Jet any shit.

Light, Iri. What happened to you?

Jet sighed again, feeling sad and strangely empty. Then she begin to put on her public face.

CHAPTER 12

IRIDIUM

As with legitimate businesses, criminals have their hierarchy. But when legitimate businesspeople get fired, there usually isn't as high a body count.

Lynda Kidder, "Flight of the Blackbird,"
New Chicago Tribune, July 2, 2112

Iridium didn't panic when an unmarked groundcar pulled up next to her, and a fat cop with a shaved head leaned out the driver's door. He said, "There's my favorite supervillain."

She shifted the case of chips to her other hand. "Detective Ostraczynski. Handing out parking tickets for fun?"

"Need to talk to you," he said, and jerked his head. "Get in."

"You can give me a ride," Iridium said. "What's the problem?"

Ostraczynski's motor-pool car smelled like day-old fast food and was littered with empty cigarette packs and energy-drink cans. The detective himself was mussed, discordant, and worn-out, just like the precinct he patrolled.

"You know Momo the Shark got hit last week," Oz said.

Iridium nodded. "Retaliation from the yakuza in Little Shinjuku. My sources confirmed it."

"Well, I don't know what kind of half-assed operation Momo was running, but his replacement is some crazy fuckstick named Deke O'Connor, and the kid is bad news."

Iridium watched the housing blocks roll past while she considered how to answer. The mobs were part of Wreck City, like rats were part of a garbage dump. She stayed out of the gang leaders' businesses, and they knew the rules—no open warfare, no rapes, no attacks on honest, taxpaying citizens. Gambling, loan-sharking, and prostitution. *Let them have their money, and they'll let you have peace,* Lester always said.

It was when the gang leaders got it into their heads to challenge her—and one did, every so often—that Iridium started to get a headache.

"He beat up one of my girls real bad," said Oz. Oz was a crooked cop, as if you could find any other kind in Wreck City, but he was also fair and actually prevented crime rather than wallowing in it like the former lead detective, Marcia Sloan.

Sloan should be getting out of the burn unit any day now, Iridium recalled. She'd send flowers.

"I'm sorry to hear that," Iridium said. They passed the Moscow Grand, the hotel that Yuri Pritkoff and his Russians ran numbers out of, squatting next to the Blarney Stone, Momo's former tavern. It was juxtaposition that made Wreck City, gave it a soul—cops and criminals, rabids and gangsters. The only thing pretty much everyone agreed on was a distinct distaste for the Everyman Society. Totalitarianism went over poorly when your flock was broke, hungry, and scrabbling to survive.

"He won't see reason," said Oz, meaning that O'Connor wouldn't pay him his 10 percent for the New Chicago PD's blind eye. "I need your help before he starts screwing up the neighborhood."

Iridium sighed. "Let me out at the corner. I'll talk to him."

Oz pulled his car over with a wheeze and Iridium got out. "Thanks, Iridium," he said. "There were a few more like you, I might actually get behind the Squadron."

"Trust me, Oz . . . there's nothing to get behind." Hefting the case again, she pushed open the door of the Blarney Stone.

Deke O'Connor wasn't hard to spot. He was the loudest, the biggest, the most tattooed, and the most obnoxiously Irish. Black hair and blue eyes, like her, the Snow White complexion that would scorch under five minutes of sun, and Celtic symbols inked on every inch of his arms.

"Top of the morning," Iridium said.

O'Connor looked up at her balefully. "If it isn't Wreck City's own little mascot."

Iridium bit back a snort. He may have looked like he hailed from the Emerald Isle, but his accent was pure South Side.

"I hear from Brian Ostraczynski that you've been messing with his streetwalkers," Iridium said. "Since Brian doesn't lie, I'm here to tell you it stops now."

O'Connor shoved back from his table, his chair toppling over. Momo's crew watched, but they didn't make a move. Momo and Iridium had an understanding, a peace agreement, and nobody wanted to get a strobe in the face if their idiot boss didn't order it.

"You've got a set of brass ones," Deke O'Connor declared. "Coming into my place of business like this."

"Thanks," Iridium said. "Goes with the outfit."

"I know Momo was afraid of you. I'm not. You're just a skinny bitch who can do a magic trick."

"Listen," Iridium said. "I'm not putting a suggestion in your box, Deke. I'm *telling* you. No women get hurt on my patch. No one gets in Oz's way, and you can be damned sure that if you *do,* I will roll over you like a transport hover through a flock of pigeons."

O'Connor went white around the lips and reached into his waistband. Iridium rolled her eyes, lifted the case, and slammed it into the side of his head. *There's a time for diplomacy, and a time to beat a bastard senseless. You'll know which is which, with a bit of practice.*

Deke lay on the floor, bloody from the nose and the temple, a bruise already distorting his face. Iridium stepped forward and put her boot lightly on his neck, just enough to make it hard to get air.

"This is my city," she said. "If you don't like it, I suggest you get the hell out."

CHAPTER 13

JET

When the going gets tough, the tough get going!
Closing of every *Jack Goldwater Show*

The following is a partial transcript from the *Jack Goldwater Show*, "More Human Than Extrahuman," which aired on Oct. 30, 2112:

Jack: So, if you just joined us, we're here with Frank Wurtham, a doctor of psychiatry and chairman of the popular Everyman Society, who has also just written the best-selling book, *Seduction of the People*, a blistering account of the extrahumans and the Squadron.
(Audience: "Woo!")

Jack: Dr. Wurtham made it very clear that he sees the extrahumans as a threat to society, to the whole world. That in his opinion, the best thing for people would be for the extrahumans to just go away.

Wurtham: Or to swallow cyanide capsules, whichever's more convenient.
(Audience: Laughing, lots of applause.)

Jack: Now, now. No need to condone suicide. And there's two sides to every story, even to *Seduction of the People.* So let's welcome our next guest. Billed as New Chicago's Lady of Shadows, she's the face of the Squadron and has saved the city twice so far this calendar year alone. Boys and girls, give a warm welcome to Jet!
(Audience: Applause and cheers, sprinkled liberally with booing.)
(Jet comes onstage. Awkward moment as Jack goes to kiss her cheek, but she stops him with the strategic offering of a handshake. Jack kisses her glove, to audience "Oooh"ing and some applause. Jet offers her hand to Wurtham, who ignores it. Jet sits to Jack's right; Wurtham is on Jack's left.)

Jet: Hello, Jack. Thank you for inviting me to your show.

Jack: Great to see you, Jet. You're looking lovely. You just come from a sponsor photo op? Maybe posing with the mayor? Or more than posing?
(Audience: "Ooooh!")

Jet: Jack, you know that I prettied myself up just for you.
(Audience: Laughter, some applause.)

Jack: Well, I'm flattered. But more than that, I'm curious. Have you read *Seduction of the People*?

Jet: Actually, I've been so busy stopping Hellion from poisoning the reservoir that I've had little downtime available.
(Audience: Applause.)

Jack: And we're all grateful to you for your actions.

Wurtham: Speak for yourself, Jack.

Jack: All right, not all of us are grateful. Doctor, do you mean to say you're upset that Jet saved the city from certain death?

Wurtham: What I'm opposed to is these freaks in spandex running around and doing the police's job for them. I'm opposed to a handful of so-called people lording it over us as if they were gods. I'm opposed to them convincing society that we need them, that we're too weak to exist without them.

(Audience: Wild cheers, some boos. Jack throws a hand up in the air.)

Jack: Hold on. You're saying that the heroes are muscling out the police?

Jet: That's insane. I've always supported our fellow crime-fighters.

Wurtham: They're not your fellows. It takes true courage for a normal man or woman to put themselves in harm's way to serve and protect, knowing they could take a bullet or worse, to protect the innocent.

(Audience: Cheers.)

Jet: You're saying I *don't* do that?

Jack: Now wait—

Wurtham: The police don't have devilish abilities to aid them. They just have their beliefs and their training. The police are people.

Jet: Extrahumans are people.

Wurtham: Extrahumans are freaks, misanthropes.

(Audience: Cheers.)

Jet: *(Angrily)* We've been given special abilities and we choose to use them to help society, so that makes us freaks?

Wurtham: Your so-called special abilities are anathema!

Jet: So now you know the mind of Jehovah?

Wurtham: You work with shadows.

Jet: I do.

Wurtham: "Every good and perfect gift is from above, coming down from the Father of the heavenly lights, who does not change like shifting shadows." James 1:17. I say again, you are anathema!

(Audience: Applause.)

Jet: Actually, I'm an agnostic.

(Audience: Some laughter; more booing.)

Jack: *(To Wurtham)* Now Doctor, you're making some wild claims here.

Wurtham: Like what?

Jack: You said—you just said that the extrahumans lord it over people as if they were gods, that they convince regular people that we're too weak to exist without them.

Wurtham: Exactly.

Jack: How so?

Wurtham: By seeing their faces everywhere. By hearing of their exploits nonstop in the liberal media.

Jack: Uh-oh. Guess I'm on your You Know What list, eh?
(Audience: Laughter and clapping.)

Wurtham: To be fair, not all of the media has bought into the Corp-Co party line about how the extrahumans are really superpowered teddy bears. Lynda Kidder got it right. *(To Jet)* Are you familiar with Ms. Kidder?

Jet: Reporter for the *New Chicago Tribune*. Been out of touch for three days. Her editor put out the word that she's on some hush-hush assignment.

Wurtham: Like maybe finishing her Pulitzer-prize-winning Origins series, eh? You know she didn't publish the final article.

Jet: What happens in the workings of the news media is outside of my expertise.

Wurtham: I'm sure. But Ms. Kidder had the gumption to tell the world the truth about you people.
(Audience: Bursts of clapping.)

Wurtham: She said, "It seems unfair that an extrahuman would take on mere mortal criminals. What chance does a standard human, a normal, have against someone who can fly, or can bend steel, or can dazzle you with light?"

Jet: I'm very familiar with her work, sir. The rest of the quote is, "But then again, as many extrahumans would tell us, life isn't fair." It's from part eight of her Origins series. May 14, 2112.

Wurtham: I suppose along with your shadows, you also have a photographic memory?

Jet: I'm well-informed.

Jack: She watches the liberal media.
(Audience: Laughter and applause.)

Wurtham: Say what you will, but Ms. Kidder got it right. She was on to the extrahuman crusade against humanity.

Jet: What crusade?

Wurtham: You're looking to make us defenseless against you.

Jet: Of all the—

Wurtham: How many crimes have you stopped recently? Not against other extrahumans. Against mere humans. How many?

Jet: I don't make it a habit to count all my victories...

Wurtham: False modesty. How many?

Jack: Come on, Jet. I'm sure you must have an idea. Let's say in the past three days alone. Have you busted up any crimes committed by regular folk?

Jet: Yes, of course.

Wurtham: Of course. How many?

Jet: Five.

Wurtham: And the police couldn't do it...why now?

Jet: Why...of course the police could have. I just got there first.

Wurtham: So you think you're better than the police.

Jet: I'm not saying that at all.

Wurtham: But you just said the police could have done the job that, oh, they're supposed to be doing. But instead, you show up with your flouncy cape and do the police's job for them.

Jet: It's not *for* them. It's . . . Look, you're misunderstanding my role.

Wurtham: And what is your role, exactly?

Jet: To serve the people of the world and protect them however I can.

Wurtham: Hmm. To serve and protect. Now where have I heard that before?
(Audience: Laughter.)

Jack: Have to admit, that does sound familiar.

Wurtham: And this is just the first step. They're making our own police and firefighters irrelevant. Soon they'll make our soldiers irrelevant. And then, with no way to fight against them, they'll take over.
(Audience: Boos.)

Jet: You're being unreasonable. We're here to *help* people.

Wurtham: We don't *want* your help. What will it take before your kind understands that we mere humans can take care of ourselves? We've done just fine without your kind, and we'll do even better once we rid ourselves of you!
(Audience: Cheering wildly.)

Jack: *(to Jet)* He's saying that you're not wanted.

Jet: I understand that's what he's saying, Jack.

Jack: How does that make you feel?

Jet: Like I'm wasting my time. If you'll excuse me, I have a job to do.
(Jet walks off the stage. Roaring applause from the audience.)

Jack: Well, I guess what they say is true: When the going gets tough . . .

Audience: The tough get going! *(Wild applause and cheers.)*

CHAPTER 14

IRIDIUM

According to a recent poll, most teenagers today say that while they'd like to grow up to be a superhero, the supervillains are infinitely cooler.

Lynda Kidder, "Flight of the Blackbird,"
New Chicago Tribune, July 2, 2112

The half-burned warehouse on the pilings above Lake Michigan wouldn't attract the eye of the most desperate junkfreak, and Iridium liked it that way. She patched herself in with her modified wristlet and waited as the antique fluorescent tubes flicked on one by one, all the way down the length of the skeletal structure.

Patched and acrid though it was, and even with the stench of the lake ever-present, the place was home enough, and the old-style steel walls kept out most of the newer scansweeps that the Corp outfitted New Chicago's Squadron with.

The chatter of the tele from the living quarters floated an echo down to Iridium, of Jet's voice.

"Boxer, turn that crap off!" Iridium shouted. She put the

case of digichips on the workbench and popped the locks, slipping on sterile gloves to handle the chips.

A moment later, Jet's electronic voice—"Thank you, Mr. Mayor. It's a real honor to be receiving this award today"—cut off, and Boxer popped his head over the railing, pushing his fedora up with one finger. "Hey, hot stuff," he called. "You got 'em!"

"You sound surprised."

"Well, bank and all," said Boxer. "Not like knocking over the home safe of some corporate fat cat."

"Boxer," Iridium said with a sideways smile, "have I ever let you down before?"

"That you haven't, honey," he agreed. Boxer was pushing fifty, but he still wore the zoot suit and fedora of the Bugsys, his old gang. "Not even when you threatened to singe my eyebrows off that first time we met."

"You were trying to mug a couple of kids, Boxer." Iridium popped the latches on the case and looked at the small digichips, dark green and packed with enough data-pushing juice to handle a grid of New Chicago's power. The rich used them to improve the resolution on tele sets.

Just for a second, Iridium allowed herself to think what it would be like to pocket the money from fencing the chips—get herself a real stronghold, with security and a soft bed she could sleep through the night in. Hell, even a new unikilt would be nice.

"Hot damn," said Boxer, quashing Iridium's train of thought. "I'm a product of my misspent youth, Iri. Being the idiot brother of a big damn hero will do that to a man."

She dug under the workbench for a box of plastic post sleeves and, wrapping the chips individually, began to slip them in. The hackers of Wreck City would get what Iridium had promised them, because the last thing she needed was pissed-off geeks on her ass.

"Your youth called," said Iridium. "It wants its purple cummerbund back."

"At least I'm not monochromatic, doll."

"When the chips are ready," she said, "drop them in the PS box on 170th that doesn't have a camera attached to it. The terminals will get the upgrades in the next day or so."

"You know, doll...Just throwing out a hypothetical here. If we sold these chips, we'd make a nice chunk of E's and could maybe quit this petty criminal racket for a little bit."

Iridium's hands stopped moving.

Boxer didn't drop his genial smile, but he backed up a step out of habit.

She took a deep breath, so Boxer wouldn't know how close he'd come to the truth. He was a lot smarter than he looked, in his tie clip and fedora and thinning slicked-back hair. "After this, we're taking the show on the road," she said. "I've spent five years being a thorn in Corp's boot, and I'm tired of it." She slammed her fist down on the workbench. Her neural inhibitor, purchased from the estate of Baron Nightmare, fell off it and rolled away into a corner.

"What are you talking about, Iri?" said Boxer cautiously. "You know how I feel about getting too visible on Corp's radar. If my brothers or my nephew ever found me, it'd be seriously down times for ol' Boxer."

"I'm saying I'm tired of being a thorn," said Iridium. "I want to be a fucking nail." A red halo blossomed around her hands, her hair, in the corners of her eyes. "We're going after Corp and its army of badly costumed minions, effective now. If you have a problem with that, motor before it gets rough. Got it?"

Boxer swallowed. "Got it."

"Good. Now go out and get me a sandwich, will you? I'm half-starved. Jet caught up with me and got in a lucky hit."

"That low-down dirty hero," Boxer commiserated. "Oh, boss, before I forget...you got a message from the leader of the Undergoths."

"Wonderful." She wrinkled her nose. The Undergoths

lived in the abandoned subway tunnels, not to mention any other holes in the ground...most of which were seeping with raw sewage.

Boxer jerked a thumb over his shoulder. "You want me to tell 'em to get lost?"

"Not until you find out what they want," said Iridium. "Wouldn't be the first time some junkfreak gang leader tried to bribe his way into my neighborhood. If he's going to make trouble, let's get rid of him now."

"He wants to meet with you," said Boxer, lighting an old-fashioned cigarette.

"Well, that's new." She wondered exactly how crazy the leader of the Undergoths had to be. "What's his deal?"

Boxer grinned at her through a cloud of blue smoke. "I know you're done with the do-gooder stuff and all, but you might like this: He says he's got a vigilante problem."

CHAPTER 15

JET

Not even two minutes after Jet stormed into her apartment, the door chime sounded. Still fuming from the
debacle that had been the Goldwater show, the last thing
Jet wanted to deal with was ... well, anything. Barring some
cosmic emergency, all she had on her schedule for tonight
was curling up with a good romance novel. Maybe—
maybe—she'd even allow herself to have some chocolate.

Thinking of which book she'd lose herself in later, Jet
opened the door. And right there, cover-model gorgeous,
was Bruce Hunter. As her gaze locked on his handsome
face, she forced herself to smile, even though she really
wanted to squeak and slam the door shut. Her heartbeat
jitterbugged in her chest, and she was breathing too fast.

Damn it all to Darkness, how could one man fluster her

so completely—and so quickly? He was just a man. A civilian, at that. Normal. Not a threat.

Except her instincts told her differently.

"Hey there," Bruce said, his voice a sexy rumble that sent tingles running up her arms like electric shocks. He smiled broadly, his teeth bright enough to qualify him as a Light power.

When she remembered to speak, she said, "Hi."

After a moment, he cleared his throat. "So, this is the part where you let me in..."

Hating the heat she felt in her cheeks, Jet stepped aside and threw the door open wide. There he stood, Bruce Hunter, Academy Runner, tall and dark and handsome in his black trencher and slacks, the dimple in his right cheek turning his grin into something boyish and altogether touchable, his blue eyes sparkling.

No, Jet thought, staring into his eyes, *they're nothing as soft or magical as that. They ripple with energy. They're dangerous eyes. Sexy eyes.*

She could almost hear Meteorite's voice laughing, telling her she really needed to get laid.

And the truly sad thing was, Jet's body agreed with the assessment. The tremors she felt in her belly had nothing to do with the aromatic smells emanating from the bag in Bruce's hand.

The tremors shifted into small pulses, sending tiny waves of heat up to very sensitive parts that usually were very carefully hidden by her cloak. But she'd hung up her cowl and cape when she'd entered a moment ago. Telling her body to stop reacting *like that* to Bruce's presence, she said, "Please come in."

"Thank you." He strode through the doorway, then turned to face her.

She tore her gaze away from his handsome face, forced herself to look anywhere but at those captivating eyes. Down. Torso covered by his black coat, but she imagined him with a broad chest to go with the shoulders his duster couldn't hide. Hints of a bright green shirt flashed in the gap of his unzipped jacket. Long legs, wrapped in black slacks. Black combat boots. Not Runner standard, but Jet had seen a number of the gophers sporting them. She assumed they were comfortable and, indeed, allowed their wearer to run quite fast. Her gaze slid back up his long legs and paused for a split second by his crotch.

Stop that. Light, where was her brain?

Apparently, it was on sabbatical, because even that moment of imagining him without his pants sent a stab of desire straight through her.

Enough. You are a hero. Heroes do not fantasize about their civilian helpers.

In her mind, she imagined Meteorite chuckling, whispering: *But maybe* heroines *do.*

Bruce's arms were burdened with two bags. As he stood by the table with her gauntlets and belt, the tantalizing smells of sautéed onions and garlic wafted from one of his packages.

"That isn't roasted chicken I'm smelling," Jet said, frowning around the saliva pooling in her mouth.

"Not tonight." His eyes twinkled with mirth.

In response, her own eyes narrowed. Well, *that* was rather forward of him. Finally, a feeling she could understand and take hold of: annoyance. Much better than the unsettling arousal that Bruce stirred within her. Yes, she'd be annoyed, would reprimand him (politely, of course), and extinguish the embers smoldering in her blood before they were stoked into a steady, burning flame. A hero didn't have time for romantic flings with civilians. They barely had time for flings with other heroes.

She thought of a towheaded boy, remembered his gentle smile and strong hands. Her chest tightened, and she forced the feelings, the memories, aside.

Jet closed the door softly, deciding that it would be

unkind of her to reprimand her new Runner with the door open for anyone to hear. Clearing her throat, she said, "I would have thought, by now, you'd have read my file."

"I did." He actually chuckled, like she'd said something cute. The gall!

Voice crisp, she added, "Then you should know that each night at six, when I'm not on assignment, I have three ounces of roasted chicken—"

"White meat only." His smile was far too innocent for her to trust it. "You prefer the breast, but once in a while you have a craving for wings. And you have a cup of cooked carrots or string beans, and a half cup of Jasmine rice or a hard roll. I know. Like I said, I read your file."

She cocked her head as she looked up at him. He was so tall... "Then why didn't you bring the meal that I prefer?"

"Because I thought it would be nice to surprise you." He hefted the larger of the two bags, and the heady aroma slammed into her like a culinary hit-and-run. "Chicken enchiladas, Mexican rice. Small garden salad. And..." Lifting the other bag, his smile hinted at something wicked. "Wine. Pinot grigio."

Jet blinked. "But that's not what I have for dinner."

"Tonight it is." Without waiting for her approval, he walked into her kitchen and started unloading the bags. "Where do you keep your plates and glasses?"

"Just a moment," she said, flustered. "I haven't approved this yet."

"That's okay. Doesn't bother me any."

He was slighting her? In her own home? How *dare* he!

She planted her hands on her hips. "What do you think you're doing?"

"Getting your dinner ready."

"I told you, I didn't approve this meal. This," she said, sweeping her hand to take in the unorthodox food and drink, "is completely unacceptable."

He paused, one covered tray half-out of the large bag.

Looking directly into her eyes, he said, "Part of the Runner's job is to anticipate an extrahuman's needs and to fulfill them. I don't need your approval on this." The smile on his face offset the casual tone of his words.

Her mouth opened, closed. Opened, and she spluttered, "What on the scorched earth makes you think you don't need my approval?"

"Your file specifically mentions that on special occasions, you treat yourself to Mexican food and a single glass of white wine." His smile broadened. "You received the Humanitarian Award today. Sounds like one for the 'special occasions' column."

After a pregnant pause, she admitted, "That's quite thoughtful of you."

He tapped his forehead with a finger. "That's me. Always thinking."

Humph. Maybe he was thoughtful, but he was also arrogant. Which was thoroughly unappealing, no matter how sexy he was.

Crossing her arms, she watched him open and shut her kitchen cabinets and drawers until he found the shelves with the stacked plates and glasses. He was certainly making himself at home, wasn't he?

He's a Runner, Meteorite's voice whispered in her mind, almost as if Jet were wearing her comlink. *He's supposed to know where everything is.*

"Technically," Jet said, "I didn't receive the award."

"No?"

"I left before the mayor could give it to me."

Bruce chuckled as he set the small kitchen table for her. "Minor technicality. Luckily, I know the judge in this case, so you're still eligible for the special occasions dinner."

A smile flitted across her lips. "How considerate."

"Where's the corkscrew?"

"Third drawer, left side."

He set the table—for one, of course; Runners didn't eat

with their clients—and poured her a glass of wine. When he offered it to her, she said, "I'm on duty."

"What, with your cape and belt all hung up, and your gloves and boots stripped off? Maybe I missed the memo that said you'd changed your look."

Damn it to Darkness, she was blushing again. What was wrong with her? "I was just about to change into my casual clothing when you arrived."

His smile stretched, bordered on something sinful. "Don't let me stop you."

"Excuse me?"

"The food will stay warm." He placed the glass on the table, positioned just so. "And the wine needs to breathe anyway."

She sniffed. "I'll change after I eat."

"Worried about staining your casual clothes?" Playful now—a quirk of his eyebrow, the smile still on his face.

"I prefer to eat while my meal is hot."

"Like I said, it'll stay warm. Hot, even," he said, his eyes telling her something altogether different, telling her that he wasn't speaking of the food at all.

He wasn't flirting with her. She was misreading his signals. Absolutely.

But the electric look in his eyes, the way his body practically hummed with energy, with tension...

Fisting her hands on her hips, Jet said, "You are the most impertinent Runner I've ever known."

"I just have a personality. Most Runners don't."

Insulting his fellows? Or speaking plainly? Jet couldn't tell, which truly upset her. Usually, she was quite astute at reading people. "Most Runners follow code."

"So do I."

"In spirit, or to the letter?"

He laughed softly, a rumble that did maddening things to parts of her way down low. "Whichever works best. Should I put the wine on the table for you?"

"Please," she said coldly. Jet dearly wanted to change into her nightclothes, but she'd be damned to Darkness if she did so while Bruce was there. The man would probably think that she'd done it because it had been his idea.

Then she sighed and rubbed her neck, wincing from the sudden pain in her left shoulder. She was just cranky because her body was sore, and she desperately needed a good night of sleep. And really, Bruce was being nice. He was her Runner; she should at least attempt to be polite.

Trying to make amends, Jet said, "Thank you for bringing dinner. And the wine. It was very thoughtful."

"Happy to serve." He dipped his head in a small bow, but when he looked up at her his forehead creased. Frowning, he said, "What's wrong with your shoulder?"

"Hmm? Oh, nothing." She dropped her hand from where she'd been massaging the kink from her neck. "Just stiff. From the workout before." It was a weak spot; ever since she'd dislocated it years ago, the shoulder tended to act up.

"That's what you call fighting for your life? A workout?" He laughed, his broad shoulders bobbing. "I'd hate to see what you called something strenuous."

"Really, the thing with the Grendels was nothing. Just kids playing at being toughs." She wasn't about to mention what had happened with Iridium.

"It still impressed the hell out of me." His eyes softened from their sizzling electric blue to that of a summer sky. "Here. Let me."

Before she could say anything, he was behind her, his large hands touching her, pressing down on her shoulders. With every stroke, her skin tingled, even with the layer of protection her skinsuit offered between his fingers and her flesh.

"Stop that," she said, her voice breathy.

His hands froze. "What's wrong?"

"You shouldn't be touching me. Like that," she added, feeling like a prude.

"I'm sorry," he said, removing his hands. "I didn't mean anything improper. Runners are trained in massage."

"I'm well aware of that."

"I just thought I'd help. You're hurt."

Worse than that, she was horny. "I'm fine. It's nothing, like I said. Just tension."

A long pause, filled with strained silence. Then Bruce stepped around her. "I'm sorry," he said again, not looking at her. "If you want to register a complaint with Ops, I understand."

She sighed. As much as she should make an official complaint, she didn't want to see him reprimanded. The Academy would dock his pay, strip him of his privileges for two weeks. He didn't deserve that. "There's nothing for you to apologize for," she said. "It's just been a long day. I need to unwind."

He stole a glance at her, like a schoolboy with a crush, then he drew the kitchen chair back and motioned to the seat. "Please?"

She smiled, feeling tired and stupid and wishing she could start the evening over. "Thank you."

As she sat, he moved her chair in, smooth as any server at a top-notch restaurant. Then he stood by her side, waiting. She unfolded her napkin and placed it on her lap. "Thank you," she said again, looking up at him.

He smiled—nothing wicked or sexy about it now; just a pleased smile of someone who's happy to have been complimented. "You're welcome. I meant what I said before. I'm a huge fan, and it's a true honor to be your Runner."

"You're very sweet." Her mouth felt dry, and her breath caught in her throat. He was more than sweet. He was so damn sexy that she could barely think.

His eyes darkened, and in a very soft, very low voice, he said, "If I may say . . . it's really nice seeing your face for a change."

What . . . oh, right. She still wasn't wearing her optiframes.

Or her cowl. Looking up into his blue, blue eyes, she said, "That's nice of you to say."

He offered her the wineglass. As she took it, her hand brushed his. Once again, she felt shocks jumping from his skin to hers, tingling through the sensitive pads of her fingers. She almost thought it felt too controlled, too precise, and just as she wondered if maybe he wasn't a normal after all, those shocks worked their way to the core of her body, and her mind whited out in a moment of utter pleasure.

"Jet?"

She wetted her lips with her tongue.

"Jet?" He leaned down, peered into her eyes. "Are you okay?"

"Fine," she murmured, thinking about kissing him. "Just fine."

She tilted her head up, and he leaned down more—

—and that was when her vidphone chimed.

Jet let out a startled breath. What in the Light had she been thinking?

Bruce straightened up, started to move toward the vidphone.

"Excuse me," Jet stammered, "I have to get that." She flew to the phone, nearly bowling Bruce over in the process, and silently berated herself for almost doing something unforgivable. Heroes didn't take advantage of their Runners. It was a lawsuit waiting to happen. Worse, it was just wrong.

But that hadn't mattered; she'd wanted to kiss him. To be kissed by him. Among other things.

Freaking great. Now she'd have to tell Ops to get her a new Runner.

Jet spat out a "Hello" when she answered the call, angrily punching the VISUAL button.

And then she paled when she saw who was on the other end of the connection.

CHAPTER 16

IRIDIUM

When walking the streets of New Chicago, give the sewers a wide berth. It's the city's worst-kept secret that the sewers are part of what the locals refer to as the Rat Network...and it's said that gang-related activity occurs in those tunnels on a daily (and nightly) basis.

The Street-Smart Guide to Illinois, Eighth Edition

The Undergoths' tunnels were lit by naked bulbs that hissed and flickered when Iridium passed by.

Boxer jerked at his tie, chin weaving from side to side. "This place gives me the damn creeps, Iri."

Iridium didn't slow her steps at all, but she created a light globe that floated gently through the dank, stinking air over hers and Boxer's heads.

His mouth twisted up at the side. "Thanks."

"This guy better not be jerking me around," Iridium muttered. "There won't be anything left of him for this purported vigilante if he is." She cracked one gloved fist against the other. White unikilt, black stockings, black gloves, black boots. Say what you wanted about the rest of the Academy, their Hero Branding and Fashion course was solid. Iridium knew that at almost six feet, in her costume, she looked positively intimidating—and she intended to use that to her full advantage against the Undergoths.

A solid-steel access door loomed up out of the gloom, flanked by two gangsters in the colored battle kilts and leather vests accented by bolts and other found metals that characterized the Undergoths. Iridium could recite gang lore in her sleep, but all that mattered now were the bullet points.

The Undergoths were an old gang, populating the tunnels after the waters from the Flood of '09 receded. They followed a single leader and a council of generals. They tended toward edged weapons, petty larceny, and hit-and-run heists. Far from their Rome-sacking ancestors, the Undergoths were major power players in New Chicago's criminal faction in only one way: They controlled every tunnel, every illegal access port, every trapdoor and passageway that ran through the ruins of the old city.

And they stank to high heaven.

"Stop," said the gangster in the blue kilt.

"We have a meeting," said Iridium, cocking her hip. By her side, Boxer moved his hand to the butt of his plasgun pistol. Iridium held up her hand to him. "I'm sure we won't need it, Box. These boys don't look old enough to shave, never mind fight."

As New Chicago had rebuilt grid after grid and closed off square miles of ruined blocks, the Undergoths' territory had grown exponentially. Rival gangs that ran in the sewers and transport tunnels without leave told stories of bodies ripped limb from limb, pipe trees with severed hands for fruit, and screams that echoed for days through the Rat Network. Frankly, Iridium thought their reputation was highly overrated.

The Undergoth clenched his fist. "Shut your mouth."

"I know you're not being rude to a guest of your leader," said Iridium. "That'd just be bad for business."

"Be quiet and let me pat you down," he snarled, pulling a Talon cutter from his belt.

Iridium let one eyebrow go up. Talons were police-issue rescue weapons, designed to bite through the tilithium hides of floatcars and cleave brick like butter.

"Freudian hang-ups are an ugly thing," she said. "You should channel that aggression into something productive, like holohockey. Or taking a shower. I can smell you even in this rotten air."

"Shut up," said the Undergoth for the third time, and reached for her.

Iridium *pushed* at him, felt her power sizzle against the oily fog of the air, then the Undergoth was encased in a column of light, as if he'd been a statue on a podium in Heroes' Hall.

He started screaming almost immediately as the light burned white-hot around him, snapping dully as the Undergoth beat against it. The skin on his face and bare torso started to blister, then to flake away.

"UV rays," Iridium told Boxer, when her companion's lip curled in disgust.

Boxer shrugged and focused on a lizard skittering along the tunnel's ceiling, its seven-toed feet tapping out a syncopated rhythm and its rat's tail swishing as the gangster's cries floated around them.

Iridium felt the sweat creep over her again. Just as Jet had to fight to reel in her idiotic shadows, pushing light waves from the nonvisible spectrum was a task Iridium didn't attempt if she could help it. The further away her power was, the harder it was to grasp. And that left her tired, wrung out, like she'd just hit a punching bag until her legs went out from under her.

Only the limit of your imagination, her father had whispered to her, just before the Senator slapped stun-cuffs on him and hauled him away to face the Executive Committee. *Your power is controlled only by that, Iridium.*

"I'm . . . sorry . . ." the Undergoth moaned. He sank to his knees, red as a summer sunset all over his exposed skin.

"You're damn right, you're sorry," Iridium said. She let go of the ultraviolet throbbing along just beyond her eyes and turned to the other Undergoth, who had watched the proceedings with the childlike expression the Academy had taught her to associate with hash chuffers. "You want to try and pat me down, big boy?"

He gulped. "N-no, ma'am."

"Good lad," said Iridium. "Take us to see who we're here to see, before we're late. Being late is very rude, I hope you know."

Boxer whistled under his breath as he stepped over the burned Undergoth. "Who pissed in your corn product this morning, Iri?"

Iridium favored Boxer with a tight smile. "I'm just not in the mood. Never am, for gangs."

"Who is? Especially for these freaks," Boxer muttered.

The Undergoth banged on the metal door with the side of his fist and it rolled back to reveal a much older tunnel, rounded at the top. Construction halos were spiked up at intermittent intervals along the tunnel. Iridium had to bend over, and the hulking gangster ahead of her was hunched almost double.

A greenish light gleamed ahead, and the tunnel opened up into an old water main, the exchange an arched chamber that housed a few fires and makeshift shelters from metal and old sheets of plast. Green plas burners gave off steam like the smoke of a funeral pyre, and the only sound was the low hiss of static. An Undergoth sat at a bank of pirate radar controls, twisting dials between hits on a junk pipe.

"Radar transmission," said Iridium to Boxer. "Jamming the sweeps from up above."

"This way," murmured the Undergoth, pushing aside a curtain made of chains. "Alaric is waiting for you."

"I'm all aquiver," Iridium muttered as she stepped through.

Behind the curtain, a skinny figure with long, white limbs like tentacles and black hair like a grease-stained waterfall reclined on a lopsided chair made from bones. Animal or human, Iridium couldn't tell, but she pulled her power a little closer and felt Boxer close in behind her.

"Iridium," Alaric rasped. "Nice to finally meet you."

"What's your problem, Alaric?" Iridium said, as a hulking Undergoth blocked her path. "Afraid of little old me?"

"Everyone in Wreck City with any sense is." Alaric smiled, revealing filed teeth. "Come closer. Hugo, stand aside."

Iridium came to a stop a few feet from Alaric. If his black kilt and the bolt through his eyebrow wouldn't stop most people, his pointed teeth and smell would.

"As I told your associate," said Alaric, "we down-dwellers seem to have acquired ourselves a vigilante admirer."

"Not in my grid, you didn't," said Iridium. "Freelance justicers know to take their issues elsewhere, if Corp doesn't tag them and put them in Blackbird." Or get them as kids and send them to the Academy, which was exponentially worse.

"Oh," said Alaric, stretching his mouth into a wider grin still. "But I have proof." He sat up straight and moved his leather vest away from his heart, pointing at the twin black marks there. "Come closer, Iridium."

"She can see fine from right here," said Boxer.

"No, it's all right," said Iridium, looking at Alaric. "He knows what happens if there's a misunderstanding."

Alaric wheezed a laugh. "Indeed I do. Hugo, go get me a chuffer. It's damper than a whore's ass after she just rode a waterslide."

"Show me," Iridium said, stepping to the Undergoth

leader. He reminded her of a spider, crouched in the center of a wispy, rotted web.

"It caused me great pain. I won't lie to save face," he purred.

Alaric's chest was red and swollen, and a mark like a lightning bolt had been burned into his pectoral, cauterized fast so that the flesh had gone black and dead. It was too stylized to be a lightning bolt, Iridium realized—more like a pictograph that you saw around power stations, warning of high voltage.

"This is supposed to convince me that you had a run-in with a vigilante?" Iridium said.

"Well," Alaric said, "I didn't brand *myself* with this symbol. We don't deal much in light and heat down here." He sighed and moved a hand through his greasy hair. "I was at an entry point to the Rat Network, minding my own business, when your typical black-clad figure of justice swooped in, assaulted me and my underlings, then disappeared after he'd given me a warning."

"About what?" said Iridium. "You Undergoths aren't exactly criminal masterminds. No offense."

Alaric laughed softly, like steam boiling against skin. "I'm just passing information and seeing if aid will be given."

"Let me guess. You boys get tired of holding flashlights for the streeties and decide to get a piece of the pie? Because I admire enterprising spirit, I really do, but if you're surprised that you've attracted a vigilante, then you're in for further rude fucking surprises down the road." Iridium tapped her finger against her chin. "Or...you've got someone holding your bankroll, someone a justicer would actually be upset about." She leaned in. "That's it, isn't it? You're a bunch of errand boys, just like the Squadron."

Alaric stopped smiling. "You're a bright one."

"Certified genius," said Iridium. "Now, are you wasting my time or do you have something to offer?"

"Like what?"

"Get out of Wreck City, and I'll look into rousting this man in black. Divorce yourself from this new sponsor, because he's obviously more trouble than he's worth. Go back to crawling around in the dark. It's what you're good at."

Alaric sat forward, propping his skeletal elbow on his equally skeletal knee. "Or you'll what, Miss Firefly?"

Iridium finally returned his smile. "Or I will come down here and personally put the power of the sun down every filthy hole that you freaks call home. I'll make it so damn bright, your eyes will burn out of your head. I'll light up the Rat Network like Yuletide Eve. And then there really won't be much use for you anymore, will there, Alaric?"

Hugo, who had reappeared holding a junk pipe made from an empty cola bottle, made a move toward her, and Iridium formed a strobe around her hand, light snapping.

"It's all right," said Alaric. "Hugo, no need to be cross." He considered Iridium, who kept the light high, spilling brightness into corners that hadn't been touched by it for a very long time. More bones glowed under the strobe, and more eyes than Iridium felt entirely comfortable with shone.

"You don't need to be thinking about this for such a long time, Alaric," she said. "Everyone on the surface knows Wreck City is mine. You and your pasty band really want to test me?"

"No," said Alaric slowly. "No, I don't believe we do. Go roust this vigilante, Iridium. We'll stay out of your grid."

"And knock off whatever got you attention," said Iridium. "It's clearly not worth it."

"Have a pleasant journey back to the light," Alaric said, reclining on his throne.

Iridium turned her back on him, a move she wouldn't

pull with many gang leaders, but Alaric needed to be taught that she wasn't afraid of him, filed teeth and bone throne or no.

"Come on, Boxer," she said loudly. "Let's get back to where you can't see the air."

"Good luck, firefly!" Alaric called after her.

Iridium turned on him with a bright gaze. "I may need a lot of things, but luck's not one of them."

CHAPTER 17

JET

Intrepid Reporter Still Missing
Headline from *New Chicago Tribune*, October 30, 2112

Hello, Joan."

"Hi, old man," Jet replied, the code sounding smooth, natural. Night wanted a clean channel. Grinning broadly at the screen, Jet said, "It's nice to hear from you." As she spoke, her fingers flew over the vidphone's touch pad, tapping a specific sequence of keys.

"I had a few minutes free, so I thought I'd say hello."

That meant to hurry. She tucked a stray lock of blond hair behind her left ear, brushing her fingers against her lobe as she did so. Then she bit back a grimace. She'd taken her comlink out hours ago; Ops wasn't perched in her ear, ready to listen in. One final tap on the keypad, then she dropped the overeager smile. The line was secure. "Clean channel. Go ahead."

Night's face also shed its uncharacteristic smile. "Good to know you're home, safe and sound." He stared at her, and even from the flat monitor and without the benefit of his retired cowl, his gaze was piercing. Night's eyes were brown like the darkest of chocolate—not hazel, as Jet had once believed with all the adamancy of a schoolgirl crush—and his pupils seemed to absorb light. His gaze wasn't wrong, exactly, but something about it made most people uneasy.

Including Jet. But she was too tired—and, to be honest, too off-center with Bruce right there—to be intimidated. Besides, Night was many things to her—her onetime mentor, her former proctor, a current colleague and even, sometimes, a friend. But he wasn't her father.

She said, "I had to get ready for the Goldwater show."

"Yes. I saw you. You let Wurtham get to you."

He's lucky I didn't punch his capped teeth in. "Sorry," she said demurely. "I should have handled myself better."

"Indeed. And I expected your call earlier today."

"I just got back."

Okay, only minor stretching of the truth, that. She'd been just about to do something incredibly stupid with Bruce, but then she would have called Night.

Thank the Light he'd called when he did. Had she really been about to kiss Bruce? A man she didn't know at all—a man who worked for her? Just thinking about him made her body do very unsettling things. She noticed peripherally that Bruce had come into the kitchen to stand just out of view of the vid, but easily within her eye contact: unobtrusive, but ready in case she needed him. The perfect Runner. With such sensual lips...

"I wouldn't have called you again if it weren't important," Night said, his voice brusque.

At that, Jet stopped thinking about Bruce and instead focused entirely on the vidscreen. "I know. Is everything okay?"

His eyes narrowed, and Jet suddenly felt like she was a twelve-year-old at the Academy. "Let's see. Besides letting the head of Everyman fluster you so badly that you stormed off the set of the most popular talk show in the Americas, you also allowed a rabid to escape, along with e-seventy-five thousand in digichips, after publicly declaring you had to rein in a villain." His dark eyes glittered with anger. "What do you think, Jet? Is everything okay? Or are you in so far over your head that a life preserver is pointless?"

"I *did* have to rein in a villain," she said, more than a little defensive. She hated having to explain herself. "She got away."

"Mayor Lee's having conniption fits over the aborted ceremony. All the vids caught him floundering. He's full of so much self-righteous ire, Everyman's thinking of recruiting him for the cause."

She rolled her eyes. Freaking politics would be the death of her. "It's not like I snuck out to go dancing," she said. Not that Lee would have noticed if she had quietly slipped away; the mayor was so full of himself that she was surprised there'd been room for her on the stage. But the police officers would have ratted her out. Loudly.

"I know, but you made him look bad."

Deep breath. Hold it. Release. Now, speak without shouting. "I did no such thing."

"Worse, you don't even have a rabid to show for it."

"The paperwork's all been filed." She shot a meaningful look at Bruce, who nodded. Translation: *Yes, all the forms are in order.* Thank the Light. That would have been all she needed after this fiasco: getting cited for breaking code.

"Jet, understand that you humiliated the mayor—"

"I was doing my job."

"—and now you can't even prove you went after the bad guy. Yes," he said, cutting her off before she could speak, "I know, you filed the reports. But anyone can do the actual filing, and Runners have been known to elaborate when persuaded by the right extrahuman."

That stung. "I'm not a liar!"

"I know that. But the mayor..." Night shrugged. "He's a little one-track minded. It's an election year. He's out for blood. Or headlines. He'll take, either."

"My skinsuit reeks from where I got hurled into the Dumpster," Jet said, seething. "Maybe we can use it to prove my word."

"He's not interested in your innocence. You know that. And he's calling in favors. Threatening to pull New Chicago's sponsorship."

Damn Iri to the never-ending Darkness.

"He'd never do it," Jet growled. "He was all but declaring his undying love for me this afternoon."

"And now the honeymoon's over, and divorce is on the horizon. This is serious, Jet." Night paused, and Jet steeled herself for the worst. "The EC's toying with putting you on probation."

Fury shot through her. *"What?"*

"Corp doesn't want to lose New Chicago's resources. The EC will do almost anything to keep Lee in their pocket, including sacrificing you."

Her head began to pound, right behind her eyes. Dizzy, she sank down into a kitchen chair. "After all I've done for them? For the city? The world?" Her voice was a strangled whisper. "How could they even consider doing this to me?"

"Jet," Night said quietly, "you know by now that heroing is just as much about the politics as it is about justice."

"Politics should have nothing to do with it."

"Should doesn't matter." He spoke through clenched teeth; his voice was cold, but his face suggested that inside, he was boiling with fury.

"It's not about how many *constituents* I help," she said,

the anger rising in her blood to match his own. "It's about how many *people* I help. Who cares if they're eligible voters?"

"The mayor does," Night replied. "And so does Corp. You're in trouble, little Shadow."

The old nickname blunted her rage. She closed her eyes and massaged the bridge of her nose.

"Want some advice?"

"Yes," she said. "Please."

"Do something to get back in everyone's good graces, most especially the public."

"I'm open to suggestions."

"Give the media a story they can't ignore." Night lowered his voice. "You heard about Kidder?"

The second time today she was hearing the name Lynda Kidder: New Chicago's own fearless reporter and resident thorn in the side of both Corp and the Academy. Most journalists assigned to the extrahuman circuit were happy to report whatever Corp told them, without digging for additional verification. Not Kidder. Jet opened her eyes. "Sure. She's on that quiet mission for the *Tribune.*"

"That's the party line," Night said, voice dry.

"You suspect there's more to it?"

"I find it odd that after a vid-hog like Kidder did nothing to conceal her actions as she dug around for the Icarus piece, now she's suddenly on the q.t." He paused. "It goes against her pattern."

"Why would the *Tribune* cover up their star reporter's disappearance, if that's what this is?"

"Why indeed?" he said.

So Night felt that either the *Tribune* editor was in on Kidder going MIA, or the editor had been strong-armed into a cover-up. Jet frowned. Night had never been one to see a conspiracy where there were just cold, hard facts. "If that's the case, why not go through the official channels? The police?"

"On what grounds? No one's reported her officially missing."

"Then send in one of the Squadron's S&R teams to do the recon."

"Not an option," Night said, tension etched on his brow. "The Mind powers are in high demand these days. Can't waste any on search and rescue for a lone reporter who technically is on investigation."

She arched a brow. "You asked Corp?"

"I did."

"And Corp said no."

"Of course they did. Kidder's been practically black-balled since that Origins feature."

"Won her a Pulitzer," Jet said.

"And made the EC very unhappy. They don't like any-one snooping around their heroes, especially when it has to do with Icarus."

"Bad for the secret identities?" Old joke, that. Heroes didn't have lives outside of Corp and the Academy; the con-cept of a secret identity was right out of Hollywood.

"Bad for business."

Jet stood, began to pace. "There are other options avail-able, if you want to pursue this. Doesn't have to be a Mind power. How about the trackers? Maybe Ranger?"

"Somalia."

"What about Bloodhound?"

"Undercover in the European Union."

"Sniffer?"

"Allergies. Trust me, going through regular channels on this one won't work."

"Maybe she really is deep undercover."

"Or in the hospital," Night said mildly. "Or in a ditch."

"I'd be happy to talk to her editor—"

"Don't bother. He's laid up in the hospital. Apparently, he overdosed on his anxiety meds. Convenient, wouldn't you say?"

"Not for the editor."

"Jet, this is what you need right now. It'll get you out of the doghouse with Lee, and the media will love you forever, again, for saving one of their own."

"Sir," she said, "if you truly suspect something, then of course I'll look into it. Kidder is a good reporter."

"Tell that to the EC," he snorted.

Jet had trained with and worked with Night far too long for her to miss the subtext: Night believed that Corp didn't want Kidder back on the beat. One way or another.

She turned to face the vidscreen. "Surely you're not suggesting that Corp had anything to do with Kidder's disappearance?" The thought made her head pound. Of course Corp had nothing to do with it; Corp were the good guys. The idea that Corp was somehow involved was insane.

"The very notion could lead to probation," Night replied. The right words...but his eyes gleamed darkly, feverishly. And now he was nodding, ever so slightly.

Utter lunacy. But then, everyone knew what happened to Shadow powers eventually.

Poor Night.

She'd humor the old man. It was the least she could do. And once he was happily distracted, she'd quietly inform Ops that Night needed help. He'd looked out for her for so long; now it was time for her to stand by him. "So Ops, and other Squadron resources...?"

"Unavailable for this mission."

"Understood."

"Can I trust you?"

Startled, and somewhat guilty, Jet replied, "Of course, sir."

"Excellent. You report to me directly for this, Jet. Keep the Squadron out of it."

"Yes, sir."

"I pulled together the basics—police reports, mostly, and parts of her EC file. I'll upload to your wristband."

Not her comlink—her old Academy portadata. He really was paranoid about Corp's involvement. Her chest squeezed tight, and she couldn't breathe for a sudden, overwhelming sense of sadness. "Understood."

"Good luck with this, little Shadow. In every way. Find Lynda Kidder. And Joan? Be careful. It's not too much of a stretch to go from scapegoat to Blackbird."

"Thanks, old man," she said, then disconnected.

She leaned back in the chair, her mind whirling. Before anything else, she'd do what Night had asked. She owed it to him to take him at his word—even though the idea that Corp was the bad guy here was enough to make her head hurt. First, she'd pore through the files Night was sending. Then she'd examine Kidder's home, a routine sweep. Maybe visit the editor in the hospital . . .

"Anything you need me to do?"

Bruce's voice yanked Jet out of her thoughts. "No," she said, giving him a smile as she strode past him and into her bedroom. "But thanks."

"You should eat," he called after her.

"I'm on a mission."

"You're in recon mode," Bruce chided. "I heard him. He's sending you the files. So you'll have time to wolf down your enchiladas. Which are getting colder by the second."

"I really don't have time." In her closet, she pawed through her school things and dug out the old wrist-receiver. With a touch of her finger, it turned on. And sure enough, a large file was waiting for her.

When she turned, she saw Bruce leaning in the doorway to her bedroom, watching her. Her heart leapt into her throat, and she had to swallow it down before she could speak. "What are you doing in here?"

"Convincing you to eat before you dash off to save the day." His blue eyes sparkled with mischief. "I'll wave the enchiladas under your nose until you're overcome by the smell and drool all over your costume."

Thinking about all the Mexican food made her stomach growl. "Well, maybe just a little..."

"That's a good little extrahuman." He led her out of the bedroom and into the kitchen, over to the table. Once she was seated, he handed her a napkin for her lap. "I'll put the wine back in the fridge. Water okay?"

"Yes, please. Thanks." She smiled at him, then set to the food. *Oh, by all that's dappled in sunlight, it tastes sublime.*

"I've got other errands, but if you need me, just call." He motioned to his own Squadron-branded wristlet. "I'll come running."

She arched an eyebrow at her Runner. "Truth in advertising?"

"Hey, it's what we're supposed to say." He winked at her, then headed for the door.

Jet lamented that he was wearing a trench coat and not a bomber jacket, then turned her attention to the wristband and started to read.

It was well past midnight before she finished.

CHAPTER 18

IRIDIUM

Police, Corp-Co Still Searching for Lynda Kidder
Headline from *New Chicago Daily*, October 30, 2112

Iridium looked down at the owner of the pawnshop, who was bound and gagged on the floor, and tipped him a salute. Pawnshops were about the only place in the civilized world where you could still get cold, untraceable paper cash. Every other place, except the diviest of the dives, was strictly digital.

"Mrph grn flarg," said the pawnshop owner.

"Hush up," Iridium said, nudging the man with her toe. "Half of this stuff is stolen, anyway. You fence for the Kleptos in exchange for their protection, right?" She prayed that Boxer had given her the right intel. Usually he was good for precise and reliable information, but there were memorable mix-ups, like the one with the gang of transvestite priests who knocked over liquor depots—but never on Sundays.

After a moment, the man rolled his eyes and nodded.

"Right. So I'm thinking that you probably won't involve the cops in your business. You'll just take this loss," she said, waving the wad of paper cash, "out in trade like any somewhat crooked businessman."

"Mmmph," he agreed.

Iridium walked to the door, which sported an old-fashioned holosign reading CLOSED with a sad-faced clown spouting big blue holotears next to it. She looked back at the pawnshop owner regretfully. "That's why I hate to do this."

The alarm began to screech as Iridium smashed the emergency panel with her fist and jerked the lever within. The fuzzy screen flashed blue and a robotic voice announced, "This is the New Chicago Police Department. You are experiencing a robbery or other felony crime. Please remain calm. Help is on the way."

Iridium chucked the cash into a mail drop and mounted the fire ladder to the top of the tall, narrow prefab buildings that composed most of Grid Sixteen. The roof was covered in junk needles, pigeon droppings, and sputtering holopapers from flyover advertising and leaflets. She sat on the electrical box and waited.

Any justice freak worth his cape would come sniffing around to see who, exactly, would be robbing a ganged-up fence's pawnshop. In the middle of territory belonging to a known rabid, on top of it.

Iridium yawned and checked her wristlet. As she was about to give up and go find a taco stand still serving, a whisper of air teased the hairs on the back of her neck.

"Waiting on me?" someone asked.

Iridium turned. "Yes, as a matter of fact. And may I just say, your response time sucks. You can't even call yourself a justice fanboy with that kind of performance."

The vigilante smiled, or at least his costume crinkled up over the mouth area. A black stocking covered his entire face, and flat black welding goggles did the job for his eyes. He was decked out in tactical gear with ceramic plating and lightweight Kevlar straps that could only have come from Corp. No skin was visible, his marking a lightning bolt spray-painted across his chest plate.

"You all talk, sweetie, or are you gonna come along peaceably?"

Iridium cocked her head. "Fan of the cowboy flatfilms, I see. Not a surprise. Your type always thinks they should have a white horse."

"Darlin', do you see a horse?"

"No, though admittedly, a horse would add that certain something to your ensemble."

"Just give back the cash," said the vigilante, "and we'll all go on with our nice quiet evening."

"You leave the Undergoths be, and we'll all go on with our flesh free of third-degree burns." Iridium crossed her arms. "You picked a bad patch of city to set up shop, buddy. This is where you roll up the carnival and move on to someplace where they welcome costumed freaks doing Corp's job with open arms."

She couldn't be sure, but something seemed to close off and darken behind the vigilante's goggles. At the same time, the hairs on her neck went stiff and she tasted burned ozone on the back of her tongue.

"I'm not with Corp," the vigilante grated.

"Obviously," said Iridium. "If you were, you'd have learned how to dress yourself by now. And you wouldn't go after a gang on their turf without four or five of your brightly dressed friends for backup." Not that Corp cared about gangs, or anyone in Wreck City. Slumlords and petty crime didn't make sound bites. It didn't give action footage. If the Senator had a choice between saving a block of residents in Wreck City from sliding into the lake and rescuing a kitten in a middle-class mom's tree, the cat would win every time.

"Give me the cash," the vigilante said again. Iridium raised a hand and summoned a strobe, the size of a spinning, glowing globe.

"I know you think this is the right thing, but you should ask Wreck City who really looks after them." She launched the strobe, aiming directly for the vigilante's face. He dove sideways, goggles irising shut, and rolled, coming up on one knee.

"I don't think. I know. You're Iridium."

"You're very athletic."

"I'm Taser," he grunted as Iridium snapped a kick at his head, only to have it bounce off his arm guard. "I gotta say, it's a real pleasure to finally meet you."

"Pleasure's all mine," said Iridium, punching him in the mouth.

Taser doubled over with a grunt. "Christo! You take body enhancers?"

"Not me," said Iridium. "I just enjoy my work." She tried to knee Taser in the face while he was down, but he grabbed her foot and tossed her away. Iridium windmilled and hissed as her back impacted with the edge of the building's steel utility box.

"A rabid," Taser said. "At least, that's what's on your wanted holoposter. Dead or alive."

"Believe everything you read? I'm practically an honor scout."

Taser swung at her, a sloppy outside punch, but fast, and he was a lot bigger than her. Iridium ducked and let her shoulder absorb the blow while she drove the heel of her boot into Taser's knee.

He cursed and let go of her. "Yeah, you're honorable enough to skim money off every gang in your grid and beat on Corp heroes for exercise."

Iridium swatted away his next attempt at a grapple and

hit him twice, neck and face. "And what fine exercise it is. A lot better than what you're dishing up."

Taser choked. "Is that so?"

Iridium regained her stance, a little impressed. Normally, the blow would drop anyone this side of a comic-book superhuman, but Taser just swayed slightly and massaged the spot where she'd hit him.

"Would you have done any different?" Iridium asked. "Corp has no love for justice freaks who color outside the lines. I hear most of 'em don't even make it to Blackbird."

"No, darlin', I surely wouldn't have," said Taser. He ducked Iridium's next swing, dropped, and knocked her legs out from under her.

Iridium's creative curse flew out along with her last breath as she hit the rooftop, holopapers flying away as Taser landed on top of her.

"I must be getting old," said Iridium. "Either that, or you're just a damn dirty fighter."

"Probably the second one," said Taser. "Now, I have no quarrel with you, but you keep dealing with gangs and getting in my way, and it'll turn ugly real fast. Pack up and find another grid to flip your middle finger at Corp from."

"Oh, I apologize," Iridium said with a smile. "Were you under the impression that the getup and the gravelly voice make you intimidating?"

She shifted her weight to her shoulders and jerked her leg to knee Taser in the crotch, but he slammed his knee down on top of hers. Iridium heard a *pop* and felt the pain that went along with it.

"Christo-damned vigilante justice jacker son of a bitch!"

Taser laughed. "I heard you were a handful and figured you wouldn't go easy, so I planned on asking you nicely." He extended his free hand over her face and Iridium saw silver pads on the palm and each of his fingers. She watched in horror as electricity began to jump from pad to pad, tiny sparks at first, then electrical storms the size of pennies, swelling until Taser's entire hand was wreathed in blue crackling lines. "And then," he said, "I planned on persuading you. You see..."

Taser faltered, and Iridium managed a rigid grin as she saw a sweat drop hit the inside of his goggles. Taser let go of her and jerked his mask up over his mouth with his free hand. Underneath, he was soaked and turning red. "What... what are you..." he gasped.

Iridium felt her hand heat slightly where it glowed white against Taser's ceramic plate armor. "You fry me and I boil you, Taser. Poetic, after a fashion."

After a long second of both of them not breathing, Taser let her go. Iridium scooted out from under him and sat up, massaging her knee.

"Well, hell," said Taser, smacking the utility box and discharging a shower of sparks from his hand. "This isn't getting us anywhere. How'd you do that?"

"Radiant light-heat," said Iridium. "You?"

"I make electricity," said Taser.

Iridium raised an eyebrow. "You *make* electricity? You use your body's electrical charge and expel it? You'd be dead."

"I pull in the ambient electrical charge in the atmosphere and store it until it gets released as one big old jolt," said Taser. "You always this picky?"

"Just smart," said Iridium. "Why'd you come to Wreck City?"

"I heard there were a lot of gangs running wild and a chance to do some good," said Taser. "So I moved in."

"Cowcrap. You thought to muscle me out and take over Wreck City for your own little playground. Make everything shiny and new and everyone going to church on Sunday. You angling for a job with Corp?"

"I already told you," he growled. "I don't work for Corp." He pulled his mask back down. "Anyway, I don't see you doing anything of the sort."

"That's because I'm not stupid. So tell me, Taser...the first time Corp sends a *real* hero to tag and bag you, are you going to knuckle under and go along to prison, or Therapy? Because unlike our little dance number, some of those wastesacks *can* fight, and they love beating up on people they're authorized to beat on. It's cathartic, or something."

Taser turned his head away. "I won't let them take me."

Iridium smiled and held out her hand. "Then I think we can work together."

THEN

YEAR 2

CHAPTER 19

JET

*Jet continues to display an aptitude for tactical instruction
and heroic theory, but her social level is well below that
of her peers. Branding may be difficult.*

Internal progress report filed by
Academy Assistant Superintendent Gabriel Graves

She dreaded this.

Standing outside his office for nearly two minutes, Jet
forced herself to run through the new Focus sequence before she could summon the courage to announce her presence. Right out of Mindset Basics: deep breath, taking in
the surroundings; hold it, absorbing the data and allowing
the mind to make assessments based on initial impressions
cross-referenced with knowledge and experience; exhale,
reviewing possible next steps, textbook cases with examples. A second deep breath, picking a course of action; hold
it, analyzing all probable outcomes; exhale, either selecting
that action or rejecting it to review another. And again, until the next step has been decided. And then: Act.

Except, Jet realized, none of that really applied when it

came to meeting your assigned mentor. There was only one course of action, and that was to press the door chime and wait for admittance. And then...

Beneath her Second Year jumpsuit, she started to sweat. How bad could it really be? He was a proctor, for Jehovah's sake. A certified hero. His deeds were recorded for history; his dedication to fighting crime in all its forms was nothing less than impressive. Feared by his enemies, respected by his allies. Praised by the civilians and admired (so she'd heard) by Corp.

Even so...

A bubbling unease filled her belly, and she squirmed as she stared at the closed door. She'd only seen him a handful of times during First Year, and other than that one time on her first day of Academy, she'd never made eye contact with him. He wore intimidation like a skinsuit, and his shadowed glower was a thing of nightmares. The man completely terrified her.

And yet something about him was...compelling.

Just thinking about that made her palms itch and her breath quicken. What did he look like beneath his cowl? She knew he had a strong chin—she'd seen that much—but when he smiled, did it reach his eyes? Hazel, she decided. His eyes were hazel. She'd always liked the color, ever shifting between green and brown, with flecks of blue. Tamed wildness. Safe chaos.

She felt her cheeks burn. *Jehovah, get a hold of yourself!*

Let me hold you, Joannie.

She bit her lip, frantically thought: *Go away, Papa!*

Let me hold you.

She squeezed her eyes shut and pushed the voice that sounded so much like her father's out of her head. The whispers had gotten worse in the past two months, ever since she'd started her Mental Preparedness units. Forcing herself to be aware of her own thoughts had made her realize just how much static was in her mind...and how, sometimes, that static formed words and sentences and started to speak to her.

When she'd first heard the voice, she'd almost asked her instructor about it. There was nothing in the textbooks about hearing things—other than a footnote about the warning signs of schizophrenia—and no one else in the unit ever mentioned such a condition. Or symptom. Granted, none of them were Mental powers; those rare individuals were trained in a quarantined section of the Academy. So Jet had little choice but to decide that the voice she heard had to do with being a Shadow power.

And everyone knew how that would go. Eventually.

Outside of her new mentor's office door, she swallowed thickly. *I'm not crazy. Not yet, anyway.*

Let me hold you, Joannie . . .

Shut up!

Hold you hold you **hold you squeeze you tuck you in at**—

"Jet?"

Her eyes flew open and she gasped aloud. That hadn't been Papa's voice. That was something darker, colder.

"Jet!"

Something much scarier than her father ever had been.

"Jet. Snap out of it, girl!"

A flash of white, like a star shattering the darkness. The voice receded until it was an ugly memory, already fading to the stuff of nightmares.

Blinking, Jet realized she was crouching on the floor, her back against the wall, her cheek stinging . . . and Night was staring into her face, his hands firmly on her shoulders.

"Jet. Do you hear me?"

She squeaked out, "Yes, sir."

He gazed at her, *through* her, and Jet dared to meet that gaze. *Hazel,* she thought, her mind locking on to those features and blocking out the hints of dark whispers. Definitely hazel. Not that she could see his eyes, but still . . .

Night nodded, then dropped his hands quickly, as if touching her had burned his hands right through his gloves. Standing straight, he said, "Good. Come inside. You're late for our one o'clock." Without another word, he walked into his office, his blacker-than-black cape billowing behind him.

Biting her lip, Jet followed. She jumped when the door slid shut behind her.

His office was stark to the point of being spartan. Other than his desk, his laptop computer and two chairs, there was nothing—just steel walls, a steel ceiling, and a plain dark carpet on the floor. No las-art or paintings hung on the walls; no holos decorated his desk. Just the standard Academy pledges, lased onto the wall: DUTY FIRST; PROTECT THE WEAK; PROFESSIONAL, POLITE, POWERFUL. He gave away nothing of himself here.

Jet nodded to herself; she approved. Showing personality also showed weakness. And Night was many things, but weak was not one of them.

"Sit."

His tone brooked no argument. Her rear hit the seat in record time.

Night tapped on his keypad, then grunted at the computer screen. "Excellent grades."

She brightened.

"For regular school." Night snorted. "Figures. Time to get you moved into something where you can actually use your brain."

Stung, she said, "I *do* use my brain. I'm a straight-A student. I've read all my textbooks already, have done all my assignments for the year."

"There's a world of difference between repeating information and actually having to think things through." He glanced at her. "Are you a parrot?"

She swallowed, stared down at her boots. "No, sir."

"You sure? You don't want a cracker?"

A whisper: "No, sir."

"Then learn to say 'thank you' when someone does you a favor. I won't have you wasted, little Shadow. We have to keep that mind of yours challenged." He paused, let the silence grow thick before he added, "You know what happens when your mind is too quiet, don't you?"

Not daring to speak, she shook her head.

"Oh really? So what happened in the hall, Jet?"

"I . . . I don't really know, sir."

"Wrong answer." The venom in his voice terrified her; she tried to shrink away to nothing as he spat, "What you mean to say is, 'I slipped and hit my head against the wall, sir.' Let's hear it."

"I don't understand."

"Of course you do." Now his voice was quiet, a thing of pending doom, and Jet bit back a scream. In his very soft, very deadly voice, he said, "Because hitting your head explains the vacant stare you had when I found you in a heap outside of my office. Anything else would mean a full examination. And that would mean Therapy. And that would be very bad. Very, very bad."

Her memory flashed to when she was five and the man in the white uniform was holding her, comforting her as he led her away from the closet and her mother's body, away from where her father had tried to . . .

"Come on, Joannie," he had said. *"Let's go, my girl. I've got you."*

"Where's Papa?"

"He's . . . he's off to Therapy," the man in white had said, his voice strained around his smile. *"He won't hurt you. I promise."*

Night's quiet voice shattered the memory, blew it to dust. "Do you understand me, Jet?"

"Yes, sir," she whispered.

"So, what happened in the hallway before?"

"I slipped. I think I hit my head."

"Better." He frowned at her, saying nothing as his hidden

hazel eyes regarded her. Finally, he cleared his throat and turned back to his computer. "What do you do to keep them at bay?"

"To keep . . . ?"

"You're an intelligent girl, so I've heard. Puzzle it out, little Shadow."

He meant the voice. He understood. He *knew*!

Did he have a voice too?

She bit her lip, then said, "Light. I keep the lights on. Or I use my goggles. The optiframes are good for sealing in the light, even after Lights Out."

Night nodded. "A good distraction. White noise is better. Constant talk or background chatter also works." He typed on the keypad. "And challenging your mind is the best technique of all. A busy brain doesn't have the luxury of listening to things it shouldn't be hearing. Effective immediately, you're in the advanced units."

"Yes, sir," she said, her thoughts whirling. He'd said keep "them" at bay—did he hear more than one voice? If he did, what did they whisper? But Jet wasn't stupid, so she bit back on her curiosity and held her tongue.

Night was a Shadow power. Night was a respected extrahuman hero.

Night wasn't insane.

For the first time in years, she felt a glimmer of hope for her future.

He closed his laptop and turned to her, folding his hands across the desk. "As your mentor, I have a certain . . . perspective . . . that others lack. If you're smart, you'll treat our meetings, and what we discuss in them, as completely confidential. If you're smart, you won't tell anyone, not even a trusted roommate, the extent to which we discuss certain matters." Night peered at her, his own face hidden, unreadable. "Are you smart, Jet?"

Translation: *Can you keep what we discuss to ourselves? Can you keep this even from Iridium?*

Meeting his gaze, she said, "I'd like to think so, sir."

"Excellent." He steepled his fingers. "I think you're meant for great things, little Shadow. You understand the power of the dark. You know why people are afraid of what goes bump in the night."

She nodded.

"As you get older, you'll learn to use that fear. Let it do your work for you. Let your reputation as a Shadow power knock the fight out of your opponents before you have to raise a hand."

"But sir," she said meekly, "I don't want people to be afraid of me."

He smiled, thinly, and without mirth. "That will change."

CHAPTER 20

IRIDIUM

The idea that children can be molded into soldiers for a great and noble cause is both obscene and untrue. Children can no more be expected to know what "justice" is or how to meter it than a normal human can sprout wings and fly.

Editorial entitled "It Worked for the Nazis, Too,"
printed in the *New Chicago Century*,
an alternative daily published from 2099 to 2107

Iridium sat on the cold plast bench and listened to the drumbeat her feet made on the base. *Thud-thunk. Thud-thunk.*

The door to the Superintendent's office stayed closed, and Iridium blew out a puff of air, ruffling the few pieces of hair that always managed to escape from her school bun.

Down the long white hallway, the voices of happy students bounced off the arched ceiling, taunting Iridium with the fact that she'd be stuck in detention until Lights Out.

After a year of constant detention, extra work, and re-taking tests so "We can assure ourselves you're not manipulating the system," Iridium came to one conclusion: The Academy had it in for her.

The students, with their whispers and idiot insults,

were bad enough, but most of the proctors gave her the exact same stony-eyed looks. They just saw a rabid waiting to happen.

It pissed Iridium off enough that, sometimes, she deserved her punishments. But only sometimes.

"At least I'll miss Self-Defense and Tactics," she muttered.

A tall, skinny form flopped down on the bench next to her. Iridium didn't move...no need to seem too interested...but she caught a flash of a smile and a shock of blue hair. "Amen to that," said the boy.

Iridium glared at him. He was tall, but his jumpsuit marked him as a Second Year, like her. "Did I say you could sit next to me?"

"I didn't see a NO PARKING sign on this bench, sweetheart." He grinned at her.

Iridium balled up her fist. "Get lost. Do you know who I am?"

"Callie Bradford," said the boy.

She blinked. "We're not supposed to use given names."

The boy pointed to the closed white door. "The Superintendent is right there. Gonna report me?"

Iridium lowered her fist. The boy was still grinning, like he wasn't afraid of her at all. "Why don't I bother you?"

"Because you're not scary," said the boy. "You're just angry." He stuck out a hand. "I'm Derek Gregory. Frostbite, if you want to go by the book. I make ice."

"Yeah, I kinda got that. I'm Iridium. You better call me by my designation if we don't want our butts permanently welded to this bench."

"What are you in for?" Frostbite asked.

Iridium knitted her hands together, then she realized she was doing the nervous thing that Jet always did when she thought they were going to get into trouble. "I punched Sunbeam during a biology lab."

"Sunbeam...wait, don't tell me." Frostbite blew a gum

bubble, popped it, chewed. "Blonde, skinny. Has big teeth. Pals around with a bunch of other Lighters?"

"That's her," said Iridium. "She tried to copy off of my pop-quiz screen, so I decked her."

Frostbite laughed, loudly. "That's it? Usually they let you Light-power divas get away with a lot more than hair pulling."

"I knocked her unconscious."

"Oh."

"What about you?"

"Underwear."

Iridium blinked. "What did you say?"

"I froze a proctor's shorts while he was showering in the locker room after my Phys Ed class. Man, when he slipped those things on . . . The screams are still echoing the hallowed halls."

Iridium smiled, then started to laugh. "That's pretty good. Hey, Frostbite?"

"Yeah?"

"I'm not one of those 'Light divas,' " Iridium snarled. "Don't *ever* make the mistake of lumping me with those other girls. I am *nothing* like them."

"Relax, girl," said Frostbite. "I can see that. We're cool here. No pun intended."

The Superintendent's door hissed open. "Iridium," his voice rang. "In my office. Now!"

Iridium stood and straightened her jumpsuit. "They're playing my song. See you around, Frostbite."

She sauntered inside, acting as if she'd decided to just stroll into the Super's office. Then she stood politely in front of his desk, smiling, as the Superintendent slammed the button to shut the door.

"Your behavior is completely unacceptable," said the Superintendent, jabbing a finger down against his data-screen. The incident report their proctor had filled out glowed and slithered away from the impact.

"Did you bring me here just to tell me that, sir? Because I have to say, this is getting predictable." Iridium delivered the speech with the sweetest smile she could muster. *Anger frightens people,* her father's voice whispered, *but smiles confound them. Remember the power in that.*

The Superintendent turned pink from the top of his shaved head all the way down to his Mandarin collar, like a giant strawberry. "You..." he sputtered. "You..."

"I know, I know, detention," said Iridium. "I'll go do my time with a spring in my step, like a good little hero."

"Oh, no," said the Superintendent, his fingers rubbing droplets of sweat away from his forehead like pudgy erasers. "No, young lady, you've stepped over the line. Hopefully, you'll be outright expelled when I convene the board of proctors. You think that your IQ and your history make you special, but what they really make you is a menace. I want you out of my school!"

"That won't be necessary," hissed a voice behind Iridium. The air around her lowered ten degrees, like someone had opened a window and let in a winter wind.

The Superintendent paled. "Night. You finally got my message, I see."

Night laid his hand on Iridium's shoulder. She fought the urge to squirm. Night wasn't as bad as some of the proctors—he was certainly no Lancer—but there was something about him, how he always seemed to be fading back into shadow just a bit, never wholly present, that bothered her if she really thought about it.

That, and she'd never actually seen the guy's face. That was just plain creepy.

"What is the problem here?" said Night softly, and Iridium knew somehow he was using the exact same tone on the Superintendent that he used on street criminals when he was on active duty.

"This...*girl*...has repeatedly flouted authority in her time here," the Superintendent sputtered, getting wound up again. "And today she assaulted another student and rendered the girl unconscious. Her attitude is appalling, she has anger and aggression problems, and I am placing her in Therapy."

"What?" Iridium shrieked. Therapy was for mental cases and rabids who went off the reservation and killed people. "I don't deserve Therapy!"

"You deserve a prison cell next to your father!" the Superintendent snapped.

Night held up a hand. "Enough. Iridium, what class were you in when you knocked out the other student?"

"What does her *class* have to do with any of this?" the Superintendent squealed. "In a few more years, she'll be a rabid just like the rest of her family..."

"If my father heard you say that..." Iridium started.

The Superintendent reached across the desk and grabbed Iridium by the front of her jumpsuit. "But *he's not here,* is he, you silly little girl? You're just a little dog, yapping at something you can't possibly hope to sink your teeth into, and it's time you were *silenced*!"

"Expel me, then," Iridium shouted back, "because I'm not shutting up!"

"QUIET." Night's voice rattled every piece of furniture in the office that wasn't molded directly into the walls and floor. "Now," he said. "Superintendent, I believe you are out of line."

"Damn right," Iridium said.

"Let go of the girl," said Night, and to Iridium he added, "When he does, young lady, you will apologize for your appalling manners."

"No," said Iridium. "He doesn't deserve my respect."

Night leaned down and whispered in her ear, and his voice seemed to carry with it the whispers of a thousand nightmares lived alone, in the dark. "He doesn't. But you will give it to him just the same, until such time as you are strong enough to take it back. That time is not now, little firefly, so smile and apologize before I break your arm."

Iridium listened to Night's breath hiss in her ear for a split second before she looked back at the Superintendent. "I'm truly sorry, sir. What I said was unforgivable."

"You've got that right," he said, crossing his arms.

"Now," said Night, "answer my question, Iridium. What class were you in when you hit the other girl?"

"Biology."

"Just biology? Not molecular or applied, but plain middle-school biology?"

"Well, yeah," said Iridium. "I'm *thirteen.*"

"Superintendent, this girl has an IQ of over 160, and she is the daughter of Lester Bradford—a fine hero, regardless of his later conduct. She is unique. Putting her in regular classes is asking for this sort of behavior. Transfer her to the gifted program and don't bother me again."

Night turned on his heel and exited the office in a swirl of Shadow-chased cape. Frostbite watched him go, then gave Iridium a thumbs-up through the open door.

THREE MONTHS LATER

The physics lab was quiet except for the *bleep-bleep-plip* of students taking a test on their datascreens, styluses scrolling across the crystal display in an almost coordinated movement.

Iridium answered question thirty-two, threw down her stylus with a clatter, and announced: "I'm done. Can I go?"

The proctor, a retired heroine named Labyrinth, said, " 'May I,' Iridium, and you may be excused from class once you clean up your workspace."

Iridium looked down at the litter of books and holo-papers in her workspace, along with her Corp schoolbag, which she'd decorated with patches and purple iridescent ink.

"That's what this school has Runners for," she said. "My test is finished. I'll wait around while you grade it, if that will help."

Labyrinth raised an eyebrow. "Runners are not your personal maid service, young lady."

"Darn, because seeing them in those little aprons and hats would be hilarious."

"Young lady, do you *want* to go to detention?" Labyrinth hissed.

Iridium winced as she felt the deadening pressure of Labyrinth's telepathy roll outward. A few of the more sensitive students moaned unconsciously.

Mental power or not, Iridium would have kept up the argument if it weren't for Jet. She was standing at her workspace with her shoulders hunched, her lips moving in the same phrase over and over again.

She was only on question fifteen.

"No, ma'am," Iridium said. "Forgive me. I'll clean up right away and report to the meditation room until fifth chimes."

"You better believe you will," Labyrinth huffed, then picked up her datareader, scrolling to the next page of her daily news.

Iridium took as much time as she could cleaning up her papers and books, then she repacked her bag. The big clock in the corner slowly ticked toward the red zone. Finally, it buzzed.

Labyrinth put down her pad. "One minute, students."

Jet's shoulders began to shake, and she lost her grip on her stylus. It skidded down the screen to the wrong answer and entered it into record. "Christo," Jet hissed.

"I know that wasn't foul language I heard, missy," Labyrinth snapped. "Frostbite, what did Jet say?"

Frostbite whipped his spiky blue head up, the goggles he kept on his forehead for vidgaming between classes sliding over his eyes. "She said 'Crisco,' ma'am."

Labyrinth's lips pursed. "Crisco?"

"Yes, ma'am. Shortening? We're all a little hungry here. This test overlaps lunch period."

The chime sounded, and Jet stabbed the last answer into her datascreen as the rest of the gifted students grabbed their bags and piled out of the room.

Jet was gripping her console, her knuckles white. Iridium shouldered her bag and went over to her roommate, nudging her arm. "Hey. We're safe until the end of term. That was our last exam."

Frostbite waved a hand in front of Jet's face. "She okay? She looks like she just got a bad hit of junk."

"She'll be fine," said Iridium. "This happens sometimes. Come on, Jet, let's get to the meditation hall and see if a Runner will bring us some leftovers from lunch."

"I'm all about that," said Frostbite.

Iridium cocked her eyebrow in a glare. "I say anything about you coming along, Popsicle Boy?"

"No," said Frostbite. "But today's taco day, and I'm not missing that for anything. Not even the oh-so-terrifying Callie Bradford."

"Frostbite," Labyrinth bleated, "we use only code designations in this classroom."

"Sorry, ma'am," he said with a sweet smile. "Iridium just got me a little carried away. She's so very scary."

"Class is over," said Labyrinth. "Get out."

"With pleasure," Iridium muttered.

They made their way to the meditation room, Frostbite in front, Iri leading Jet, who shuffled her feet. Second Years weren't allowed to use the meditation room, except for those in the gifted program. Iridium didn't give a damn about meditating, but she liked having separate space from the other Second Years. The room itself was largely empty, its tatami mats and wooden tables embedded with datascreens set at discreet intervals. Iridium settled Jet on a cushion and buzzed for a Runner.

"I failed," Jet moaned.

"You didn't fail," Iridium said with a sigh. "Those tests are a load of cowcrap anyway. I covered fluid dynamics before I even came to the Academy full-time."

"Kiddie stuff," Frostbite agreed.

Jet began to bang her forehead against the table.

"Stop it," Iridium hissed. "Do you want to get dragged off to Therapy? Just relax for a damn minute!"

Jet hid her face with her hands. "I can't do this. Night told me I could, but I can't. I don't know things the way you and Frostbite know them, Iri. It doesn't work that way in my head."

Iridium rubbed Jet between the shoulders, knowing her friend was hiding her face so no one would see her cry. "I'll tutor you. You won't get kicked out of the program."

"I . . . You will?" Jet looked up, her eyes red but dry.

"Of course," said Iridium. "Think I'd let you leave me alone with Derek the Dork?"

Frostbite wadded up a leftover menu from the cafeteria and threw it at Iridium, who ducked, giggling.

"Well, if it isn't the mental patient and friends," said a voice from Iridium's back. "What does it mean when a Shadow, a rabid, and a blue fairy all get together? Six more weeks of winter?"

Iridium spun around. "Go bend over and bite your own ass, Dawnlighter. What in Christo's name are you even doing in here? You don't have access."

"Yeah, I thought they kept all you yappy poodles on a leash," Frostbite said.

Jet ducked her head and looked like she wanted to melt into the shadows under the table.

"I'm authorized for the sponsorship track today." Dawnlighter tossed her head. "My mother and father are here for my costume fitting."

"We don't get fitted for costumes until Third Year. It's procedure," Jet murmured.

"It's procedure," Dawnlighter mocked. "Maybe for freaks who don't have parents and spend their time with their noses plastered to datapads instead of thinking about branding." She did a pirouette, and the short unikilt she was wearing turned the shade of a sunrise, red at the bottom fading to the most delicate pink against Dawnlighter's pale skin.

"Morphing fabric, biolinked to my vitals," said Dawnlighter. "The best kind of fabric. Mommy pays only for the best."

The unikilt faded back to white, with a large *D* in script on the chest.

"That's the ugliest costume I've ever seen," Frostbite stated unequivocally. "Good luck getting a sponsor with that eye-bleeding mess."

"Why don't you go drink some of your hair dye?" Dawnlighter hissed. "You and the Shadow both. Get out of the extrahuman gene pool and do us all a favor."

"Screw you," said Iridium. "Besides, I already got my costume." She dug in the bottom of her bag and pulled out a plastic package.

Jet goggled at her. "How do you have that?"

"Night gave it to me early," said Iridium. Night had shoved the package into her hands with a sonorous, "No one is to see this until the end of term." Iridium didn't question why she, out of all the students in Second Year, got lucky, but now she was glad of it.

She shook out the white unikilt with the black belt and collar, holding it up with a smug smile to Dawnlighter. "It doesn't turn the color of puke when I see you, Dawnie, but I guess you can't have everything you want, right?"

"You can't be white!" Dawnlighter hissed. "*I'm* white!"

"You're an idiot, too, but you don't see me boarding the Freakout Express," said Iridium. "Run back to Mommy and Daddy and leave the smart people alone, huh, Dawnie?"

Dawnlighter began to shake, and Iridium saw a thin

trickle of blood start from one of her nostrils. "You think you're so funny, Iridium. You think that you can make everyone forget that your father is a filthy rabid criminal. And *she* thinks that if she's perfect enough, everyone will forget that *her* father went crazy because he was a Shadow." She was glaring at Jet now, and she hissed, "Well, you're *not* perfect. You're nothing but a *filthy Shadow.* And I'm going to stop you from spreading your filth!"

Dawnlighter raised her hands to the skylights of the meditation room, and all the weak sunlight filtering through the pollution layer flowed into her, her costume fading from pink to yellow to a deep, bloody red as she screamed and pulled power into her.

Iridium blinked in shock. Dawnlighter had an expression she'd only seen on the faces of bodystim addicts in news broadcasts. She had eyes like an Everyman, or the religious fanatics who burned themselves in front of the Corp headquarters in New York Metropolis.

The eyes of someone who hated what they saw of the world and wanted to watch it burn.

Then Dawnlighter opened her mouth and started to laugh as the sunlight she'd absorbed grew around her fists. Still laughing, she focused on Jet.

"Oh, shit." Iridium was dimly aware of other screaming—Dawnlighter's mother and father, she guessed, and students—but she ignored them and threw herself across the table and onto Jet, taking them both to the mats.

Dawnlighter's blast hissed overhead and burned a hole in the wall, smoke billowing out to cover everything. Fire-containment alarms started to howl and extinguisher mist came from the ceiling with a hiss.

"Unauthorized use of power detected," blared the Power ward over the PA. "Stand by for Containment."

Underneath Iridium, Jet was sobbing. "I'm not filthy. Make them shut up! I'm not filthy—I'm *not!*"

"Jet, for Christo's sake, button it!" Iridium shouted as

the other girl lined up for another blast. Dawnlighter wasn't pretty anymore. Blood gushed from both nostrils now, and one of her eyes was red and filmy where the vessels had burst. And her costume, Iridium noticed with a blink, was beginning to melt.

Iridium craned her neck and saw Derek crouched on the other side of the table, the tops of his spikes singed away. "Frostbite!" she yelled, pointing her free hand at Dawnlighter.

"On it!" he said, and cast ice at Dawnlighter, encasing her hands first and sending a fine layer of icicles and frost over the rest of her body.

Dawnlighter staggered, going down on her knees, tears and blood streaming from her eyes. "Filthy...filthy... filthy..." she muttered, before Iridium stood up and kicked her once, hard, in the face.

Dawnlighter slumped on her side, still mumbling feebly through her split lip.

The lights in the room flickered, died, then burst into full illumination.

"Make them shut up," Jet whispered, her hands covering her ears.

Before Iridium could comfort Jet, a Runner burst through the door, closely followed by a Containment crew in full tactical gear and a host of proctors drawn by the alarm.

Night came sweeping over, his cowl covering the floor in an inky wake. "What happened, Iridium?"

"Dawnlighter flipped out," she said. Her teeth were chattering and her hands were shaking. "Jet...Jet is..."

Night clapped a hand on her shoulder. "Breathe. You, too, Frostbite. Breathe until you can speak normally, and don't move from that spot."

He bent over Jet, his cape hiding her from view, and whispered something that Iridium didn't catch. A moment later, Jet stopped sobbing with a long gasp and hiccup.

Then she sat up, wrapping her arms around Night. He stiffened, then put one massive, gauntleted hand against her back, letting her cling to his body armor.

"Go with the Runners to your rooms," he said to Iridium and Frostbite, his voice like death. "The Superintendent will want to see you later."

"Jet . . ." Iridium started, moving to her friend.

"Maybe I didn't make myself clear," Night said in a tone that was colder than Frostbite's ice. "Leave. Leave now. Jet will recover."

Two Runners in white scrubs came in with a float and put Dawnlighter onto it, strapping her down and giving her a pulse injection. Whatever the drug was, it made her stop muttering and giggling and jittering.

"What happened to her?" asked Iridium, feeling more unsettled than she could recall since the day the Bradford front door had blown inward and a squad of heroes dragged her father away.

"She needs Therapy," said Night brusquely. "If you don't want to follow in her footsteps, both of you put today out of your mind."

"Yeah, that'll happen," Iridium muttered, watching Dawnlighter disappear through the doors of the meditation room and into the lift, going up. The only thing above this level was the Mental wing of the Academy. Iridium shivered.

"I'm serious," Night said. "Go with a Runner before you become an annoyance. I'll see to your roommate."

"She's not my roommate," said Iridium. "She's my friend."

Night didn't comment, but she felt his gaze sear her.

She picked up her bag and moved toward the Runners with Frostbite, but then she stopped and took the small flashlight off her strap. It was the one the Academy had issued in their survival kits the day they'd first joined.

"Here," she said, walking over to Night. "Give this to her. I don't use it, anyway."

Night took the small tube and nodded, tucking it somewhere behind his cape. "I'll make sure she gets it."

Only then did Iridium allow the Runners to walk her back to her room.

Even though she knew it was her imagination, she thought she could hear Dawnlighter's screams long after the Runner had deposited her safe and sound in her room, locking the door behind him as he left.

She was still hearing echoes when it came time for Lights Out.

CHAPTER 21

JET

In my opinion, the patient will be a danger to all those around him until the day he dies.

Internal psych report circulated to
the Executive Committee regarding George Greene,
Code name: Blackout

She couldn't keep them out.

filthy filthy Shadow filthy Shadow filthy

No matter how hard she pressed her hands against her ears, how she silently screamed the Academy Mission Statement and ran through the periodic table of the elements, their voices whispered to her, giggled their accusations and promised what was to come.

filthy and crazy and crunchy sweet

Shut up! Please, Jehovah, make them shut up!

But Jehovah either was busy or wasn't moved to help, because the voices whispered, and giggled, and slowly got louder.

Hands on her shoulders—strong, comforting. A voice,

his voice, soft and commanding, cutting through the dark echoes in her head:

"Jet. Joan. Hear my words, Joan. Hold on to them, Joan."

Night, saying her name, her real name, over and over again the way that Papa did the way he did before he—

"Hold on to my voice, Joan."

sweet and sickly and screams oh yes the screams she makes she makes she screams she

A burst of white, like a star going supernova behind her eyes. The Shadow voices hissed, receded.

And suddenly, like a switch had been flipped, Jet could think. Her eyes focused, and she gasped as she stared into Night's hooded face.

"Good girl," he said, and for the first time in two years, he smiled at her.

She threw herself around him, hugged him tight. After a moment, he hugged her in return. He said something, to someone, but Jet didn't listen. The only thing that mattered at this moment was holding on to Night, clinging to him as if he were her last shred of sanity.

Because the thing was, she was convinced that was spot-on.

She was going crazy.

Shivering against Night, she tried to believe that everything would be okay, that just because her father had . . .

Dawnlighter's voice sneered: *Gone bona fide nutso and murdered your mama and tried to kill you, too, and he should have succeeded, you filthy little Shadow . . .*

Jet took a deep breath, pushed Dawnlighter's voice out of her mind. One day, she'd have to confront her, make her shut up about her father. Iri had been telling Jet that for almost two years, and Jet knew her friend was right. But still, the thought of telling Dawnlighter anything made Jet's stomach roll.

One day, she thought, and clenched her fists.

Night murmured, "You need to be strong now, little Shadow. Do that for me."

She would. She would do anything for him.

Pulling away from him, she wiped her eyes, sniffled. He was frowning at her, but she could tell it wasn't because he was angry or disappointed. No, he was concerned. The thought made her squirm.

Blinking, she glanced around the empty meditation chamber, then stared at the smoking hole in the wall. "Sir? What—"

"Nothing for you to concern yourself with."

She whispered, "Iridium? Frostbite?"

"Both fine. Runners escorted them to their rooms."

Swallowing thickly, she said, "Dawnlighter?"

"Off to Therapy."

Jet took a shuddering breath. Part of her screamed, *Serves her right! Talking trash to me, about me and Papa! Hope they put you in a room right next to him! Have him teach you to be afraid of the dark!*

But the rest of her was horrified. Dawnlighter was only thirteen. She was a snotty, self-entitled princess, yes, and she had enough attitude to make up for what she didn't have in finesse, smarts, or ability. But none of that explained what had happened just now. What could make someone like Dawnlighter . . . slip?

And why did Jet feel guilty?

"Jet."

She hiccuped, realized she'd started crying again. Grimacing, she brushed away her tears, looked up into Night's face.

"What happened?"

Lifting her chin, she said in a monotone: "Iridium saw the threat and threw herself over me, knocked us both down to avoid getting incinerated. I must have hit my head."

"No, Joan," he said softly. "What *happened*?"

She bit her lip, looked down at the mat. "They're getting louder. Sir."

A strained silence, then: "You're getting straight A's."

"Not in Physics," she muttered. Stupid, freaking physics! She didn't care what the formula insisted, there was no way that one item could exist in two spaces simultaneously. That wasn't physics. That was magic.

"Even so. I was going to wait until Third Year, for you and your roommate both. But sometimes things get moved up. Come with me."

They both stood, and she followed Night silently, out of the blasted meditation chamber, down the hall, and through numerous corridors and one flight of stairs until they were in his office. He had her stand while he rummaged through a large box.

She waited, her hands clasped, staring straight ahead, chewing her lip as she wondered if she was in trouble. She read the Squadron declaration, lased into the wall: DUTY FIRST.

Finally, Night pulled something out of the carton and tossed it to her, with an offhand "Catch."

Startled, she caught the package neatly, cradled it to her chest.

"For you, Jet."

She looked at the transparent wrapping, saw the bundle of clothing folded into a soft rectangle.

"Go ahead, take it out."

Her fingers numb, she pulled out the costume. The unikilt was a glossy black—not the dull blackness of an absence of light, but a true, rich ink that seemed to wink and shimmer—with bright white by the collar and a matching white belt.

Exactly like Iri's, but reversed. Yin and yang.

She bit back a giggle and said, "Sir, it's wonderful! But I'm not supposed to get fitted until Third Year. It's procedure."

He let out a sound that was suspiciously close to a snort. "Procedure for those not in the gifted curriculum. Optional for those who are. You deserve acknowledgment of how far you've come. But you missed part of the uniform. The most important part."

Something else gleamed at the bottom of the plastic wrapping. Jet reached into the bag and scooped up a metallic earpiece.

"Tap it twice for white noise," Night said. "Once to shut it off. You'll need to charge it about once a month, so plan accordingly. When you're old enough to go on missions, the comlink will connect you directly to Ops."

Operations. She swallowed, blinked away tears. Only the front-runner extrahumans, the ones selected by Corp to join the Squadron and be the face of the Academy, got a direct connection to Ops.

Only the elite held such an honor.

"Sir," she breathed, "I don't know what to say."

" 'Thank you' will suffice," he said dryly.

She squeaked her thanks.

"Don't lose the earpiece. It should help you focus, even when you're under a great deal of stress."

Translation: It would help keep the voices away.

"Thank you," she said again, stronger this time. "Sir . . . does that . . . particular stress ever go away?"

After a very long moment that felt like forever, Night said, "You're thirteen, Joan. Your mother was a Light power. Anything can happen."

"Oh," she said weakly.

"Iridium was very protective of you today."

"She's my friend."

"Yes." He steepled his gloved fingers. "Is she also your confidante?"

Her eyes narrowed, and before she remembered that this was Night, her mentor and Academy proctor and someone who was altogether frightening, she said, "I didn't tell her anything I wasn't supposed to. You told me not to, and I haven't."

They locked gazes, and Jet thought she saw something bright sparkle beneath his cowl, like a wicked thought. "A young woman of her word."

"My word matters, sir."

He smiled thinly. "That's good to know."

CHAPTER 22

IRIDIUM

Also present at the scene were the suspect's daughter and wife. After attempting to assault an officer and damaging several police floatcars, VALERIE BRADFORD was taken into custody. The child was remanded to social services and later removed by Corp.

Police report concerning the Corp-sponsored
raid of 3445 Marigold Street

History was the one thing that Iridium could immerse herself in, dive deep below the lines of text on her datascreen and forget that she was at the Academy. Which was the only reason why the proctor was able to sneak up on her.

Iridium felt the tap on her shoulder, and she shrugged away, throwing up her hands. "I didn't do anything!"

Frostbite raised his head from the chapter on the Fourth World War, grinning. The other Light powers like Iridium, who were arrayed across the front of the classroom like bright, mostly blond suns, smirked at her.

"Calm down, Iridium," said the proctor. Celestina, the only proctor other than Night who still pulled active duty with the Squadron, never raised her voice to the class, which was why Iridium respected her. And she was the only proctor, in their Second Year, to not give Iridium detention— which was why Iridium liked her. Celestina's purple eyes sparkled with concern as Iridium glanced up at her. "I've been instructed to have you report to the Superintendent's office. You're excused from classes and training for the rest of the day."

Iridium felt her glare slip into confusion, so she quickly composed herself. To be summoned for something other than an infraction made a cold feeling start in her stomach. No one got called in to the Superintendent's office for candy and balloons.

"I don't know why," said Celestina, putting her hand on Iridium's shoulder.

"I wasn't going to ask," Iridium said, tossing her head as she shouldered her bag. She noticed that Jet was staring at the datascreen in front of her, but the text had stopped scrolling. She was listening.

"We'll miss you," said Celestina, with the smile that graced every Lyman's Department Store in New Chicago. But their spokesmodel ads did not do justice to Celestina's violet hair and amethyst eyes, just like her commercials for Whitecap Toothpaste couldn't capture the mischief behind her smile.

"Whatever," Iridium said with an affected sigh. She turned and strode out of the classroom, down the white hallways with their embedded screens that flashed the Academy logo along with the short, recorded messages from active heroes.

"Be true to the Academy," declared Megaplex, a Light power like her, known for his illusions.

"The Academy made me what I am today!" said Fly Boy, the youngest hero on active duty within the Squadron. He was fifteen, and a supergenius—who still didn't know enough not to strike a ridiculous pose, an artificial wind billowing his yellow cape.

"The Academy stands behind its heroes, and heroes stand behind the law." Night's cool voice rolled out at her from a dozen screens as she walked the long hall to the Superintendent's office. The words twisted, and now she heard an echo from her memory, pronouncing doom.

"Lester Bradford. You are hereby ordered to submit to the authority of Corp and appear before the Executive Committee on charges of robbery, fraud, and murder. You are a criminal and are in violation of the law."

"Move it, Iridium. You're late."

She jumped a little bit. Night appearing out of the thinnest slice of shadow was a trick only Jet seemed to find amusing. It still gave Iridium the creeps after a year.

"The Superintendent will explain."

Iridium blinked. "Explain *what*?"

After a pause, Night said, "The Superintendent has arranged a special meeting for you. Today. If you choose to accept it, that is. I'm to serve as witness to your decision."

Some of it made sense then—the withdrawal from class, the quiet, quick appearance of Night, probably the only person in the Academy besides Joan, Derek, and Celestina who, as far as she could tell, gave a crap about her. As for the rest, what this optional meeting could be . . . Iridium felt a headache worthy of the ones Jet sometimes complained of grow behind her eyes.

They walked in silence, until they reached the Superintendent's door. Night put a hand on her shoulder. It chilled Iridium's skin beneath her uniform. "Think long and hard before you agree to the meeting."

"Yes, sir," she said, trying to act like she wasn't burning with curiosity.

The Superintendent gave a resigned sigh when they entered his office. "You're fourteen," he said to her.

"Have been for two weeks now," she replied.

He narrowed his eyes. "Watch your mouth, young lady. You're eligible for visiting rights at Blackbird Prison."

She could have sworn her heart stopped beating. "Sir?"

"You can see your father. If you decide to." The Superintendent leaned forward in his seat and met her gaze. "Or you can decide not to and turn your back on that rabid part of your family. Show the Academy and Corp that you're looking forward, not holding on to your past or on the path to throw away a brilliant future, like your mother."

She thought about it for all of a nanosecond. "I want to see my dad."

The Superintendent deflated. "Of course you do. I didn't expect anything else from you."

"So witnessed," Night said coldly. "I've discharged my obligation here. I have to get back to work."

The Superintendent glanced at Night. "How's the reclamation coming?"

"Favorably," Night said, bowing his head slightly. "I thank you for allowing me to turn the meditation room into my training capsule. The room never really served any purpose, even when I was a student."

"Christo knows the last thing these children need is more time to contemplate their lot in life," the Superintendent muttered. Then he remembered that Iridium was right there. He visibly shook his head and said to her, "Iridium, a prison transport is waiting for you on my landing pad. You are to be back in two hours." He jabbed a finger at her. "Don't cause trouble, or the next time you see your father will be when they carry his body out the prison gates."

"I understand," said Iridium. Her stomach flopped. Five years...how much had Lester changed? Would he even remember her?

The ride to the prison was a long blur. Once they arrived, Iridium was scanned and swept and patted down, and led into a plain white room. One chair was normal. One had hookups for stun-cuffs.

"Inmate walking," said a robotic PA. "Lester Bradford, formerly known as Arclight."

Her father, when he came in, looked startlingly the same. His hair was even combed back in the old style that had made *Underground* magazine proclaim him the Sexiest Supervillain Alive just before he was arrested. Then he saw her.

"Callie?" he gasped, nearly falling against the guard holding his elbow.

"Dad!" she cried. For the first time since she'd left Abbie, Iridium felt something close to joy swell in her. She jumped up and ran to him, only to be held back by the guard's baton.

"No contact with the prisoners."

"It's all right, my girl," her dad said. "Sit down. We have ten whole minutes to talk."

His sarcasm was not lost on the guard, who snorted and backed out of the room. "Freak."

"Pay him no mind." Her father smiled at her, the crow's-feet around his eyes deep. "They let you come. I feared they wouldn't."

"I wanted to, for a long time," said Iridium. "I miss you, Dad."

"And I you. My stars, Callie, but you do look like your mother."

"Don't say that." Iridium shifted uncomfortably. "Everyone at school says I look like you."

He laughed. "And how is life in the world's most posh concentration camp? Have they indoctrinated you to hate me yet?"

"Never," Iridium cried. "I wouldn't."

"Beware of what you think you would and would not do," he murmured. "The Academy has a way of twisting that, like looking into a dark mirror."

"I'll keep visiting."

"See how long they let you keep that up, once you're a star student on the hero track." He smiled at her. "I know you will be. You've got my smarts and your mother's tenacity."

"I'll never stop," Iridium promised. "It's been so hard to be away from you, Dad. No one's going to stop me now."

Lester reached out to take her hand. "That's my girl."

CHAPTER 23

JET

Get it through your head—the average criminal on the street wants to kill you. It's up to the hero to act first, to neutralize, to both stay alive and discharge their duties. The criminal has no such concerns.

Manual of Basic Self-Defense, **Third Edition**

Jet sensed Lancer behind her, but she didn't acknowledge him. Taking her eyes off of the Boy Moron for even a second would give him the opening he'd been looking for. Besides, after two years of self-defense with the Daft Family (as she and Iri had taken to calling Hornblower and his uncle), Jet knew what the instructor was going to do.

You'd think by now he'd have stopped being so freaking predictable. A sobering thought checked her from rolling her eyes: Maybe this was another lesson. Everyone, from the most revered heroes to the vilest of archenemies, had a tell. Learn what that giveaway move was, and you learn your adversary's weakness.

Or maybe Lancer really was just that stupid. The thought made her smile.

Crouching lower, she crab-walked on the mat, circling the large teen. Beneath her black unikilt, she was sweating like a First Year during finals. The fabric of the costume was gorgeous, and just wearing the outfit made her feel confident, even dangerous. But did it have to be so hot? Ignoring a bead of sweat that was working its way down her nose, she made a mental note to ask one of the Runners about breathable material.

Matching her movements (if not the sweat), Hornblower snarled at her. *Oooh. How intimidating. Not.* Jet decided that he must practice making scary faces; no one could naturally twist their mouths into something that made them look like a lion coughing up a hairball.

Around them, the rest of the class stood in a loose circle, watching. Some were taking bets—that was Iri's voice she heard, laying twenty-to-one odds that Hornblower would get flattened with a TKO. Then Frostbite asked, "Does it count if he trips over his own big feet?" The laughter that followed was like the sweetest music.

People weren't laughing at her anymore.

In her ear, the white noise of a waterfall played on—just loud enough to give any Mental powers a case of the nerves...and to drown out any other voices she didn't want to hear. In the three weeks since Night had given her the earpiece, Jet had been sleeping better than she had since she was a kid. Her studies weren't a struggle anymore; even the thrice-damned Physics units began making sense. Most of her instructors chalked it up to budding confidence, brought to light (ha-ha-ha) by her wearing her costume almost a full year before others in her grade. She'd gotten praise from teachers who she'd previously thought had hated her.

All because she didn't have to be afraid of the dark anymore.

Thank Jehovah for Night.

In front of her, Hornblower snarled impotently. Jet

wondered if he knew he looked like a poster child for junk abuse. Probably not. Hey, maybe the American Medical Union would sponsor him when he graduated. *Kids, stay away from junk, or this is what will happen to you! Brought to you by your friendly neighborhood medical spinners.*

"Time?" someone shouted.

"Two minutes twenty," Iri answered, sounding smug.

Hornblower's biceps and thighs strained against his Second Year jumpsuit, all but screaming his need to break and rend and tear. All the circling was making him impatient.

Excellent.

Jet slowed the pace of her steps while slightly increasing the radius of their circle. Now Lancer was in her peripheral vision—flexing his fists, the idiot. He might as well wear a holosign that announced I'M GOING TO HIT YOU FROM BEHIND.

Of course, none of the Taft family were known for subtlety. Or, really, for anything other than being walking, talking punching bags. Or, in Boy Moron's case, a windbag. Jet allowed herself a smile.

That pushed Hornblower into addressing her. "Any day now, skank."

She said nothing, but her smile stretched wider.

"Christo! Come on, already! You going to hit me, or what?"

Jet said nothing, kept circling.

"You're a creepy skank, you know that? Think you're so hot." He leered, which made him look like an advertisement for date rape. "You're nothing but a dirty Shadow. Why don't you crawl under a rock, where you belong?"

She batted her lashes. "If that's the best you've got, I recommend you take Battle Banter as an elective next year."

His face purpled, and baring his teeth like a rabid dog, he barreled forward.

Too easy.

She let him come. *Five, four, three.* She dropped low and spun around, right leg straight as a pylon. *Two.* Her leg leading, she completed the spin. *One.*

Contact.

She swept his legs out from under him, and he pinwheeled wildly. She followed through, getting her body out of the way before he lost his balance and landed heavily on his back.

The students whooped and cheered—cheered for *her,* for Jet. Probably it was because most of them despised Hornblower and his whole "I'm Jehovah's Gift To Extrahumans" attitude. But maybe, just maybe, some of them actually had been rooting for her instead of against him.

She grinned. That would be sort of cool.

"Two minutes fifty-one!" Iri chortled her glee. "Horny didn't even last three minutes!"

"Got to work on that stamina," Frostbite laughed.

Oh, how the other students ate that up.

On the mat, Hornblower glowered at her. Couldn't attack her, though; rule of the unit was if you land on your back, that's a kill for your opponent. In a battle situation, Hornblower would be either incapacitated or dead.

No great loss.

Standing up, Jet gave her back to Lancer as she smiled grimly at the Boy Moron. *Come on,* she thought, *I'm right here, not seeing you, practically helpless...*

Behind her, Lancer charged.

She pivoted right, her arms bent and up. Lancer's fist sliced the air where her back had been. Grabbing onto his overextended right arm, Jet yanked down and to the left, and Lancer, as off-balance as his nephew had been, tumbled to the mat.

"Two for the price of one," Iri cheered.

Jet offered her hand to her instructor, but Lancer sneered at her. "Get your stinking hand away from me!"

Someone whistled. "Bad form," Frostbite said.

Jet withdrew her hand and stepped back. *He's a jerk, he's a jerk, don't show him that the insults still hurt.*

Lancer pulled himself up and rotated his shoulders, his small eyes glittering as he stared at Jet. Behind him, Hornblower climbed to his feet. "Today's lesson's about overconfidence. Just because you may win a battle, that doesn't mean you win the right to be smug. Because you never know when the next fight's going to come."

As if on cue, Hornblower opened his mouth and let out a sonic blast.

Oh, cowcrap—

Jet threw herself to the left, but the sound wave grazed her. Intense static in her mind, angry bursts of power reverberating, but washing away—a combination of its being a passing blow and her blessed, blessed earpiece.

Furious, she scrambled to her feet. "No powers in Street Defense," she shouted, pointed at the towering boy. "That's the rule!"

"And you should have learned by now that in street fighting, there are no rules." Lancer sneered at her, let out an ugly laugh. "Take her, boy."

Hornblower cut loose again, but this time Jet was ready for it. Reaching inside herself to where her power lived, she raised graymatter to form a shadowshield. The sonic bolt hit it square on—and her shield absorbed it. She felt the impact rattle her bones.

Before he could attack again, Jet took the offensive. Her brow furrowed as she reshaped the shadowshield into a creeper, one of her new toys. It hurt—a lot; damn, she needed an aspirin—but as Night had told her again and again, she'd never know the full extent of her powers if she didn't push past the pain. When she'd shown her mentor the creeper last week, he'd encouraged her to practice it, no matter what her Power tutor otherwise instructed.

So she had. Quietly, of course; unauthorized use of powers was a major offense. She wouldn't have dreamed of practicing on the sly, but Night had given her explicit permission. He'd explained that mentors had the authority to override Academy procedure—but even so, she should practice cautiously. And she did, every chance she got. In the past week, Jet had gotten very good at morphing Shadow into a creeper. It would be her signature move, Night had said.

It was that thought that allowed her to focus past the building agony in her brain as she manipulated Shadow. When she was a fully certified hero, the creepers would be her signature move.

And the really neat thing was, no one else knew about it.

Until that moment. Her graymatter shield darkened and bubbled out, slinking forward like a living thing—a shadow seeking its own Peter Pan to adhere to.

Hornblower's eyes boggled, and he stepped backward. "What is that? Get it away from me!"

Hearing the panic in his voice made the agonizing headache worth it. Grinning madly, she nudged the creeper forward.

"Uncle Erik! Make her stop!"

Lancer aimed his fist at Jet's face. A glow of power outlined his hand. "Call it back, girl. Right now."

Sweat beading on her brow, Jet summoned the creeper back. It flowed into her, leaching away her headache but leaving her so drained that she almost toppled over. But she would be damned to the darkest hell before she let the Daft Family see her stagger. She lifted her chin and waited.

Lancer didn't lower his fist.

"Um . . . sir?" That was Iri. "Shouldn't you, you know, power off now?"

If he heard Iridium, he ignored her. His dark gaze

drilled into Jet, and she clearly saw that while she may have thought other instructors hated her, Lancer actually, truly, despised her.

"You are damn lucky that I swore I'd never intentionally harm a student," he said. His voice was low, and breathy, and Jet saw his arm tremble. *Holding himself back,* she realized. *He's forcing himself not to attack me.*

And that utterly terrified her.

She swallowed, lowered her head. Whispered, "Yes, sir."

"If you ever—*ever*—use your filthy Shadow powers in this unit again, I swear by all that's holy I'll forget you're a student. Now get the hell out of my classroom and report to the Superintendent for detention."

Around her, the students muttered. A few—including Iri—opined that Lancer was being unfair. And then one of the students, a boy, asked, "What did she do?"

Still glaring at Jet, Lancer replied, "She used her filthy power against my flesh and blood. And I won't stand for it."

"But sir," the boy said, "all she was doing was defending herself. You're the one who let Hornblower attack first with his power."

At that, Lancer cut his gaze over Jet's shoulder. "Samson, you questioning how I run this class?"

A pause, and then: "In this case, yes, sir."

A collective hush fell over the room.

"Well then," Lancer said through clenched teeth, "you and the Shadow can both go to the Superintendent. Rot there for all I care. You think about returning here, you better have an apology at the ready. You hear me, boy?"

"Yes, sir."

"Then get the hell out of here. And take this trash with you." Lancer glared at Jet again, then lowered his arm. "The rest of you wannabes, pair off! Hand-to-hand combat!"

Jet took a deep breath, caught Iri's eye. Her roommate shrugged, mouthed, *He's an asshole.*

Jet couldn't argue that point. She nodded to let Iri know she was okay, then turned to walk out of the room.

A large boy was waiting for her by the door. Samson. Big, bigger than big—at least six feet tall and a good two hundred pounds of muscle. Short blond hair that called attention to the way his ears stuck out. A lantern jaw in the classic superhero tradition; dazzling green eyes that crinkled in the corners when he smiled. Like now.

Jet smiled at him, said, "Sorry to get you in trouble."

He shrugged, an easy movement of his shoulders. "All I did was tell the truth when I was asked. Basic heroing."

"A real good guy."

"I try. Race you to the Super's office?"

She cocked her head, considered him. "No running in the halls."

"What're they going to do, send us to the Super's office?"

Running in the halls was against procedure. She was about to open her mouth to quote the code, but then she noticed how his eyes were twinkling as he waited for her answer, and she saw a mischief there that reminded her of Iri.

If Iri had been a very, very cute boy.

Logic shorted out as hormones kicked in.

"You're on," Jet said, then dashed away.

NOW

CHAPTER 24

IRIDIUM

Ever since the Squadron took down the Code Red villainesses more than a decade ago and disbanded the Ominous Eight by force, there's been no superclub for extrahumans who scorn the law. Do they prefer to work independently? Or are they organized into clandestine cells, run by an elite few? Or something else entirely?

Lynda Kidder, "Flight of the Blackbird,"
New Chicago Tribune, July 2, 2112

Iridium was pushing it. Visiting her father twice in three days would set off Warden Post's obsessive-compulsive sense of security, but she had to.

"What the *hell* are you doing here?" Lester demanded. "I told you I'd be in touch when my man delivers."

"About that," said Iridium. "I don't want some shadow figure dealing with us. Who is he? How do you know you can trust him?"

"His name is Ivanoff. And he's a prisoner of Corp, the same as I am," said Lester. "Don't question me again, Callie. Have I ever led you wrong?"

Iridium bit her lip. "No."

"You saw what Corp did to our family firsthand. Drove my friends over the edge, threw me in prison, destroyed your mother's career when she wouldn't abandon us. Are you wavering?"

"No!" Iridium snapped. "I know what they did, Dad. I saw what the Academy does firsthand. I just..." She stopped, fighting the urge to summon a strobe, expel her nervous energy.

Lester softened, extended one hand as far as he could in his shackles toward her. "What's wrong, girl?"

"I got hit with a vigilante." Iridium sighed. "The Undergoths have a new backer. Wreck City is going to shit and Corp is just going to keep coming. I'm not having a good week, Dad."

"Nor will you, until Corp is put in its place," Lester said. He didn't believe in pity, or, in many cases, sympathy. Iridium wondered at her fellow students who'd had the family existence, with birthdays and school pictures. They all seemed so insulated, so removed from what the world really was.

Which was why they were heroes, and she was here.

"Gangs will always be gangs, Iridium." Using her designation made Iridium snap her head up. Lester gave her a rueful smile. "Justicers will always be too eager. But you can change Corp hunting you. I suggest you focus on that."

"I asked him to meet me," Iridium said. "The vigilante."

"I forbid it," Lester said instantly. "Corp will be hunting him and it will expose us to too much risk."

Iridium nodded. "You know best, Dad."

"I don't like this, Iri," Boxer said, fidgeting with his watch chain.

"There isn't much you do like lately, Boxer," Iridium said. "Will you knock that off? You're making me nervous."

"Gee," he said, looking over the edge of the hoverpad. "We're perched on an aerial lander illegally, waiting for a guy who shoots electricity out of his hands—and is on the side of justice—to question his motives. And if I know you, you'll still insult at least one of his ancestors. Can't see why you're nervous, Iri. Not at all."

"Button it." The hoverpad swayed gently in the wake of a passing bus and Iridium deliberately looked up, at the pollution layer, and not down at the street five hundred feet below. Her father would kill her. But there was something about Taser, something that suggested it would be a bad idea not to get him on her side . . . after all, they shared no love of Corp. Backup could be useful, when Lester's mystery man Ivanoff delivered.

"He's late," Boxer said finally, snapping his watch shut in a huff and tucking it into his lime-green vest.

"Yeah, he seems to make that a habit."

"You're talking about my dashing good looks, right?"

Iridium turned and saw Taser dismount a small black hover, sans license tag and flight markings. He swiveled his head toward Boxer. "You didn't tell me we were going to have a chaperon, darlin'."

"Somebody has to make sure you don't get fresh," said Boxer, patting his plas pistol.

Taser's eye goggles irised and refocused. "I know you."

"I don't think so," Boxer said, tilting up his fedora with his finger.

"You're the third Taft brother." Taser cocked his head. "How about that. Heard you were dead."

Boxer's jaw went tight. "Fanboy, are you?"

Taser snorted. "Not hardly. Nice to see you've found something to keep your hands busy." He looked toward Iridium with his blank glass gaze. "Does she? Keep your hands busy?"

Iridium snapped her fingers in Taser's face and a prism flashed, shorting his goggles. They sparked and clamped shut. "Can we focus, please?"

Boxer snorted. "Good luck with this sewer rat's ass, Iridium. I'll be at home." He tapped his wristlet and signaled a taxi, which floated to a stop at the pad. Boxer got in with-out another word.

After it had whirred away on its lift fans, Taser grinned. "You gonna pay me for these goggles?"

Iridium feigned shock. "You mean to tell me you're *not* a rich playboy during the day? I'm so disillusioned."

Taser shocked the goggles and they opened again. Iridium saw a hint of light eyes beneath. "Why'd you really bring me up here? Because I gotta be honest—a woman who banters is not one of my turn-ons."

"How about a woman who throws your ass off a hover-pad?"

Taser shook his head. "We did this dance, remember? It'll just end in tears, Iri."

Iridium pressed her lips into a line. "Only my friends call me that."

"Then tell me what you brought me up here for so we can move down that road."

The lights of downtown blinked softly at Iridium as she turned away from Taser. "I'm going to cut ties with the gangs in Wreck City soon. I want you to stop messing around with the Undergoths and make an alliance with me."

Taser laughed. "You and me against the world? Romantic, Iridium. Never expected that out of you."

"No," said Iridium. "You and me against Corp."

Taser canted his head. "But I'm a fanboy, remember?"

"If you were really a wannabe, you would have turned me in to Corp the first time we tussled. You would have tipped the active duty squad to the Undergoths." She turned to him. "You would have had a pair of stun-cuffs on you so you could haul me to the prison gates and get a pat on the head from Corp."

Taser shrugged. "Got me there. All that, and I did tell you that I wasn't a Corp lover."

"Yeah, but I just assumed you were a liar," said Iridium.

"Sort of a dim view of the world."

Iridium smiled thinly. "It's a dark world we live in, Taser. Do we have an accord?" She stuck out her hand, trusting him not to simply shock her, tag her, and take her to the hero squad.

Taser gripped her hand, firm and warm. "Against Corp? We do for now."

CHAPTER 25

JET

*Together we stand, a united front against injustice.
Together we fight, a Squadron dedicated to expelling evil
from our world.*

Squadron Mission Statement

One thing Jet could say about Lynda Kidder: The
woman had an ego the size of Old Texas.

Amid the occasional holos and traditional paintings and
posters on the walls were dozens—hundreds—of shots of
the reporter. Candids. Formals. Ads and product place-
ments. Two professional caricatures. And one life-size card-
board cutout of her, wearing an old-fashioned fedora with
the word "Press" on a scrap of paper tucked into the hat-
band.

Well, at least Jet would know her when she saw her.

Lips pressed into a grim, determined smile, she continued Shadow-walking through the missing woman's apartment, making sure not to leave any trace of her visit. Her
feet cushioned in boots of Shadow, Jet kept moving just

slightly above the floor, searching for any hint of where Lynda Kidder could have gone. Or, as Night would insist, where she had been taken to.

Her heart lurched, and Jet forced herself not to think about her mentor losing his mind. *Maybe he's right,* she told herself gamely. Night always had a penchant for Sherlocking things. Perhaps something really had happened to Kidder.

Jet felt a pang of guilt as she realized that part of her fervently wanted there to be something wrong, all so that Night would be correct. Well, enough. If Night was going mad, so be it. Duty first—and that duty was to the citizens of New Chicago. Kidder would be fine.

But because Night, too, was a citizen, Jet continued to give him the benefit of the doubt. So she kept examining the apartment.

The furniture, to Jet's eye, was tasteful yet common; it served its function while not drawing attention away from the important pieces in the apartment: items about Lynda Kidder. Along with all the pictures, framed copies of her articles lined the walls of the small apartment, as well as even larger framed pictures of articles *about* her. "Fearless Reporter Unmasks Rabid Killer" got the top spot in the living room; "Kidder Takes New Chicago" was the pièce de résistance in the bedroom.

And over the mantelpiece, of course, was the coveted Pulitzer for her work on the Icarus investigation, showcased in the Origins feature that ran over thirteen weeks in the *Tribune.*

Jet ran her fingers over the old-fashioned engraved award, a Shadow-layer between her gloved hand and the plaque. On the base, the Pulitzer read: "Awarded to Lynda S. Kidder of *The New Chicago Tribune* for her persistent, painstaking reports on Icarus Biological and its controversial connection to Corp-Co and its affiliated Academy of Extrahuman Excellence."

Icarus.

Jet frowned. She knew precious little about the fertility clinic from the end of the twentieth century; the Academy didn't encourage studies in that direction, and getting information from Corp about the clinic that reportedly was connected to the first-ever wave of "superheroes" was nigh impossible. Students who attempted to learn more were gently—or forcefully—steered to another topic of interest.

Until the Origins piece, the most that Jet could have said about Icarus was that Corp bought the company, Icarus Biologicals, back around the turn of the twenty-first century. Public information about the pre-Corp Icarus facility was all but missing; other than a one-paragraph description of the clinic's purpose and its founder, there was nothing. It wasn't as simple as the records being confidential, or top secret, or even code black.

The records had been expunged. From both public and private databases.

That tidbit came from the data Night had sent her yesterday, and it nagged at her as she moved through Kidder's cozy apartment, taking in tiny details of the missing woman's life. As she noted the small collection of kitten figurines—*kittens,* how very adorable—Jet wondered how Kidder could have gotten any real leads on Icarus.

She blew out a frustrated breath. The only ones who had access to the information were from Corp. Kidder, therefore, had to have an inside connection to Corp.

It was after the Origins feature started running that Corp had openly frowned on Kidder's work: a press release officially censuring the investigation; a few well-placed opinion pieces on the net; sound bites making the evening news. That sort of thing. Obviously, Corp didn't want Kidder snooping around the extrahumans' origins.

So why would Corp have helped her with that information in the first place?

Jet pictured New Chicago's fearless reporter on her beat, shamelessly waving a mic in front of Superintendent

Moore from the Academy, or Dawnlighter as she left one of her innumerable cosmetics sponsorships, demanding answers about where the heroes had come from—and why the heroes had come at all. It wasn't like there was a *Where Do I Come From? The Extrahuman Edition* available at the library.

Kidder wasn't the sort to be easily cowed. So how did one shut up an investigative reporter?

One gave her some information.

A red herring, perhaps, Jet thought. Or just insipid background material that the EC had carefully vetted and deemed irrelevant. *Give her some answers, pat her on the head, and send her on her merry way.*

But Kidder wasn't the sort to stop with only a bare handful of answers. Kidder craved the truth—or, more likely, craved the attention that came from uncovering the truth. One look at all the kudos framed around her apartment was proof of that.

Did the reporter do her job too well? Had she learned something about the extrahumans that Corp didn't want her to know?

Feeling a headache kick up behind her eyes, Jet kept moving through the apartment, her mind working even as she took in the details of Kidder's life. Jet couldn't investigate Kidder's possible connection to Corp, because (A) Night was certain someone from Corp was behind Kidder's disappearance, and (B) unless you were on the Executive Committee, there was no way, nohow, you could tap into Corp records.

Unless you had an in.

"In your face," Ops had snarked just an hour ago, when she'd requested the personal time so she could investigate Kidder's apartment. It had been too much to hope that Meteorite or Two-Tone or one of the other former heroes had been on call. "Oh, damn, she was in your face! Iri wiped the floor with you!"

Jet gritted her teeth and bore the humiliation. He had reason, after all. "Can you please refrain from the comments and just log the personal time for me?"

"Aw, poor Lady of Shadows got her panties in a knot?" Frostbite laughed, sounding bitter and angry. "The golden girl is slipping off her pedestal, finding out that the ground where we mere mortals walk is hard and uncaring and cold?" He paused, and Jet felt the hatred flowing from the comlink. "Sound like anyone you know, Jet?"

"I know you're glad she escaped," she said quietly. "I understand."

"No, Jet. I don't believe you do."

"Will you file the request? Or do I need to come in and do it personally?"

A snort. "Can't have our precious heroine all plumb tuckered out from doing such mundane tasks as filing a request, can we? I'm on it, Ms. Jet, ma'am! Let me go ahead and type in the painstaking code of numbers and symbols that indicate that you, Ms. Jet, ma'am, have requested two hours of personal time, effective immediately, ma'am! I would be remiss, ma'am, if I didn't remind you that you have a ten-thirty appointment with Rabbi Cohn, ma'am, and that if you miss it, you would be in deep shit, ma'am!"

"Thank you," she said politely.

"Drop dead. Ma'am."

Remembering the earlier conversation with Frostbite, Jet sighed. She understood why he despised her. But that didn't make coping with his hatred any easier. It never did.

Yet if there was anything Frostbite hated more than Jet, it was Corp itself. If she had to, she could turn to him. Not that he would actually help her.

And not that she would actually need to go to him at all. Because Night was wrong. Corp wasn't involved in Kidder's disappearance. Corp *couldn't* be involved.

Night had to be wrong.

Enough, she told herself as she entered Kidder's bedroom. Worrying about Night was pointless. She was here as a favor to the old man; she should at least give the apartment a thorough search. There was still some time before she had to get over to Cohn's for her ten-thirty.

In the small bedroom—with a lonely twin bed, she noticed—Jet stared at a framed picture on the nightstand. It showed Kidder as a young woman—twenty, maybe, looking happy and ready to take on the world—with her arms around the neck of an older man who had features similar to her own. Kidder's father, probably.

Jet picked up the picture. And she smiled at the easy way between daughter and father, at how proud the older man looked.

You're a bad girl, Joannie. You broke the rules, didn't you?

Her hand trembled. *Shut up, Papa.*

In her mind, her father laughed.

She didn't realize she'd broken the picture frame until she heard the crunching of broken glass. Freed from its frame, the photograph of Kidder and her father floated down to the carpet, where it lay atop a pillow of gleaming shards.

Cursing, she glared at the warped frame in her hand. And there, sticking out of the bent silver, was a black square.

Jet plucked the object from the broken frame. It was a memory stick—a tiny thing, no larger than her thumbnail. Frowning at the electronic device, Jet absently summoned Shadow to suck up the broken glass.

A hidden file.

It was probably nothing; just family photos or some such, placed inside the picture frame for easy storage.

When the carpet was once again clean, the Shadow folded in upon itself and flew to Jet's outstretched hand, the one holding the memory stick. The black shape shuddered, then flowed into the leather gauntlet and, beneath that, into Jet's flesh. She didn't notice the sudden chill of Shadow against her skin.

It's nothing, she told herself again. Even so, she padded over to Kidder's desk, sandwiched between the bed and the window, and fired up the computer there. She connected the device. And then she accessed the contents.

An hour later, she slipped out of Kidder's apartment. In one of the bulging pouches of her belt were the remains of the picture frame. In another was the memory stick.

The photo remained behind, on the nightstand. In it, Kidder grinned and her father beamed, as if they were thrilled that a secret had been uncovered.

CHAPTER 26

IRIDIUM

What do villains do when they're not trying to take over the world? Do they ever get a chance to relax? Or are they constantly looking for a new opportunity to get rich, or to seize power, or to make a statement?

Lynda Kidder, "Flight of the Blackbird,"
New Chicago Tribune, July 2, 2112

Iridium waved her wristlet at the warehouse's big doors and they rolled back, silent in their tracks. Taser followed her in, close but not too close—arm's length, the distance it would take to reach out and snap her neck.

"Who trained you?" she asked.

Taser faltered and cocked his head. "Nobody trained me. I'm a one-man show."

"You move like military," said Iridium as the lights flickered on. "Or maybe cop. You an ex-cop with a beef, Taser? Trying to reprogram the system?" There were other, less savory possibilities, of course—the explanation of how he'd evaded Corp long enough to grow to adulthood couldn't be all rainbows and roses. There were rumors of gene therapy to keep you off the scanners, back-alley surgeries in places like Bangkok 10, removal of the portion of the brain that gave extrahumans that *extra*.

Taser laughed. "You're adorable when you're interrogating someone."

Iridium took off her wristlet and rubbed the joint underneath. Her comm followed, her belt with its old-fashioned picklocks, cash, credits, and fake ID, and the steel baton she kept strapped to her leg under the unikilt.

Taser whistled. "For a renegade antihero, you sure pack a lot of crap."

"At least I didn't steal my crap from Corp," said Iridium with a pointed look at Taser's armor.

"This?" He tapped his breastplate. "Fell off a truck. I bought it in the gray market. Got the bill of sale right here." He started to unstrap the armor but she held up her hand.

"Never mind." She mounted the rickety metal stairs to the enclosed second floor.

Taser sauntered around the workshop, stopping by the large table near the back. He picked up the neural inhibitor lying there and turned it over in his hands. "These things are illegal."

"Yeah, and so is dressing up like a ninja and playing hero, but you don't see me complaining." Iridium turned back at the door of her bedroom. "Make yourself at home, as long as it doesn't involve touching my things."

She slid the opaque glass door to and watched Taser's shadow move away to explore the rest of the workshop.

Iridium took her time undoing her unikilt and sliding it off, courteously ignoring the shuffling and muffled *thud* as Taser searched her hideout.

She'd do the same, in his position.

Iridium pushed Light into the bioluminescent gel on the walls, causing it to glow with green undertones and illuminate her bedroom in soft contrast to the tube lighting in the warehouse.

In her plain white underwear, Iridium unpinned her

hair and let the black waves fall and brush her shoulder blades. Her curls were sticky with sweat and pollution. Staring at herself in the mirror over her dresser, she touched her fingertips to the two-inch puckered scar on her breastbone. Corp had offered to remove it when she came of age and went on active duty; scarred female heroes didn't brand well.

She'd told them exactly where they could stick their removal surgery. She had other scars, too—a Talon cutter in her lower back when a motorcycle chieftain in Little Shinjuku took exception to a rabid on his turf; the pale line across her knuckles where she'd fallen off a hover and dragged her hand along the pavement back when she was six.

Her memory flashed to that day—her father had carried her into the house, and while her mother chewed on her lip and worried about the carpet, he'd slapped a cauterizer patch on her hand and held her close when she screamed. The bandages were usually worse than the cuts themselves, but it had healed almost completely.

Taser rapped on the glass. "You alive in there?"

Iridium grabbed a T-shirt and cotton pants from a drawer and slipped them on. "You finished searching my place?"

Taser slid the door open. "No booby traps. I'm disappointed, darlin'."

"I'll have the gas-deploying wall sconces and the pit of live tigers up and running next time you visit me, I promise."

"So, I've been wondering," Taser said, following Iridium into the small square of mats that served as her practice area. "What exactly are we planning?"

Iridium shrugged as she took a practice swing at the heavy bag. "I'm not sure yet. But big. It will be big. Public. And embarrassing."

Taser stopped the bag with one arm. "Do you ever relax?"

Iridium glared at him. "Having a masked vigilante trailing after me isn't very conducive."

"What do you do for *fun*?" he asked. "Do you *have* any?"

She imagined that if she could see Taser's face, it would have one of those smarmy smiles that heroes like Lady Killer made sure to flash in the cameras anytime press got close.

"Are you here to help me, Taser, or hit on me?"

"Is there some law against both?" His mask crinkled along his smile lines.

She regarded him for a moment before she spoke. "I spend most of my waking hours looking over my shoulder for heroes desperate to drag me in for fame and a fifteen-second sound bite on the evening news. I spend the rest keeping Wreck City from turning into another slum like the rest of the flood grids. I keep the gangs from burning Wreck City down and I keep the cops from bleeding it dry, which is more than I can say for the rest of the grids. Everything I take, after expenses, is either funneled back into Wreck City or goes to bribing the administration at Blackbird to keep them from overdrugging and torturing my father." She strobed the bag and it sprouted a singed hole, sand running out. "So no, Taser, my life is not all rooftop escapades and an adrenaline rush from dressing up and running around under Corp's nose. My life is hard. It's too hard. Corp made it that way, and it's time they paid."

Taser held up his hands. "Iri, I didn't mean—"

"I told you not to call me that."

"Iridium." He said it very quietly, the word muffled by his costume.

She turned away from him, pushed past him. Taser came after her as she walked to the industrial kitchen and got a glass of water.

"When I was seven years old," he said, "my mother and I were living in this shitty block housing in the Manhattan Quarantine—you know, before they firebombed and started over." He blinked, his goggles irising. "This rabid came in, one of the Mental ones, and he took my entire block hostage ... made us see things. Terrifying things."

"Doctor Hypnotic," said Iridium. The Siege of Manhattan was a standard in tactics training for Corp.

"Anyway, that's not the point." Taser sighed. "After five days, the heroes broke through Hypnotic's henchmen. When they caught him, he was on top of our block."

Iridium remembered the plain photographs on her datascreen—no 3-D printing back when she'd been a student. Ruined, burned, twisted metal. Screaming civilians. Chaos.

"They fought," Taser said softly. "They destroyed our block. My mother and a few of my friends were crushed in the wreckage from the fight between Hypnotic and some musclehead extrahuman. Corp didn't let in rescue workers, regular cops. Three months later, I got an apology and a check for e3,000 from the New York Squadron branch." He laughed once, bitterly. "And that was it."

"They took something from both of us, then," said Iridium. "I'm taking it back."

Taser nodded slowly. "And I'm right there with you."

CHAPTER 27

JET

While certain leaders have shown a marked hostility toward the extrahumans, in the religious communities, there is more often than not a cautious tolerance. But, safe to say, no reverence. Religious leaders, after all, answer to a higher authority.

Lynda Kidder, "Heroes Among Us,"
New Chicago Tribune, March 5, 2112

Thank you, David," Rabbi Cohn said, taking the cup of coffee his assistant offered. "Unless Jet needs anything, I believe that will be all."

"I'm fine, thank you," Jet murmured, holding her own cup. She was far from fine; what she had read was still screaming in her thoughts.

David nodded and closed the door of the rabbi's office behind him as he left.

Jet forced herself to smile pleasantly and pretend she wasn't fighting a migraine. Feigning interest in the rabbi's office, she glanced around. Small room, somewhat cluttered with a large desk and leather chair, as well as a cluster of smaller, plush chairs around a circular coffee table, where she and the rabbi were seated. Somber colors dominated the room, accented with thoughtful paintings here and there. But the true attraction for her was the dilapidated bookcase, overstuffed with titles. She and the rabbi seemed to share an affinity for old-fashioned books. If she hadn't been so distracted, she probably would have struck up a conversation about what they liked to read.

But she had done too much reading in the past hour. Her head throbbed, and she bit back a groan. Hoping the caffeine would help, she took some hasty sips of coffee, scalding her tongue.

"I'm sorry you missed the sermon yesterday," Cohn said.

Pushing aside thoughts about Lynda Kidder and Corp, Jet replied, "As am I. But duty called."

"I understand." He regarded her, as if studying her features. Out of respect, she had pulled back her cowl and removed her optiframes. All she needed was light makeup and no perfume, and she could do another Goldwater appearance.

"How did the sermon go?" she asked, to be polite.

"Well, I think. You'd be surprised how receptive people are to the notion that whether human or extrahuman, we're all children under *HaShem*."

"You're right," she said, thinking of Wurtham, of Everyman, of all the citizens too happy to boo whenever she appeared. "I would be surprised. But it's nice to hear."

Cohn smiled at her, his light eyes twinkling. With his long white beard, comfortable fat, and spectacles, he looked more like a Santa Claus candidate than someone from the rabbinate. "I take it you've been subjected to the opposing viewpoint?"

"Loudly. And in public."

"Yes. But what a blessing it is that we live in a society that allows such freedom of expression."

"A blessing," she muttered, sipping her coffee.

"A responsibility too."

"I understand responsibility."

"You better than most." Cohn watched her for a moment, his smile easy, his eyes inviting. "Another blessing is the ability to question."

She frowned. "How so?"

"Well, political relevance aside, questioning is one of the joys of Judaism," he said with a wink. "Oh, we declare ourselves to *HaShem,* of course. But then we question."

"Question what?"

"Why, everything," he said, laughing. "We have a hymn, '*Ein Keloheinu.'* After we say there is none like *HaShem,* we ask, Who is like *HaShem?*"

"With all due respect, sir, if you've already said there's none like your god, then why question?"

"Because we can. Because questing for answers is one of the ways we show our humanity."

She nodded, thinking, *But the problem with seeking answers is that sometimes, you find them. And then what?*

In her belt pouch, the weight of the memory stick pressed down on her.

Wurtham had been right. There was a final, unpublished Origins article that Lynda Kidder had written. It had been there, in the memory stick. Encrypted. After more than forty minutes of tinkering, Jet had broken the code. And then she'd read the seven paragraphs.

And her stomach had dropped away.

Unlike the pompous, self-righteous tone of the previous Origins installments, this final article had been clipped, perfunctory. Jet had sensed the reporter's nerves as she'd read the damning paragraphs—ones that tenuously linked Corp-Co to the New Jersey–based Icarus fertility clinic in the late 1980s, as well as to disease-control facilities in Hong Kong and Mumbai.

If Kidder was right, then Corp-Co hadn't merely bought Icarus Biologicals at the turn of the twenty-first century. They'd played a larger role. And *that* meant...

No. She couldn't think about what that meant. Kidder had to have been wrong. Speculating. Looking for controversy.

Jet's head pounded, pounded. She didn't know what to do with the information she'd uncovered. Give it to Corp? Turn in the article to the *Tribune,* even though Kidder had hidden it?

Destroy it?

"If you don't mind a personal question, Jet, are you religious?"

Pulled out of her confusion of thoughts, she answered, "Agnostic."

The rabbi nodded. "Were you always?"

She remembered a blond-haired boy, his warm smile, his easy laugh. "No."

"I see." He paused. "Usually, when people have been greatly hurt, they turn away from *HaShem* completely, become atheists. But not you."

"Not I."

The rabbi seemed to measure his words carefully before he spoke. "People sometimes do evil things. But that doesn't mean people are evil."

"No," Jet said. "They just choose to be."

"Some, yes. And that is a tragedy." He put down his cup, then met her gaze and smiled proudly—reminding her, for a moment, of the photograph of Lynda Kidder's father. "But others," he said, "ah yes, others have wondrous gifts. And they choose to use them to help make the world a better place."

"Of course," she said, surprised. "It's what we do."

He reached out and clasped her gauntleted hand in his bare ones. "No, Jet. It's what *you* do. There is always a choice. And for choosing to help us all, I say thank you."

His words touched her, soothed an ache she hadn't known was there. This wasn't the almost mindless dedication of her fans, the vocal adoration of thousands who never dared come close. This was one man's genuine thanks.

Her eyes stinging, she flitted a smile and gently removed her hand from his. "You're too kind, sir."

"I call them like I see them," he said, winking again.

And in that moment, she knew what she had to do. And with that thought, she could breathe again. Her headache receded, and she smiled.

Over the next fifteen minutes, they talked on a wide array of things—books, mostly, and the city, and the nature of good and evil. When she had to go, Rabbi Cohn invited her to come back anytime she wanted to talk. And as she left, Jet thought that perhaps one day, she would take him up on that offer.

But now, soaring over New Chicago, there was something else she had to do. Taking a deep breath, Jet tapped her comlink.

In her ear: "Operations."

"Frostbite, it's Jet."

He clucked his tongue. "What now? You need a Runner to massage you after the beating you took yesterday, maybe?"

"I need your help with something."

The pause was filled with tension thick enough to strangle an elephant. When Frostbite finally spoke again, there was no mistaking the fury in his voice. "Oh, do you now? Let me guess. You want to tag Iri and bring her in for Therapy."

"No. It has nothing to do with her."

"Like the way you had nothing to do with her getting onto everyone's most wanted list?"

"Believe what you want," she said tightly, "but Iridium did it to herself."

"Right."

Remembering the rabbi's words, Jet said, "It was her

choice, Frostbite. Just like it's your choice now whether you want to help me."

"Why should I? So you can betray me too?"

Rage washed over her, cold and unforgiving, and she trembled as a black nimbus glowed around her fist.

Calm. Stay calm.

The dark aura faded, causing a headache to thud behind her eyes. "Help me because you're still a hero, and heroes help each other."

"Fuck off."

Jet closed her eyes. "That's the song you're singing, huh?"

The words felt stale on her tongue. How long ago since she and Iridium and Frostbite and Samson had come up with the Canary Code? A memory flashed, and she was in Third Year, in Study Hall, and she and Iri were giggling over how Sam pitched spitballs at Hornblower and Frostbite would ice them just enough to make them sting—completely against code, but when Iri and Sam and Frostbite put their minds to doing something, Jet couldn't help but go along with it. Whenever a proctor strode into view, either Jet or Iri would loudly ask about that song they'd been singing earlier.

Canary Code for "Danger."

Frostbite was silent for so long that Jet was positive he'd severed the connection. He was serving as Ops; he didn't have to keep the line open for a personal favor.

Maybe he'd forgotten the code. Or maybe he was still so furious with Jet that it didn't matter even if he had remembered. But then a burst of static sliced through her ear, followed by Frostbite's muffled voice. "Clean channel. You have thirty seconds to convince me why I should help. Go."

Her voice low, she said, "I have reason to suspect that Lynda Kidder was taken out by Corp because she got too close to the truth behind Icarus."

A beat, then: "Why?"

"She got the Pulitzer for her Icarus investigation. But all the Icarus files weren't just sanitized—they were expunged. They never existed. So how did she get her information?"

"That's not enough. Reporters have sources."

"There was another article," she said quietly. "Unpublished. I found it. It strongly suggests that Corp had something to do with Icarus."

"Corp bought Icarus."

"No," she said through clenched teeth. "Before that." She wanted to say more, but her headache kicked into high gear. *Tension,* she thought, pinching the bridge of her nose. Entertaining this insane idea was practically blasphemy. Corp stood for justice. Corp sponsored the Squadron and the Academy.

Corp was in the business of saving the world.

Of course Corp wouldn't have removed Lynda Kidder. The thought was insane. Kidder had to have been wrong.

But then, she'd thought Night had been wrong when he'd asked her to look into Kidder's disappearance. And that's what this was about right now: finding Lynda Kidder.

Jet could almost hear the gears of Frostbite's brain turning. Tempting him with the possibility of a Corp cover-up was the one thing that might get him to override his hatred for her. Maybe. She hoped.

"What do you want from me?" Frostbite said.

"I need you to give me access to Corp's original files on Icarus."

He barked out a laugh. "All the glory's gone to your head. If you think I'm taking that kind of risk for you, you're crazier than your father was."

The barb struck home. Grimacing, she said, "If you do this for me, and I see there's something concrete that links Corp to Kidder's disappearance, I promise you I'll stop hunting Iridium."

Silence over the comlink.

Hovering over New Chicago, Jet waited.

Frostbite finally said, "You have to do better than that, if you want me to do this for you." Jet could hear the smile in his voice, and despite his words, she knew she had him. "If there's something that links those bastards to Kidder's untimely disappearance, you publicly renounce Corp and the Academy."

Damn. "No."

"No deal. Be talking to you ..."

"Wait. If I find anything that definitively proves Corp was behind Kidder going MIA, I promise to make that information public." Her mind whispered that she was a traitor for even making such a suggestion.

He snorted again. "What, interviews?" A subtle mocking in his tone now. "Public outcry? A revelation on Talk Circuit, where you announce the evils of Corp and throw away your cowl and burn your goggles?"

"Completely anonymous," she said. "But with backup so everything can be proven. Including Kidder's final article."

Frostbite laughed softly, and Jet could picture his light eyes sparkling with humor. And rage. Frostbite's eyes had always given away his emotions. "Considering you need my help, Jetster, you're not being very accommodating."

Through clenched teeth, she said, "I can't change who I am, Derek."

"I know, Joan. You're Corp's lapdog."

"No," she said, "I'm the Hero of New Chicago. And I believe what we're doing is good, that people need heroes to save them."

He laughed at her, the sound brittle and grating to her ears. "And heroes need the spotlight, don't they?"

"It's not like that."

"Right."

"It's *never* been like that, no matter what you may think." Her words poured out of her, thick and full of the quiet rage she'd borne for more than five years. "I'd give all that up in a heartbeat if I would still be allowed to do my job. But that's not the way of the world, Frostbite, and you know it. If I'm going to hero, I need to do it by the hero rules. And as screwed up as it is, that means sponsors, and politics, and asinine pep rallies and talk shows and Light help me, photo ops!"

She shut her mouth, surprised to realize she'd been yelling. *Great,* she thought. *Bad enough to soliloquize. But at full volume?* Jet exhaled slowly and tried to force her blood pressure down.

"You hate it so much," he said, "go vigilante. It's in vogue, so I hear."

Her words a whisper, she said, "I can't." Even if she'd wanted to, she couldn't.

"Right, I almost forgot." The sneer was all too clear in his voice. "You'd have to give up your Runners, your cushy spot as the Hero of New Chicago."

"Don't put words in my mouth," she spat. "I said I can't. But take that as you will, Derek. You will anyway."

Frostbite was quiet for a moment, and then he murmured, "Holy shit, they've got something on you."

She didn't reply. Her heartbeat drummed wildly in her chest.

"How long've they had you on a leash?"

"Not your concern." If he thought she was going to tell him about the true purpose of the comlink, and the voices she could barely keep at bay, he was...well, as crazy as a Shadow power.

"Was that what happened in Fifth Year? Did they force you to sell her out?"

"We're not discussing Fifth Year," she hissed. No more games; no more backing and forthing. "Are you going to get off your high horse and help me? Or are you going to let Lynda Kidder rot because you hate me for something you're convinced I did five years ago?"

Frostbite cleared his throat, then said, "I'll get back to you." Then he cut the connection, leaving angry static in his wake.

Hoping against hope that Frostbite would come through, Jet began the day's patrol.

CHAPTER 28

IRIDIUM

*Even locked away, the villains are not defeated. You can
see it in their eyes, in the way they hold themselves,
even drugged or wrapped in a straitjacket. Caged, yes.
But not defeated.*

Lynda Kidder, "Flight of the Blackbird,"
New Chicago Tribune, July 2, 2112

The guard who ushered Iridium down the hallways,
past the blank cell doors, each branded only with the
designation of the rabid within, turned to her with an apolo-
getic smile. "He's been yelling and carrying on for the last
hour, demanding to see you, Doctor. Sorry for waking you."

"It's not a problem," Iridium murmured, feeling the
cold snake of fear twist and coil in her gut. "I'm always here
for my patients." For Lester to risk drawing attention to
their arrangement, something was very wrong.

"You're a saint, Doctor," said the guard, sliding his key
through the pass slot outside the interview room. Iridium
heard her father ranting from inside.

"Motherless sons of whores!" he shouted. "You let me
out! We'll see who's rabid and who's not!"

The door slid open, and Iridium pressed past the guard. "Mr. Bradford, that's quite enough of that noise."

Lester sobered immediately when he saw the expression on her face. "About time you got here, missy," he snarled.

"Show the doctor a little respect," said the guard, raising his nightstick in warning.

"Not to worry," Iridium said through a fake smile, sitting at the lone table. "We're fine here."

"You got ten minutes." The guard glared at Lester as he walked out the door.

As soon as she heard the lock click into place, Iridium watched the enormous clock ticking down the seconds. As soon as the requisite thirty had passed, she snarled, "What, Dad? What is so all-fired important?"

Lester exhaled and slumped backward in his chair. "You have any idea how tiring yelling obscenities for a solid hour is? I'm knackered."

Iridium slapped the table with her palm. "Focus, Lester."

His face flickered with a smile. "You sound like your mother when you call me Lester."

"Dad," Iridium said through gritted teeth. "What. Is. The. Problem?"

He leaned in, even though they were alone, and spoke so low that Iridium had to bend her ear almost against his lips. "We've got a message from Ivanoff."

"Great," said Iridium. "That still doesn't explain why I had to rush down here to take in the wisdom of some Corp flunky."

"Ex," said Lester. "He was their commnet programmer until he got caught skimming from the accounts heroes use to fund their Runners and cushy little cages and Christo knows what else. They tossed him in here with the rabids rather than go through with one of those bothersome trials with evidence and the like. Nice bloke. Plays chess with me."

Iridium narrowed her eyes. "Where are we going with this?"

Lester's worried face re-formed into the sly grin she remembered from his WANTED holopapers, which at one time had covered New Chicago like flickering snow.

"Ivanoff let slip to me during one of our games that he programmed the communication systems that the heroes use from the ground up in the good old days." He laced his fingers behind his head. "Everything that the skinsuits use to talk to each other, he built."

Iridium felt her throat tighten. "What did he give you, Dad?"

"Everything."

Iridium sighed in frustration. "Assuming that he isn't jerking you around—and may I say that embezzling Corp scumbags aren't famous for telling the truth—what could we do with some outdated passwords into superhero email?"

"Callie," he said, shaking his head, "you're not thinking, girl. Ivanoff programmed *everything*. Including that little voice inside your head when you strap on the costume and go out into the field."

Iridium's eyes widened. "Ops? You mean he programmed Ops?"

"Ops," said Lester, grinning. "He knows every code key, every back door into the program." He shrugged, the grin still on his face. "I figured it was my duty to pass the information along to my brilliant daughter."

Iridium felt her heartbeat quicken, heating her up inside the cheap suit. She told herself to calm down. She didn't have enough information to get too excited. Yet. "Dad, even with pass codes and the like, I can't do anything with this. Ops is run from a stand-alone mainframe *inside* Corp headquarters."

"Then your part of this is to find a way in, isn't it?" He leaned forward in his chair, as much as the cuffs would allow. "This is it, Callie, and you know it. I've been cultivating Ivanoff for months. He thinks we're friends, partners in crime. Thinks we're going to siphon off some of Corp's E and that'll be the end."

"If Ops goes down, every hero in this city will be defenseless," she said, her mind racing. "They'll have no way to call for backup, no access to GPS, if something goes wrong—"

"If something goes wrong, they should have paid more attention in their field training," said Lester with a sniff. "In my day, we didn't have some squawk box in our ear telling us when to duck and when to punch." He arched a brow. "Don't tell me you still hold feelings toward any of those people, Callie. They don't deserve pity. They deserve *nothing.*"

"You think I don't know that?" Iridium said softly. "I don't miss anyone from the Academy, Dad. I hate them, just like you do." *Even Jet, damn it. Even her.* "But if I do this—if I hack Ops and take the hero network down, they're going to know it was me and you. They'll hurt you, Dad."

Lester folded his hands. "Callie, I'm in bloody prison for daring to speak my mind. There is nothing in the next world worse than being trapped in a cell, knowing that the people who put me there are out flying around pretending to protect the world." He reached out, palm up, and Iridium put her hand in his. "We're going to do this, Callie. You're going to do it for me. Right?"

"Right," Iridium said.

"No mercy."

"No mercy," she agreed. "I'll get Ops down."

"Good girl," Lester said, sitting back. "Good girl, Callie."

"We have to do it when something big is going down, though," Iridium said. "Otherwise, they'll buy a new mainframe, sweep the mess under the rug, and it will be situation normal."

Lester tapped his finger against his lips. "This city is ripe for anarchy, girl. It won't be that easy."

Iridium thought of the Undergoths, of the ripples through the underworld, the swelling tide she felt under her feet in Wreck City. "I'm not responsible for what happens after," she said.

"The natural order will happen," Lester said. "No one will be cleaning up humanity's messes. It's time the people of the world learned to think for themselves."

His words sent a shiver up her spine. Her voice soft, she said, "You sound like an Everyman."

"Ironic," he said, laughing. "They hate heroes as much as I do. Too bad we couldn't work something out with them."

She narrowed her eyes. "I'm not working with the Everyman Society, Dad. *Ever.*"

"We'll see. I'll be thinking of you, Callie," Lester said as the buzzer sounded. The guard was already sliding open the door. Her father whispered, "Send me a message when you've done this." He made like he was shaking her hand, then pulled her into an embrace, the first they'd shared since Iridium was a child.

She thought she did a fine job of hiding her shock.

"There is a postal box in Looptown, inside the Apex Mall," Lester hissed. "The number is 2285. The digichip with the programming you need to hack Ops is in that box. Ivanoff smuggled it out in a letter to his wife."

The door slid open, and Iridium pulled back. "No contact with prisoners," said the guard reproachfully.

"I'm so sorry," said Iridium. "It was a very intense session." She smiled at the guard. "Trust me, it won't be happening again."

CHAPTER 29

JET

Not everyone is enamored of the extrahumans. The civilian police bear an open hostility, even more so than they do for the FBI. And then, there's the Everyman Society.

Lynda Kidder, "Heroes Among Us,"
New Chicago Tribune, March 5, 2112

Midnight in New Chicago.

Jet perched on the windowsill outside of Martin Moore's apartment, debating if she should break the window to scare the bejesus out of him or if she should Shadowslide and go for the silent approach.

She decided to opt for Shadowsliding. Technically, it wasn't breaking and entering that way.

Inside, Moore was shuffling around. He'd been home for only five minutes; hazard of pulling second shift at Corp. Jet would give him a little more time to get comfortable, maybe even climb into bed. He was an older man—late sixties—and he'd just pulled a ten-hour shift. He had to be exhausted.

Best to let Moore collapse into bed, then . . . wake him up.

She'd have felt bad about it if Frostbite hadn't been convinced Moore was the one who'd spilled information to Kidder.

"You want to talk to a man named Moore, Martin G.," Frostbite had told her six hours earlier. "He's the connection between Kidder and Corp."

Jet was more than a little skeptical; it was distinctly possible that Frostbite was about to lead her on a wild-goose chase—or, worse, on a course that would lead to a wrongful arrest. "How can you be so positive?"

"He's the on-site tech guru for the EC. He's got access to all the files that Corp ever created. And," Frostbite added with relish, "he has a bank account a little too padded for a Corp man. His car's a little too nice. His apartment's a little too well furnished. And he has expensive habits."

"Circumstantial," Jet said. "I can't interrogate him based on that."

"Something else. There's a mention about a brother, deceased. Based on the birth date, a twin."

"Anything suspicious?"

"Not unless alcohol poisoning during Rush Week at college is suspicious."

"Then there's nothing," she said glumly.

"No? How about this: His first cousin was an active hero killed in the line of duty. Maybe you heard of him. Green Gaze."

She frowned. "Not ringing a bell."

"Mental power. Before your time." Jet could hear the shrug in Frostbite's voice. "Hell, before Night's time. This was back around the flood. He got taken down by the Santini Family, if you go by the official reports."

"And if you go by the street?"

"There were accusations, quickly covered up, that it had been a case of friendly fire."

Jet hissed through her teeth. "Not good. Everyman pick it up?"

"Nope, but you'd think so, right?" Even though they were—supposedly—on a clean channel, he lowered his voice. "Instead of joining the Everyman Society for a good ol' public round of righteous anger against the extrahumans, GG's family, for all intents and purposes, went underground."

"What do you mean, 'for all intents and purposes'?"

"They were suspiciously quiet—didn't seek remuneration from either Corp or the city, didn't make waves in the media. It was like they just went away. Maybe they did."

"Maybe," Jet said, unease bubbling in her stomach.

"But then they surfaced publicly, all Orwellian and Corp Is Our Friend. Almost fanatical. Became loud defenders of Corp and the extrahumans, and led some short-lived outcry against the Family and the gangbangers. Soon that quieted down, and they became regular civvies. Anonymous. Moore himself hooked up with Corp directly and worked his way through the techie ranks. Been there now going on forty years."

Her voice quiet, Jet asked, "You think Moore's family had Therapy?"

Frostbite said nothing, but his silence answered for him. Green Gaze's immediate family, and probably the outspoken extended family, had been . . . reeducated.

And if Frostbite was correct, and Moore had been the one slipping incriminating data about Corp to Kidder, then the Therapy was breaking down . . . or it had never taken, and Moore had just blithely played along. Either way, the man had a motive to want to see Corp taken down.

And based on where he worked, and in what capacity, he had the means.

"Forty years," she mused aloud. "That's a long time to build up resentment."

"I wouldn't know." Any drier, and Frostbite's voice would have been the perfect martini. "I still have thirty-four to go."

Jet ignored that. "If Therapy wears off after time, then the EC's going to have problems."

"Makes me all warm and fuzzy just imagining it."

She just bet it did. "Thanks for the information, Frostbite. I truly appreciate your help."

"Don't." The clipped humor shriveled, died, and all that was left in his voice was a cold, brutal fury. "Don't you dare thank me. We're not buddy-buddy, and we sure as hell aren't good."

She sighed. "I know."

"Just do what you said. If there's a connection to Kidder's disappearance and the EC, you go public with it."

"I will. You have my word."

"Yeah. And we know how important that is to you."

Jet frowned as Frostbite's words lingered in her mind. Her word *was* important. She meant to keep it.

And that meant disturbing Martin Moore's sleep.

Jet nodded to herself in the predawn light, her black cape allowing her to blend easily with the heavy shadows. Effectively, she was invisible to any passersby on the street, or in the air. And now she was about to take that one step further.

Reaching inside herself, Jet touched Shadow . . . and *slid.*

The world oozed gray, all other color leached away by the power of Shadow. One of her long-gone instructors once referred to the ability as morphing or ghosting or—to appease the scientists among them—molecularizing. But to Jet it was simply Shadowsliding.

And, truth be told, it was a lot of fun. Phasing through solid objects gave her such a rush. Not to mention the look on people's faces when she appeared out of nothing.

Not exactly heroic, she knew. But at least she was honest about it.

Smiling, she slipped through the locked window and stepped inside Moore's apartment. She'd entered through the bedroom window—and the man himself had settled down in his bed, ready for the express to Dreamland. His face was seamed with age; his hair—what remained of it— was as white as Iridium's costume. Next to the bed was a small table, with an old-fashioned framed photograph of two teenage boys. Jet couldn't make out the details in the dim room, but it looked like the boys were grinning with all the impertinence of the young.

Like you're so freaking old. In Jet's mind, Iri's voice chortled. *Twenty-two. Positively ancient! Then again, you act like an old biddy, so the confusion's understandable.*

Hovering by Moore's bed, Jet froze.

What, am I interrupting something important? Here you are, sneaking into an old man's apartment to scare information out of him. Maybe you and I aren't so different after all, Joannie.

At least I'm not a rabid, she retorted.

Oh, what a comeback! They teach you that at the Academy when I was gone?

Enough. I have a job to do.

It's all about the job with you, Iri said with a laugh. *Isn't it?*

Iri's laughter faded. Face set in a determined mask, Jet approached the front of Moore's bed. The old man must have just settled down; his breathing was far from the steady, restful pattern of someone truly asleep.

Get it over with, she told herself.

"Martin Moore." She pitched her voice low, filled with subtle menace. "Wake up, Martin Moore."

The old man startled, blinked his eyes. Rolled over to face her. And screamed like a girl.

"Shut it," she hissed.

His mouth slammed shut. He stared at her, his eyes wide and terrified.

Jet could almost hear his heartbeat thumping madly. *Light, don't give the man a heart attack.* "Where is Lynda Kidder?"

He paled dangerously, or maybe that was just the

contrast of his skin against the darkness in the room. His mouth gaped like a fish. Then he whispered, "Why . . . ?"

"You're the leak in Corp," she said, her voice almost purring. "You've been feeding Kidder code-black files. You're her Icarus source. Now she's missing." So what that she was accusing him without the benefit of proof? If he was innocent, he'd say so. And if he was guilty, he'd crack.

They always did.

He let out a cry, then buried his face in his hands.

Jet let him sob for a minute, watched dispassionately as his shoulders heaved. So it was true: He'd been leaking sensitive information to a reporter. People like him incited riots, caused wars. Behind her optiframes, Jet's eyes narrowed. "I hope her payoff was worth it, Moore. Corp's none too gentle on those who clandestinely work against it. I'm curious: What was your thirty pieces of silver?"

"It's not like that," he stammered.

"Right."

It struck her, then, that this was the same conversation she'd had with Frostbite—only now she was on the other side.

Softening her voice, she said, "Then what's it like? Explain it to me."

Moore dropped his hands and met her goggled gaze. "Yes, I shared information with her. But not for the money."

"Then why?"

"To get the information public." He took a shaky breath. "To get the truth out about the extrahumans."

She remembered Rabbi Cohn's words about seeking truth, and something cold worked its way up her spine. "What truth would that be, citizen?"

"That you're ticking time bombs. The lot of you." As if his words had given him courage, he set his jaw. "Some are just wired to blow before others."

"I see," she said, her voice giving away none of the panic rising in her. He was lying. He had to be lying. The epitome of calmness, she said, "And this was spelled out for you, in Corp's files?"

"Not in so many words," he admitted in his old man's wavering voice. "But there's clearly an early connection to Icarus, and it's reasonable to assume that Corp-Co sponsored the fertility project—"

"So there's nothing definite about your claim." She gritted her teeth, forced herself to keep her voice steady. "Paranoid, baseless accusations that could lead to full-scale panic. You're a model Everyman, Mr. Moore. You should consider joining."

He sniffed, as if she'd wounded his dignity. "I'm a proud member of the Society. And you're trespassing in my home."

"I'm pursuing a lead on a very important missing person." Jet leaned way, way into his personal space, until she was nose to nose with him. She smelled the stink of his fear. "You know where Lynda Kidder is. And you're going to tell me. Now."

He squeaked, his bravado bleeding away. "I can't!"

Light, he *did* know where she was. Jet was going to have to thank Frostbite. Somehow. Voice pitched dangerously low, she said, "Can't what?"

"If I tell you, they'll do me next!"

Uh-oh. "What happened to Lynda Kidder?"

"No, I—"

She got in his face and shouted: *"What happened to Lynda Kidder?"*

Whimpering behind the fragile shield of his fingers, he groaned, "The Society took her."

Better than Corp, at least. "Where is she now?"

"The tunnels," he said meekly.

"What tunnels?"

"Below the city." He hiccuped, said, "The Rat Network."

Oh . . . damn.

She debated for all of two seconds whether or not to call

this in to Ops, and decided against it. Night had stressed that she do this on her own, to redeem herself in the eyes of the media.

Besides, how hard would it be to haul Kidder out of the tunnels? The Everyman Society, as fanatic as they were, were only human. Not a true threat.

Unlike the dark, where Kidder was trapped. Helpless.

"Get dressed," Jet said. "We're going to the sewers." Down into the dark, where shadows thrived. Where the voices would whisper, and caper, and giggle. "And Mr. Moore? You'd better pray that Lynda Kidder is alive and unharmed. Or I'll leave you there, in the sewers, for the Undergoths and the rats to find. Do you understand?"

He swallowed loudly. Nodded.

"Now move."

THEN

YEAR 3

CHAPTER 30

JET

Creating a Heroic Identity is not merely a marketing tool—it is a new life that the extrahuman in question will adopt totally, for the remainder of their career and often beyond. It is a new skin that they must blend seamlessly with the old.

An Introduction to Alternate Identity, Chapter 2

Jet breathlessly ran into her room to get Iri. "Come on, they've posted the results!"

Iri arched a brow, then turned back to her chem text. "So? It'll keep."

"Come *on*," Jet said. "Don't you want to see?"

"What, the idiot they've paired me with? Why'd I want to see that?"

Jet felt her mouth gaping open, so she shut it with a click. Crossing her arms, she glared at Iri, who was freaking *ignoring* her. "I don't know, maybe because this is the first step in our careers, in becoming full-fledged heroes?"

"Yeah, great. Go ahead and order me a big pile of cheer, because I just can't be bothered to do it myself."

"Christo, what's with you? Don't you want to see who you're getting teamed with?"

"Not really."

Mind-boggling. Utterly mind-boggling. "Why not?"

Iri shrugged, kept her gaze on her computer. "Like I said, it'll keep."

If this had been First Year, or even Second Year, Jet would have caved and left Iri to stew in her blatantly false apathy. But ever since getting her blessed, blessed earpiece, then becoming...friends...with Samson, Jet had discovered an inner strength she hadn't known she'd possessed. So she grabbed Iri's arm and bodily shoved her out of their room, with Iri squawking, loudly, that Jet was crazy.

Well, yeah, she probably was. But what did one thing have to do with another? Grinning, Jet pulled Iri along. As she led them down the hall, a number of students chuckled, and one girl clapped.

"At least let me get my boots on," Iri yelled.

"And let you lock yourself in? No way, Princess."

"Princess?"

Looking over her shoulder, Jet flashed Iri a toothy smile. "You're so concerned about your boots, I thought maybe it was an accessory issue. You know, your bare feet clashing with your hairband, or something."

"You've lost it," Iri muttered, giving up. "Utterly lost it. I have a psycho for a roommate." She raised her voice and called out to anyone listening: "A psycho for a roommate!"

Of course, that was when one of the proctors, Stretch, crossed their path. She elongated her arm to halt them in their tracks. "And what in the hell are you shouting about, Iridium?"

"Ma'am, my roommate just kidnapped me, which, I believe, is a Code Seven offense." She gestured down to her bare feet. "Code Nine if I get a splinter."

Stretch blinked at Iri, then at Iri's feet. And then she

glared at Jet, who smiled meekly and said, "Just excited to see about the pairing results, ma'am."

Stretch sighed and shook her head. "Fine. But get there quieter. Some people actually are studying."

"I *was* studying," Iri muttered as Jet grabbed her arm again and led the way. "I was studying just fine until my psycho roommate kidnapped me. In broad daylight. In the freaking Academy. There's no justice in the world. None."

"Come on, I bet the crowd's not so big yet."

"You know, this is a total role reversal. You're the one who's always cooped up, trying to get ahead of the curriculum."

"And you're the one always telling me to lighten up," Jet said, steering Iri toward the stairs. "I'm lightening."

"You can't lighten up, you psycho Shadow! You're the dour one. I'm the obnoxious one."

"You're not allowed to have a monopoly on obnoxiousness."

"This is because of *that boy*," Iri said, making sure to sound like every adult who ever disapproved of teenage romance.

"That boy," Jet said, doing her best to ignore the warmth in her cheeks, "has nothing to do with wanting to see who we're getting paired with."

"You know that you won't be partnered with Samson, right? I mean, not that you and he haven't been doing your own style of partnering when no one's looking . . ."

"Shhhh!" Jet darted her glance around, but there was no one else in the stairwell. For the moment. "Come on, keep it down!"

"What? You started."

"Did not. Besides, Sam and I don't do anything of the sort," Jet said primly, holding the stairway door open for Iri. "We're just friends. After you, Princess."

Iri glared at her, then stood rooted to the spot until Jet sighed and marched through the door first. Iri followed.

The two girls walked together down the main hall of the first floor, heading toward the assembly hall.

"Friends, she says. Hah." Iri rolled her eyes. "If you ever kiss me the way you kiss him, I'm going to shove a strobe down your throat and boil your tongue."

Jet giggled. "Admit it, you like him."

"Sure, I like him. But you're stupidly in love with him. It's making you positively chipper. Hurts the whole sullen angsty almost-heroine thing you have going for you."

"You've got Frostbite. I've got Samson."

Iri burst out laughing. "Oh Jehovah, trust me, Frostbite and I are absolutely not friends the way you and Samson have redefined the word."

Jet arched an eyebrow. "You really mean to tell me after all this time, you guys never...?"

"Nope."

"Not once?"

"Nope."

"Huh." Jet paused, thinking about Samson's lopsided grin, his rumbling laugh. His hands, so huge yet so gentle. "Sam and I haven't. You know. Done it."

"Christo," Iri said, "if this is how you act from just kissing the big dope, I'm so freaking doomed when you actually let him in your pants. You'll be all giddy and happy and shit. I won't be able to take it."

"I *am* happy," Jet said, feeling a goofy smile on her face. "I really like him, Callie."

Iri's mouth twitched, then she let out a dramatic sigh. "I'll have to tell Derek that our Joannie's in *lurve.* He'll cry, you know. Kids grow up so fast these days."

Jet's blush deepened. "I think I am. In love."

Iri draped an arm around her shoulder. "No shit, my friend. No shit. But you tell the big lug that if he breaks your heart, I'll break his kneecaps."

"You're so good to me."

"What are friends for?"

"Friends in the you-and-me way? Or in the me-and-Samson way?"

"Friends in the you-and-Samson way are for me to make fun of," Iri said. "Oh goodie. We're here. Now we can see who we're stuck with for the rest of our Academic lives."

The lobby outside of the assembly hall was swarming with Third Year students eager to see who they would be paired with for the duration of their studies, all buzzing over the posted results. Numerous instructors and a handful of proctors were all trying to keep some semblance of decorum. Jet wished them luck: a superpowered mob wasn't a pretty sight.

Instead of shoving their way through, Jet and Iri hung by the back. As much as Jet was dying to know whom she'd be working with, training with, she sensed that Iri needed to talk.

Getting an Everyman to preach about the wonders of the extrahumans would have been easier.

"What's eating you?" Jet asked softly. "All kidding aside, Iri, this isn't like you. What's wrong? Don't you want to know?"

Iri pressed her lips together into a thin white line. For a moment, Jet thought she wasn't going to tell her, but then Iri spoke, her voice clipped and quiet, sounding faintly British. "I'm not eager to make nice with some wet-eared hero wannabe. There are exactly two people I'm comfortable with, and one of them's impossible for me to be paired with because the Academy is more mixed-gender phobic than most convents." She slid a glance at Jet. "And the other one's acting like she's insane."

Jet smiled. "In love."

"Same thing."

"Whoever you get paired with, you're going to be great." Jet bit her lip, then said, "How can you be anything *but* great? I wouldn't have made it to Third Year without you."

Iri waved her off. "You'd have found yourself another tutor."

"No, dummy. Not that." She lightly punched Iri's arm. "Come on, you're the smart one. You know what I mean."

"Yeah," Iri said, rubbing her arm. "And fucking ow! What's with you?"

"I'm trying to make a point. You've made Academy bearable. Hell, Iri, you've made it almost fun. And that doesn't stop once we get paired with other people."

"But I don't *want* to be paired with anyone else." Iri scrubbed a hand through her black hair. "Christo, could you imagine me covering Steele's back?"

"Steele's okay."

"Yeah, but she's more freaking by-the-book than you are!"

Jet smiled sweetly. "See? You won't miss me at all . . ."

"I'm going to strobe your sheets when you're sleeping."

"And I'll put creepers on your pillow when you're not looking."

The two girls shared a laugh, then grew quiet. Soon Iri said, "Seriously, Joannie. I like being myself around you and Derek the Dork."

"You can still be yourself, even around a new partner."

"Yeah, that'll happen."

"Why wouldn't it?"

"I don't want to have to break in another hero-in-training."

"You know," Jet said dryly, "you're not so impossible to get along with. For a criminal."

Iri smiled, but it didn't reach her eyes. "So says the kook."

"Come on," Jet said, pushing Iri forward. "Let's see who we got. I'm sure it won't be that bad."

"It'll be worse. Christo, they probably put me with LightBright . . ."

"And I'll probably get Lady Luck. Let's go."

They weaved their way through the crowd, Iridium snarling at people who tried to block their path and Jet slinking between people like a snake. Or a shadow. Finally, they got to the results board.

And stared at their names, linked.

"Holy Jehovah in a minihover," Iri breathed. "I don't believe it!"

"See?" Jet's grin stretched so wide that her cheeks threatened to fall off of her face. "*See?* Sometimes things work out better than we hope!"

"Yeah, yeah," someone behind them called, "congratulations! Now get out of the way already!"

The two allowed themselves to be pushed out of the crush of students. When they were on the periphery of the crowd, they both whooped for joy, and to hell with the proctors.

"Light and Shadow, working together," Iri crowed, pumping her fist. "I want to know who you slept with to get us paired."

"Me?" Jet giggled. "I thought maybe you threatened someone."

"This is going to be great!" Iri's eyes lit with passion, and Jet practically saw her roommate's—no, her partner's—mind working on how the two of them would take the Academy by storm. "Light refraction and casting shadows... Damn, Jet, we could really make this thing work for us!"

"Striking terror into the hearts of villains?"

"You know it! Black and white, Joannie. You and me."

"And Samson?"

Iri groaned. "I'd do almost anything for you, Jet. But I am absolutely, positively not agreeing to a threesome. But maybe I'll let him sidekick."

" 'Let,' huh?"

Grinning hugely, they both nodded to Night, the proctor at the assembly hall's entrance, who nodded in return. In his cold voice, he said, "Happy with the results, I take it?"

"Couldn't be happier, sir," Iri said brightly. "It's almost enough to make me believe in guardian angels."

Night smiled. Sort of. "And you, Jet?"

"I'm really happy, sir." And she meant every word.

"Good." This time, Night really smiled—wide enough for Jet to see his shockingly white teeth. "Enjoy the moment, girls. Because now the hard part is going to begin."

CHAPTER 31

IRIDIUM

You have to ask yourself what will happen when one of these heroes snaps—and we're not talking about spousal abuse, drunk driving, or a public display of aggression. I'm talking nuclear meltdowns, whole cities wiped off the map because an extrahuman decided he wasn't going to take it anymore.

From the *New Chicago Century*,
an editorial entitled "Mad as Hell"

Single file. Paired students together. No talking." The Superintendent looked at Frostbite and Chen Leung, his paired hero, code name: Red Lotus. Their heads, shocking blue and red respectively, were bowed together.

"I said no talking!"

Frostbite jerked upright. "Sorry, sir."

"While you are in the city, you are representative of the Academy and of Corp," the Superintendent said sternly. "So behave yourselves, or the consequences will be swift and dire."

" 'Swift and dire,' " Iridium mocked. She saw Jet bite the insides of her cheek to keep from smiling. "He's going to make us listen to one of his speeches if we misbehave."

Night walked by and tapped her on the back of the head. "Be quiet, Iridium."

"Sorry, sir."

Night looked down at Jet. "Are you looking forward to this, little Shadow?"

She nodded silently, favoring Night with a bright, soft smile. Iridium almost rolled her eyes. If her roommate hadn't been so head over heels about Samson, Iridium would have thought Jet had a serious crush on Night. *Yuck.*

From the front of the line of students, Celestina clapped her hands. "This way to the transport, everyone."

They all filed in, sat down, and belted up, like the good little heroes-in-training that they were. And then they were off.

The hover took them through the towers of the new downtown, over the reclaimed grids, until they parked on a glassed-in stationary platform in Little Shinjuku. Even in the middle of the day, neon characters and signs glowed; somewhere far away, fireworks popped.

"Now, this area is very safe," said Celestina. "But—"

Iridium raised her hand.

Celestina gave a small sigh. "Yes, Callie?"

"If it's so safe, how come there's bulletproof glass around the lander?"

Night clapped his hands together. "Here's all you need to know. This is your first training patrol. You've each been assigned a sector of the neighborhood on your wristlets. You'll patrol for one hour, then report back immediately. Any of that too complicated for you hormone cases?"

"No, sir!" Jet exclaimed.

A few of the other students snickered. Iridium shot them black looks. No one razzed on Jet for being all perfect except for Iridium.

As Celestina punched a code into the door of the lander, Jet nudged Iridium on the shoulder. "I've got our grid. Let's get to the door. I bet we'll be the first to complete the exercise!"

"Hey, hold up." Iridium pulled Jet back by the sleeve of her uniform. Outside, the stairs unfolded, forming a path from the lander to the street. "This is a bad idea."

"Little Shinjuku is safe," said Jet. "Night said so."

"I'm telling you, this is a bad idea." As they filed out of the lander and down the stairs, Iridium glanced around to take in the surroundings. And she frowned deeply.

"It's training, Iri." Jet's voice was full of happy thoughts. "It's preparing us for when we'll be heroes."

"Yeah." Iridium pointed to a hunched, shaking bum sitting on the curb. "And that's a junkfreak." She rotated to the cluster of buzzing hoverbikes and their satin-jacketed riders. "And that's a speed gang. All preparing for when they'll rob, rape, or kill us." She looked back at Jet. "The city is a dangerous place. My dad at least taught me that."

She felt more than heard Night at her back, his shadow blocking out the faint light from the pollution layer.

"Problem, Iridium? I know we aren't discussing rabids during a class exercise."

"No, sir," Jet said, shoving Iridium forward. "No problem at all. We were just strategizing the best way to proceed."

"Get moving," said Night. "You don't want to fall behind."

Jet blanched, then hissed at Iridium, "I can't believe you're messing this *up*!" Furious, she stalked away.

"Christo, Jet," Iridium called, hurrying after her. "I'm sorry."

"It's fine," Jet muttered as she paced rapidly along the alley, wristlet flashing data. "It's just that..." She took a deep breath. "If Samson and the others have a more complete report because they started on time, that will be reflected in our scores."

"No one is going to have a more complete report," said Iridium. "We're the best, remember?"

Jet sighed, relaxing. "Yes. I know. I'm sorry."

"Forget it," said Iridium, smiling so Jet would know she'd forget it as well.

"It's a straightforward infogather patrol," Jet said, reading the data. "We must collect information on illicit activity, which will be quantified by Ops, and then—"

"Perfect," Iridium said, starting in a random direction. "Let's do a look-see and get back to the hover."

"We have one hour, remember?"

"Let's finish, before the hour's up. Dad told me stories about this neighborhood that'd make your toes curl up."

A man's voice said: "Stories about the boogeyman?"

Iridium whipped her head around and saw two men in ragged old-style clothes with yellow sunburst patches on the breast pockets. She hadn't heard them approaching. "Shit," she said clearly.

Jet frowned at them. "I'm sorry, citizens. This is a training area. You must not have been notified."

"Who do you think you're talking to, brat?" demanded the younger of the two. He had a blunt, dangerous face and glittering dark eyes.

"Jet," Iridium said as the men walked closer, "I don't think they're part of the training exercise."

"But . . . they can't be here otherwise," Jet stammered. "It's not procedure."

Iridium started backing up, forming a strobe in her hands. *Find an exit, make a hole, and get the hell away.* It wasn't Academy training, but it was good common sense.

"Listen to the little freak. You think we let *things* like you tell us where we can and can't go, freak?"

"I don't understand," Jet started. "Who . . . ?"

"Everyman," said Iridium, the sunburst insignia finally clicking into place.

"Look at that," said the older one. "The tall freak's got a brain."

The younger drew out a Talon cutter. "You're not welcome around here, little girls."

Jet was frozen in place, chest fluttering rapidly, her hands shaking. Iridium cursed under her breath but stood her ground. As long as Jet wasn't moving, she couldn't either. Partners never strayed.

"You think you're scaring me?" she spat at the Everyman with the cutter. "I've seen more frightening things in my lunch tray."

"Shut your mouth, you little bitch," he hissed. "A time's coming when all of you are going to see how weak you really are. But I'm gonna teach you a lesson right now." He slashed the cutter close enough to Iridium's face that she could feel the heat from the vibrating edge. "Maybe you'd like that big mouth even wider?"

Iridium released the strobe like a baseball, straight at the man's face. It exploded on contact. He screamed, dropping the Talon. Iridium kicked him in the crotch.

"*Jet*," she snarled. "*Help* me."

"Training," Jet panted. "Just supposed to be training..." She started to gather a Shadow cloak around her, but not quickly enough. The older Everyman grabbed her around the waist and hoisted her into the air in front of him, like a human shield.

"Let her go!" Iridium screamed. She sent a fury of strobes at the man, but they all got absorbed into Jet's Shadow cloak.

The man with the Talon was getting up, rubbing at raw red eyes running trickles of blood from the corners. "I'll blind you, you piece of filth," he snarled. "Every last one of you mistakes of nature is going to pay!"

Iridium saw the knife swing down toward her face...

...and then it just didn't matter. A sense of well-being settled over her, and a faint lavender mist twinkled at the corners of all her senses. Dimly, she noted the Everyman setting down his knife, turning his face upward to the faint sun.

Celestina walked in front of Iridium, the woman's hands shining like rays, her eyes glinting pure like amethysts. A small part of Iridium cried out that something was wrong, they should be fighting, struggling, someone should be dying...

"Put the child down," said Celestina, her voice musical and quiet.

The Everyman complied, a broad smile on his face. He released Jet, who just stood there, the perpetual worry line on her brow soothed away.

"Jet, come here."

Jet walked over at a measured pace to stand beside Iridium.

At Iridium's feet, something chill and slick as the fabric of night passed over the ground.

Celestina snatched Iridium and Jet back, pulling them behind a Dumpster. "Clear!"

Night surged forward, his creepers wrapping the Everymen in blackness. As Celestina's mind mist lifted, Iridium heard their screams. She turned her head away from the sight, but Jet kept staring, more transfixed by Night than by any Mental trick Celestina could muster.

"Get to the hover," said Celestina low in Iridium's ear. "We're evacuating. You're responsible for Jet, Iridium. Make sure she's all right. Do you understand?"

"Yeah," said Iridium. Her voice came out papery and very young. "Yes, ma'am," she barked louder, to cover it up. "Come on, Jet."

Jet didn't move.

Iridium turned to see what had captured Jet's attention: Night closed on the two men, wrapping them in layer upon layer of Shadow, and now he was snarling at them, bellowing, "You like to frighten *little girls*?"

Iridium shivered, then tore her gaze away. "JET!"

She blinked and turned toward Iridium. "What...?"

"We gotta motor. Come on. Just run for the hover and don't look at anything else." She gripped Jet's hand. "I've got you."

Apparently that was enough, because Jet followed her as they jogged back to the hover. After they were safely inside and the Runner pilot had punched a heading back to the Academy, Iridium let out a very relieved sigh.

"I told you this was a bad idea," she said.

Jet pressed her nose against the window, looking down on the firefly lights of Little Shinjuku with the rest of the students. "What's going to happen to Night and Celestina?"

Iridium shut her eyes as the hover lurched into traffic. "Somehow, I think they can take care of themselves."

CHAPTER 32

JET

We have declined to prosecute the Everyman Society as a whole in this instance.

Statement issued from the
New Chicago District Attorney's Office

FIVE DAYS LATER

"So then I say, I don't know, go ask your mother!"

Were cracked up on the punch line, as usual, and Samson followed suit, ditto the usual. Even Frostbite and Red Lotus were chuckling. Iri exchanged a look with Jet that clearly said "Boys are freaking stupid" far louder than any words. Jet absolutely agreed.

But they were also really cute. At least, Samson was. And he was a toe-curling-good kisser. She tried not to blush as she ate her salad.

Iri reached across the table for the catsup. "You kissed your mother with that mouth, Were?"

"Just before I ate her, babe." He howled laughter and

high-fived Red Lotus, who almost spewed his lunch from laughing so hard. Samson and Frostbite snickered, even though Sam looked like he was trying not to (and failing miserably).

Iri elbowed Were in the ribs. "Gross!"

Jet didn't get it, but she knew better than to call attention to that, so she took a cue from Iri and frowned at Samson until the big teen blushed redder than his skinsuit. Smiling sheepishly, he said, "Come on, Jet. It's funny."

She sniffed. "Must be a guy thing." Then Sam blew her a kiss, and she giggled, utterly ruining her cold disposition.

An appreciative whistle from Were dampened Jet's laughter. She glanced at the wiry teen, who was kicked back in his seat and had thrust one large, booted foot on the table—right next to his lunch tray. *Yuck. How can he eat like that?* His hands were propped behind his head, and he had a crap-eating grin on his face. The picture of insolence. His black skinner shimmered beneath the cafeteria's fluorescent lights, much like Jet's own skinsuit, but there was one crucial difference between a skinner and a skinsuit: Were's costume morphed with him when he shed his human form. Couldn't have a werewolf running around in an Academy-standard pre-Squadron outfit; that would be tacky. And expensive to clean. Not to mention bad PR.

Jet smiled to herself. She was getting positively cynical. She arched an eyebrow at him. "What?"

Were shook his mop of long, brown hair out of his eyes and grinned toothily at Jet. "I swear, babe, if I didn't know better, I'd say you and Fright Night were bloodkin. You have his haughty cold shtick down pat."

"If I *were* related to Night," she replied—coolly, of course—"you better believe I'd freeze you with a look."

"Hey," Frostbite said, affronted, "that's *my* line."

"Signature quip," Red Lotus agreed around mouthfuls of Salisbury steak. "He's working on the patent."

"You can't patent a quip," Iri said. "I checked."

Frostbite rolled his eyes. "You would."

"Hey, I'm just getting a leg up on Branding."

"Yeah? What are you thinking of—doing the Snow White thing to the extreme?" He motioned to Iri's black hair, her pale skin, her white unikilt with black piping. "Maybe getting Disney to sponsor you? You'd need cartoon forest creatures in your entourage."

"And dwarves," Samson said, taking a bite of steak.

Iri smiled innocently, and Jet prepared to duck. "Actually," Iri said, "Jet and I are thinking of doing a collaborative sponsorship."

Jet blinked, mouthed, *We are?*

Frostbite scoffed. "You are?"

"Sure." Iri grinned hugely. "Oreos."

They all chuckled over that. Even though it was Iri who'd made the joke, Sam smiled at Jet. She felt a leg wrap around hers beneath the table—and Sam winked at her.

Jet's heart flip-flopped in her chest as she winked back at him. After all these months, she still couldn't believe that Sam was really her boyfriend. He was kind, strong, good-natured, and great-looking; he could have his pick of any girl in their grade—hell, any girl in the Academy. But he'd picked her—a smallish, thinnish, quiet girl with a freaky Power and excellent grades. She wasn't as pretty as Iri, or as smart. Or, as the training session the other day proved, able to think as fast on her feet. Jet was strictly a background player, someone who, appropriately, kept to the shadows.

But Sam had picked her. She could still feel the tingle on her lips from when they'd kissed before joining the others for lunch.

Fourteen and in love. Life was good.

Sometimes, like now, Jet thought she was blessed. She had a best friend who was also her crime-fighting partner-in-training. She had a mentor who encouraged her strongly and helped her quietly. She had a method of keeping the voices at bay, so she didn't have to worry about going boogity-boo crazy, or getting Therapy and having her brain sliced open. She had a boyfriend who liked spending time with her, even when they just held hands and didn't talk at all. And now she had a small group of acquaintances who were slowly becoming friends.

Okay, in Were's case, maybe not friends. Maybe more like someone to put up with. But he was Sam's partner, so Jet just rolled with it.

Yeah, she thought, smiling and feeling ridiculously happy. *Life is good.*

Red Lotus was laughing over something that Were had said (and Jet had missed because she had been thinking about Sam and how good everything was), and laughing so hard that he started to choke on his lunch. Frostbite, seated next to him, pounded the slight boy's back a couple times. On the last thump, Red Lotus pivoted to block with his forearm. He was slight, yes, but a strong and willowy sort of slight. From the loose yet tailored fit of his red (of course) belted skinsuit, to his black almond-shaped eyes and golden skin, to his usually serene disposition, Jet thought Red Lotus was the picture-perfect *wuxia* expert.

If those legendary *wuxia* swordsmen had really been extrahumans with Earth power, that is. And had shockingly red hair.

"Bad form to hit your partner," he said to Frostbite, who shrugged.

"Next time, I'll let you choke."

"You're a pal."

"I'm nothing if not considerate of my partner's needs," Frostbite said innocently.

"Christo, the steak tastes like feet," Iri muttered.

"You suck a lot of toes, babe?"

"Shut it, Were."

"Or what?"

"Or I'll sic my partner on you."

"Don't drag me into this," Jet said. To Were she

somberly added, "For the record, she's never sucked my toes."

"Hey! You're supposed to be on my side!" Iri threw her spork at Jet, but Samson caught it before it could bean her on the head.

"My hero," Jet murmured, batting her lashes.

"Oh puke, get a room already," Iri said. "And give me my spork back."

"I have a room," Jet said primly. "But it comes with an obnoxious roommate."

Iri rolled her eyes. "You know, I think I liked you better when you were all withdrawn and antisocial. Can't you scowl at me or something? Where's the Jet I know and love?"

"Girl love!" Were hooted. "Where's the mud?"

Jet and Iri both glared at him, at least until Sam gave Iri the utensil back. "For the food. Don't use it to stab Were."

"Why not?"

"Blood's a pain to wash off a skinsuit."

"Nice," Were lamented. "Red Lotus's partner looks out for him. My partner sells me out to the 36-C Lighter."

Iri blew him a kiss, then attacked her Salisbury steak with gusto.

"Holy Jehovah," Frostbite said. "Is that who I think it is?"

Jet looked up from her salad to where Frostbite was pointing. And then her jaw dropped.

Standing in line for lunch, smiling brighter than any of Iri's strobes, was Dawnlighter. She looked just as sparkly clean as she had back in First and Second Years. Her red hair was vibrant, her green eyes sparkling, and, Jet noticed with dismay, she was way more developed than Jet had remembered. Beautiful, body of a supermodel—a *true* supermodel—and looking pleased as punch to be in the Academy cafeteria, as if seven months hadn't gone by since anyone had last seen her.

"I can't believe it," Iri said, frowning. "Dawnie's back, lighter than life."

"Hey," Sam murmured in Jet's ear, "you okay?"

Jet blinked, tore her gaze from Dawnlighter to smile at Sam. "Why?"

"Your hand's getting black."

She glanced down at her left hand, and sure enough, Shadow had begun to seep out of her pores. Whoops. She pulled the darkness back inside of herself, thankful that Sam had spotted it before any of the proctors had. Or before the Power wards had been breached.

Great. When she was out during training, she'd frozen quicker than you could say "Frostbite." But here, when she wasn't supposed to use her powers without authorization, she was practically leaking Shadow.

"She looks so normal, it's killing me," Iri said.

Frostbite nudged her. "You think she's been in Therapy this whole time?"

"Probably. The way she was hardwired, I'm stunned they let her out at all."

"What's the big deal? Other than the big rack, I mean?" Were eyed Dawnlighter, clearly impressed by her physical assets. "She's just another Lighter. Dime a dozen. Present company excluded, babe," he added to Iri.

"Bite me, wolf boy."

"You wish, firefly."

"Now now, children," said Red Lotus. "Behave or the proctors will get you."

Jet barely heard them banter. Her gaze was fixed on Dawnlighter, who looked so freaking happy and perfect that it turned Jet's stomach.

In her mind, she heard Dawnlighter's voice, clear as the day she'd snarled it at her in Second Year: *"Get out of the extrahuman gene pool and do us all a favor."*

Jet's hand trembled. *Shut up.*

"You're nothing but a filthy Shadow."

Shut up!

"I'll stop you from spreading your filth!"

Jet stood and started to march over to Dawnlighter. She heard Iri exclaim "Oh, shit!" and the scrape of chairs behind her, but she didn't care. It was far past time for her and Dawnlighter to have words.

And if they weren't loud enough, actions too.

She sauntered up, legs loose, arms dangling easy by her sides—she was sure she didn't look like she was summoning Shadow and getting ready to let loose the creeper brigade. When she was in spitting distance of Dawnlighter, she spoke the girl's code name.

The redhead turned to her . . . and smiled in delight.

"Jet!" she chirped—*chirped,* could you believe it?—and stepped out of line to squeal. "Eee, look at you! Love your hair, it's so pretty! Do you get it highlighted? I don't remember it being that honey-blond."

Jet blinked, said, "Excuse me?"

"Oh," Dawnlighter laughed, "sorry, didn't mean to offend you. If you say it's natural, then I believe you! Only you and your hairdresser will know for sure, am I right?"

Jet was pretty certain someone had slipped something into her lemon water, because she had to be high if she thought this . . . Barbie doll . . . was Dawnlighter.

"So how's it going?" Dawnlighter said, all bubbly enthusiasm. "I've missed quite a bit, but Celestina tells me that I can make it up quick enough if I really focus." She giggled, covering her mouth with her hand. "But between you and me, that's going to be tough. Look at the guys! When did they discover muscles?"

"Um . . . Jet?" That was Iridium, behind her. "Is . . . everything okay?"

"I honestly don't know," Jet said, feeling rather lost.

"Iridium!" Dawnlighter squealed. "Wow, look at you! Your acne's all gone, and you've gotten so pretty! You're going to be a poster hero for the Academy in no time!"

Iri and Jet exchanged a troubled look. "Dawnie," Iridium said. "You're . . . different."

"Am I?" Dawnlighter's eyes clouded for a moment, and a vertical worry line marred her brow. "Bad different?"

"Um, no, just . . . different."

"Well, it's been awhile," she said with a huge smile. "And I know we haven't been close, but that's all water under the bridge now. We're all on the same side—the side of justice." She stuck out her hand and said to Jet, "Friends?"

Stunned, Jet stuck out her hand, remembering last minute to make sure no Shadow had seeped through before clasping the other girl's hand. "Uh, sure."

"Terrific," she beamed. "But boy, your hand is cold! You need to improve your circulation, Jet. Can't be at the top of your game if your circulation is sluggish. Drink more water."

"Or something stronger," Iri mumbled.

"Well, I have to get my lunch. Growing heroes need their nutrients, you know! Good seeing you girls," Dawnlighter said, then turned to head to the back of the line instead of pushing her way back to where she'd been before Jet had approached.

"What on the scorched earth was that?" Jet said.

"That," Iri replied, "is why we never, ever want to get sent to Therapy."

Staring at Dawnlighter's retreating form, Jet said, "I'd sooner kiss an Everyman."

"Considering you already danced with one, that's not such a big step . . ."

Jet hissed between her teeth. "Don't remind me."

"Well, look at the bright side," Iri said, leading them back to their table. "Next time we tangle with Everyman, you won't freeze."

"Oh no? How can you be so sure?"

"If you do, I'll strobe your ass."

"Deal."

But through the rest of lunch, Jet kept sliding looks over to where Dawnlighter sat, amid her old friends, chatting happily, and Jet frowned and fretted when she realized that she'd preferred the snotty, elitist girl to the chipper impersonation wearing her form now. At least the old Dawnlighter had been . . . real.

This one was like a walking ad for the Academy.

No way will I ever—ever—get sent to Therapy, if that's the result, Jet swore to herself.

I'd sooner die.

CHAPTER 33

IRIDIUM

No citizens should interfere with the discharge of your duties. If one does, simply recite the prepared statement about your work for Corp protecting your city of residence and send them on their way.

Squadron Field Patrol Manual, Section III

THREE MONTHS LATER

Frostbite inhaled the dingy air of Looptown and crinkled his nose. "This sucks."

Red Lotus grinned through the wrap on the lower half of his face. "Doesn't bother me."

Frostbite punched him on the shoulder. "I hate you, man."

"Could we focus, please?" Jet said, tapping her wristlet.

Iridium laughed. "Chill, Jet. This is just another stupid training op."

"So what? We still have to do our best."

Iridium rolled her eyes.

After the disaster in Little Shinjuku last semester, the

hover had dropped them off in the safer but equally dingy Looptown. Passing pedestrians gave the six teenagers curious looks. A New Chicago cop on a speedbike glared at them from behind mirrored sunglasses.

"Training is preparation for real combat," said Jet in the prissy tone that reminded Iridium of a female, high-pitched Night.

"Honey, I think Iri is right," said Samson, sliding an arm around Jet's waist. "Nothing is going to happen today. It's a good day."

"But—"

He shut her up with a kiss. Which lasted until Were made pig noises. Jet disentangled herself, blushing.

"You're a walking, talking evolutionary mistake," Iridium told Were. "You know that, right?"

"I know you want me," he said, waggling his shaggy eyebrows, then yelped. Iridium coughed to hide her laugh at seeing Were's feet covered in ice.

"We're supposed to be acting like heroes," Frostbite said. "Pretend, can't you?"

Were snarled and lunged for him. "You better pray you grow wings, fairy!"

Red Lotus held up one palm, which was slim but calloused from his hours of *wuxia* practice. "Do not touch him."

"Hey!" Jet stuck her fingers in her mouth and let out a piercing whistle.

The boys paused in their posturing and looked at Jet, who hissed, "I'm not failing because you're trying to outtestosterone everyone, Were. Could we please do the assignment and get back to the transport? We're supposed to be star students. This isn't helping."

Iridium was impressed. When had Jet grown a backbone?

Samson shot Were a glare that could have derailed an express train, and Were looked at the ground. "Yeah, sorry," he muttered. "Can't have your girlfriend getting upset. She might not give it up if she's pissy, right?"

Iridium snapped her fingers, and a strobe appeared between them. "You want to stop that train of thought right now, Shaggy." He growled at her, and she winked.

"Let's go, Were," Samson said, giving Jet a kiss on her cheek. "I'll meet you back at the lander, babe."

Jet smiled at him. "I'm counting the seconds."

As the boys walked away, Iridium arched an eyebrow and looked at Jet. "What's gotten in to you? And if you say 'Samson,' I'm going to hit you in the head to reengage your brain."

Jet shrugged. "I don't know. I just feel . . . I feel *good,* Iri. For the first time in a long time." She paused. "And I won't let Were mess up my grades." She touched her earpiece, tucking her hair behind her ear.

Iridium touched her own, which was linked to Celestina, who watched them from the hover's monitors to make sure they weren't writing graffiti or urinating in public. The earpiece gave a squeal of feedback as she brushed the volume control. Damn, she hated the thing.

"Okay, well, euphoria and Were aside," Iridium said, "the training data indicates that we're supposed to observe this street for twenty minutes and record suspicious activity." Iridium surveyed the sad expanse of auto shops and bars that breathed the population of the street in and out.

"I'm recording to my wristlet," Jet said. "Let's do a slow pass down the north side and see if there's anything going on in the alleys."

"Whatever," Iridium said. "Do you think the Squadron spends its days tromping around Looptown? I mean, really?"

"Great heroes come from humble beginnings."

"You are a walking platitude. You know that, right?"

"I prefer 'hero-in-training'."

They passed a café, an electronics store with one sad tele in the window playing a news broadcast, and three pawnshops lined up in a row.

"Yup," Iridium said, looking into the last pawnshop's window. The centerpiece was a decommissioned creeper 'bot that gazed at her with sad headlamp eyes. "This here neighborhood is a hotbed of crime, all right."

Jet didn't chastise her—didn't respond at all.

"Jet?" she said, looking around.

"Iri! Look!" Jet was half a block down, standing in front of a thrift-shop window. A faded, curled poster decorated the glass, a man in a red skinsuit, orange cape, and goggles. "It's the Firebolt. He was always my favorite when I was a kid."

"I thought your heart belonged to our tall, dark, and creepy teacher." Iridium mimicked Firebolt's hands-on-hips pose. "But I can see why that turns you on."

"Iridium, I can hear you," said Celestina in her ear. "Watch what you say about your proctors."

"Sorry, ma'am," said Iridium sweetly, then took her earpiece from its cradle and tossed it into a passing trash 'bot. "How do you work with that thing in your head?" she muttered. The hiss of static was maddening, and the frequencies never worked right when she brought up her powers, anyway.

"They've got all kinds of memorabilia!" said Jet, excited. "Look at the toy goggles. I wanted a pair so badly when I was a kid ..."

"I was more of a Persephone fan myself," said Iridium. "She was the same year at the Academy as my mother. Came to the house a lot before Dad got arrested."

In the glass of the shop window, she saw Frostbite and Red Lotus across the street. Frostbite stuck his finger down his throat and pantomimed gagging. Behind his face shield, Red Lotus was probably smiling serenely. A garbage loader cut across traffic lanes. Horns sounded.

"I wonder how hard it would be to get a pass to come back?" Jet murmured.

"Pretty hard, considering you'd have to be a nut to ever come back here voluntarily."

"I'd like to check out this store. When we're not on duty," Jet added. She glanced at Iridium, a smile on her face. "Do you think they have Night stuff? Like action figures? Wouldn't that be neat?"

"It'd be creepy," Iridium said absently. "Just like Night. Jet, aren't garbage loaders 'bot-operated?"

"With preprogrammed routes," Jet agreed, still looking in the shop window. "Why?"

The loader slowed, and its rusted doors rolled backward. Iridium saw the gleam of the plasgun barrel appear from within, caught in the light like an old flat snapshot.

"Move!" Iridium screamed at Jet, grabbing her friend by the arm and dragging her around the corner of the shop. The bolt shattered the window where Jet had stood. The merchandise inside caught fire with a *whoosh*.

Iridium pelted down the alley, Jet behind her, and nearly slammed into the solid back of someone much larger than herself.

Samson spun, his big fists closed, and when he saw it was Iridium, panic crept into his eyes. "What in the hell is going on?"

Behind him, a construction hover pulled up and disgorged more men, all of them wearing yellow sunbursts on their clothing, some with it painted on their faces and hands.

"Power to every man!" one of them shrieked. "Death to the freaks!"

Footsteps pelted behind Iridium, and she whirled around to see Red Lotus and Frostbite running down the alley ahead of a horde of Everymen. They had guns, Talon cutters, fixed metal knives. The weapons were all different, but the hatred on their faces was exactly the same.

Iridium looked at Jet. Her voice tight, she said, "I think we're a little bit fucked."

Jet tapped her earpiece. "Celestina! Celestina, come in!"

A plas bolt splashed off the brick above Iridium's head and she ducked, cursing.

"Guys, I don't mean to alarm you," said Frostbite, pointing at the crowd of Everymen, "but I don't think the cavalry is going to make it in time."

"Told you little freaks you'd get what was coming to you," growled one of the men at the head of the column. "You think you can come into *our* city, tell us how to live our lives, like fucking guardian angels gone wrong?"

Iridium touched Frostbite on the shoulder with one hand, Jet with the other. "When they get close enough," she said in a low voice, "freeze them. Blind them. Do whatever you have to do. We have to get out of this bottleneck."

Were snarled and doubled over, his lanky body growing and re-forming into a wolf. Samson struck his huge fists together, the sound like thunder.

The men at the front of each column howled and charged, raising their weapons.

Were launched himself at the first Everyman group, teeth bared, just as Red Lotus whipped his foot around, faster than Iridium could see, and cracked the leader of the second group across the skull hard enough to send him backward into the alley wall.

Iridium waited a second longer, then created a handful of strobes and flung them indiscriminately, the light washing back over her. Next to her, Frostbite sent out wave after wave of ice, rendering the plasguns useless and slicking the floor of the alley. In front of them, a flock of men with suns on their chests fell over one another.

On Iridium's other side, Jet unleashed her power, Shadow creepers winding around legs and feet, climbing up and over everything, drowning one Everyman at a time like an inexorable black tide.

Still, they came, screaming insults and swinging their weapons like they were attempting to trim unruly weeds. Iridium kept strobing them, harder and faster than she'd ever done before.

Red Lotus blocked the swing of a baseball bat, then cried out as Iridium heard bones crack. Frostbite, half-dragging his partner away, froze the arm of the boy's attacker so that it shattered, crystalline shards raining to the ground.

Jet whirled to face Iridium, her face flushed, creepers writhing around her head. She pointed and screamed, "Behind you!"

Iridium turned, nose to chin with an Everyman, and it was too late to do anything but stare.

She felt the Talon cutter slide through her skin, underneath the breastbone, hot and foreign and numbing. She felt air where no air had drawn before, felt her left side fill up with something liquid and heavy.

"Iridium!"

Jet's scream came from down a tunnel as Iridium slumped to the ground, the cold pavement pressing against her cheek.

"One down!" the Everyman cheered. "Press 'em in good, boys!"

"No," Jet's voice hissed, very close to Iridium's ear.

Iridium tried to draw breath and spat blood instead.

"No," Jet said again. "You stay *away* from her!"

"We'll hold them off!" Frostbite shouted. His voice echoed, high and tinny. All Iridium could see was the sky. "Help Callie!"

Iridium felt someone pull her unikilt aside. Fingers touched her, cold as stone. "Oh, Christo. You're bleeding, Iri. You're bleeding . . ." To Frostbite, Jet cried, "The wound's too deep! We need a medic!"

"Sure, I'll get right on that!" Frostbite yelled, and more ice sizzled to rest on the stones of the alley.

"Jet." It hurt so very much to speak, more than anything

Iridium could remember or conceive. "Jet." Blood flowed freely from her mouth with the word.

"Oh, Iri..." Jet moaned. "I'm so sorry...I can't stop it..." Her hands pressed on Iridium's chest, cold and useless.

"Let...me..." Iridium gasped.

She reached into herself, past the pain and the dull, deadening feeling as her lungs filled up with blood. She reached for power, for the very brightest part of herself and forced it outward, into her hands, her fingers.

She pointed them toward the wound and, inch by inch, let the power escape.

The burning started, worse than the wound, and Iridium heard herself scream. Her power seared her skin and slowly, slowly closed off the gash. Then it was done, and she collapsed in Jet's arms, gasping. Her heart fluttered, then stabilized, thudding hard enough to break her ribs. Sticky warmth flowed from her nose.

"You did it," Jet whispered. "Sweet Jehovah, Callie, you did it!"

"Yeah!" she heard Frostbite shout. "You want it colder? I can make it colder, you pieces of crap!"

"Get out of here before we hurt you," someone— Samson, she thought—yelled.

Jet gently laid Iridium down on the ground, then stood and shouted, "That's right, you better run!"

Iridium's eyes slowly refocused, her burned nerves shutting off. She saw Jet to one side, Samson to the other. And beyond Samson, an Everyman turned and raised a gun.

She didn't have the strength to call out a warning, but she tried.

Samson fell silently, his body breaking the vacuum with a boneless *thud.*

Jet screamed, and went to her knees beside Samson, and in the midst of her crying, Academy hovers overflew the alley, spewing heroes, who flew or landed in the street to disband the rest of the Everyman group.

"Wake up," Jet told Samson. "Please, Sam, wake up."

Someone swept Iridium into their arms, and a float slammed into her back. "Careful," a gravelly voice growled. "She's just a kid."

"We've got one unresponsive!" another hero shouted. "Miss? Miss, you're going to have to move now."

The last thing Iridium saw as the ambulance doors hissed closed was Samson, prone in the alley. Not moving.

CHAPTER 34

JET

In the line of duty.

Epitaph on Samson's gravestone

Everyone had shown up for the funeral. The entire Academy, from students to instructors to support staff; all members of the Squadron who weren't currently out battling evil or posing for their sponsors; the mayor and his City Hall entourage; the governor of Illinois and her assorted posse. Various other government officials, looking properly grim. Corp muckety-mucks, talking loudly about the "terrible tragedy." The media, already branding the event as "Death of a Hero."

And the dead hero, of course. He was there too.

Jet sat straight in her hard-backed seat, chin high. Eyes dry. Next to her, Iridium held her hand, squeezed tightly. Jet barely felt it.

She barely felt anything anymore.

Samson was dead.

The world had taken on a slow, syrupy feel—Jet sat, and breathed, and sometimes someone would say a word or a phrase that would capture her attention, then it would slip away and Jet was alone, sitting, breathing. She knew Iridium was on her right, poor Iri in her bandages and her pain, and next to her was Frostbite, with his fresh scars so livid compared with the bright blue of his hair, and Red Lotus next to him, his broken arm set and mending. She knew Were was on her left, as untouched as she was herself. Unmarked. Unhurt.

Undead.

She knew these things, but none of it really mattered. After the funeral, life would return to normal at the Academy; they still had to finish Third Year and apply for preliminary sponsorships. She knew this, too, and it mattered even less.

Even Night didn't matter, not anymore.

"He's gone, Jet," Night had said to her after they had returned yesterday, Jet wearing blood that wasn't hers and still feeling the ghost of Sam's lips on her own. "He's gone, and you have to accept it and move on."

And when she hadn't responded, Night had gotten cold, even for him, and told her that true heroes weren't stopped by death. They held their heads high and did their duty. When she still hadn't responded, he said curtly: "If you let this break you, Joan, then you weren't worth the effort."

She remembered turning her back on Night, actually turning her back on the man she'd emulated and maybe even loved, remembered walking away from him, then finding herself in the Infirmary by Iridium's side, her hand in Iri's just as Iri's hand would be in hers at the funeral the next day. And when it was well past Lights Out and they were alone, Jet shed her Shadow cloak and became visible and cried. She'd dimly realized that she'd used her power when she was not authorized to, had used it and no one had noticed and none of the Power wards had been tripped, but that didn't matter.

She cried, softly so as not to disturb Iridium, who was so medicated that even if Jet had wailed, she probably would have slept through it. Jet cried, feeling her heart slowly shred and drift away, leaving behind a hole in her chest that ached all the more for its emptiness. Jet cried, and lost herself to her grief.

Her fault.

She'd been too slow, again. Iri had gotten hurt because Jet hadn't reacted fast enough, then she couldn't stop the bleeding.

She hadn't even heard the shot that had killed Sam, cut him down so cleanly, and he'd been standing right next to her.

She was no hero. She was just a scared little girl in a skinsuit who'd thought she had a chance at being happy.

Iri was hurt and Sam, oh holy Jehovah, Sam was dead, and if Jet had been a real hero, it wouldn't have happened.

And now she was at Sam's funeral, the whirring of the vids and the feedback from the speakers wreaking so much havoc with her earpiece that she'd had to shut it off.

Nothing mattered anymore.

Not Night in his cold arrogance, not even Iri, who'd almost died as well. Not the voices with their whispering and giggling—and maybe it showed how cruel Jehovah truly was, because this was the one time she would have surrendered herself to the dark and come what may, but today the voices were silent. In mourning, perhaps.

It didn't matter. Nothing mattered.

She'd hand in her skinsuit and earpiece after the funeral. And if that meant she was resigning herself to Therapy, that didn't matter, either.

Onstage, the Superintendent was blathering about the state of the world today, and why the Squadron was needed more than ever. Jet blinked and now it was Mayor Moulton droning on about the senseless hatred that had brought about this horrific event. She blinked again to find Mister Marvel speaking about how death is the risk every hero takes every time he walks or flies into the field.

None of this is about Sam, Jet thought, and that realization shattered her numbness.

This should be about Sam.

She thought she felt his arm around her shoulder, and she leaned into his touch. Iridium whispered something nonsensical about whether Jet was okay, and Jet ignored it because she didn't want to lose this last feeling of Sam next to her, Sam touching her and kissing her and laughing with her and telling her . . .

. . . telling her . . .

"It's too soon," he says, stroking her face, "I know it's too soon, but Joannie, I gotta tell you this before I burst, and I hope to heaven that you won't run away."

"You can tell me," she says, a fluttering in her belly and a strange light sensation in her chest. "You know you can tell me anything."

And he smiles—oh sweet Jehovah, his eyes are so bright—and he says, "I love you."

She cries then, a little, and he's afraid he's scared her off, and then she starts laughing and she's kissing him and telling him that she loves him too . . .

"Jet? Come on, answer me."

Iridium again. Jet lifted her head and didn't reply. Sam was talking to her, the memory of Samson was holding her and telling her it was all going to be okay . . .

"I swear," Jet says, hearing the whine in her voice and helpless to stop it, "I'll never get this right!"

"Of course you will." Sam's hands are strong and soothing, massaging away her tension.

"I won't! I go by the book, follow the moves exactly how I'm

supposed to. But then Iri goes and improvises, and I land flat on my back with her heel on my neck!" Jet lets out a wretched laugh. "How'm I supposed to study improvisation?"

"You're doing great, honey. Iri's used to thinking outside of the text. And she's okay with fighting dirty."

"We're not supposed to fight dirty."

"I know. But I think that's just in the Academy. I think in the real world, we're supposed to fight to win."

"If the real world doesn't do what I expect, then I'm in trouble." She closes her eyes, leans back against his broad chest. "I'm terrible at this. I'm no hero."

"You are, Jet." He turns her around and tilts her head up until she's gazing into his eyes. "We're heroes, all of us. We've got these powers for a reason. We're meant to help people."

She says, "But I can't do what Iri does."

And he smiles and strokes her cheek. "So do what Jet does."

"I have no idea what Jet does."

"And you have plenty of time to find out. You are a hero, honey. Even if you don't feel like one. Don't worry. It's all going to be okay."

The Superintendent was speaking again, getting ready to introduce someone else who would talk about how important heroes were and why they all need to be strong and not saying a damn thing about Sam.

That was the only thing that mattered now: Today had to be about Sam.

Jet stood.

"What are you doing?" Iridium hissed. "Sit down!"

Jet walked out of the row of seats, stepping over feet that didn't shuffle out of her way, leaving a wake of buzzing voices. The vids didn't swarm to her until she started walking down the main aisle and headed toward the stage. Then they were on her, their lights glaring and the sudden silence so thick that she barely heard the cameras' mechanical whirls.

It didn't matter. Only doing right by Sam mattered.

He would have done the same for her.

No one stopped Jet from ascending onto the stage, and when she approached the podium, the Superintendent said to the room, "But first, one of our Third Years wishes to speak a few words. Jet, go ahead."

She stared at the audience, but all she could see was the lights from the vids and the overheads. And even though she had no idea why she was onstage at all or what she was going to say, she opened her mouth and spoke.

"This isn't about why we're heroes." Her voice was soft, and if the microphones weren't there, even the people in the first row would not have heard her. "This isn't about the way things are in the world. This is about a fifteen-year-old boy whose designation was Samson. But his name was Joseph Rogers."

"You can call me Joe," he says to her Second Year, that day when he followed her out of Lancer's class.

"We're not supposed to use names," she replies.

"Yeah, and teachers aren't supposed to break the rules whenever they want." His smile is big, huge, and it eats his face. "And we're not supposed to talk back to them. If you don't like Joe, you can call me Sam. Lots of people do."

She laughs softly and offers her hand. "I'm Joan. Joannie."

"Joe was an Earth power," Jet said, using his given name on purpose, even though it was foreign on her tongue. "And he was as strong as you'd think. But he was also kind. And sweet. And he always, always helped out whenever he could. And he wasn't afraid to speak up when he thought something was not fair or just."

"But sir," Samson says, "all she was doing was defending herself. You're the one who let Hornblower attack first with his power."

At that, Lancer cuts his gaze over Jet's shoulder. "Samson, you questioning how I run this class?"

A pause, and then: "In this case, yes, sir."

"He was my friend," Jet said, her voice caught on a sob.

"And I loved him. And I'm going to miss him terribly. Without him, the world isn't as good as it was when he was in it."

She took a deep breath. "We're heroes, even if we don't feel heroic, or if we're scared, or if we want to quit and walk away. And we're told that we can't let death stop us, that it's a risk we all face daily." Jet paused, and when she spoke again there was an edge of steel in her voice. "But Joe died a stupid death. He shouldn't have died. That was horrible and wrong, and nothing will ever make it right."

"Nothing is going to happen today," Sam says, sliding an arm around Jet's waist. "It's a good day."

"Joseph Rogers would be the first person to say that we're heroes for a reason, that we're meant to help others. Well, he didn't get a chance to show the world what he could do as Samson. But he helped me, more than I could ever say. And for that, I say to him: Thank you, Joe. Thank you, Samson."

"I love you, Joannie," Sam says, and everything is right with the world, and she could never imagine that it's all going to fall apart not even a week later.

"Thank you for being my friend," Jet said softly, "for helping me when I needed help. For making me laugh. For having my back. For holding my hand." Tears streamed down her face, but she didn't acknowledge them. "Thank you for your courage, and for your strength. Thank you for your smile, for your good humor. Thank you for being a true hero, and a truer friend."

She bowed her head. "Good-bye, Samson."

Brushing the tears from her cheeks, Jet exited the stage. No one stopped her when she left the assembly hall. She walked out of the Academy, her head high, breathing the cool autumn air. She thought she felt Sam squeeze her shoulder, but it wasn't him at all.

"Jet," Night said, not at all cold. "I'm so sorry for your loss."

"Thank you, sir." Was that her voice, so curiously flat, sounding so unlike herself? "You could have said so to me yesterday."

A long pause before Night spoke. "Yes. That was insensitive of me, and I regret that. But you were in shock, and I said what I did to try to snap you out of it." He sighed. "Even heroes make mistakes."

Oh yes, they surely do.

Night said, "Your tribute to Samson will probably be repeated by the media for the rest of the day. Maybe the rest of the week. What you just did back there was the best thing you could have done for Samson's memory. And," he added softly, "for yourself."

She couldn't bring herself to thank him; she wouldn't have meant the words.

"You've more strength in you than you realize," he said. "Your speech just now made that very clear. You'll heal, Joan. You'll move on."

"Maybe I don't want to move on, sir."

"Maybe not right now. But you will. You're a hero, Jet. And if you want Samson's death to have any meaning at all, you'll let his dedication to helping others be your beacon. Your guiding light in the dark."

Her fist trembled, and that was when she realized she'd been about to lash out and hit Night. Hissing out a breath, she unclenched her hand. "Yes, sir."

"Put the earpiece back in, Jet. And then let's get you back inside."

The device back in her ear, Jet allowed Night to lead her back into the Academy, safe behind its walls.

CHAPTER 35

IRIDIUM

The psychological toll on extrahumans in training is sometimes severe, but with very few exceptions our conditioning enables them to cope with the demands of heroism. No counseling support is deemed necessary at the time of this report's publication.

Internal report circulated to the Executive Committee

Iridium sat down across from Frostbite, and jerked her chin at the hunched, silent figure on the other side of the cafeteria. "Any change?"

Frostbite refroze his blueberry slush and sucked on it through his straw. "That's a big negatory. Not tears, not smiling. Just sitting, and staring. Sorta creepy, honestly. It's been what, two weeks?"

"Her grief is weighing her down," Chen said. "You can see it in her body, in the way she moves."

"I'm going to try again." Iridium picked up her tray, winding between tables until she sat down across from Jet. "Hey, stranger. We've missed you at lunch."

Jet pushed her vegetable stir-fry from side to side on her tray but didn't take a bite. "I just want to be alone."

"Okay, but it's been two weeks," Iridium said, echoing Frostbite. "Do you want to talk about it, maybe?"

Jet looked up, her eyes flat. "About what?"

Iridium sighed. "Samson dying was terrible, it's true—"

"Heroes aren't stopped by death," Jet said shortly. "We hold our heads up and do our duty. For Corp, and for the people."

Iridium rolled her eyes. "Is that what Night said, to try and placate you?"

"It's the truth. The sooner you realize that, Iridium, the better off you'll be."

Iridium picked up Jet's chocolate milk from her tray and dumped it down the front of Jet's unikilt.

Jet shrieked, jumping away from the table. Glaring at Iri, she snapped, "What was that for?"

"To wake you up!" Iridium shouted. "Stop acting like Samson dying doesn't bother you! I hear you crying at night, Jet. I hear the nightmares. His death was wrong, so drop the act!"

Jet raised her chin. "Death is a fact of life when you're a hero. All it does is strengthen your resolve."

"We're not heroes," Iridium said through clenched teeth. "Not yet. Our friend—your *boyfriend*—died pointlessly. How can you can actually stand there and say that it doesn't bother you?"

Jet trembled for a moment, then Iridium watched her friend visibly shed her emotions. It was utterly terrifying to watch. "What's done is done," she said coldly, sounding just like Night. "And speak for yourself, when you say we're not heroes. Corp's been begging for my attention lately."

"Because of the passionate speech you gave. At your boyfriend's funeral."

Jet's eyes narrowed. "You should be careful of what you say, Iridium. The child of a known rabid has to work extremely hard to find sponsors and build her image."

"Oh, *fuck* image," Iridium hissed. "The only image you

have is of the little girl with the crazy father." She knew that it was a horrible, hurtful thing to throw at Jet, but she kept going. She hoped Jet would cry, slap her, summon Shadows and destroy the cafeteria—anything to show she wasn't brainwashed.

Because if Iridium hadn't known better, she would have sworn Jet had gone to Therapy.

"That's preferable to the image of the immature child with the felon father," Jet said in that same dead tone, the Nothing-to-See-Here tone. She picked up a napkin and blotted at her unikilt. "I have a press conference with the Squadron tomorrow, and then Night mentioned that the city wanted to talk with me about doing a public-service announcement." She tossed the napkin onto her tray. "I'm excused from field training for the next week. You'll have to find a new partner until I get back."

She grabbed her lunch tray—her food still untouched—and started to walk away.

Desperately, Iridium said, "Don't you miss him?"

Jet paused. With a struggle, she ground out, "No." Then she deposited her tray by the designated return station and walked out of the cafeteria.

Iridium slumped back in her seat, tears that she hadn't shed in her entire time at the Academy brimming. No matter how much it hurt, she never cried. But this was a different kind of pain, an insidious, ephemeral type she couldn't guard against.

If this was being a superhero, she didn't want it.

NOW

CHAPTER 36

JET

The Everyman Society is the Squadron's most vocal opponent. A humans-first activist group, Everyman purports to hold a 48% approval rating among populations in the United and Canadian States of America. If you believe their stats, more than 39% of Greater America are in or have family members in the Society. That must be very sobering to Corp.

Lynda Kidder, "The Plight of Everyman,"
New Chicago Tribune, September 10, 2112

They walked beneath the city, slowly, with Moore leading and Jet following, picking their way through the tunnels of the Rat Network. Around them was nothing but gloom that receded into damp shadows; the rounded passages hinted at what might have once been plast, or maybe steel, which was now nothing but water-smoothed blackness festered with mildew and rot. Eye-watering stench—raw sewage; filth; sodden decay—turned breathing normally into an Olympic feat. Sounds were both amplified and muffled, overriding the steady white noise from Jet's comlink, filling her ears instead with the *plunk-plunk-plunk* of their footsteps, the constant drip of unseen water, and the buzzing spurts from overhead that must have been early-morning traffic on the streets of New Chicago.

All in all, Jet would rather have been in bed. Or curled up in her rocker with a paperback romance. Or doing something altogether inappropriate with her new Runner.

The sewers, she thought morosely. *It had to be the sewers, didn't it?* Why were hostages never held for ransom or for torture in penthouse apartments?

They sludged forward, and Jet tried not to think about what diseases were in the water they stepped through. Moore carried a lightstick, which he held like a holy object. For her part, Jet saw well enough. Perk of her optiframes. But they did precious little to block out the voices, which even now she heard pressing around her, waiting for her to get careless. Which was stupid; even now, her comlink hummed its white-noise hum. The voices couldn't touch her. Not even here, in the pit of the world.

She pressed her lips together and marched on, pretending that she wasn't afraid.

You scare easy, Iridium's voice hissed.

When it came to the dark? Oh, yeah. She knew what went bump in the night. And it had teeth.

But she was the damn hero. So on she went.

More to distract herself from the looming threat of the whispers in the dark than out of actual desire for conversation, she said, "So you believe that I'm a time bomb?"

If Moore responded, she couldn't hear it over their plunking footfalls, over the slow but maddening drip of water. Maybe his reply got eaten by the odor, which was rancid enough to be its own life-form. Her nostrils flared as she exhaled sharply. Damn it to Darkness, she was going to have to burn this skinsuit after they got Kidder out of here. Probably the cape and cowl too. Maybe Bruce would be a dear and get the whole enchilada dry-cleaned.

Enchilada. Heh.

She smiled, remembering the taste of the spicy food on her tongue. That really had been sweet of him. Bruce Hunter hadn't been kidding when he'd said he'd read her file. Mexican food. Jet shook her head, the smile softening. He was ... sweet.

She wondered what it would be like to kiss him.

"All of you."

Jet blinked, lost the pleasant daze of imagining Bruce's lips on hers. "Pardon me?"

"It's not just you. All of you extrahumans are set to go off."

"And ... what, explode? Have a mental breakdown? A stroke?"

"Yes."

She arched an eyebrow, which he couldn't see. To his back, she asked, "Which is it, then? If I'm a doomsday machine, I'd really like to know which symptoms to look out for. I fully believe in prior planning."

"It's different for each of you, depending on your genetic structure." He risked a look back at her, over his shoulder. She saw fear in his eyes, yes ... but also something else. Incredulousness? Or ... Light help her, pity? No, she had to be misreading him.

And she had this nagging sense that he looked familiar.

He said, "You really mean to tell me you don't know any of your kind who inexplicably started breaking down, either mentally or physically?"

A flash from Second Year: Dawnlighter bleeding from her nose and ears, shooting fireballs at Jet because she was a filthy Shadow, at Iri because she dared to have a costume that was also white ...

Jet tripped, but quickly righted herself before she stumbled into the murky water. "Of course," she said primly. "But that's nothing more than an unfortunate side effect. This isn't exactly a low-pressure occupation."

"No," he agreed, sounding grave. "It's suicide. Or, depending on how many humans are around you when you finally go, homicide."

Jet swallowed the lump that had formed in her throat. What Moore said made a frightening kind of sense—the kind that had nothing to do with logic and everything to do with a primordial instinct that explained the ways of the universe. An extrahuman race memory, perhaps. The sun brings light; the gods bring destruction.

Get ahold of yourself, woman!

Schooling her face to impassivity, she said, "You're awfully sure of yourself, considering you've admitted you don't have the hard data to back this up."

"I see things." Moore stared ahead as he kept walking. "Files that never existed. Conversations that never happened. Anything that once was data in Corp's systems, I've seen it before it was obliterated. And I know how to connect the dots."

Clearly, the man had issues. But that was understandable; losing a family member could easily have turned him into someone driven by vengeance. While she didn't condone that, she certainly understood. "Mr. Moore, don't you think that if extrahumans truly were wired to explode, as you so charmingly put it before, Corp would be working to resolve the issue?"

At that, he spun to face her. "Who do you think did this to you in the first place?"

Her heart dropped to her toes.

No. He was wrong. Kidder had been wrong.

Moore pivoted and started walking again, this time splashing through the watery filth. "This is why it was so vital for me to help get the truth out there. It's not just to educate the citizens of the world. It's to educate our so-called saviors as well."

A burst of rage shattered the fear that had been icing her limbs. " 'So-called'?" she spat. "I'll have you know that

I've personally saved New Chicago twice in the last calendar year!"

"Yes, how very noble of you." He shot her a look. "But maybe we mere mortals should be left to save ourselves."

She scowled at him. "You're infuriating."

"We didn't ask for superheroes."

"*And* you're an ingrate."

Moore shrugged. "I've been called worse. But at least I'm not being deluded by a megalomaniacal organization bent on ruling the world."

Jet shook her head. "Now you sound like Mister Invincible."

"I'm not the villain here. Nor am I the threat to the public good."

"No, you just kidnap reporters. Why'd you do it? Why Kidder?"

"I didn't do a thing."

"Everyman, then," she gritted.

Moore paused as he considered a fork, then headed down the left-hand tunnel. Jet wondered if he really knew where they were going. Once she had Kidder safely in hand, she'd tap Ops to maneuver her out of the Network. "The problem with intrepid investigative reporters," he said, "is that they don't know when to leave something alone."

"Do tell."

"What do you want me to say? Ms. Kidder started looking too closely at the Society. Or, more accurately, at a small part of the Society. And that made some people very unhappy."

Thinking about the memory stick she'd found in Kidder's picture frame, Jet wondered what other things were carefully hidden in Kidder's apartment. "Did it make you unhappy, Mr. Moore?"

He wheezed out a laugh. "Me? I'm an old man. I'm interested in the truth, not in power plays."

"I take it Everyman's planning another attack against the Academy." She frowned, remembering that day in Third Year, and Iri bleeding in her arms, Iri screaming...

screaming

...and Sam—

screams sweet screams

No. Her hand pulled into a fist. *Get back.*

so sweet

Back!

Giggling, the voices receded. For the moment.

Light. She blew out a quiet breath, ignored the sweat dripping down her face. Forget the safety of white noise; she had to get out of the dark.

Soon. They had to be close to Kidder already.

Realizing Moore had been speaking, she focused on his words: "...crude as all that. But of course, it's like your kind to jump to such conclusions."

"My kind," she said, "has saved humanity more times than you can count."

"And again, we didn't ask for your help."

"Maybe not you, citizen. But many others have. Thousands of them. Hundreds of thousands." More like millions.

"And how many of your kind are there? Ten thousand?"

She had no idea; Corp kept the exact number confidential. "Why?"

"How many extrahumans would it take to rule the world? To crush humanity under its feet?"

"We wouldn't do that."

"Of course you wouldn't," he agreed, not deigning to look at her. "But if, one day, you decided to do just that— say, that internal wiring of yours melts and leaves you more likely to, shall we say, wreak havoc—what could we humble civilians possibly do against you?"

Tension, thick in the foul air as she imagined the

extrahumans declaring war on the innocent. It would be full-scale slaughter. "You read way too much science fiction."

"And you, girl, are willfully ignorant. Ah. Here we are." They'd come to a halt in front of a steel-reinforced plast door.

Too easy, despite the darkness and the voices licking at her mind. "Convenient that none of the Undergoths interrupted our little journey."

He shrugged. "The Society has an understanding with them."

Of course. "How much per month?"

"I have no idea," he said, sounding appalled she would even ask such a question. "I'm not a moneyman."

"Just a mole. Open the door."

He patted his pockets helplessly. "I'm afraid I don't have a key."

Of course not.

She approached the door, touched it. Tried the old-fashioned knob. Locked. She could Shadowslide through the crack between the doorjamb and the wall, even though she was loath to use her power in the dark. But duty first, always. Yes, Shadowslide, then see about opening the door from the inside. Worst case, she could pummel the thing with a Shadowbolt—

The blow hit her at the base of her skull. She staggered, whirled in time for the lightstick to clip her in the temple. The world tilted, and she stumbled to her knees.

Moore tinkered by the knob. "I lied about the key. But I didn't lie about the reporter. She's inside."

Blinking away her dizziness, Jet let fly a runner of Shadow. It wrapped snugly around Moore from shoulders to knees, trussing him tightly. He teetered to the left, then toppled like a felled tree.

"That was a mistake," Jet said, pulling herself up.

"Leaking information from Corp was bad, but at least it was for a decent purpose. But attacking me from behind? Moore, you just bought yourself ten to twenty."

Behind her, the door creaked open.

From inside, a rumble, like a bear's growl, made Jet's stomach knot and her knees turn to rubber.

She whirled around, but all she saw inside the doorway was shadow. The growling continued—low, almost musical. "What in the Light is that? A pit bull?" She hated dogs almost as much as she hated the dark.

Stomping from within. And the growl deepened.

Jet drew back. She couldn't cut loose inside the room, not without knowing where Kidder was inside. Hitting her with Shadow could put her into shock, especially after her ordeal.

She called into the room: "This is Jet. I'm here for Lynda Kidder. Release her, now."

Chuffing laughter—from the trussed form of Martin Moore.

Jet couldn't spare him a glance; in front of her, a person was lumbering into view—obscenely muscled, the clothing shredded in its attempt to contain the body beneath it. It was a mountain of a human, someone so overly padded with bulging muscles that walking should have been simply impossible. Towering, hunched over to avoid hitting the roof of the tunnel, the figure almost vibrated with murderous fury. A string of pearls strained around the bulging neck.

"Oh Light," Jet breathed, staring up at the monstrous person's face.

The hulking shape paused in the doorway, blinked stupidly at the feeble glow from the lightstick on the ground, then focused on Jet.

"Freak," wheezed Martin Moore, "say hello to the new and improved Lynda Kidder."

CHAPTER 37

IRIDIUM

*You never know what you'll find down in the dark, but
the dark will always find you.*

Taser jumped down first, crinkling his nose under his
mask as the smell of the Rat Network drifted out of the
grate. "Remind me why we're doing this again?"

"Dortmunder and Burke," said Iridium, taking his prof-
fered hand and jumping down. She stumbled a little until
Taser caught her, his arm around her shoulders.

"Supervillains distinguished by their silly surnames?"
he said.

"Architects. They designed a lot of the new downtown
after the flood. They also designed the Academy complex."

Taser stopped walking. "You can't think that they'll have
plans for the Academy lying around."

"If we're going to hack the Ops network, we have to do
it from inside the Academy," she insisted, moving past him.

"And by law, the firm that designed the complex is required to keep plans on-site."

"Don't know if you noticed this," he said as he caught up to her, "but Corp isn't bound by any law except how much cash and how many extrahumans it can toss at a problem."

"I also know that Johann Dortmunder was indicted about ten years ago for conspiracy. He sold *his copies* of the Academy plans to the Everyman Society. They'd planned a bomb, or a raid, or something before Corp stepped in. Dortmunder got off with conspiracy, but..." She threw him a glance over her shoulder. "Would you get rid of an insurance policy like plans to the hallowed halls?"

"No, I surely wouldn't."

They walked in silence for a few minutes through the patchwork light. When they rounded a corner that led them farther into the darkness, Taser said, "What do you hope to accomplish by hacking Ops?"

"I don't hope to *accomplish* anything," said Iridium grimly. "I hope to show the Squadron that they're just as vulnerable as the people they're supposed to protect. That if they don't have their little voices and Corp behind them, they're fallible, and nothing for people to be afraid of. I want people to see that. I want—"

Taser held up his hand, and as she stopped, Iri thought once again that he all but radiated military. "You hear something?"

Iridium stilled herself and listened, over the drips and echoes of the tunnels, and the slow sliding trickle of the stagnant stream in the gap in the floor. Voices bounced off the curved walls and came back.

"What did you..."

"Say hello... Lynda Kidder..."

CHAPTER 38

JET AND IRIDIUM

Everyone bleeds.

Lancer to his first-year students in
Basic Defense Techniques

JET

Jet slowly backed up, her gaze riveted on the monstrous form of Lynda Kidder. To Moore she spat, "What did you do to her?"

Moore chuckled wetly, the sound of an old man drowning in laughter. "Ms. Kidder was kind enough to test our defense against your kind. A serum designed to augment the human physique."

Just what she needed: a mad scientist wannabe. Jet took another step back. "Was she kind enough to volunteer?"

"Under duress, absolutely."

In front of her, Kidder snarled. She still hovered in the

doorway of her cell, a dictionary definition of violent potential. But as threatening as she appeared, she hadn't made a move against Jet. Perhaps there was enough of Kidder's mind left to stop her from attacking.

But based on the way she was frothing at the mouth, and how she kept flexing her bulging muscles, probably not.

"Easy," Jet said to the hulking reporter. She couldn't risk hurting Kidder; the reporter wasn't the bad guy here. Just posing as one. In a very, very convincing manner. "Lynda, I'm here to help you."

Kidder's lip curled into a sneer. Saliva leaked down her chin, and her low growls grew louder.

"She can't understand you, you know."

Eyes on the huge woman, Jet said to Moore, "So this is your way of opposing Corp? A drug that turns people into mindless monsters?"

"We won't be easy meat for you."

Jet didn't pull her gaze away from Kidder, so she didn't see Moore as he spoke, but she had no doubt that his eyes were gleaming with the fervor known only to psychotics and religious fanatics. She did, however, see a ripple of tension wash over Kidder's body.

"We'll fight back with everything we've got," Moore said. "With everyone we can get our hands on."

"You're insane."

"I'm committed to defending humanity against your kind."

"*My kind* helps humanity." She would have said more, but Kidder took a lumbering step forward, growling like the pit bull Jet had thought was in the cell. Jet's heartbeat slammed in her chest. Light, she hated dogs. She hated rabids. She hated Iri for getting her in this position.

Hate later, she told herself, forcing her breathing to remain steady. *First defuse the situation.*

Moore, oblivious to or uncaring of his own danger, said, "We don't want your help, freak. We don't want *you*."

Jet put her hands out, palms forward, to indicate that she didn't want to fight Kidder. The malformed reporter's growling increased. *Damn.* "And you'll destroy innocent people to make your point?"

"There are always casualties in any battle worth fighting." He paused, then said, "Acceptable losses."

The growl kicked up into a roar of challenge, and Kidder charged—meaty fists raised overhead, ready to slam them down like sledgehammers.

Jet didn't dare go on the offense, let alone use Shadow as a weapon. Kidder was an innocent, no matter how freaking huge and insane she was. So instead, Jet threw herself to the left, felt the wind from the enormous fists slicing the air.

She landed on her feet, spun, and dropped to a crouch as Kidder stormed forward, her right arm pulled back for another swing. Jet ducked under the punch, trusting Kidder's momentum to carry the huge woman forward a few paces. *Careful. Enclosed area. Not a lot of room to maneuver.*

Jet spun to see Kidder already charging her, fist already careening toward her. *Damn it, she's fast!* With a grunt, Jet threw herself to the right. She heard Kidder's hand connect with the wall, and turned to see the misshapen woman pull her gigantic fist free . . . Jet blinked at the damage to the tunnel wall.

Fast, and unnaturally strong. Like Earth-power strong. *Oh boy.*

IRIDIUM

A spillway door rumbled free ahead of Iridium and Taser, and she put a hand on his arm. "Somebody's down here."

"You think?" he said humorlessly.

Iridium created a twin pair of strobes, no larger than marbles, to shed light just ahead of them, and started to walk.

"Maybe we should go a different way," Taser muttered behind her.

"No," she said. "Something's wrong." Voices were rising, distorted by the tunnel walls but definitely shouts.

"And you say you're not a hero."

Iridium smiled at him before peering around the junction in the tunnel. "I never said I was the bad guy, either."

"Don't mind if you are," said Taser. "A vigilante and a villain. That's kind of hot."

"My mother thought so."

"And the mood keels over, dead."

Iridium poked him on the shoulder. "Shh. Someone's coming."

An old man in pajamas rounded the corner, so busy looking behind him that he slipped into the slough. With a curse, he pulled himself up, soaked from waist to ankles. He launched into a run again—and shrieked when Taser stepped in front of him.

"I'm innocent!" he cried, shielding his face with his hands.

"Settle down!" Taser said, grabbing the old man by the arm.

The civilian looked between Taser and Iridium, his eyes going wide. "Oh Christo, not more of you people. What do I have to do to get away from you freaks?"

"Nice," Taser said. "You don't see me insulting you about how you just wet yourself, do you? What're you doing down here, anyway?"

"Getting away. Now let me go!"

"Hey," Iridium said, staring at his wrinkled face, "do I recognize you?"

He turned to her. "I highly doubt that, freak."

"I do. You're that doctor," she said, placing him. "You

worked in the Mental wing at the Academy. You used to assist with Therapy." She spat the last word.

"I never worked at the Academy," he sniffed. "And I'm not some wannabe brainwasher."

She leaned into him, got in his face. "No? Then how do you know what Therapy is?"

"I do not have to suffer the insults of a rabid girl wandering around in some filthy tunnel," he warbled. "You're mistaking me for someone else."

Taser lifted the old man off his feet by the front of his pajamas, and the old guy squeaked like a trapped mouse. "Want me to beat the hell out of him, Iri?" Taser gritted.

Iridium was about to tell him not to bother when a crash came from farther down the tunnel, followed by the distinct sound of a body hitting brick.

JET

Maybe slamming her monstrous hand into the wall had hurt Kidder, because the woman bellowed and charged forward.

Jet leapt up, landed on Kidder's massive shoulder, and vaulted off, landing a couple of yards away. Crouching on the ground, Jet was sweating. And Kidder was already turning, getting ready to come at her again.

Forget pulling punches. Take her down, fast.

Jet summoned a floater of Shadow and used it to catapult herself, feetfirst, into Kidder's chest. Kidder staggered back as Jet landed heavily on her feet, her boots splashing in the debris-filled water.

And then Kidder barked out a laugh.

Uh-oh.

Jet tapped her comlink, about to tell Ops where she was and to request backup, but then Kidder was right there, swinging at her, and all Jet could do was dodge. And again. Still Kidder attacked, punching almost lazily with huge fists. Jet ducked in and rabbit-punched Kidder in the gut, one two, one two three—

—and grimaced as she backpedaled. Damn, the woman was solid muscle! And the punches hadn't done anything, other than make Jet's hands sore. Sparring wouldn't work; Jet was breathing hard, and Kidder only looked annoyed. The gigantic woman raised her fists overhead, ready to slam them down like the monstrous weapons they were.

With a grunt of effort, Jet threw Shadow at Kidder, shaping it into viselike bonds to pin the woman's arms to her side. Kidder growled, flexed . . .

. . . and snapped the bonds.

Jet gasped from the pain. It felt like something in her head had snapped along with the Shadow, like a hot blade had seared her and cauterized the wound before the blood could flow. Tears blurred her vision, and she blinked them away to see Kidder stomping toward her with murder in her eyes—her fists already raised for striking.

Lips peeled back in a snarl, Jet reshaped the broken Shadow into a graymatter shield, threw it overhead just in time to deflect the sledgehammer blows. The impact sent Jet to her knees, but she kept her arms raised and her shield up.

Kidder slammed her fists down again, and Jet cried out when the shield cracked—a sudden, stabbing pain in her head overrode everything else. She doubled over, clutched her head in her hands. Her body trembled, and her mind screamed that Kidder was *right there, damn it, keep fighting*! But she couldn't move. Light, she hurt so badly, she almost wanted to die.

Something wrapped around her left arm, brutally yanked her forward.

Jet's eyes snapped open, and she stared into her opponent's face. If there was any part of New Chicago's fearless reporter left, it was buried far beneath the monstrous beast that possessed Lynda Kidder's body. Nothing remotely human stared back at Jet; just animal eyes, filled with a mad desire to rend and tear and maim.

"Lynda," Jet whispered. "Don't—"

Kidder grinned, and Jet's words shriveled on her tongue.

Gripping Jet tightly by the arm, the massive woman swung her back. Jet screamed as her shoulder popped from its socket. Kidder pitched her like a fastball, and Jet hurled backward through the air, still screaming as she flew—and then crashed into the wall.

IRIDIUM

"Hey—hey, damn it, get back here!"

Iridium turned to see the old man darting down the tunnel, heading away from the commotion.

Taser let out a snort. "That'll teach me to get distracted by the sounds of certain death. You want I should go after him?" In the other direction, the screams and grunts continued. The walls of the tunnel shook, and the lights flickered as another crash echoed.

"Never mind him," she said, turning back to whatever lay ahead. Part of the wall had caved in; a gaping hole, easily large enough for her to step through, yawned between the bricks and plast. Iridium slowly walked toward it. "The Undergoths will find him before he finds the surface."

"Fine by me," said Taser, falling into place beside her. "What on the scorched earth is that racket?"

"Jet," said Iridium in surprise, staring through the hole in the wall. Careful to avoid the ragged pieces of broken brick and pipe, and especially the dangling wires, she watched Jet launch herself out of view.

Iridium turned to see who Jet was fighting...and her jaw dropped as Jet impacted against something far too big to be a person. The creature lost ground, and Jet landed on her feet in front of it, breathing hard.

Christo, Iridium thought, her eyes wide. *What is that thing?*

The monster laughed, then charged Jet—who dodged the enormous fists, then maneuvered close enough to jab the creature with small punches. Jet stepped back, out of the thing's reach.

Iridium bit her lip to keep from shouting out. *Shadow, Joan. Use your damn superpowers instead of proving how tough you are.*

"That...thing is..." Taser shook his head. "What *is* that?"

"Some sort of sewer mutant."

Taser turned to her, the eye slits in his goggles narrowed.

"What?" she demanded, glaring at him. "They exist. I saw it on *Mysterious Chicago.*"

"If you say so."

She turned back to see Jet finally getting smart—the hero had bound the mutant in strips of Shadow. About time. Iridium was about to suggest that she and Taser quietly back away when the monster snapped her bonds and charged. Jet got a graymatter shield up in time—barely—to avoid getting flattened by the thing's huge fists. The impact sent Jet to her knees. Another blow, and Iridium flinched when Jet cried out, doubling over.

"We going to help her?" Taser asked, his voice low.

All you have to do is use one strobe, Iridium thought, *and it would all be over. Jet would never even know you were here.*

And in her mind, Lester's voice spoke, harsh as stone. *Don't tell me you still have feelings for those people.*

"No," Iridium said aloud. "No, we're not getting involved."

"I think the sewer mutant is lining up to kill the hero."

"Well that's not really our problem, is it?" Iridium hissed

at Taser, using harshness to cover her moment of weakness. "Just let them finish and get out of our way."

"Your call," Taser said.

That was when the mutant grabbed Jet and pitched her like a baseball. Iridium watched Jet crash into a wall, and told herself that she didn't care.

"Use your damn Shadow, you stupid girl," she whispered.

JET

Jet crumpled to the ground, her shoulder blazing, her head spinning, her right leg screaming. She cradled her dead left arm, tried to push past the agony. She didn't want to think about her leg, which was twisted beneath her. Over her ragged breaths, the comlink whined in her ear feedback loop.

And beneath that, the voices giggled. And began to whisper.

Kidder was still grinning as she lumbered forward, her fist cocked.

No choice.

Teeth clenched, Jet unleashed Shadow and wrapped it in a blanket around the reporter. *Just for a moment,* Jet told herself. The cold blackness would steal Kidder's breath and knock her out—and if the woman saw anything in the dark that made her piss her pants before she succumbed, oh well. She could get therapy. The traditional kind.

Kidder struggled against the Shadow, punched at it, but it squeezed her and squeezed her, forcing her into submission. Still the woman fought, and roared a muffled roar.

IRIDIUM

Iridium watched as Jet wrapped the giant in Shadow, and shuddered as she remembered the feeling of the cold nothingness pressing against her, suffocating her.

Hidden in Shadow, the mutant began to scream. The sound reverberated off the tunnels and inside Iridium's skull. Peripherally, she saw Taser press his hands over his ears.

A scrim of frost stole across the water and the damp tunnel walls—that was Jet, pushing more and more effort into her Shadow prison. The mutant writhed in a black cocoon, twitching and convulsing as the darkness got under her skin.

Iridium shivered, and watched.

JET

The Shadow *squeezed,* and Jet's eyelids fluttered. Another squeeze, and the world dimmed. For a long moment, all Jet could do was breathe around her pain, and pray that the voices stayed locked away. Her shoulder and leg screamed at her, and she felt like she had to vomit. The dimness threatened blackness. Jet had a sense of drowning, of losing herself in that blackness...

...and then a burst of white clawed her back to consciousness.

She blinked, and the world came back into focus. She was propped against the damaged wall, sitting amid the floating debris, clutching her left shoulder. In front of her was a black bundle.

Kidder.

Jet released the Shadow, called it back into herself. It caressed her in a cold, comforting embrace before it dissipated, giving Jet a sorely needed energy boost. Now she didn't feel like she was already dead; instead she merely felt like she was dying. Something was better than nothing...

Kidder swayed on her huge feet, then toppled forward. She hit the ground with a tremendous crash.

IRIDIUM

The giant fell. Jet stayed where she was—on the ground, clutching her left arm, her leg twisted beneath her. Iridium watched Jet breathe, the small woman's ribs heaving like butterfly wings as she sucked in air.

She was hurt. Bad.

Iridium shut her eyes, felt the bright hot place in her mind that would keep out cold and dark.

Then she pasted a thin, nasty smile on her face and stepped into Jet's line of sight, clapping.

JET

Kidder was prone on the floor. Not moving.

Ambulance, Jet thought dimly. *Got to get her to the hospital.*

Using her right hand, she pulled herself to a sitting position—oh, Light, her leg was on fire—and nearly fainted from an overwhelming wave of dizziness and nausea. Leaning against the wall, Jet took deep breaths, forced her sickness down. *Vomit after. First get help for Kidder.*

Her hand was halfway to her comlink when she heard the clapping.

Jet pivoted right, her left side shielded, her right fist out.

There, looking like she'd just come from a cover shoot for *Extrahuman Weekly,* was Iridium. Behind her stood a man in black, his face in a ski mask affixed with goggles, his arms folded, his manner suggesting boredom.

Iri grinned. "A nine, definitely. I'd give you a ten, but the blood really detracts from your style."

CHAPTER 39

IRIDIUM

*There's no one more dangerous than a criminal with a
grudge . . . except for an extrahuman with a grudge.*
                    Lancer to his third-year students in
                    Advanced Street Fighting

Jet's face, what little Iridium could see under her cowl,
was whiter than the skin of a drowned corpse and her
lips had a ring of blue around them. Blood trickled from her
nose, and Iridium gritted her teeth when she saw Jet's skinsuit was ripped and bloodied across the abdomen.

She stuck out her hand. Maybe this didn't have to turn
into a fight. If she was lucky, Jet was too concussed to remember she even saw her. "The sewer mutant really did a
number on you."

Jet made like she would take Iri's hand, and then scis-
sored her legs out. Iridium fell backward, landing in the
slough and on the concrete at the bottom, water made icy
by Jet's shadows soaking the back of her unikilt. "Christo!"
she shouted. "You bitch!"

"You had something to do with this," Jet hissed. She braced one gauntlet against the tunnel wall and pulled herself up, protecting her left side. The blood from her nose flowed more freely with the effort. "You set me up."

Iridium rotated her head to Taser. "A little help?"

"All this water is going to fry my circuits, darlin'," he said, leaning down over the fallen mutant—from Iridium's quick look, the thing seemed like a grotesquely muscled corporate type, complete with pearl necklace straining against a huge, corded neck and a permawave that was the latest style. "I think you're on your own with the nutso hero."

"Swell," said Iridium, jumping up to face Jet.

"You and Everyman set me up," Jet barked. "You think I'm stupid, Iridium?"

"No," said Iridium, drawing out the syllable, "but right now you are acting a little crazy, Joan."

"Don't call me Joan!" Creepers of Shadow writhed around Jet's feet, and Iridium created four strobes in front of her to keep them back. They hissed, nothing but toothy little mouths made of darkness.

"Fine," said Iridium. "But that doesn't change the fact that you're rambling about nothing, *Jet*. How hard did you hit your head, anyway?"

"Holy Jehovah," Taser said. "Is this Lynda Kidder?"

Jet made a noise halfway between a laugh and a sob. "Pretending like you don't know, Iridium? That's cute. But it won't work. Not after this."

She swung at Iridium, a movement far slower than Jet usually managed, and Iridium ducked and blocked, letting the blow bounce off her forearm.

"Stop it," she warned Jet. "I'm not down here for you. You...why are you down here, anyway?"

"As if you didn't know," Jet hissed. "How could you? How could you be working with Everyman?"

Her words shocked Iridium enough that Jet landed a

solid blow to her face, snapping her head back. Iridium spat blood and pulled her unikilt aside at the neck, exposing the white line on her breastbone.

"Bitch, does this scar make you think I'd *ever* work with Everyman?"

"Scum always floats together eventually," Jet snarled, sending a creeper across the space between them. Iridium fried it with a light beam and Jet grunted, swaying on her feet.

"Catchy," said Iridium. "The banter writer who came up with that must be so proud. Now stop it, Jet. You're hurt, and I'm not keen on beating up invalids."

"So pithy," Jet said. She attacked Iridium again, a basic combo that they learned their first year of field training, but Iridium didn't fight back, just deflected, because where was the fun or point of hitting someone who should be on an ambulance hover headed to the hospital?

"Damn it, Jet, knock it off!"

"Always so superior," Jet growled. "Thought you were so much smarter than me!"

She hit Iridium in the gut, and Iridium let her, then grabbed Jet's fist and twisted her right arm into a restraining hold. The only way out of that would be for Jet to break her arm to wriggle free. "I *am* smarter than you, Jet, especially now. I'm not going to warn you again. Let's *talk* about this."

Jet thrashed against her, the water around their feet turning black with creepers. Iridium sent light refracting through the water to scare them off.

With a grunt, Jet twisted violently, and a *crack* echoed in the tunnel as she pulled free. She didn't seem to notice her newly broken arm.

She's really lost it, Iridium thought, grabbing Jet in a bear hug to stop the small woman from hurting herself even more. *Blackout all over again.* "Jet, stop!"

Then she cried out as Jet slammed her head backward into Iridum's nose. Iridium felt the give, the hot rush of blood, and pain exploded like supernovas in front of her eyes. She released Jet to clasp both hands over her nose.

"Who's the genius now?" Jet panted, raising her broken arm. "You may not be so pretty after this, Iri. But hey . . . at least you'll still be smart." She slid into her textbook stance, Shadows growing around her.

Iridium tried to focus on a way to end the fight through the pain. Jet had fought dirty, and she'd gotten her. *What a time for Joannie to finally grow some balls.*

"Hey," Taser remarked conversationally, from where he'd been ministering to the fallen mutant. "Kidder's dead."

Jet slackened, her hands dropping and her eyes behind her goggles going wide. She turned to face Taser. "What?"

Iridium spun-kicked, her foot connecting with Jet's jaw. Jet crashed into the wall and slid down it. She landed in a heap, and didn't move.

"Yikes," Taser said. "Remind me never to whack your nose."

"You, I'd just kill," Iridium said. She bent over Jet, pushing her goggles aside with her fingers to peer into Jet's eyes. "Joan?"

Jet's jaw was swelling into a ball-shaped bruise where Iridium's kick had made contact. She muttered something unintelligible.

"That's enough," Iridium said. "Stop fighting me."

Jet whispered, "Leave me . . . 'lone."

"No. You have to stop this."

Jet tried to sit up, and Iridium pushed her back down.

"Joannie, you're hurt. Bad. Is heroing worth tearing yourself apart?"

Jet's mouth set in hateful lines, and Iridium felt like she'd been headbutted all over again. Whenever Jet re-minded her that she hated Iridium, that she *believed* Corp's lies, it started Iridium's memories and her own hate all over again. "I'll die if it means I stop you," she rasped. "All of you rabids."

Iridium felt the air chill again and saw the creepers Jet had formed behind her back grow into a Shadow tree. "Have it your way." She sighed, and hit Jet across the face.

Jet's head snapped back, and she fell against the wall.

"Come on," Iridium said to Taser, standing up. "We gotta move."

"She's barely awake," said Taser. "You smacked her good."

"Yeah, but if she managed to signal Ops before she and I danced, in about two minutes her backup is going to be here." She stared at Jet's crumpled form. "I've had my fill of Corp lackeys for the day."

"We'll split up, meet at the downtown junction," he said. "It'll be faster than trying to evade the heroes and the Undergoths together."

"One hour," said Iridium. "If you're not there, I'm going to assume you're dead."

"Likewise," said Taser, turning and jogging down the tunnel past Jet.

Iridium gave her fallen friend one last look, then started running.

CHAPTER 40

JET

The one thing you can count on is that heroes tell the truth—even when those around them don't.

Lynda Kidder, "Origins: Part Twelve," *New Chicago Tribune*, June 11, 2112

Jet tried to pull herself up, but she didn't have the strength. Pain streaked across her battered limbs, leaving behind a miasma of sensations that made her hiss—a sharp stabbing in her leg and arm; a steady agony in her shoulder; an almost gentle throb in her jaw. Her body must have been five shades of purple beneath the skinsuit, bruised to the point that just breathing made her want to weep. And her head felt like Colossal Man had used it for a soccer ball. But none of that mattered.

Lynda Kidder was dead.

No, Jet thought, trembling. *He lied. The man in the black mask must have lied.*

I didn't kill her.

She tried to move again, to go see for herself, but her

body simply refused to obey. Between Kidder's abuse, then fighting Iri—*again,* twice in a handful of days, and damn it all she got away *again*—Jet's body was on strike. And broken in at least two places, to say nothing of her freaking shoulder.

Or her head. When she realized her vision had doubled, she focused on the large body on the ground. And got horribly dizzy.

Okay, focusing wasn't such a terrific idea.

Bile rose in her throat, and she swallowed thickly. No way was she vomiting. She was so exhausted, she wouldn't even be able to turn her head away so that she didn't puke all over herself.

Grunting, she lifted her broken right arm just enough for her to tap her comlink. A man's voice replied, and she whispered, "Backup. Fix on...coordinates..."

Things got a little gray, and she swallowed again. She didn't hear anything in her earpiece; they must have disconnected.

All she had to do was wait. And pray the Undergoths didn't stumble across her.

Backup will be here soon, she told herself. *Ops will dispatch the local S&R team for the city.* Someone was coming.

They'd see Kidder wasn't dead.

Get up, she told herself. *You have to get up. The Undergoths might be scurrying this way. And what if Iridium comes back?*

Iri gently nudging Jet's goggles up and looking into her eyes, Iri telling her to stop fighting...

Jet gnashed her teeth.

"Joannie, you're hurt. Bad. Is heroing worth tearing yourself apart?"

Yeah, it would be just like Iri to circle back and kick her when she was down.

Iri sighing, then clocking Jet in the jaw, the right hook so fast that Jet hadn't seen it coming...

Iridium.

Jet's fist clenched, and a snarl curled her lip. Iridium, claiming she didn't know what Kidder was doing there. *Right*. Like Iridium had any other reason to be in this section of the Rat Network, with a masked lackey in tow.

Jet tried to move again, but her body wouldn't have any of it. Almost sobbing from the pain, she groaned as her thoughts danced in slow circles around the idea that Iridium had sold out to Everyman. So what that she had history, bad blood, with them? She was rabid ... and Iri always had a fondness for chemistry. Maybe she'd helped the Society with their damned serum, hooked them up with rogue scientists who got their kicks by selling their brains to the highest bidder.

Maybe Iridium had *created* the serum.

That backstabbing ... rabid ... bitch!

Fueled by anger, Jet rolled herself onto her right side, then bore down and propped herself up on her broken right arm. Oh Light, it hurt! Shaking, nauseated, she pushed herself back until she was leaning against the ruined wall.

Tears streaked down her cheeks, and she panted as she clutched her dead left arm to her chest, the pressure of squeezing a limb she couldn't feel taking the edge off the glassy pain of her broken right arm. Her left leg splayed at an angle she didn't want to think about.

I should change my handle to Rag Doll, she thought numbly.

Over the sounds of dripping water that she couldn't see, of her heartbeat thudding in her chest, a man's voice called out: "Jet?"

Him. Iridium's lackey in the goggled black mask. He'd come back. Probably to finish the job his mistress didn't have time for.

Jet gripped her left arm tightly, but that did little to dampen the pain of summoning three creepers of Shadow. Oh, Light, she was hurting. Bad. The creepers pulsed by her feet, waiting for her command.

"Jet? Where are you?"

A light from the far end of the passage marked his presence. Certainly was smug, letting himself be seen like that. Jet braced herself to throw the creepers at him. Hearing him scream like a girl would do wonders for her bruised ego, if nothing for her equally bruised body.

The light brightened. "Jet? Answer me if you can!"

Sweat rolled down her face, stung her eyes. When had she taken off her optiframes? Oh, right—*Iri* had. When she'd tried to convince Jet to stop fighting.

Damn Iri to the never-ending Darkness.

Panting, Jet bit her lip to keep from crying out. The creepers tried to slip away from her, but she reined them in. Barely. *Signature move,* she told herself with a wretched laugh.

Everything tilted to the left, and she squeezed her eyes closed. *Hold it together just a little longer,* she thought, feeling light-headed. *Just enough to take him down. Backup will be here soon...*

"Jet? Oh fuck, what happened to you?"

With a gasp she opened her eyes, saw not the masked henchman but Bruce Hunter, her own Runner, right there in front of her... well, almost right there. He was giving the creepers a respectable radius. Swathed in his black trencher, black shirt, and black slacks, he looked like one of her groupies. Except she could see his eyes, so blue and electric, even from this distance; her fans always wore goggles. She'd have to give him the official Jet Fan Club dress-code handbook.

Light, she was losing it. She whispered, "Kidder. Help Kidder."

Bruce took a step toward her, but the creepers reared up. "Jet? Honey, can you call off your shadowdogs?"

Closing her eyes again, Jet pulled the creepers back, absorbed them. For a blissful moment, she felt better. Then she opened her eyes and the room canted to the right and started spinning lazily, and she had to fight the urge to vomit again. She shut her eyes again, which was better. Slightly.

His hands on her face now, so wonderfully cool. "Hang in there, Jet. Help's on the way."

"'M fine." Her tongue was so thick, she could barely get words out. "Kidder. Get Kidder."

He murmured, "Don't worry about Kidder."

"Go," she said. "Hurt. Needs help."

"I told you, honey, help's on the way."

"Not me. Kidder. Needs..." What had she been saying? Ah, Light, it was so hard to think. Bruce was here, and that was...wrong somehow. "Why you? Backup. Not you." She was too dizzy to worry about sounding rude.

"You contacted me instead of backup. You must have put me on speedlink. I guess that means you like me."

She heard the strained humor in his voice. "Mistake. Dangerous. Iri."

"Iri? Iridium did this to you?" The humor was gone, replaced by a flatness she found oddly appealing. It reminded her of Night. "Jet? Did Iridium do this to you?"

"Kidder," she said faintly. "Help. Kidder."

"Shh. It's okay. I'm here. Help's on the way. Should be here any minute to get you out." His hand on her bad shoulder now, but instead of adding to the agony it felt...warm. Soothing. "Tell me what happened."

She tried. But even to her own ears, she sounded rambling, incoherent. Finally she gave up and said, "Shoulder."

"I know, I see. Separated or dislocated."

"Dislocated. Old problem. Pop it back."

"No, honey. The S&R team will be here in a minute, they'll float you up to the surface, get you to the hospital."

"Pop. It. Back."

She heard him hiss through his teeth, then he said,

"Fine. On three." Both of his hands on her, now, one on her dead shoulder, the other on her good one. "Brace yourself. One."

Then the bastard popped her shoulder back in its socket.

Pain, so raw and overwhelming that it was almost exquisite.

Jet slipped away, then, and faded in and out of consciousness. When she first came back to herself, she felt her head cradled in someone's lap, heard Bruce speaking softly, urgently.

"Not good," Bruce was saying. "Pretty broken up, maybe internal bleeding...no, S&R'll be here soon...want her now?" A pause, and then: "No problem, you give the word... yeah, she's dead..."

Dead. Kidder was dead.

No, he was lying, the man in the black mask was lying, and oh Light, the man had come back and was going to...

She slipped away again, only to open her eyes to a familiar face.

"I've got you, Jetster," Steele was saying. "You just hang in there, I'm getting you out now."

The feeling of being lifted, then floating. Jet whispered, "Kidder."

"We've got her, Jet, don't worry."

"Good," she said, then passed out again.

The next time she woke up, she was getting wheeled down a corridor, with people running alongside her, talking quickly over her. She thought she heard Bruce, or maybe Night, and someone was trying to cut off her skinsuit, which was foolish because everyone knew the material was so densely woven with Kevlar, it made it almost impossible for a blade to penetrate. But the costume pulled away, and the person cutting through hissed and said something about bruising and internal damage, but then Jet slipped...

...and woke up in a room with horribly bright lights

and shrilling *beeps* and a person was smiling over her and telling her just to breathe, honey, just breathe deep and then there was a cloying sweet smell that carried her away . . .

She awoke to the sound of crickets.

After listening to their soothing *chirps,* to the sound of her own breathing, and to the faint but consistent sound of *beeping,* Jet opened her eyes. Dim lights overhead. Soft sheets under her; warm blanket over her. The perfume of flowers around her. She felt like she was floating, distant from her own body, which she couldn't feel. And while she knew that should bother her, she just didn't give a damn.

"Hey, you're awake."

She tried to turn her head to face the person who'd addressed her, but her neck wouldn't cooperate. Shame.

A man swam into her field of vision: dark hair, blue eyes, chiseled features. Ruggedly handsome. Terrific smile, if a tired one. A name clicked into place, and she smiled at Bruce. At least, she tried to smile; her face didn't want to work.

The feeling of pressure where her hand should be. "How're you feeling?"

She tried to answer, to no avail. She'd have been frustrated if she didn't feel so warm and floaty.

"I'll take your silence to mean you're feeling peachy." His smile softened, and she felt something like a dim stirring around where her chest was. Presumably. Bruce said, "From what they told me, they're keeping you higher than a kite while your body finishes healing. You shouldn't even be awake now."

Healing?

Maybe he saw the question in her eyes, because he said, "You were pretty busted up. Broken bones. Internal bleeding. Concussion. You gave the Faith Healer a run for her money. Apparently, she's out of commission now for at least a week. And so are you."

She didn't like that; even the pleasant haze she was in now couldn't fog a sense of anger.

Bruce laughed softly. "Don't complain. She fixed you in record time, but she said you won't be up to full strength for a while. And she's the one who said you're temporarily grounded to make sure you don't rebreak what she fixed." A brushing feeling where her cheek probably was. "Lucky you, you have your own personal Runner to make sure you do what the good extrahuman doctor says."

Oh really?

"Jet," said another voice.

She couldn't turn, but she didn't have to see Night to know who had spoken. Or feel Bruce's hand to know he'd removed it from her face.

"You shouldn't be awake," Night said. "Your energy is better spent on completing your healing."

Bruce said, "She's stubborn."

"Indeed. Excuse us, won't you?"

"Of course, sir." To Jet, he said, "I'll be seeing you." And then he was gone.

"I only have a minute before they come in here, see you're awake, and dope you senseless again," Night said, staying out of her limited field of vision. "So I'll make this quick. Your Runner reported that on your way home from nighttime patrol, you'd communicated with him that you'd seen some movement by one of the sewers and were going to do a cursory pass, make sure the Rat Network was quiet. And the next thing he heard was you requesting backup." Night paused. "This is the official report, Jet. Do you understand?"

Yes. Bruce had lied for her, hadn't said anything about her actively seeking Lynda Kidder or her pursuing the connection between Corp and Kidder—even though he'd known what Night had asked her to do.

But why had Bruce lied?

"From what Steele reported," Night continued, "there

had clearly been a battle where she'd found you and Kidder. From what she and the Runner puzzled out, it looks like you'd accidentally found where the Undergoths were keeping Kidder, whom they'd tortured hideously before they killed her. And then Iridium found you."

Kidder. She'd killed Lynda Kidder.

"Corp will be grilling you once you're healed, but they're ready to send the Squadron in full force to clean out the Network once and for all. At least, that's what they're feeding the media. Should be interesting if that's actually true," Night said dryly. "That would tie up a good chunk of active extrahumans for the near future."

Gentle pressure around her shoulder.

"The media's already picked up the important parts. You found Kidder and nearly died trying to save her. Iridium, a known rabid, was apparently working with the Undergoths. You're back in the City's good graces, Jet. This time, when the mayor tries to give you an award, I suggest you stick around to accept it."

Night's plan had worked. Jet knew she should be satisfied, but she kept seeing Lynda Kidder's monstrous form, heard the reporter's wet chuckle before she'd slammed Jet against the wall.

She'd killed Lynda Kidder.

"You're tired, I can see that. We'll talk when you're healed. For now, rest up. Your Runner will be staying close to you." Softer, by her ear: "You can trust him, Jet. I helped place him in his latest assignment."

She'd killed a civilian. An innocent.

Night cleared his throat. "Is the white-noise setting adequate? Would you prefer something else? A waterfall, maybe?"

She didn't answer, couldn't even if she wanted to.

"Excuse me, Night, but I have to ask you to leave." This from a new voice, a woman's voice. "Jet needs her rest."

"Of course." The pressure around her shoulder vanished. "Sleep well, Jet."

Jet wanted to cry, to scream, to beg for forgiveness. She hadn't meant to kill her. But then something warm rushed through her, soothed her, wrapped her up and held her.

And then Jet didn't want anything at all.

THEN

YEAR 4

CHAPTER 41

IRIDIUM

Since partnering with Corp-Co to facilitate the branding of a Heroic Identity, we have seen a 40% net profit increase across all divisions.
—Quarterly report, Chicago Consolidated Hauling,
September 2106

Iridium knew about Career Day, in an abstract way—it was what kids who didn't have superpowers got. Normal kids, deciding on their normal lives. She hid a yawn behind her hand. She was fairly sure normal kids didn't have to sit through dozens of corporate presentations vying for her application to be the face of everything from cars to cat food.

No more regimented classes on theory, here in Fourth Year—now it was practice, training patrols, and practical instruction on heroing. Iridium was always covered in bruises and scrapes from the full-contact sessions Lancer ran, and she was always tired from memorizing page after page of criminal code.

But today was different. Today was the lottery.

Frostbite's head dipped, and she jabbed him. Night was

standing at the end of the row of chairs set up in the cafeteria, and she could feel his eyes sweep over the crowd at regular intervals. Derek would kill her if he got sent to detention for sleeping and ended up sponsored by hemorrhoid cream.

Jet was in the front row, of course. She was always front and center these days, it seemed. Iridium had lost count of the number of practices and classes that got interrupted by press. The press loved Jet. Face like an angel, powers like a nightmare. Tragic origin story. She couldn't have been more perfect if she'd planned it.

"That concludes our presentation," said the Superintendent. "Please put your name in the datapad for all sponsorships that have piqued your interest. The preliminary lottery is in one week."

Iridium knew that the chance portion of the branding lottery was a sham at best—how else did you explain how her father, Blackout, and Night had walked off with the three biggest sponsorships in their year—Lester, the City of New Chicago; Blackout, Mid-Atlantic Petroleum; and Night... well, you couldn't walk past a bus stop without seeing Night's face these days.

Three best friends, three plum jobs. Iridium knew she'd never get the same treatment. She followed Derek and Chen down the row of corporate booths, putting her name in for anything that didn't repel her too much.

She'd never get past the interview, anyway. Once the sponsors drew five student names, they interviewed the candidates and picked the most marketable. The one with the biggest muscles or smile (or hell, even breasts), the one with the cleanest-cut past and best party line.

Iridium was none of those things.

"This sucks," she told Derek. "My entire life is depending on some corporate wankstick liking the way I pose."

"Careful who hears you say that," he said, as the representative from Kensington Semiconductors glared at Iridium.

"These wanksticks are all that stands between us and some paper-pushing job in Ops."

Iridium curled her lip. What was worse—being at the beck and call of Corp and her sponsor, or sitting in a stifling room with the other washouts who couldn't get a sponsor in the first place?

After a stultifying hour, the Superintendent called them back. "We have a special announcement before you are dismissed," he said. "Here to present the news is Vice Mayor Petrelli."

The vice mayor bounded up and took the PA, to polite applause. "Thank you, Superintendent. On behalf of the City of New Chicago, I'm delighted to announce that we've signed an early deal with a student here today to be our official Hero."

Murmurs ran through the room, along with groans from heroes who'd hoped to pluck the prime spot in their city. Hornblower cursed under his breath. Dawnlighter pouted.

Vice Mayor Petrelli extended his hand. "The city is very pleased to recognize . . . Jet."

Iridium felt like someone had kicked her in the gut. *"Jet?"* she hissed.

Frostbite blinked in shock. "Whoa. Guess you won't be doing a cosponsorship, huh?"

Iridium set her jaw. "I guess not."

Jet took the PA. "Thank you, Mr. Petrelli, and thank you to the entire city for putting this enormous trust in me. When I graduate, I will *not* let you down."

Iridium stood up and left rather than listen to the rest of the speech. In the hallway, the temperature dropped, and Night stepped out of a shadowed door.

"You should try being happy for your friend."

"Hooray for corporate lackeys," Iridium said, deadpan.

Night leaned in, the way he had the day he'd threatened to break her arm. "You need to be careful, Iridium. Some at this school are seeing entirely too much of your father in you."

"And that's a bad thing why, exactly? Heroes are supposed to help people, not pose and ape for money."

Night shook his head. "You talk like him, but you're not nearly as smart. The world turns on poses and public faces, Iridium. The sooner you realize that, the better off you'll be."

"With all due respect, sir," Iridium said, stepping around him, "I hope I never do."

Night didn't reply, but she felt him watch her until she turned the corner toward the dorms, eyes cold and hard as a knife in her back.

CHAPTER 42

JET

Trainee heroes rely on us to mold them, to shape them and to define appropriate behavior for everything from eating to dating.

Night, in an interview for the *Chicago Sun-Times*

Jet knocked on the door—two perfunctory raps—before she let herself in.

The huge man seated behind the desk looked up from his computer and scowled at her. The metal pin connecting his left arm to his shoulder gleamed in the light. "My my," Lancer said. "The darling of the Academy has come to pay a visit. Go away, girl. I'm busy."

No longer the scared mouse, Jet ignored the hostility in his voice as she also ignored his words and shut the door. She needed him. He was the only one who could help her. Smiling brightly, she sat in the seat opposite the desk. "Thank you for seeing me, sir."

His scowl pulled into a snarl. "Maybe you need your hearing checked. I said go away."

"Sir, I'm here to ask for your help."

Lancer sneered. "Why don't you go ask one of the other instructors or proctors to give you what you need? With the way Corp's been shining to you, and now with the city practically in your pocket, anyone would bend over backward to aid the little Shadow."

Hearing Night's name for her on Lancer's lips made her seethe, but she quashed the feeling and instead turned up the brilliance of her smile. She'd been practicing. She knew that her smile was reflected in her eyes, even if inside she wanted to rip his prosthetic leg from his body. She was becoming quite the actress.

Night was very pleased.

Jet said, "But sir, you're the best there is at teaching aggressive and defensive fighting tactics."

Lancer's eyes narrowed. "Flattery, girl?"

"No, sir. Simple truth. You're the best martial-arts and street-fighting instructor the Academy has. I'd be a fool to turn to anyone else."

And never mind that he was a washout who'd barely clocked three years with the Squadron. Jet smiled demurely.

After a moment, Lancer leaned back in his chair. "Well, I suppose I can hear you out before I send you on your way."

"Thank you, sir," Jet said, and meant it. "When I'm engaged in battle, my response time is too slow. I need to increase my reaction speed. Can you help me?"

"That's just practice, girl," he said, snorting. "More you do it, the better you'll get. Or you'll get yourself hospitalized, or dead."

"I do practice, sir. I put in hours in the gym and on the mats, sparring with anyone and everyone. I know the forms, I've studied the moves. In the Academy, I'm fast. But out there, where it matters, I'm slow." She took a deep breath. "Will you tell me what I'm doing wrong?"

He looked at her, his dark eyes searching for something in her own. Finally he grimaced and said, "When you're out there, and someone approaches you, what do you do? First thing. Tell me."

"I run through the ABCs of Peacekeeping. Analyze, battlescan, confront."

"Good. Next?"

"That's just it, sir. I seem to be in the middle of reviewing battlescan when I get attacked. There's not enough time for me to make a sound decision before I'm locked into combat. And then I'm forced on the defensive."

"So you're taking too long to determine next moves." He shrugged. "That's common at first."

"I try to think of all the possibilities before dedicating myself to an action. That's the logical way to move forward."

"Sweetheart, there's nothing logical about a dirty fight. On the street, you've got to survive."

"But there's honor to battle. Rules to physical engagement."

He snorted again. "Now you sound like you're dating me. You want rules, Jet? Simple. First rule: Survive. Second rule: Don't be your own enemy. Everything else is just practice, until your body knows what to do even as your mind is still processing the situation."

"But—"

"No buts!" He slammed his fist onto the table, and Jet jumped in her seat. "Don't try to rationalize it. Don't paint the real world into pretty shades of pink. It doesn't work like that. You go in there with your black skinsuit looking all slick, and your ideals about battle, thinking it should be glorious and chivalrous or anything other than staying alive no matter what, and you will get killed. Make no mistake about that, girl."

Chagrined, Jet kept silent.

"Out there, the bad guys don't give a rat's ass if you're doing a photo op because some stupid agreement with your sponsor says you can't pass up an opportunity when the press is on the spot." His eyes flashed, and a bitter smile played on his face. "If you think the world is going to accommodate your vision of it, think again. Arrogance is death."

"Sir," she said, her voice soft, "I'm sorry, I—"

"Shut it. Worse than arrogance is compassion. With arrogance, at least, you've got the right attitude. You're a strong fighter, a warrior dedicated to protecting civilians from the scum of the earth." His lips pulled into a sneer. "But compassion is death, girl. Far more so than arrogance. Compassion will get you a skinning knife in your ribs, a plasgun blast to your head. You want a mantra, Jet? Here's one: They don't matter."

"Who doesn't, sir?"

"Them. The enemies you're fighting. Once you start thinking of them as people, your heart's going to screw up what your head's telling you to do." He jabbed a finger at her. "Overthinking it slows you down. Overfeeling it will get you killed."

"I see," she said slowly, not liking the advice but appreciating that it held a note of ugly truth.

"No, girl. You don't." He barked out a laugh, a harsh sound that grated on her ears. "You think you know better. You think that you're different, that you can go out there and be sympathetic and yet firm. It doesn't work like that, sweetheart."

"Then show me what to do."

He paused. "Excuse me?"

She leaned forward in her seat. "Teach me. One-on-one. Show me how to fight the way a Squadron hero should fight."

"You've got Fourth Year instructors for that," he said, scoffing. "Madame Marvel and Fisticuffs, I believe. They can even hook you up with tips on how to smile for the vids as you take out a villain."

"They're not the best," she said plainly. "I want the best, sir. I want you to teach me."

"Bullshit," he spat. "I'm not the best and I know it. I got

taken out of the field in my prime because of a stupid mistake on my part. So tell me the real reason why you're here, girl, and maybe I won't shove a detention band down your throat."

She lifted her chin. "You hate me, sir. And that means you wouldn't hold back when we spar."

"You want me to really fight you? To pull all stops? To beat you down if you don't get it right?"

"Yes, sir."

"And this would be in addition to your regular Peacekeeping and Defense units."

"Absolutely, sir."

He stared at her, his gaze merciless, his face set in stone. "You're a filthy Shadow. But you've got guts. And you've got gumption. You want me to do this, you make sure you sign a waiver and get it to your mentor and to Academy Records. When I break you in half, I don't want the responsibility of paying your funeral expenses."

"Yes, sir," she said, grinning. "Thank you, sir."

"Go ahead and thank me, girl. I promise you, tomorrow you'll be cursing me. Five in the morning, main obstacle track. Every morning, rain or shine. You ever don't show up, I'm done with you. We clear?"

"Yes, sir!" She stuck out her hand. "Thank you, sir!"

He stared at her hand like she was holding a steaming pile of dog turds. Finally Jet lowered her hand. *It doesn't hurt,* she told herself, keeping the smile pasted on her face. *It doesn't hurt.*

"Tomorrow, girl. Don't be late." With that, he went back to his computer. He didn't look up when she rose from her seat, nor did he acknowledge her final "Thank you, sir."

Jet thought she saw him look up when she closed the door softly behind her, but she decided that she was mistaken.

CHAPTER 43

IRIDIUM

No comment.

Response from Assistant Superintendent
Neil Moore when asked if the Academy
forbids same-sex dating among students

The tele blared a reality program about the Squadron. Darkmancer was fed up with Kinetic Lad's recklessness and they were yelling at each other in the kitchen of the Squad House—the mansion financed by Corp and completely wired with cameras.

"How hard up do you have to be to do one of these programs?" Iridium asked. Frostbite and Red Lotus, sprawled on the sofa, paid her no attention.

"I don't care if he is a Mental power, I'd kick Darkmancer's ass," said Frostbite. "He's a total prick. How does Kinetic Lad put up with that?"

Chen vaulted to his feet and struck a fighting stance, moving his mouth slightly out of sync to mimic a bad dub job on a kung-fu movie. One of the many things he and

Derek shared, Iridium had noticed, was a love of flatfilm. "Only when you defeat me will you become the master."

The door from the classrooms swished open, and Jet crossed silently into her room, studiously ignoring Iridium and the boys. Iridium stuck her tongue out at Jet's back.

Frostbite jumped up and struck an equally ludicrous pose. "But my crane kung fu is strong! You will never defeat me!"

They began to wrestle, and Iridium clicked up the volume on the set to drown them out. Frostbite finally won over the smaller Red Lotus and pinned him to the ground, letting out a cowboy yell.

Hornblower stomped into the common room from the gym, sweat beading on his muscles, unshapely on his still-stubby teenage body.

"Fairies," he sneered. "Misplace your wings?"

Iridium pushed a footrest into his path without taking her eyes off the projector, and Hornblower almost fell on his face.

"Watch it, you bitch," he snarled, "or I'll make sure you can never put that face on an endorsement poster."

"I am shaking in my fashionable shoes," said Iridium. "Why don't you go drown in a vat of protein shakes, *Tyler*?"

He pointed a stubby finger at her. "You don't get to use my name, bitch."

"Stop calling me 'bitch' or I'm going to get irritated."

"You're going to get a smack across the face."

"Oh, *knock* it *off*." Frostbite sighed, standing and helping Red Lotus to his feet. "Everybody in here knows that the only reason you pick on girls is because your teeny, tiny, shriveled 'nads aren't big enough to stand against someone your own size."

Hornblower rounded on Frostbite. "You wanna start something, faggot?"

Chen winced, but Derek stuck out his chin. He'd grown every which way in the last year, and Iridium realized with a start that he was taller than Hornblower.

"I don't start fights, Tyler," he said. "But I'll sure as hell end this one. So why don't you go look at porn or pump iron or something, and leave us higher life-forms to our afternoon?"

Hornblower made a move toward Frostbite, but Derek stood firm, his hand in Red Lotus's.

Iridium jumped up to join Frostbite and Red Lotus in their standoff. "Fuck off," she told Hornblower. "Unless you want me to get Night and your uncle in here."

Hornblower's eyes flickered between the three of them, and Iridium knew he was weighing them up: Derek with his eyes nearly as bright as his hair, cheeks flushed, spoiling for an excuse to hurt Hornblower; Chen like a golden, trapped animal tethered by their intertwined fingers; and Iridium herself, her arms spread and palms up, the beginnings of strobes in each hand.

"Like any proctors would side with you people," he sneered. "Rabids and queers."

"Report this," Frostbite said quietly, "and I will do things to you that will render you useless to everyone except the Janitorial division."

Hornblower's lip quivered, and he looked like a very small boy wearing a muscle suit. Then he turned and practically ran out of the room.

Red Lotus jerked his hand from Frostbite's and stormed off into the boys' dormitory.

Frostbite raked his hands through his hair. "Shit. *Shit.* Chen, wait!"

"Whoa, there!" Iridium grabbed Frostbite's arm.

He spun around, and she saw ice-crystal tears imprisoned in the corners of his eyes. "Just leave me alone, Callie."

"I don't care," Iridium said. "You need to know that."

Derek blinked. "You don't?"

She lifted one shoulder in a shrug. "Why should I?"

Frostbite slumped back on the sofa. "In case you missed it, Corp's not keen on the love that dares not speak its name. Especially when it's between heroes. You know how many 'retirements' over the past ten years have been Corp quietly getting rid of us?"

"Screw them," she spat. "You're my *friend*. Hell, I was best buddies with the girl voted Most Likely to Hack Somebody Up and Mail the Parts to Their Family." She smiled thinly. "I think I can handle you making out with guys instead of chicks, Derek."

"If anybody finds out..."

"No one's going to, not from me," said Iridium. "Now go talk to Chen. I'm sure it'll be okay."

Frostbite sniffled again. "He was the only one... in my entire life. What if I've blown it, Iri?"

"Not possible." She reached over and ruffled Frostbite's spiky hair. "You know, Derek the Dork, you turned out pretty irresistible. Chen would have to be some kind of idiot not to see that."

He smiled and brushed the frost away from his face. "Thanks, Iridium."

"Go," she said, putting her feet up again and changing the channel on the holo. "And tell Chen the two of you make a cute couple."

"You'll be the only one we *can* tell," Derek muttered. "The sneaking around puts a cramp in the romance, let me tell you."

"Well, at least you don't have to find a date for the graduation formal," said Iridium. "I can see it now... matching tuxes, corsages, a floatlimo... are you going to get a hotel room? Chen will slap you around if you get fresh."

Frostbite's smile was less rigid this time. "You're crazy. Corp would have a heart attack. Night would probably fall right out of his creepy cowl."

"Worth it for that alone," said Iridium, grinning.

Frostbite started to go into the men's bunkroom, and then turned to face her. "You're a good friend, Iri."

"Thanks," said Iridium. "I guarantee, you're the only one who thinks so."

CHAPTER 44

JET

If you don't override your pain, you're dead.
Lancer to his first-year students in
Basic Defense Techniques

Jet knelt in the Academy confessional, trying not to play with her sling as she waited for the priest to slide open the screen and signal that she should begin confessing her sins.

Top of the list: pride.

Her left shoulder throbbed, and she grimaced. Lancer hadn't been kidding when he'd said Jet would be cursing him. She'd done that, quite loudly, when he'd gotten the best of her and had dislocated her shoulder just a few hours ago.

She shuddered, remembering the impact as she'd hit the ground hard—and the acute pain that had accompanied it. Lancer had stared down at her, his gaze implacable, as she'd writhed on the floor.

"You're dead," he'd said coldly. "Next time, don't bother with the pretty follow-through. Bad guys don't give a shit if your form is correct. Guard your left. Now get your whining Shadow ass down to Infirmary."

The staff nurse had given her a local, even though Jet had adamantly said no. At fifteen, Jet was still a minor, and so the Academy had the final say on her medical treatment—and that meant all patients were anesthetized when treating severe injuries. Jet had wanted to feel it when her shoulder had been popped back into its socket. Maybe that agony would help remind her of Lancer's lesson today.

Instead, she'd gotten a sympathetic smile, a brightly colored sling, and a mandatory pass from physical activity for seventy-two hours, then moderated physical activity over the next four weeks. Lancer had scoffed and called her a pansy... but he agreed to keep working with her once Medical approved.

Small favors. Dejected, Jet sighed. She was a lousy excuse of a hero.

You're a filthy Shadow, Lancer told her.

Jet closed her eyes, told herself to let it go. That it didn't hurt.

Jehovah, she prayed, *why am I a Shadow?*

But instead of some invisible god, it was Night who whispered: *You understand the power of the Dark.*

Yes. But she hated it. Despised it.

Feared it.

You'll learn to use that fear, Night crooned. *Let it do your work for you.*

Her heart danced; sweat beaded on her brow. Her throat constricted as she grappled with an idea that kept trying to slip out of reach.

How could the Dark work for her? It utterly terrified her.

Sam's voice, now, filling her with warmth, with love: *We've got these powers for a reason.*

Sam.

Tears slipped down her cheeks as she waited for a priest to come and absolve her of all her sins. To tell her that it was okay that Sam was dead.

"Those dead, who believed in him, shall be raised and live, and those living who believe, shall never perish. Death will only be a change to a better existence."

Maybe it's better, she thought bitterly, *but I still want him back.*

. . . *those living who believe* . . .

Her lip curled into a snarl. *Tell me, how will chanting Our Fathers and performing penance make Sam come back?*

How could Jehovah be so cruel?

Night again, his voice cold and yet soothing: *If you want Samson's death to have any meaning at all, you'll let his dedication to helping others be your beacon. Your guiding light in the dark.*

My guiding light.

Light.

Her heart leapt, and her mouth opened wide—in surprise, in delight. Her shoulder still ached, but it was a minor pain, easily overlooked in the face of an epiphany.

Light she could understand. Light was her personal savior, the thing that banished the darkness.

Forget Jehovah and his heart of stone. Forget Christo the Son. Forget Heaven and Hell, and all those things that demanded people believe in unconditionally, even with no proof that they existed at all.

Light was real.

Darkness was real.

It was all the religion that she needed.

Letting out a laugh, Jet climbed to her feet just as the screen slid open.

"I'm sorry for the wait, my child," the hidden priest said.

"It's okay," Jet replied, feeling lighter than air. "I've already found what I was looking for."

And in a weird way, she had Lancer to thank for it.

CHAPTER 45

IRIDIUM

Mentally gifted extrahuman students should consider a
Therapy internship to hone their skills.

Promotional booklet published by
the Executive Committee

Normally, Iridium would be glad for the interruption, but her stomach sank when the Containment team shuffled into their Applied Extrahuman History class.

One by one, the students stopped moving their styluses across their datascreens, staring at the silent faces under the riot shields.

Beside Iridium, Frostbite's breath hitched.

He and Chen had made up in the week since Hornblower's scene in the common room. Nobody had started looking at them strangely, or sending hate messages, and no proctors had so much as turned a hair. Derek and Chen were partners. It was natural for them to be together.

"Is something the matter?" said Charisma, their instructor.

The Containment worker at the head of the column pushed past her and they filed through the classroom, massing around Red Lotus.

"Derek Gregory," said the Containment worker in a flat tone. "He in this class?"

Frostbite laid his stylus aside, his fingers shaking so that it slipped off the podium and rolled away. "Yeah. I'm Derek Gregory."

The Containment worker tightened his grip on his stun blaster. "You need to come with us, son."

"He's not going anywhere," Iridium spoke up, holding her arm out between Frostbite and the team.

The Containment worker frowned at her. "Stay out of this, girl. There are some very serious allegations leveled at Mr. Gregory. We need to get to the bottom of them."

Iridium stuck her chin out. "What allegations?"

"That's between Mr. Gregory and the Superintendent, miss." He lowered his voice. "Get out of the way before I stun you."

"Get out of mine before I blind you," Iridium hissed. "You're not taking him."

The Containment worker jerked his head at one of his companions, who reached out and yanked Iridium's right arm behind her in a submission hold. She struggled, but unless she wanted to break her arm, she wasn't going anywhere.

"See here!" Charisma snapped, leaning on her cane and starting forward. "You can't just come into my classroom and manhandle my charges."

"Stay out of this," snarled the Containment worker. "You have no idea what this boy has been accused of."

Iridium glared at Hornblower, who was watching the scene unfold with a slack-jawed equanimity.

Frostbite must have had the same thought, because he rounded on Hornblower. "You are so fucking dead, Tyler. I'm going to freeze your tiny little prick off and feed it to you!"

"Me?" Hornblower squeaked. "I didn't report you! You think I'm stupid?"

The Containment team traded looks. "I guess we weren't wrong," the leader said.

"No," Frostbite said, his voice rising. "No, you weren't wrong. I'm gay. I like men. When I'm in the shower, I think about Keanu Reeves. I kiss men and someday I'll fuck men and you all can just quit whispering about me, because you're all absolutely right—I'm a big old queer!" He glared around the room, daring the other students to say something. "There. That's what you wanted, right?"

Iridium squirmed, tried to break free. "Derek . . ."

Frostbite ignored her and turned to Chen. "I'm sorry. I know this wasn't how you wanted it. Please believe me."

Red Lotus looked at the floor, slowly backing away from Frostbite. "I'm sorry, too, Derek."

Another Containment officer put his hand on Chen's shoulder. "You did the right thing, son. We'll take you up to the Mental wing after your classes let out for the day to begin your treatment."

Iridium felt the floor drop away from her feet.

All the blood drained from Frostbite's face. "Chen," he rasped, "*you* reported us?"

"I can't get a sponsorship if I don't agree to Therapy," Chen said quietly. "I need to be able to survive in the real world, Derek. How can I be a hero without backers? When everyone is looking at me and whispering?"

"How could you do this?" Frostbite shouted. "I love you!"

The Containment officer held Frostbite back with his baton. "It'll pass."

"*Fuck* you." He ducked under the man's arm, running to

Chen and grabbing his hands. "This doesn't matter. We can drop out and go live with my aunt in Hawaii. The Squadron there is friendlier—"

"Yeah," said Chen coldly. "Because I'm going to have a great damn career protecting surfers from sunburns."

"Move it," said the Containment officer, pulling them apart. "You're going upstairs, Gregory. Now."

"I don't need Therapy!" Frostbite yelled, struggling against the Containment team. One of his punches landed on the man's riot shield and it snapped backward, causing a red spatter to erupt from his nose.

Two more Containment officers shot Derek with their stun blasters, and he collapsed, twitching, to the floor.

"Stop!" Iridium shrieked, summoning a strobe.

An alarm triggered as she accessed her power, and the rest of the students cried out, hands over their ears.

The Containment officer holding Iridium pushed her to the ground next to Derek, who was still feebly fighting against stun-cuffs.

"Tell Chen..." he groaned. "Tell him...I'm so sorry."

The Containment workers dragged Frostbite up and out, and a flash of blue was the last Iridium saw of him for nearly a year.

CHAPTER 46

JET

You misunderstand. The Academy is not here to hurt its students—it's here to help them. Unfortunately, sometimes help comes too late, and that is my greatest regret.

Celestina, in an interview given to Channel 1

Jet sighed loudly as Celestina ushered her down the hall to the Girls' Dormitory. "I still don't see what was so urgent that you had to pull me out of Public Speaking, ma'am." Jet still had a long way to go before she was comfortable in front of the vids. Everyone seemed to think that because of what she'd done at Sam's funeral, she was a natural. Except that day, she'd been possessed by her grief. Now all that gripped her when she had to speak publicly was stage fright.

She rolled her eyes. Some hero she'd be if she turned green every time a camera shone in her face.

Next to her, Celestina huffed out, "There are some things that are more important than work, Joan."

"Ma'am," Jet chided, "you're supposed to use my designation."

"And you're not supposed to correct a proctor. Now move it, Ms. Greene."

Jet blanched and increased her pace. They walked the rest of the way in silence.

When they stopped in front of her room, Jet threw Celestina a pointed look. "Ma'am?"

"Go inside," Celestina said, her voice soft as lilacs. "Help her."

"What? Help..." Jet's eyes widened. "Iri? Is she in trouble?"

"That's for her to say." Celestina motioned toward the door. "Go."

Jet swallowed. She and Iridium had been pulling away from each other for the better part of ten months now. It was natural, Jet had told herself on those nights when she'd hear Iri laughing in the common room with Frostbite and Red Lotus; she and Iridium had different worldviews. Jet was focused on her studies, on her career as a hero. Iridium was focused on... well, on Light only knew. Iri didn't care about the Academy. Iri didn't take her studies seriously—which truly irked Jet, who had to work for every A; it was grossly unfair that Iridium just seemed to absorb information and process it at lightning speed. They'd remained roommates Fourth Year because they were already paired, and it made the most sense.

But it would have been a stretch to say they were still friends.

There were times that Jet missed Iri so much, it felt like her heart was torn in two. Those were the times when she almost would set aside her texts or would beg off an hour at the gym to go find her and listen to whatever Iri had to say—probably something cynical about the Academy, or the Squadron, or even Corp, as blasphemous as that was.

Those were the times when Jet missed hearing Iri laugh with her, when she missed Iri's wicked grin.

But those times were few and far between. A fledgling hero had a lot on her plate as it was; friendships were nice, but they simply weren't a priority. Night had said so last year, and Jet firmly agreed.

So why did Jet suddenly, overwhelmingly, feel ashamed?

"Ms. Greene," Celestina said, her soft voice rimming with frost, "are you going to stand there all day?"

"No, ma'am," she said. And then she pressed the palm-pad to her room, and the door slid open.

Iridium was on her bed, lying prone, with the pillow over her head.

The door slid shut behind Jet. It sounded like a coffin slamming home. A glance behind her told her what she'd already known: Celestina had left her alone with her roommate.

She listened to the soothing white noise in her comlink for a moment, then cleared her throat. "Iridium? Are you sleeping?"

Iridium said nothing.

"Well, technically, there's no way for you to answer that in the affirmative," Jet said, fighting her sudden bout of nerves by babbling. "So either yes, you're sleeping, and you don't hear me talking, or no, you're awake, but you're ignoring me."

"Go 'way," came from under the pillow.

Well, that answered that question. "My room too."

"Fine. Leave me alone."

"Iri?" Jet had never heard this tone before, not from Iridium. She was used to hearing the other girl sounding brash, even arrogant. And there were times when she'd sound coldly professional. Not to mention the times when she'd sound as furious as the Bulldozer with a shard of glass in his foot.

But this was the first time she'd ever heard Iri sounding resigned. Defeated.

"Iri?" she said again, alarmed. Jet strode over to Iridium's bed, sat on the edge, and put a hand on the girl's shoulder. She felt it tense under her fingers. "What's wrong? Is it something with your grades? Your parents? Did they move Arclight to another wing?"

"What do you care?"

Ouch. "Iri, of course I care."

"Please. You haven't said shit to me in the better part of a year, not unless it has to do with training, or classes." Iridium yanked her pillow off of her head and pitched it at Jet, who easily dodged. "So leave me alone. Go throw shadows or something."

Jet wanted to argue, to tell her that she had to be focused because otherwise she'd fall behind—and that meant she would earn Night's disapproval. But this wasn't about her. It was about Iri. "Callie," she said. "What happened?"

Iridium said nothing, just wrapped her arms around the back of her head and shook with silent rage.

"I know I've been...preoccupied," Jet said softly, "but I'm here now. There's something wrong. Tell me. Let me help you."

"Always the hero, aren't you?"

"No. A friend."

"You've been a shitty friend lately."

"I know," Jet said, the truth of the words making her chest feel too tight. "But let me be one to you now. Come on, Iri. Tell me. This isn't like you. Are you sick?"

"Christo, yes. I'm sick to my stomach." Jet was about to grab the trash bin for Iri to puke into, but then Iri continued speaking. "It's this place. It's rotten. It gets inside of you and festers in you, and there's nothing we can do but lie here and feel sick."

Hearing those words about the Academy sent an

irrational surge of anger through Jet, but she pushed it aside. "What happened?"

"They took him. Took both of them."

"They?"

"Derek and Chen. They're gone."

Jet felt the blood drain from her face. "What do you mean, gone?"

"Containment pulled them out of class today. Took them to Therapy."

"What? Why?"

"Because they're gay," Iridium growled. She sat up and shrieked, "They love each other, and this place is going to tear their brains apart because of it!"

Frostbite was gay? And Red Lotus?

Jet could quote the policy that expressly forbade same-sex relationships at the Academy and in the Squadron. Corp wouldn't dare ostracize its ultraconservative support base by putting a known homosexual onto the front lines; it was bad for business. If Derek and Chen really were gay, then they had taken a huge risk.

For love.

Jet wanted to tell Iridium that the boys had done something that was considered a crime, and they were being reprimanded according to procedure. But...

...but that would be the absolute wrong thing to say. And damn it to Darkness, this was Derek and Chen. Jet liked them. She thought of Dawnlighter, who was still the perfect plastic Academy student. In her mind, she saw an Academy-approved version of Red Lotus, perhaps not as serene as he used to be, but Chen was someone who could adapt. She tried to imagine Frostbite without his perpetual snark, without the evil gleam in his eye.

But she couldn't. He was who he was.

"Oh, Iri," she said, "Light, I'm so sorry."

Iridium stared at Jet with tear-swollen eyes. *Iri had cried,* Jet thought, stunned. Iri never cried.

"Don't be sorry," Iri said. "This place is so fucking sorry already. Come on." She grabbed Jet's wrist and pulled her as she got up from bed.

"Where're we going?"

"To the Mental wing. We're getting them out of there."

Jet dug her heels in and pulled back. "Stop. Damn it, Callie, *stop!* We can't."

Iridium spun to face her. "Why not? What they're going to do to them is wrong! I don't care that Chen submitted—it was temporary insanity or something. He and Derek had gotten into a fight. He wasn't in his right mind. We have to get them out before it's too late!"

"Callie," Jet said slowly, "listen to what you're saying. We can't just waltz up to Mental and sneak them out."

"Why the hell not?"

"Because it's the *Mental* ward, Iri! Come on, think! It's as heavily guarded as Blackbird! We'd never make it five steps before Containment was on us too."

"Then let's stage a coup! Get Were and the others to back us up, make them stop this . . . this travesty!"

"Iri. No one will do that. And you know it." Jet hated saying the words, even though she knew they were true. "It's regulation, Callie. They ignored it."

"It's a stupid fucking regulation!"

"Maybe. But it's still how it is."

Iridium grabbed her desk chair and hurled it at the wall. It bounced off, unbroken. She covered her face with her hands and screamed, "I fucking hate this place!"

Jet wrapped her arms around Iri and hugged her tight, said again and again how sorry she was. Eventually, Iri hugged her back, and cried.

Together, they went to the Superintendent's office to petition for Frostbite's and Red Lotus's release.

The petition was denied.

And life at the Academy rolled on.

NOW

CHAPTER 47

JET

I'm very grateful to Jet for doing everything she could to save my little girl. She must make her own father very proud.

Harold Kidder, father of Lynda Kidder,
to the press at his daughter's funeral

And here we are," the nurse said as Jet's door slid open. "Home sweet home!"

The RN's overly bright, overly loud voice made Jet wince in her wheelchair. "Thank you, Jessica."

"You're quite welcome."

Bruce sauntered past, carrying a travel bag and a bundle of mail. "You really didn't have to come all this way," he said—and maybe Jet was mistaken, but she thought he sounded put out.

"Of course not." The nurse sniffed. Loudly. "But I wanted to make sure our favorite hero made it home, safe and sound."

"She's safe with me," Bruce growled.

"Of course she is," Jessica said, her voice the textbook

definition of patronization. "And what do you think you're doing?" That last was to Jet, who'd started to get up from the wheelchair.

"Getting up," Jet replied.

"I don't think so. You sit right back down, there's a good girl. You're on bed rest, dear. And that means you're not walking anywhere, for a full week."

Jet smiled, gritting her teeth together so that she wouldn't scream. "Surely, in my own home, I can move about."

"Absolutely not," the nurse said, wagging a finger. "Doctor's orders, both the Faith Healer's and Dr. George's."

"Don't worry," Bruce said. "If she tries to get up, I'll lace her food with sedatives."

Jessica blinked, then must have decided he'd been joking, because she laughed politely. "I'm sure that won't be necessary. Will it, dear?"

"Of course not," Jet agreed—because she was willing to bet that Bruce hadn't been joking.

"Wonderful. Let's get you set up in your bed, shall we?"

A brief, if humiliating, time later, Jet was safely tucked into her bed, pillows fluffed, comforter tucked. Her white-noise machine was set to NIGHTTIME SERENADE, and the crickets were *chirping* in the hopes of finding their mates. After a dire warning from the nurse that Jet was to stay in bed until Dr. George paid her a visit in five days' time, Jessica pulled Bruce aside, probably to give him additional instructions.

Jet sighed as she turned off her earpiece and tossed it to her nightstand; she'd ask Bruce to charge it for her. She couldn't do it herself, oh no, not with the charger in the kitchen, and her trapped in bed.

She clenched her fist. She felt ridiculous in her night-gown and bathrobe. And in bed. She wasn't sick. She wasn't hurt anymore. Sure, she was tired, but she'd patrolled when she was tired before. Light, she'd fought battles when she'd been running on empty. She wanted to get in her skinsuit and summon a floater and hum across the rooftops. She wanted to get far away from her apartment, from her bed.

From her thoughts about what had really happened to Lynda Kidder.

She'd tried to get Frostbite to put out a Code 1 bulletin about the treacherous Martin Moore, but she couldn't get ahold of him...and it wasn't like she could request Frostbite by name, not without raising flags.

Frowning, she closed her eyes, her mind whirling as if to make up for her body being confined to bed. Frostbite had said Moore was strictly the tech end. But why did his face look so familiar to her? She wanted to say that she'd seen him at the Academy, lurking in the Mental wing, a white lab coat hanging from his shoulders.

Insanity. Moore wasn't a Therapist. But then how did she know him? It was an itch between her shoulder blades, a nagging sensation that she'd seen the man before.

Of course she had. She'd been at Corp HQ enough times for her to have noticed him in the background, working on the computers. That had to be it.

A computer man, who'd leaked information to Kidder to embarrass Corp and the Squadron.

An Everyman, who'd known about Kidder's containment, who might have even been in on the reporter's actual capture and...transformation.

"How many extrahumans would it take to rule the world?" he'd asked her as he led her to Kidder. *"To crush humanity under its feet?"*

A driven man, with computer expertise...and if he had anything to do with the creation of the serum, a scientific background. Biometrics.

"We won't be easy meat for you," Moore said. *"We'll fight back with everything we've got. With everyone we can get our hands on."*

A dangerous man.

Jet had to find Moore, learn more about the serum he'd bragged about. But Frostbite was off-line for the time being, and she couldn't risk Bruce on something that could put him into danger.

And when she'd spoken to Night about it two days ago, at the hospital, and had told him the truth about her rescue attempt, his reply had been less than encouraging: "I'm not surprised, not in the least. But you have to keep this quiet, Jet. Corp is making the Undergoths the scapegoat. And you have to let them do it."

And he'd said no more about it. She almost felt bad that she hadn't mentioned the memory stick with Kidder's real conclusion to the Origins piece, but she was positive Night would have told her to hold on to it, to keep it safe.

She hadn't filed an accurate report to Corp about the Kidder mission. Bluntly, she'd lied. Same as Bruce, who Night had at least admitted was his man. So her Runner was taking orders from her old mentor, who was also telling her to roll over, for reasons unknown.

A headache bloomed behind her eyes as she wondered why Night didn't want her to tell the truth about Moore and Kidder's connection to the Everyman Society.

And what about Kidder's examination of Icarus? Did that have anything to do with her winding up in the sewer, turned into a monster?

And what was Iridium's connection?

"I'm not down here for you," Iri said. *"You . . . why are you down here, anyway?"*

Acting like she had no clue, like she'd just happened to come across Jet and Kidder.

And the thing was, after mulling it over for the past few days and reviewing what she could remember of the actual fight . . . Jet believed her. She didn't want to, but in her gut, she knew she was right. Iridium had been honestly surprised that Jet was in the tunnels.

So if Iri really had no idea that Jet was going to be there, battling for her life against Kidder . . . what had she and her lackey been up to?

Once Iridium was grounded in Blackbird, maybe in a cell right next to her dear old dad, Jet would have to ask her.

"Hey."

Jet opened her eyes to see Bruce standing over her. She managed a smile. "Hi. Where's Jessica?"

"Who, Nurse Ratched? Got rid of her."

"Didn't peg you for a classic literature fan."

He grinned, part arrogance, part amusement. All charisma. "There's lots about me I bet you have wrong."

Laughing softly, Jet said, "I'm sure you're right."

"You have about a zillion fan letters waiting downstairs, as well as your personal correspondence." He tossed a bundle of parcels onto her lap.

She stared at the pile of mail as if it would rise up and strike her dead. "Maybe later."

"All righty," he said cheerfully, gathering up the letters. As he moved over her, Jet felt a tingle run through her, especially in her lap, where Bruce's hand was slowly picking up the mail. She took a deep breath and blew it out, telling her body to calm down.

But Light, the man's very presence hit her like an aphrodisiac.

He finished picking up the letters, his fingers dragging over her thighs—safely hidden by her blanket, but oh, the feel of his fingers on her thighs . . . like a hum of electricity working through her, working up to her . . .

She cleared her throat, and he removed his hand, then tucked the mail under his arm as if nothing had happened. He was smiling at her, and his eyes were so devilish they should have been red instead of blue.

"Want me to turn on the vid for you? You're all over the news, but I'm pretty sure you're not in the mood for that."

"You know me well." At least she didn't sound too breathy; that had to count for something.

"Hey, I told you I studied your file. Want me to put on a movie? Or a sit-com? Maybe something spicier?" He grinned, splitting his face from ear to ear. "Is it too soon to get you addicted to daytime soap operas?"

"Bruce," she said, looking at him hard, "when you came to help me in the sewers, why did you tell Corp what you did?"

He measured her with his gaze, and what she saw in his eyes was both exciting and frightening, and that was when she realized that the casual flirting on his part wasn't casual at all. "It was pretty clear you were going out on your own, at Night's suggestion. I wasn't about to blow that for you."

"But you're an Academy Runner."

"No, Jet." He met her gaze, locked onto her dark eyes with his bright blue eyes. The smile on his lips softened into something sensual, and his voice deepened, as if weighted with passion. "I'm *your* Runner."

She didn't know what to make of that, so all she said was, "I see."

They looked at each other as he stood over her bed, radiating something that she was afraid to place. Her breathing had quickened along with her heartbeat, and suddenly she was far too warm and wanted to kick off the covers, shed her robe.

She wanted to kiss him. And do much more than that.

Still gazing at her like he was thinking the same thing, he said, "I'll be here until six, when Terry will come with your dinner and will stay through the night shift. Then I'll be back in the morning. It'll go that way for the whole time you're on bed rest."

And that was the cold shower she'd needed. Forcing herself to smile instead of scream, she nodded. *Bed freaking rest.* "So you're my keeper?"

He grinned so wolfishly that even Were would have been impressed. "Honey, you know you're a keeper."

Honey? "Do you always flirt with your clients?"

"Only the sexy ones."

She couldn't hide her blush, but between her thick bathrobe and the comforter, he couldn't see what his words had done to her body. "You sound like you've been Running for Lady Killer."

"Maybe I have been. What can I get for you? Something to eat? Drink?"

"See if you can get through to Frostbite, at Ops. I need to speak with him. Quietly."

"Gotcha. Anything else while waiting?"

"One of my books would be nice. They're in the living room—"

"On the small bookshelf by the rocker. The romances. I know. Any particular one?"

"Oh, I don't know. Thrill me."

He blinked, then grinned, bemused. "Excuse me?"

"Thrill me," she said, blushing again. "Pick one and surprise me."

"'Thrill me.' I like that." He chuckled, and turned to walk out of her room. "When I tell the other Runners that I got to thrill you, the rumors are going to fly."

Let them, Jet thought, her body still tingling in places she could never show in public. *Let them.*

CHAPTER 48

IRIDIUM

I have no doubt that the ones responsible for my little girl's death will be brought to justice. That's why we have the Squadron. And I know they'll do right by my Lynda.

Harold Kidder, father of Lynda Kidder,
to the press at his daughter's funeral

Iridium tapped the stolen Academy plans with her finger, and the holo fizzed, the pixels skating away from the digit. "The only way to insert is through the Runner entrance. It's the most heavily trafficked and lightly guarded."

"Right, because who cares about a bunch of wannabe grunts?" Taser said. "I never got the whole Runner shtick."

"Me, either. Half of them are fanboys or -girls, and the other half are some creepy version of Jeeves."

"I'm guessing you'll get the uniforms and IDs we need?"

"Boxer is out collecting gear right now," said Iridium. "The techhacks in Wreck City are pretty friendly with me since I gave them that load of digichips, so our clearances should check out, at least cursorily. Once you're inside the Academy complex, nobody looks twice at you unless you're flying or setting something on fire." She shook her head. "Self-absorbed little bastards."

"Didn't you use to be one of those little bastards?" Taser's goggles flickered with amusement.

"Indeed. Precisely why I'm doing this."

"Oh really?" Taser said mildly, scanning through the layout section of the plans. "I thought you were doing this because Daddy ordered you to."

Iridium slammed her fist down on the table. The projector jumped and skipped, the plans blacking out for a moment. "Are you trying to start something, Electric Eel Boy?"

"There *was* an Electric Eel," said Taser with ill-disguised laughter. "Back at the end of the twenty-first century. I've always wondered if I was related to him. Genetic passing of powers and all that."

"Don't try to change the subject," she seethed. "You just accused me of being some sort of sycophant. Is there a reason, other than your wish for a speedy and premature death?"

"I just want to make sure you're committed to this," he said, jabbing a finger at the projector. "If this goes south, Corp will make us disappear. We'll be one of those stories that gets passed around by cops and vigilantes about what creeps the extrahumans are."

She shrugged. "Blah, blah."

"They've made it happen before, Iridium. You're deluding yourself if you think a cell at Blackbird is the worst thing that can happen to us when this goes wrong."

She glared at him. "After spending five years at the Academy, I'm a hell of a lot more committed than *you* are." Iridium rubbed her arms, felt the old fears creeping up her spine. "It's not just the surface stuff, the brainwashing and the everything's-fine-citizen mentality the heroes have. It's the things you *don't* see. The homogenization. Being a hero is being without a mind of your own. It's selling your soul to Corp...*trusting* them. And they don't deserve it," she spat. "Not one iota of anyone's devotion."

"All right, all right," he said, his hands up in a placating gesture. "I was just testing you."

"Yeah, well, I was a straight-A student," she huffed. "So stop wasting my time."

Taser's mask pulled into a grin. "Bet you cheated. Anyway, here's what the whispers on the street have to tell me: your girl Jet, the nutty one? She thinks you had something to do with that reporter getting killed. You and the Undergoths, together. She's doing a pretty good job of selling it to the EC. They're talking about going into the Rat Network after you."

Iridium smiled—not what Taser was expecting, judging by his frown. "Good." She pulled a plain coat over her unikilt. "Stay here and keep reviewing the plans. There's something I have to do before we go after Ops."

"And what would that be? Pedicure? Hair appointment you can't miss?"

"You're a real smart-ass for someone I could fry with a stray thought."

"Sorry," he said, and she thought he sounded sincere. "I always get keyed up before a job." He gestured around him, the movement taking in the entire warehouse. "You leaving me all alone in your place?"

"Yeah," said Iridium, shrugging. "Don't go through my underwear drawer."

"I'm just flattered you trust me."

"Well, I can always kill you later," said Iridium with a wink, and ducked out the access door before she could overthink it. She did trust him, and while she knew that should bother her...she sort of liked having an ally who wasn't bending over backward to please her. Boxer was a good man to have behind the scenes—but Taser was the sort of man she preferred to have by her side.

Once she was in the dampening zone offered by old-style overstrung power cables, she placed a call from a hardwired telephone.

"Yo."

"Derek, it's Callie."

Frostbite stopped chewing on whatever he was eating and inhaled sharply.

"Your call could really not come at a worse time. Do you have any idea what a shitstorm you've stirred?"

"Is Li'l Bitty Jettikins blaming her fresh bruises on me still?" She sighed in exasperation. "Would that I could slap the bitch as hard as that."

"I assume you've heard that Night and the EC are panting on your heels. Talking about a full-scale raid on your Grid and the Rat Network." Derek sighed. "Why do you have to be ... you? They're going to kill you, Iridium. Really, the best you can hope for when they come for you is a full lobotomy."

Iridium ground her palm heel into her forehead and forced herself to keep her tone light. "Good thing I'm going to be having an iced mocha, then," she said. "Safely aboveground."

"Not following," said Derek. In the background, Iridium could hear a flattie television, a man's voice ringing out: "*Pop quiz, hotshot. There's a bomb on the bus ...*"

"Derek the Dork," she said with a smile, "are you watching Keanu Whatshisface again?"

Frostbite snorted. "So what? The man was brilliant. A true artist."

"He's a dead flattie actor whose most famous role consisted entirely of the word 'Dude.'"

"Not true. Have you seen *Point Break*? Pure artistry!"

"Derek. I need to see you."

"No way," Frostbite said. "I can't leave the complex. Ever since Shadow Princess got her knees scraped, we're on lockdown except for the Squadron and their Runners."

"So fake a stomachache or something." She paused, then said, "You know I wouldn't ask if it wasn't life or death, Derek."

He sighed. "Where?"

"Looptown Mall, one hour," said Iridium. "In the food courts. I'll be the one with the iced mocha."

"This better be important, Iri."

"Trust me," she said. "It is."

Frostbite was annoyingly punctual, his usual habit, and he dropped into the wire chair across from Iridium. "What? What is so Christo-damned important that I practically had to sneak away from my post?"

His hair was still blue, but Frostbite had grown lines around his eyes and mouth that made him look years older than twenty-three. His premature aging, plus the fact that he was royally pissed, didn't make for a friendly combination.

Therefore, Iridium decided to make it short. "I'm going to hack Ops in three days' time. I suggest you not be there when I do."

Frostbite blinked at her. "Excuse me? You're going to what now?"

"Ops. I'm cutting the umbilical, Derek. No more voices in your head." She set her lips. "Without it, the heroes will have to fend for themselves. Oughta be a pretty bunch of chaos."

He whistled. "I'd say so."

She smiled, the thin one that she knew didn't reach her eyes. "That bitch Jet won't have the power of the mighty Corp to fall back on anymore."

Frostbite's shock was replaced with a sad look, his eyes far away. "You know, Callie, you should cut her some slack."

Iridium cocked an eyebrow. "*Slack?* This coming from the only person who might possibly hate her more than I do?"

"I'm not saying that what happened between you two was right, by any stretch," said Frostbite curtly. "But you haven't been riding a desk at Corp for the past five years. You see things, when people consider you invisible and unimportant." His mouth flattened with a bitter twist. "Believe me, Calista, Corp's got something hanging over Jet. I don't know what it is, but it'd have to be bad for her to be...well..."

"Herself?" said Iridium. "Please. Jet's not happy unless she has a master to bring slippers and the newspaper." She drained her coffee and stood up. "I'm hacking Ops, Derek. She needs a wake-up. They all do."

"You're serious," Frostbite said.

"Duh."

"Iridium," he said, sounding for all the world like someone from the EC condemning her on the tele. "Have you really thought about this?"

"Have *you*?" she growled. "Fuck it, Derek, you're still there. You're still hanging around after what they tried to do to you."

" 'Tried' being the operative word. Obviously, it didn't take." He fidgeted in his chair. "I'm not like you, Iri."

"Shocking revelation. Never would have guessed."

He held up a hand. "Let me finish."

She settled down.

"I can't live like you do," Derek said quietly. "Knowing that if I slipped, I could spend the rest of my life in a hole, closed off from everything. That if I let the Mind flunkies get inside my head again, I might not even *be* myself anymore."

"Spare me the lecture," said Iridium, kicking back her chair. "You won't change my mind."

"Good," said Derek, meeting her gaze. "Because when you fuck Corp over, I want you to give the sons of bitches a kick for me."

CHAPTER 49

JET

*Who do heroes hold in the dark, when their job is done?
Who could love a hero more than the people who
already adore them and practically worship them as
gods?*

Lynda Kidder, "Heroes Among Us,"
New Chicago Tribune, March 5, 2112

What do you think you're doing?"

Jet gleeped and stepped back from her bedroom window, then turned to see Bruce in the doorway, arms crossed, his face set in a mask of righteous fury. Jet smiled sheepishly, said, "You're back early. Should have taken you at least another half hour to run that errand."

Bruce stormed over to her, glanced out the window and down to the street, and Jet knew she'd been busted. He growled, "Tell me you had nothing to do with the little old lady who's smacking an unconscious gangbanger with her purse."

"Um..."

"Jet..."

"What was I supposed to do, let her get mugged?" Light,

she was whining. Steeling her voice, she said, "It was just a little creeper. They didn't even notice it."

"In case you've forgotten, honey, you're on bed rest for one more day."

Her eyes narrowed. "Don't call me 'honey.'"

Ignoring her outburst, he said, "Know what *bed rest* means? Your ass is supposed to be in that bed. Resting."

Jet glared at him. "You don't get to talk to me like that."

"I sure as hell do. While you're recuperating from *almost dying,* you're in my care. And that means," he added, his voice dripping with a combination of menace and compassion, "I take care of you. Now get back into bed, Jet."

Pouting, she crossed her arms defiantly. Her Runner didn't get to boss her around like this. Period. "I wasn't going to let him rob her," she said.

"Hate to break it to you, honey, but you're not the only hero on the block. Or the entire Complex. Let them earn their paychecks."

"I said don't call me that!"

"And I said get back into bed."

They glared at each other, and damn it all to Darkness, Jet couldn't help but notice how bright his eyes were when they lit with passion. *I can't be attracted to him,* she told herself as she scowled at him. *He's an arrogant, demanding bear of a man.*

Who looked so freaking sexy that it made her panties damp.

"Jet," he said softly, his voice a low growl that did very maddening things to her, "so help me, if you don't start behaving, I'm going to lace your food with so many sedatives that you won't be able to get out of bed to go to the bathroom."

Her eyes widened from the threat. "You'll be the one changing bedpans, so I think that's a lose-lose situation."

"I'm willing to do some dirty work for you. And if you still don't behave, I'm going to spank you."

"You wouldn't *dare*!"

"Honey, there's a lot that I'd dare for the right reason. Now, are you getting back into bed? Or do I drug you up and carry you there, then swat your ass?"

And he would too. Jet knew that from the sheer determination on his face. "You're an insufferable bastard."

"No. I'm your Runner. And until you're given a clean bill of health, I'm also your caregiver. It's my job, and I'm paid well to do it." He pointed at her bed. "Get going, Jet."

She frowned at him, then grudgingly complied. "It was just a creeper. Barely cost me any energy."

"Any energy is too much energy." He wagged a finger at her, scolding her like a child. "Unless you want all of Faith Healer's work to unravel and get yourself grounded for the better part of two months while your shattered bones heal the old-fashioned way, you better stop pushing yourself too hard."

"I should fire you."

"Ah, you love me and you know it."

"As soon as Terry gets back here for the evening shift," she muttered, climbing into her hated bed, "I'm absolutely firing you."

"You said that yesterday too. And yet when I showed up to relieve Terry this morning, you didn't tell me you'd call Corp if I didn't get out of your apartment."

She ignored how his very proximity made her mind almost short out from lust. Voice curt, she said, "Maybe that's just because I wanted to give you a chance to get another job first. Line yourself up as a Runner for someone else. Steele, maybe."

"Want to know what I think?"

"Not particularly."

He grinned. "I think it's because you like that I don't fawn all over you like the other Runners did. I think you like that I treat you like a normal person, not some goddess made flesh."

At that, Jet grew quiet. When she didn't object to Bruce settling the comforter around her, he said, "Did I hit a nerve?"

"A little," she admitted. "But you're only half-right. My Runners either adore me, or they're terrified of me. I'm either the legendary Lady of Shadows, or I'm a freak that they can't wait to get away from."

"You're not a freak."

Her lips twitched. "Tell that to Everyman."

"The Everyman Society can go suck it up their collective asses. You're no freak, Jet. None of the extrahumans are."

She blew out a frustrated sigh. Mentioning Everyman reminded her that Bruce hadn't been able to reach Frostbite. And Night had proven equally uncommunicative. She hated being cut off.

Bruce sat on the edge of the bed, facing her. "You know, I can understand the adoration your Runners had." His voice was soft, gentle. "I wasn't kidding when I told you I was a huge fan. Have been ever since you stopped Crusher Jones from looting First National five years ago. I was there."

"You were?"

"One of the many on the rubble of the floor, hoping that I wouldn't be the one Crusher used as an example to all the cops outside." He smiled grimly, and his eyes focused on something Jet couldn't see. "He'd taken out the security guard with those meat hooks of his, and the main lobby was totaled. One of the tellers hadn't moved fast enough, and he'd slammed the back of her head. I still hear the crunch, sometimes."

"The sounds can be hard," she said, "especially at night." Especially in the dark.

Bruce's eyes lit as his smile broadened, transforming his face from ruggedly handsome into something truly beautiful. "I remember the room growing cold, and the shadows coming alive and wrapping Crusher like a present. And then you just appeared, stepping out of nothing, telling him he's under arrest. And like that, the crisis was over."

Jet remembered. It had been one of her first solo missions after graduating from Academy, becoming a full member of the Squadron. She'd refused a partner.

She'd never request a partner again. They inevitably left you—either they died, or they betrayed you.

"I was a kid," she murmured. "Still wet behind the ears. Looking to prove myself to the Squadron."

"You proved yourself to me that day." He took her hand, squeezed. "You're the reason I became interested in the Academy at all."

She let out a startled laugh. "You became a Runner because of me?"

"Sort of. I had an interesting run-in with Night, and he pretty much got me the job."

"Wow." She tried to imagine what Bruce could have done to capture Night's attention. "You must have really impressed him."

He loosened his hold on her hand and slowly trailed his thumb over her palm. "Hey, I'm an impressive guy."

"Among other things," she said, her voice level to disguise how her heartbeat was rocketing. Light, if this is how he made her feel just by touching her hand, what would it be like if he touched her—

"And you're a very impressive woman."

"I'm a hero," she murmured, feeling light-headed and tingly. Maybe she was having a relapse. Yes, that had to be it. She wasn't healed at all . . . "Being a woman is secondary. Duty first. Always."

He leaned in—so close now that she could barely breathe. "You're off duty for two more days."

"Yes . . ."

"So it's time for the woman in you to get the attention she deserves."

"Bruce . . ."

Then his lips were on hers, and her protest faded as she melted into his kiss.

When she woke two hours later, naked, her sheets rumpled, her body so very, very relaxed and a permagrin on her face, it was well after six o'clock. She heard someone moving around the apartment—humming a song. That had to be Terry; she liked to sing to the radio.

Bruce was long gone. But next to her pillow was a note:

If I'm not fired, I'll see you tomorrow. Can't wait. —B

Jet's grin stretched even broader. She couldn't wait, either. Tomorrow couldn't come fast enough.

CHAPTER 50

IRIDIUM

No matter where you go, the Academy will always be
your home.

Academy Assistant Superintendent Neil Moore,
to the new graduates during
the Academy's graduation ceremony

Iridium fidgeted inside her canvas jumpsuit. Her psychiatrist suit was bad; this was unbearable. The blue jumper with the Chicago Power, Light, & Antigravity patches on the shoulders was dense and smelled like day-old roast-beef sandwiches, which, she guessed, its real owner consumed with some regularity.

Taser, wearing sunglasses and a bandanna over the lower half of his face, opened the junction box with his stolen tools and examined the wires. "Fuck. You know what any of these are?"

Iridium examined the diagram. "I'm more of a chemistry girl, but I'd say if you hit that set of circuits there," she said, pointing, "it'll take out the backup city power. They won't have a shot of fixing it in time."

"Good enough." With a touch of his hand, he fried the entire junction box.

Iridium frowned at him. "Was that completely necessary?"

"Never hurts to be sure."

"Come on." Passersby were starting to cough on the acrid smoke rising from the box; she and Taser had to get moving. Now.

After they stripped out of the jumpsuits and stuffed them into a trash 'bot, Iridium breathed a little easier. Granted, not much easier. They wore white coveralls now: Corp uniforms with its imposing black concentric Cs on the breast pocket.

"See you on the other side," said Taser.

She nodded grimly.

They left the alley at opposite ends and Iridium waited for an Academy shuttle to come by. It stopped for her, keying onto the frequency of her badge. Taser would take the next one. She moved to the back, picked a seat, and tried to blend with the rest of the lapdogs.

Next to her, a woman said "Hi!" in a tone so perky it could shatter glass. Clipped to her pink blouse was an ID badge with a cursive *R* in the upper left corner.

A Runner. Just great.

"Hello," said Iridium, striving for nonchalance. Her black hair was tucked under a cap, and she'd worn her doctor's glasses and purple contacts for insurance, but she couldn't be sure the Runner wasn't a fangirl.

"You're new!"

"Uh-huh," said Iridium as the shuttle whirred along, entering the private tunnel that led to the service entrance of the Academy. The plans flickered in Iridium's mind. She was moving, like a clot in an artery, making her way to the heart of the system.

"What division are you? I'm a Runner!" The Runner lowered her voice. "*I* work for Hornblower. He's dreamy!"

"You're smoking junk."

The Runner blinked. "Excuse me?"

"I said he sure is a hunk."

"Isn't he, though?"

"Sure. This is my stop."

"Well . . . bye!" the Runner chirped, levity recovered.

Iridium restrained herself from running off the shuttle. Just another working drone, she reminded herself as she walked with a group of other Academy workers. Just another day at the superoffice.

Just before the biodetector gate, a guard stopped her. "ID, miss."

Iridium flashed it at him, and he blipped her with a scanner. "First day?"

"Yes," said Iridium, smiling brightly. "I wasn't supposed to start until next week, but apparently there's a problem with the cooling system. They're calling all the Maintenance workers in."

The guard frowned. "Temperature feels fine to me."

Iridium kept smiling, taking her badge back. "Wait for it."

She walked past the guard, through the biodetector that would scan her for metal, disease, disguise, contagion . . . and then she was joining a line of other jumpsuited workers, shuffling along at that don't-really-care pace so many people adopted when they worked too many hours for too little money.

Iridium looked at the arched white walls, familiar as if she'd last been inside the Academy an hour ago.

She allowed herself a tiny grin. "I'm back," she whispered.

Half an hour later, Iridium approached the double blast doors that housed the Academy's generator complex. She'd run a few training exercises here, as a student, with Jet and

Derek and Chen, back in Third Year. Enclosed spaces, embedded opponents. Jet hadn't been a fan; too many variables, especially with the inflatable "civilians" acting as shields.

One time, Iridium's solution had been to toss a smoke grenade into the generator room and wait for the Containment "enemies" to come stumbling out. Frostbite had frozen them, and the op was over. Celestina had failed her for not following Squadron protocol. "You could have given those citizens lifelong respiratory problems!" she'd chided. Once again, a reminder that heroes were supposed to play by the rules.

The thought made Iridium smile.

"Maintenance?" said the guard at the door. "You're not scheduled."

"Nope," she said, silently counting down. The cameras were on a thirty-second sweep. She heard a lift swish down the corridor, and Taser appeared, back in his costume, his face once again hidden by his goggled mask. Smiling at the guard, she said, "But trust me, this is where I'm supposed to be."

"Huh?" The guard cocked his head. "What do you—"

The camera cycled away, and Iridium jabbed him in the throat. He collapsed without a sound, mouth working like a hooked fish's.

Taser put his hand against the blast doors. "You're sure the tilithium coats all of the walls in there?"

"That's what the plans say," Iridium said tersely. "Hurry up. We're got twelve seconds."

Taser exhaled, and a stream of electric currents writhed free of his hand, crackling over the door. The lights flickered once, twice—and as Iridium counted *six, five, four . . .* they went out.

No red emergency lights came on. No alarm Klaxons sounded. The backup power from the city grid wasn't coming to the Academy's rescue.

Far off, above her, Iridium heard screaming as students and heroes and Runners were plunged into dark. She couldn't help it: She grinned. Looking over to where she was just able to make out the shine of Taser's goggles, she said, "Nice work, Ace."

"Light us up."

Iridium created a bobbing strobe to guide them to the lift. Taser tapped the call pad, and the box slid open. Once they were both inside, he electrified the control panel to override security protocol, then the door slid back. Iridium looked up, imagining the thunk of the security doors slamming shut as they automatically detected the power outage.

Taser followed her gaze. "Gonna be a lot of trapped, pissed-off grunts up there."

"Not as pissed off as the heroes will be when they find themselves without a way out of the Rat Network," said Iridium. "Ops still has power, and they're going to know something is up. So move this tin can."

"I love a woman who gives me orders," Taser said with a grin, then he zapped the lift control. "Going up."

CHAPTER 51

JET

Oh, I don't believe in bad news. It's all in how we process information. Keeping a good attitude is all you need to do, no matter what the circumstances.

Celestina, to a reporter during a press conference

Forgot to tell you," Terry said brightly. "Bruce is running late. Hee, I made a joke! Running late!"

Jet smiled as she accepted the cup of tea, but her stomach was heaving. Why was he late today, of all days? Was it because of what happened yesterday? No, nonsense. He was a professional Runner.

Whom she'd slept with. Oh, Light, she was in trouble.

"I'm sure he'll be here as soon as he can," Jet said casually. "If it's a problem for you, Terry, why don't you pack it in? I'll be okay on my own."

Terry grinned. "Right, I bet. Bruce clued me in on your sneaking out of bed to help save a little old lady." She clucked her tongue. "You're on bed rest, Jet."

"Just for one more day," she said around her smile, trying not to growl.

"Exactly. For one more day. You're following doctor's orders. At least, you are when I'm on duty."

Chagrined, Jet sipped her tea. Terry smiled over her victory and left Jet alone.

Oh boy, she was in *a lot* of trouble.

How could she have slept with Bruce? What had she been thinking?

Well, that was easy. She'd been thinking how sexy he was, and how horny she was, and how his lips were so enticing and his eyes so electric...

Right. It was thoughts like that, that got her into trouble in the first place.

She had to tell Corp. What she'd done was strictly against policy. Bruce could sue her for sexual harassment.

Then again, he hadn't been complaining yesterday. And he'd been the one who'd instigated. It wasn't her fault.

She let out a bitter laugh. Yeah, that would play real well. How many times had criminals wailed that it hadn't been their fault?

Grow up, Jet. When he gets here, you'll talk to him. Like a grown-up. And you'll figure it out from there.

She finished her tea and set the cup down. Nothing to do but wait for Bruce to arrive. And then they'd talk.

And maybe they'd do more than talk...

Stop that.

To pass the time, she picked up the paperback romance on her nightstand. After reading the same passage three times without really seeing what she was reading, Jet put the book down.

Instead of thinking about Bruce, her mind was focused on Iridium.

Joannie, you're hurt. Bad. Is heroing worth tearing yourself apart?

Callie had said that to her. She had been nearly deliri-
ous from pain, but it had still penetrated.

Iri had wanted to help her.

Jet's head started to throb, so she leaned back against
the pillow and closed her eyes. It made no sense. Iridium
was rabid. Iridium didn't give a damn about her, about
everything heroes stood for. She'd proven that five years
ago. All Iridium cared about was Iridium.

And yet ...

You can either get in my way and be burned by my strobe,
Iridium said, cocky and arrogant, then when Jet tried to bat
the ball of ever-brightening light away, she'd hissed:
Careful, that's over a thousand BTUs of heat!

Iridium didn't have to warn her. Iridium could have let
her get burned.

But when Jet had wrapped her in Shadow and Iridium
had cried out, had begged for her to stop, Jet let her go ...
and Iridium had sucker punched her.

Iridium didn't give a damn about her.

And yet ...

*I am smarter than you, Jet, especially now. I'm not going to
warn you again.*

Why had Iridium warned her? If Iri really cared, then
why was she a rabid? Why did she turn her back on the
Academy and Corp all those years ago? Why had she turned
her back on Jet?

And what had Iridium been doing in the tunnels? She
couldn't be working for Everyman. She couldn't. Not after
Third Year.

Maybe something with the Undergoths?

Or ...

She hissed in a breath, doubled over. Oh, by the Light,
her head hurt.

Wincing, Jet rubbed her temples, fought off a maddening urge to put in her comlink. As if that would help. She

reached over to her nightstand and turned up the volume on the white-noise setting. "Babbling Brook" filled her ears, but did nothing to ease the pounding in her head.

She grabbed the phone—audio only; she couldn't get to the actual vidphone in the kitchen, not with Terry here—from her nightstand and punched in Night's direct extension. When his familiar cold voice answered, she said, "Hey, old man."

"Joan." He sounded either surprised or irked. "How're you feeling?"

"Fine, sir. Eager to get out of bed and back into uniform."

"I understand. Did I ever tell you about the time Mister Mystery laid me up for the better part of a month? Very frustrating. I was fresh out of the Academy when it happened too. And... there we go. Clean channel. What is it, Jet?"

"Sir, I need you to tell me why I'm not pursuing Everyman. Why we're cleaning out the Rat Network."

"We've been through this."

"No, sir, not really. You haven't told me why, just what." She closed her eyes, saw Iri's face. "Why are we using Iridium like this?"

" 'Using Iridium'?"

His tone made her flinch.

"We are *not* using her. She is an excuse, yes. But we most certainly aren't using her."

"But she had nothing to do with Lynda Kidder's abduction." Or her death.

"She walked away from the Academy, from you, long ago. She's a criminal, like her father. You have to push aside old friendships and commit yourself to the only course of action that matters."

"But why aren't we going after Everyman?"

"Because that's suicide, Jet."

It's suicide, Martin Moore agreed, sounding grave. *Or, depending on how many humans are around you when you finally go, homicide.*

"Corp has a quiet agreement with the Society," Night said. "We leave them alone, and other than sound and fury, they follow suit."

"But," she spluttered, her mind unwilling to grasp what Night was saying, "but how could that be?" She remembered Wurtham's scorn when they'd appeared together on the Goldwater show, the look of pure loathing in his eyes. "They hate us. They'd never work with us. And Corp would never condone such a thing."

In her mind, Moore laughed. *Who do you think did this to you in the first place?*

"Jet," Night said, "it's been this way for years. Haven't you ever wondered why there hadn't been another assault from Everyman since Samson died?"

"But Martin Moore—"

"Belongs to a fringe organization of the Society. We know, Jet. The EC is hunting him down, with the Society's help. Quietly. This is an embarrassment to both organizations."

At least I'm not being deluded by a megalomaniacal organization bent on ruling the world.

"How could Corp work with Everyman?" she asked, her voice breaking. "It's *wrong,* it's—"

"It's business, Jet. Just business."

She clenched her fist. "It's untenable."

After a long pause, he said, "I understand your rage." His voice was quiet, and utterly terrifying. "Trust me, I understand. And a reckoning will come."

Her stomach knotted. "A...reckoning?"

"Soon. A little more patience, Jet. You concentrate on healing. I need you at full strength."

She whispered, "For what, sir?"

"To stand at my side, little Shadow. To stand at my side."

CHAPTER 52

IRIDIUM

They say there's honor among thieves. But here, in Blackbird, everyone says that honor isn't worth its weight in digichips.

Lynda Kidder, "Flight of the Blackbird,"
New Chicago Tribune, July 2, 2112

The elevator ride to Ops was interminable. Iridium tapped her fingers against the panel as they glided through blackness.

"Nervous?" Taser's voice rolled out of the dark and startled her.

"Eager," she lied. "What about you?"

He paused for a moment, and when he spoke, his tone was reflective. "Once, my unit got dropped over Siberia during a blizzard, winds about fifty, sixty miles an hour. I looked down and all I could see was white, going on forever. I was scared then. Not now."

"So I was right," she murmured. "You are ex-military."

"You win some kind of bet on that one, darlin'?"

"Just with myself," Iridium said.

Taser's hand wrapped around hers, flexible Kevlar gloves rough on skin. "I'm glad I met you, Iridium. Know that."

The lift slowed, and Iridium disentangled herself. "Now isn't the time for mushy stuff, Taser. It's not like either of us is planning to die a dramatic death."

He laughed once. "I get the feeling it's never the time with you."

"If we pull this off, I might prove you wrong," Iridium said, her voice low, throaty. She couldn't tell in the dark, but she thought Taser probably grinned.

The light panel over the lift doors turned green, and Iridium clenched her fists. She reached for the Light, pushed it outward as the door swished back.

The glow erupted into the Ops control room with a bang, light and heat surging forth. If a flash grenade could work for Keanu Whatsit in his old movies, Iridium figured it could work for her.

Taser charged into the control room, shooting electrical bolts left and right. Runners slumped over their stations; the quicker ones screamed and retreated. Someone hit the alarm. Overhead, Klaxons began to whine.

Iridium strobed the Runners hiding behind their consoles, then shouted at Taser, "Turn off the damned alarms!"

He shocked the control panel, and the Klaxons cut off abruptly. "Not like anybody can hear them."

Iridium was about to sit at the nearest console when something hit her between the shoulder blades. She stumbled and rolled, looking up into the sooty, enraged face of a dumpy, female, grounded hero—Weather Girl or Meteorology or something equally inane. At the Academy, she'd always eaten alone, studied alone, and passed Frostbite elaborately decorated love notes in the hallway.

Well, that last had turned out well for her; on any day other than today, Derek was probably stationed next to her.

The weather girl lowered her fire extinguisher and blinked at her. "Iridium?"

"None other."

"Oh no..." Twitching, she stared around the room, took in the situation with her big, wide eyes. "What did you do?"

Iridium whipped her foot up and kicked her in the gut, then got to her feet and kicked her again. The former hero collapsed.

"Something really cool, trust me," Iridium said. She jerked her head at Taser. "Load them into the lift. Lock the panel and send it to the basement."

As he did so, she pulled herself up to a console, which was locked and flashing the Academy logo. Iridium slid Ivanoff's digichip into the drive, marrying it to the console so it became the recognized processor, along with her fake access code. After a long moment, the screen popped up a password box, and Iridium waited for the crack program to engage.

"I'm in," she said to Taser, who panted slightly as he shoved the last unconscious Ops flunky into the lift.

"You sound surprised," he said, coming to stand behind her.

"Me? Never." She scrolled through the data on-screen, an icon for each active hero with GPS positioning. They spread through the Rat Network like a small, lonely constellation.

Iridium was about to enter the shutdown command when a cluster of power grids in the corner of the screen caught her eye. "Hey, Taser. Check this out."

He leaned in, putting one hand on her shoulder. Static popped between them. "What is that?"

"It's frequencies," she said. "Hundreds of them. Nothing connected to the comm network."

"And nothing receiving," said Taser. "Just broadcasting."

Iridium felt a cold twist in her gut. "Broadcasting what?"

Taser shrugged. "You're the genius."

Iridium thought about comlink, the muddled thoughts that came with wearing the earpiece. She thought about Dawnlighter's blank features. About how Jet had gone from a thin shadow to the darling of the Academy.

Jet and her earpiece.

Frostbite, his aged face grim. *Corp's got something on Jet. You can be sure of that.*

"I don't care," Iridium said out loud. "It's time to end this." She brought up the command window and typed in TERMINATE ALL.

ARE YOU SURE?

Iridium keyed ENTER and waited.

SHUTTING DOWN OPERATIONS MAINFRAME.

"Now!" Iridium snapped at Taser. "Fry the network so it can't do a hard boot!"

Taser stuck out his hand and shocked the bank of servers underneath the console.

A great hum died away, like blood had stopped flowing in and out. Every Ops screen went black.

Taser circled back behind Iridium. She could see him now, clearly reflected in her dead datascreen. "We did it," she said. Her heart was thudding, and she could feel sweat under her unikilt. Unbelievable as it was to be sitting in the bastion of her enemies, it was real. She let herself grin. "We fucking did it!"

"Never doubted," said Taser softly. "Makes me almost sorry."

Iridium frowned. "Sorry . . . ?"

Taser grabbed her by the hair and slammed her forehead against the console once, twice. Blood spattered over Iridium's vision.

"Don't fight, Calista," Taser said.

"My name is not Calista!" Iridium summoned strobes, sent them backward blindly as Taser slammed her head again. Pain overtook her, and she dimly felt the strobes fizzling harmlessly.

Taser jerked her out of the workstation chair and sent her sliding across the floor. Iridium's vision was all blurs and light, blood and blackness.

From his sleeve, Taser drew out a flat disc and shook it until it irised into the silvery network of wires and metal she recognized.

That bastard had stolen her own neural inhibitor.

"I want you to know I don't enjoy this," said Taser. "I respect you. Not many people get my respect. This is just business."

"Oh, go to—" Before she could finish the insult, Taser slipped the neural inhibitor over her brow, then she didn't know anything except nothingness.

CHAPTER 53

JET

Even heroes are fallible; even extrahumans aren't impervious to human nature. That's why rogue heroes work in the shadows...and why a Luster can become an Arclight.

Lynda Kidder, "Flight of the Blackbird,"
New Chicago Tribune, July 2, 2112

In her bedroom, Jet was pacing. Had been for a long, long while. Terry had popped her head in at one point and scolded her, but a look from Jet was enough to send Terry scampering back to the other side of the apartment.

Corp and Everyman were working together.

The very thought made Jet's stomach clench and her chest feel too tight. It was a slap in the face, a burn on her soul. Everyman despised extrahumans. And what they'd done in the past was inexcusable.

And yet Corp was working with them.

Worse, Night knew about it. And was going along with it.

Night, who she'd thought had been going mad. Night, who she'd thought was sending her on a wild-goose chase by asking her to investigate Lynda Kidder's disappearance.

Night had known all along.

It's a plan, Jet told herself, wearing the carpet thin from all her striding. *Some sort of master plan from the Corp EC, to lull Everyman into lowering their guard, then the Squadron would come in and arrest them all for their crimes against us. Against humanity.*

Corp wouldn't condone it otherwise. Corp stood for justice.

Corp supported the Squadron and all extrahumans.

Corp was good.

Corp was in bed with Everyman.

Everyman hated extrahumans. An Everyman had killed Sam. An Everyman had nearly killed Iri.

Iri, who'd tried to tell her that day, five years ago . . .

A slash of pain cut Jet's thought, made her clutch her head and bite back a cry. She tried to push through the pain, like they'd been taught back at the Academy—*the Academy, the educational branch of Corp, oh Light, everything they've been teaching has been from Corp and mandated from Corp and Corp is working with Everyman—*

Another stab through her mind, brutal, agonizing. Her world narrowed until it was just her head and the hot blade slicing through it, searing her until she couldn't think, could barely breathe.

Blindly, she staggered to her nightstand, turned the white-noise device all the way to eleven. She was drowning in a waterfall, clutching wildly to the sound, trying to stay afloat before the pain dragged her under.

It did no good; her brain felt like it was on fire.

Desperate, Jet pawed inside her nightstand drawer until she grabbed her comlink. Shoved it into her ear. Clicked it onto the white-noise setting.

Still nothing. And now just beyond the scream of torment in her mind, she thought she heard whispers. Giggles.

Rumbles of anticipation.

"No," she said aloud. She tapped her earpiece to connect her to Ops—

—and yanked the device from her ear as the deafening alarm shrilled on and on and on. Tears streamed down her face; she couldn't catch her breath. Her heart thumped frantically, as if trying to break free from her rib cage. Sweating, shaking, Jet collapsed to her knees, her hands pressed to her head.

Corp stands for justice, she thought wildly. *Corp looks out for the common citizen. The Academy teaches, the Squadron protects. Duty first, always.*

Duty first.

Slowly, so very slowly, the pain receded. She recited the Academy Mission Statement as fast as she could, and again, and a third time. And then, finally, the pain was gone, leaving only echoes in its wake.

Oh sweet Light, that had hurt.

She stared at the comlink, which was still whining in alarm. With a trembling hand, Jet reached out and tapped it. Silence, except for her rapid breathing, her slowing heartbeat.

What had just happened?

Jet pulled herself to her feet, her gaze riveted on the earpiece. Her head was a mess, and her comlink was broken.

And Corp and Everyman...

A warning buzz in her head. Biting her lip, Jet thought, *I! Serve! Corp!* She even smiled.

And the buzzing faded.

She sank down onto her bed, her eyes wide. By all that was Light, they'd gotten into her mind. Somehow, they'd brainwashed her. Corp or Everyman or both.

She saw Martin Moore, grinning. Pictured him in the crisp white lab coat that all the doctors in the Mental wing sported, saying: *"Who do you think did this to you in the first place?"*

And Frostbite, stunned and yet smug, asking her: *"How long've they had you on a leash?"*

Longer than she'd ever guessed.

On the floor, her comlink seemed to wink.

Her eyes narrowed, and she clenched her fist so hard that her nails gouged the sensitive flesh of her palm. Someone had a lot of explaining to do. Blackness seeped out between her fingers, covered her hand in Shadow until she shook it away. *A lot* of explaining.

And she wouldn't take no for an answer.

First, a shower. Get clean. Scrub away the remnants of what was starting to feel like a mental rape.

She dashed into her bathroom, ignoring Terry's outburst. No time for any of that. She showered in record time, was toweling herself dry as she raced back into her bedroom. Terry didn't try to stop her, at least.

She dressed quickly—undergarments, skinsuit—and wrapped her hair into two thick coils and pinned them back. She strode down the hall and to the front of the living room, headed straight for the low table by the front door. She grabbed her boots and yanked them on, then clipped on her belt. Her hands slid into her leather gauntlets. Oh, it felt good to be back in uniform. Ready to take action.

Jet smiled grimly as she snatched her cape and cowl from the hook by the door. *Oh yes,* she thought, fastening the cloak so that it rested comfortably over her shoulders. She was ready for action. And answers. She wouldn't stop until she got answers.

Almost ready—except her optiframes were missing.

"Terry," she called out, "where—"

The lights cut out.

Even though it was about eleven in the morning, the living room was pitch black, as if it were storming outside and the sun couldn't break through the pollution layer . . . or as if someone had reinforced the shades.

Her breath caught in her throat for a moment, then she pushed the reaction away. No time to be afraid. Get the lights on before the voices start to whisper.

But duty first: Get the civilian out of danger. "Terry," Jet called out, tugging her hood to cover her head. "Are you all right?"

"Terry's not here, darlin'," a man's voice replied—cocky, almost a verbal swagger. She'd heard that voice before, and fury swirled through her, slashed through her fear of the dark. "I gave her the afternoon off."

The voice was coming from the bedroom.

Distract him. Get the lights on.

"You shouldn't have, she's paid through tomorrow," Jet said, circling into the kitchen and pressing the lightpad—to no avail. She moved back into the living room, tried the front door—hissed as something shocked her, right through her leather gauntlets.

"Sounds like you're having some electrical issues." His voice was closer now—moving down the hall.

Aiming her hand toward the hallway entrance, Jet said, "Where's your mistress?"

"Who?" Still closer.

"Iridium," she said, lining up a shot. "You know. Tall. Mouthy. Tends to wear white." Come on, say something else, just one more thing . . .

"My mistress, huh? Now that's cute."

Jet let fly a blast of Shadow. It crashed into something, but she didn't hear a grunt or a cry, so she assumed she missed. *Damn it to Darkness, I need light.*

From behind her: laughter. "Iridium couldn't be here. She's a little tied up."

She whirled and unleashed another Shadowbolt, and she heard something crash and tinkle.

"Hope you have insurance for that," the man said, somewhere to her left. By the front door. "And by the way, I borrowed your goggles. They're real cute. Spruce up my outfit something fierce."

Jet stalked right and back, sought room to maneuver. Her legs banged against the sofa. "What do you want?"

"An all-expense-paid trip to Europe would be nice." From her right now; damn, the man moved silently. "Maybe a cup of world peace. Oh, and one order of Jet. To go."

But at least he was a blabbermouth. She hurled a black-ball at him.

"You missed," he whispered in her ear.

She elbowed him in the gut, but he grabbed her left arm, twisted it behind her back until her shoulder threatened to pop. Snarling, she slammed her head back—got his chest, which was heavily padded.

"Uh-uh, darlin'. I saw that move before." He forced her arm back to the breaking point, and with his other hand he tore her cowl away from her head, yanked the cloak free.

The voices reared up, gibbering, demanding. **hit him hit him HIT HIM HARD**

No!

She was panicking now, but not because of the man pinning her arm behind her back. In the darkness, the shadows around her seemed to gather together, rise up and form something, something with teeth, something hungry...

HIT HIM HURT HIM HURT HIM KILL HIM MAKE HIM SCREAM

"Shut up!" She couldn't think, couldn't block out the voices and fight Iridium's lackey. Writhing in his grip, she stomped down on his foot. He didn't even grunt. "Get away!"

MAKE HIM SCREAM MAKE HIM SUFFER MAKE HIM SHADOW SQUEEZE HIM SQUEEZE HIM TIGHT

On the small amount of exposed skin of her neck: a pinch, then a rush of pressure. He whispered, "You're supposed to be on bed rest, Joan."

He released her, and the darkness slipped to the left. Jet staggered drunkenly, struggled to keep the world from spinning away. But the shadows reached for her, clawed for her. Dragged her down. *No,* she thought dimly, shielding her face from the blackness with its teeth. *No* . . .

Over the giggles of the Shadow voices, she heard the man say, "Nighty night."

She was out before she hit the floor.

THEN

YEAR

CHAPTER 54

JET

I look at what Corp is unleashing on the world, and I know that the world will tremble and fall if no one stands against them.

Arclight, in an interview with *Underground* magazine

The Academy main pavilion was filled with the sounds of grunts, of blasts, of bodies hitting bodies. Not to mention whoops and shouts, and more than a little scolding and outright belligerence. If not for the harsh wind stealing the smells, the place would have reeked of sweat, and ozone, and dirt. Paired heroes trained under the watchful eyes of their instructors, with the exception of the Fifth Years; they worked unsupervised.

Which bothered Jet immensely. How would she know if she was going too slow, or if her form was off, or any host of things, if no one was watching? Palming her hair out of her eyes, she said, "Once more."

"Enough already." Iri's breath misted with the late

February chill. "We've done it ten times. We've got it down cold."

Jet rubbed her hands to keep them warm. Maybe her Squadron skinsuit should have gloves—no, gauntlets, like Night's. They'd protect her skin and keep her warm. "I just want to be sure."

"Well, *I'm* sure. We're done." To prove her point, Iri yanked the comlink from her ear and tucked it into one of her belt pouches. "Christo, I hate that thing."

"But the field test is tomorrow," Jet said. "We have to make sure it's perfect."

"It is. If we keep doing it, we're going to get tired, and that means getting sloppy. And then . . . boom." Iri popped a strobe in her hands.

Jet's goggles irised to shield her from the sudden burst of light. "Hey! Quit it!"

"We're done," Iri said. "And that means it's time to relax. Come on, *Squad House* is on in fifteen minutes."

"Fine, maybe I'll spar with one of the others, or offer to ref the Fourth Years, or—"

Iri hooked an arm around Jet's shoulders. "You, girl, are going to relax if it kills you. We're popping popcorn and watching *Squad House.* I'm betting Girl Power goes all slutty on Screamer."

Jet groaned, but she allowed Iri to steer her back into the Academy. She was constantly proving to Iridium that they were really friends again, after making up during Fourth Year. So for Jet, that meant hanging out and, among other things, watching *Squad House,* even though she'd rather pluck out her eyeballs.

Jet wasn't about to risk their friendship again. Not for the Academy, or Corp.

Or Night.

He was too busy for her, anyway. Between the close of Fifth Year and all that entailed and some proctor project he'd been working on, her mentor had been horribly scarce as of late. And he was curt to her when they did see each other. Rude...and distracted. The one time she'd seen his face before he'd adjusted his cowl, his eyes had a wild sheen—almost feverish. Whatever had captured his attention, it had nothing to do with Jet.

She pretended that didn't hurt. Or that she didn't worry about him.

Because everyone knew what happened to Shadow powers. Eventually.

But here, at the Academy, surely someone would notice if Night started acting...in a way he shouldn't act.

Thinking of her father, Jet glanced at Iri—who was grinning broadly, looking for all the world like she'd just won a tremendous victory.

Maybe Night cutting her off was a good thing. If anything, she and Iri had been closer this year than they were even back in Second Year—before Jet had gotten her earpiece and her confidence. She remembered that day, saw Dawnlighter's face twisted into a snarl of utter hatred, just before she'd tried to kill Jet.

"Jet! Wakey wakey."

Jet blinked. "Sorry. Lost in thought."

"There's a news flash."

"I can't believe you're making me watch some extrahuman reality show."

"Come on, it's good for you. Builds character."

Well, maybe it wouldn't be a total waste of time. She could think more about what her postgraduation battlesuit should look like. Maybe take a cue from Night on more than just the gauntlets. He'd like that, wouldn't he? She could go for the whole intimidation motif. If people were afraid of her, then that fear would do most of the fighting for her.

The thought made her smile.

She was still a little thin, and not exactly tall. So she'd need to make up for the lack of physical presence with other things. Add padding to the battlesuit, both for protection and for more of a figure. A hood or a cowl to shroud her face, turn it from something vaguely pretty into something secretive. And a cape, definitely, she thought, picturing how Night's cloak swirled around his legs. Maybe she'd even add height to her boots—ugh. She should have taken Femme Fatale as an elective to help her learn how to balance in high heels...

"What're you groaning about?"

Jet laughed. "Fashion. Picturing me in heels."

"Holy Jehovah, now there's a sight!" Iri snorted laughter. "Let me guess, you're considering a halter top and steel bracelets."

"Me? Light, no. I don't want to have to shave my underarms before going into battle."

"I'm telling you, heels and a halter top. Maybe a leather bikini to distract men with your womanly charms."

"Great," Jet said. "Code name: Bikini."

"Yeah. No battlesuit for you. Just acres of flesh."

"Acres? Now I look fat in the bikini?"

"Or maybe a PVC skinsuit..."

"Worse than leather," Jet said primly, biting back her giggles. "Way too stiff. Too restrictive."

"So 'Bondage Girl' is out. Fine, you'll go the body-stocking route instead of a unikilt. Between that and the heels, there'd be nothing left to the imagination."

"Uh-huh, right. Code name: Spandex."

Iri beamed. "Exactly! I love it."

"You're crazy."

"Nope, I'm the criminal. You're the kook."

Giggling, they went into the common-room annex and made some popcorn—with Iri grumbling as they waited the three minutes for it to finish nuking; by the third minute of Iri's impatient pacing, Jet was fervently wishing that Power Plant would stroll in and zap the corn with a touch of her hand. After, they walked into the Fifth Year common room with five minutes to go before the show started. A number of students had already converged, laying claim to the three sofas and scattered chairs, which meant floor room only for Jet and Iri.

"Hey," Steele said from the far corner chair, waving. "It's Yin and Yang!"

"With popcorn," Firebug declared. "Our heroes!"

A bunch of the students said their "heys" to them; the rest ignored them, other than casting a disinterested glance their way. Jet and Iri maneuvered their way to the back corner and grabbed some floor by Steele's seat, then passed the bowl of popcorn around. Over them, Firebug sat scrunched on the sofa by the chair, and squeezed by her were Windfall, Were, Colossal Lad, and Stealth. Someone nudged Jet's shoulder with a foot; she didn't have to look up to know it was Were, already chortling.

"Hey, Jetster, you hear the one about the Shadow and the Light?"

Her cheeks heated as she turned to look up at him. *Damn it.* Yeah, she'd definitely get a cowl for her battlesuit. Something to help her mask her embarrassment.

"Christo, not that one again," Windfall groaned. "You going to tell that same stupid joke every time Jet and Iri walk in together?"

"Aw, it's a good joke."

"If you define 'good' as making you want to rip your ears off and eat them so you don't have to hear it again, then sure."

Jet hid her smile behind her hand.

"You're no fun," Were grumbled. "Tell him, Stealth."

Stealth, silent as ever, shrugged.

"Yeah, what he said!" Were nodded, satisfied.

Stealth rolled his eyes.

"You guys ready for tomorrow?" asked Steele, and Jet pivoted to face her.

"Oh yeah." Iri slammed her fist into the open palm of her other hand. "We're going to blow through the field test. Dazzle them with style. Impress them with elegance."

"Bore them with a monologue," Colossal Lad said.

Iri elbowed his shin.

"We're ready," Jet said firmly. And they were. Iri had been right, of course. They had their maneuvers down cold. All that was left was to perform for a live audience.

"Me, I'm so freaking nervous, I should bring a barf bag," Firebug said.

"I keep telling you, you're terrific." Steele smiled at her partner. "I wouldn't lie to you."

"I know we know our stuff," Firebug said, "but there's so much riding on this." She gulped. "I don't want to get expelled if we fail."

Were said, "You know, if you keep worrying about it, you're going to mess up."

Windfall bopped him on the head. "Shut it, Were! The rest of us don't get an autopass because our partner got killed. Oh." He cleared his throat, muttered, "Sorry, Jet."

She swallowed the lump in her throat. "It's okay."

"You're going to be fine," Steele said, her eyes glinting like her armored flesh did when she powered up. "You'll see. As long as we go by the book, nothing can go wrong."

"Because Jehovah knows," Iri mumbled, "the bad guys always go by the book."

"Not now," Jet told her.

"It's true." Iri shrugged. "It's stupid for us to follow expected patterns. Repetition leads to predictability, which leads to ambush."

"Repetition leads to getting the moves perfect," Steele insisted. Jet nodded. Thank the Light, at least Jet wasn't alone in that belief.

"Hero Philosophy later, ladies," Windfall said. "The

show's about to start. Hey, Were, quit wolfing down all the popcorn!"

They watched the insipid show, and by the end of the hour, Jet wanted to claw her eyes out. But she laughed along with the others, and she followed their group out of the common room when the show ended. The room slowly cleared out.

She was hanging by the door for almost a full minute when she realized that Iri was inside, talking to someone. Poking her head in, she saw her roommate seated in the far front corner... next to Frostbite. They were the only two left in the room.

Oh boy. She hadn't known Derek was inside—hadn't known that he was out of Therapy. Pasting a smile on her face, she walked in to say hello.

Frostbite regarded her with cold, haunted eyes. His face was gaunter than she remembered, and his shock of blue hair was buzzed close to his scalp. He was far too thin. "Jet," he said.

"How's it going, Frostbite?"

"Same old," he replied. "Mind still works, if that's what you mean."

Uncomfortable, Jet looked at her boots.

"Anyway, you need anything," Iri said to him, rising, "you let me know."

"I will, Callie. Thanks."

Iridium grinned at him, then strode out of the room.

Jet wanted to follow, but her feet were rooted to the spot. "She missed you," she said quietly.

He stared at her with those haunted eyes. "She'll get over it," he said. "I can't hang with her anymore. With anyone anymore." His voice faded, as if he saw something that Jet couldn't see.

"Maybe if we talk to the Superintendent..."

"You stay out of it," he growled. "You don't want any

part of this, Jet." His gaze fixed on hers. "You just stay close to Iri. Make sure you two pass tomorrow. Don't fuck up."

"We won't."

"Good." He nodded, once. "You know, they kept telling us to make sure you're okay, to stay close to you. But they've got it wrong."

"What? Who said that?"

"Everyone. Instructors. Proctors." His blue eyes held her dark ones. "Since First Year, it's been about looking out for Jet, making sure the Shadow power was protected."

She whispered, "What on the scorched earth are you talking about?"

He laughed mirthlessly. "Can't make the newest Shadow go crazy too soon."

Jet swallowed thickly. "That's ridiculous."

"I agree," he hissed. "We shouldn't have been coddling you. Because you're the worst of them."

"Derek . . ."

He motioned at her, a lazy flip of his wrist. "You parrot everything. You're all about rah, rah Academy, rah, rah Corp. You're so impressionable that there's no Joan left. Just what they made you. Just Jet."

It's the Therapy, she told herself sadly. *It's made him crazy.*

"I promise you, Just Jet, if Iri gets expelled tomorrow, or worse, because she's too busy protecting you to remember to follow procedure, I'll find you. And I'll make you pay." He delivered the threat perfectly—quiet, assured. Stating simple truth.

"There's nothing for you to worry about," she said, feeling sorry for him, for what he'd lost. "I promise, we'll be fine."

"You better." With that, he turned to face the blank vid screen, dismissing her.

Outside of the room, Jet let out a shaky breath. Iri said softly, "You okay?"

"Yeah. That was just...hard."

"I know," Iri said, her voice tight. "It's not our Derek anymore."

But Jet had a feeling that it was the real Derek, just stripped of his mask.

CHAPTER 55

IRIDIUM

Police officers were good, and city workers—cleanup crews and the like, yanno? But the best was a hero... jumping a hero and winning would make you a god on the streets.

Jasper Kane, former leader of the Asphalt Kings gang, during his intake interview at the Illinois State Correctional Facility

Jet piloted the hover, and Iridium rode shotgun, tapping her fingers against the control panel in a rhythm she used to telegraph boredom to the world at large.

"Would you stop that?" Jet demanded. "I'm nervous enough as it is."

"Nervous?" Iridium snorted. "This assignment is bull. I can't believe this is all it takes to graduate and get active duty. In my father's day, they used to actually, you know, *stop crime.*"

Jet stiffened. "Keeping the city free of vandalism is important, Iridium."

"Whatever," she muttered, looking at the directive on their datapad again. *Patrol Grid 23. Remove any instances of*

vandalism, gang activity, and illegal street art. Pass three train-
ing checkpoints and report back no later than 1400 hours.

In other words, jump through hoops like the trained
seals they were.

"There," Jet said, pointing to a flagpole protruding from
the front of the grid's community center. The flag had been
replaced with a gang banner. "That's checkpoint one."

She pressed a few buttons, and the hover slowed, paus-
ing in place. "I think we can request a landing slot on the
roof," Jet mused. "And ask the citizens to allow us access to
get the art down . . ." She scanned the center's landing pad.
"Blast. They're closed today. We'll have to call the building
super."

"Christo." Iridium rolled her eyes. "I'll take care of it.
Get closer." She popped her hatch and jerked her earpiece
out, tossing it in the back of the vehicle.

Jet's eyes went wide. "Iri, what are you doing?"

Iridium swung herself sideways, the toes of her boots
standing on nothing except the street, twenty feet below.
She grabbed the stabilizer fin of the hover and pulled herself out of the cockpit, standing on the running board and
half-dangling into open space. "Hurry up, Jet!" she ordered.
"We've only got an hour to patrol this whole grid. And it's
freezing out here."

"This isn't procedure." Jet worried her lip. "Our points
could be docked."

"We could fail out of the training program if we don't
complete this assignment," Iridium reminded her. "Do you
want to sit on your butt in Ops with the other washouts for
the next twenty years?"

Jet sighed. "Hang on." She guided the hover in until the
vehicle's nose bumped against the bricks of the community
center. Iridium reached out and grabbed the flagpole with
her free hand, planting her foot on the ledge. It was icy and
crumbling, and shifted under even half her weight.

"Be careful!" Jet cried as Iridium swatted at the gang banner.

Iridium heard the rumble of the bus and felt it parting the air behind their hover. It was going too fast for a residential grid; when the wake hit, it pitched the hover sideways.

Pitched Iridium into the brick face of the center, her foot losing purchase. She fell.

She felt herself punch through the heavy-duty plastic roof of a shanty at the street level, and darkness closed in as she disappeared from the hover's view.

Iridium bounced off something—an old-style gasoline auto, abandoned along the street, and landed in a heap on the slush-covered pavement.

"Brilliant," she groaned. She looked through the hole in the plastic and saw Jet circling the hover.

"Iridium! Are you okay?"

"Bloody wonderful!" Iridium yelled back. "Land that thing and get me. I'm soaked!"

"I can't!" Jet sounded panicked. "The autopilot is programmed for the checkpoints. This is a dangerous grid—no landing without backup!"

"Override the fucking thing! I'm going to freeze to death, Jet, and then you'll have to walk alone at graduation in front of all those news cameras."

"Hang on, I'm calling Night right now!"

Iridium cursed, and rubbed her arms for warmth. And waited for Night to tell Jet to get her ass off the hover and rescue her already.

Two minutes ticked by before Jet called down: "Night says that I have to check in directly to give my report."

"WHAT?" Iridium screeched.

"He said something about getting a witness for the unconventional request, paperwork or something. It's procedure, he says—"

"Fuck that, Joannie! Get me out of here! Now!"

"It . . . it's procedure, Iri. I'm going to report this directly, and then I'll be back with help. *Stay put.*"

"Procedure? Are you smoking junk? Put the thing on autohover and help me!"

"I will," Jet shouted, "I promise! But I have to do what Night says. I don't want us both to fail for this. I'll be back before you know it!"

She righted the vehicle and sped away. Jet would go report directly, as Night told her to, before coming back to do the right thing.

"Oh, sure," Iridium muttered. "I'll just go get a latte while I wait."

"Hey." A bum shuffled out of the broken shanty. "You okay, kid?"

"Just banged up," Iridium said, brushing herself off. Her costume was soaked, and she started to shiver.

"Hell of a fall," said the bum. "You from Corp?"

"Maybe," said Iridium. "Maybe I just had a bad day and fell out of the sky. You want to tell me how to get to the metro station from here?"

The bum snorted. "Nearest metro is a good two miles away. You can walk it if you cut through Alleytown, then go up Broadway."

Alleytown appeared to be the dark warren of shacks and jury-rigged lightpoles over the bum's left shoulder. Iridium sighed and wrung out the hem of her skirt. "Thanks, Grandpa."

"You be careful now!" he called after her. "Alleytown's a rough place!"

It wasn't any rougher than the neighborhood where Iridium had lived with her family. She didn't remember living with Corp—Lester was rabid before she was really aware of anything. Most people in Alleytown were inside their shanties or instablock houses, warding off the cold. Iridium wrapped her arms around herself. The one time she needed the damn earpiece, and it was back in the hover with Jet, who was on her way back to the Academy, while Iridium froze her ass off.

She was probably more upset about the possibility of failing than about Iridium.

The uncharitable thought stole in along with the frigid wind, and Iridium focused on her footsteps and avoiding the ice rather than get any angrier.

You'll admit, girl—this was your own fault. Your little friend had the right idea about procedure.

"Shut up, Dad," Iridium muttered out loud. Jehovah, he could be annoying.

Voices started up from around the corner, one crying and one laughing. Iridium slowed her pace, reflexively putting her back to the wall nearest her and glancing toward the voices without revealing herself.

A woman in a pink fur jacket and a short skirt was sprawled on the ground, her neck and face bloody. A number of small cuts covered the deep V her stretch top left open.

The man standing over her was wholly unremarkable— short, brunette, with a sallow face and dark eyes. He was holding a Talon cutter and loosening his belt.

"Shut up, bitch!" he bellowed when she raised her hands and begged incoherently. "You won't take my money, so what am I supposed to do?"

"Don't," she choked. "I'm off a half an hour ago. I can't process the transaction..."

"You will," he snarled at her, sweat beading on his face. "You will. You bitches are all the same. In the end, you want it."

"Please," she sobbed. "I'm just making a living."

"Whore!" he screamed, and stopped fumbling with his pants to kick her.

Time for Iridium to show herself.

"Hey," she said, stepping into view. "She's got a job, at least. What do you have to show for yourself, pencilneck?"

He pointed the Talon cutter at Iridium. "Fuck off. This doesn't concern you."

The prostitute saw Iridium and started screaming afresh. "Please help me! He didn't pay. He cut me up and he's going to hurt me!"

"That true?" Iridium asked the man.

"Who cares?" he spat. "What does a hero know about hookers? Keep your middle-class Corp ass out of this, you little bitch."

"Sex workers must present valid ID at all times, as well as proof of health," Iridium recited. Thank Christo she'd paid attention in Heroic Law instead of cheating her way through like she had with Extrahuman Ethics. "If they are not accompanied by a licensed business manager—colloquially known as a pimp—and if their mandatory eight-hour shift has ended, it is illegal to process a business transaction, and their license may be forfeit."

"I'll cut you up if you don't shut your mouth," the man growled. "You think this sorry sack is the first bitch who's said no to me?"

Iridium looked at the sobbing woman and the grin on the man's face.

"You're done," she said, and was almost surprised at how cold her voice came out.

The man was surprised, too, because he blinked and started for Iridium. "You need to learn to watch your mouth!"

"And since you just threatened me, while I'm acting in my official capacity," Iridium said, dropping back to a fighting stance, "I can do whatever I need to pacify you, all without repercussions."

"I'm going to shut that mouth of yours," he sneered.

She dropped her gaze to the girl on the ground. "You might want to run."

The girl jumped up and stumbled away down the nearest alley. Iridium turned her attention back to the man with the Talon cutter. "I'm Iridium," she said conversationally. "I should ask your name, seeing as how I'm about to beat you unconscious."

"I'm Paul Collins. And after I've cut you, little girl, I'm going to fuck you." He grinned. "You're not the youngest I've ever caught, but you're definitely the prettiest."

Iridium felt the cold stealing over her again, almost as if she were wrapped in one of Jet's creepers. She knew, in that moment, that Paul Collins would never face justice in the way the Academy taught it. Prostitutes couldn't testify in open court. In Alleytown, there were probably a hundred Paul Collinses.

No one saw them. No one wanted to see. Jet and the others were exactly what Night had said to her that day in the hallway: poses and public faces. That was all the Academy wanted her to be. Corp pretended this dirty alley, this man with a blade, didn't exist.

And that meant his victims didn't, either. And it wasn't right, wasn't *fair*.

Iridium suddenly understood exactly why her father had walked out on the Squadron.

Paul Collins was on top of her.

Iridium fell for the second time that day, smelling his breath as she hit the ground. It was slightly stale, like warm beer.

"Very pretty," he whispered, clutching at her, ripping her unikilt.

Iridium strobed Paul Collins. She strobed him over and over, until he let go of her. Until he dropped the Talon.

Until he couldn't do anything except scream.

And even when he stopped screaming, she kept strobing him.

They'd have no choice but to see, now. She'd dragged it into the Light.

So why did she still feel so cold?

When Collins was still, Iridium grabbed him in a medic

carry and followed the faded signs to the police precinct for Grid 23. Before she could mount the steps to the office, a pair of officers came running toward her, their faces crinkling in disgust when Iridium dropped the burned, bloody mess at their feet.

"What the hell happened to him?" one officer asked. He didn't seem angry to see Iridium, a hero in his precinct; that was something, at least.

Now she just had to see how he felt about a dead body.

"Him?" Iridium said. She shook all over, but with a deep breath she stilled herself and looked the police officer in the eye. "Justice."

CHAPTER 56

JET

It's unfortunate that so many with special abilities feel the need to work outside the law, turning extrahuman against extrahuman. The Academy exists to stamp out such dangerous thinking and turn tomorrow's vigilante into today's protector.

Night, in an address to the
Concerned Parents of New Chicago

Jet's feet hurt from pacing so long.

She stared at the closed door, wishing for the zillionth time that Sensor Girl was with her so she could hear what was being said inside.

Iridium had been in the conference room for three hours. The Containment officers had dragged her in, still in her torn unikilt, her hands trapped inside stun-cuffs, her eyes glazed. All of the Academy superiors had already jammed inside the room, from the twelve proctors to the head instructors to the Superintendent himself. And then the suits from Corp had arrived, their faces stark, their spines rigid.

And Jet waited.

At least Iri hadn't been hurt, she thought yet again. And there were no media. Small favors.

Two Runners had tried to get Jet to leave, to go to class, to eat something, to rest in her room. She'd ignored them until one dared lay a hand on her shoulder. Then she'd allowed a creeper out to play. The Runner had paled and done as his title suggested.

Iri was going to be okay. She had to be okay.

Jet wrapped her arms around herself, shivered. Light, all of the blood. Jet had been sure it was Iridium's, when she and Night and the Superintendent had found her at the police station... until Jet had seen the man's body. Iri had killed him.

Heroes don't kill.

But this was Iri...

Her head throbbed when she tried to make sense of it, so she stopped thinking about it.

A short eternity later, the door opened. Iridium was marched out, still in her cuffs. Jet tried to catch her eye, tried to stop the Containment unit, but they bulldozed past her like she was insignificant.

A shadow.

Out came the suits, looking stern and self-important. Then the Superintendent and the other Academy officials. Last one out was Night.

"Sir," Jet said to him as the others filed past. "What did they decide?"

Night's jaw clenched. "Therapy."

Jet's breath caught in her throat. "No," she whispered. "No, they can't. They can't do that to her." She saw Dawnlighter, the Stepford Superhero; saw Frostbite with his impotent rage. "Not Iri."

"Yes," he snapped, and for a blistering moment, his fury rolled over Jet and evaporated her horror. "Damn it!" He slammed his fist against the wall; overhead, the lights died.

Jet bit back a cry as her optiframes irised to allow for night vision. Nothing to panic over. She had her goggles. She had her earpiece. She was safe from the Shadow.

"Sir," she said, touching his arm, "can't you appeal? Intervene?"

He pulled his arm from her grasp. "Don't you think I tried that? They wouldn't hear of it. Bad press, they said. All this work, all this time, wasted, because they're worried about the media. The media!" He bellowed the word and slammed his fist against the wall again.

"But Therapy will kill her," Jet whispered.

"No, it'll leave her *alive*," he snarled, as if he were as offended by the notion of a scooped-out version of Iri as Jet was. "She couldn't follow procedure this *one* time, play the wooden soldier when it mattered most. Damn her! That stupid bitch!"

"That bitch is my *friend*," Jet snarled, forgetting to be awed by his power or cowed by his ire. "And I won't stand here and listen to you insult her."

Night froze, his shadowed face a twisted mask of rage. And then, incongruously, he started to laugh. "And what can *you* do about it, Joan? What makes you think that *you* can defy the will of the Academy and Corp?"

"I won't let them destroy her," she vowed. With that, Jet spun on her heel and marched out the door, rushing to catch up to the cold men in their proper suits.

When she reached them, they almost refused to listen to her. But she was Jet, the darling of the Academy and, more important, of the press. So they listened to her words.

And to her wild suggestion.

And after a short deliberation, they agreed to her request.

CHAPTER 57

IRIDIUM

For a hero, there is no acceptable shade of gray. There are only shades of justice. Black, and white.

Captain Colossal, Squadron member for
New York Metropolis

After a day and a night of being handcuffed to the wall of her cell, Iridium watched the door roll back to reveal two Containment officers. "Clean her up," the man told the woman. "Get the blood off. There are cameras out there."

"Who cares about some rabid?" the woman muttered, scrubbing at Iridium's face and neck with a sanitary cloth.

"That Shadow bitch called the press in," said the Containment officer. "Can you believe that shit?"

Iridium blinked. Jet was holding a press conference?

She didn't know why she was surprised . . . of course Jet would be selling herself. Branding. The new Hero of New Chicago, protector of average rapists against big bad rabids.

The Containment officer threw a pair of prison blues at Iridium's feet. "When you're released from the cuffs, you'll change. Then you'll be prepped for transport to your cell at Blackbird."

"Jail?" Iridium said, stunned. She composed herself in the next second, so they wouldn't know how shocked she was that she wasn't just going upstairs to have holes poked in her brain for the rest of her natural life.

"Better than you deserve," said the male officer. The door swished shut. A moment later, Iridium's cuffs released. She dropped her arms, her muscles crying.

After she'd put on the rough cotton inmate's uniform, the door opened again.

"Hey!" Iridium yelled. "I'm not dressed!"

Instead of the Containment team, Jet stood in the opening.

Iridium curled her lip back. "You."

"I don't have much time," Jet said. "I had your guards paged away to deal with the crowd outside, but they'll be back."

"Come down here to gloat over a job well done?" Iridium said, zipping the jumpsuit over her bra.

"Callie . . ." Jet pressed her hands over her face. "Why'd it have to be this way? Why couldn't you have done the right thing?"

"See, Jet," Iridium said, crossing her arms, "I *did* do the right thing. I know it, because all the time I've been in this cell, I haven't felt one thin drop of regret for Paul Collins."

"You just proved everyone right," Jet said. "You proved you're like your father."

"Mutual," said Iridium. "You proved everyone right too."

Jet blinked behind her goggles. "Excuse me?"

"You proved that you're a lapdog who parrots the party line no matter what. Who sells out her friends for TV ratings and who will never, ever be able to grow a backbone and think for herself." Iridium stepped closer to Jet, feeling her power grow hot inside her. "And that's why I'm not sorry about this. At all."

"You're wrong..." Jet started, but Iridium made her move.

She strobed Jet in the face, the other girl's goggles flying clean off her head from the force of the blast. Jet crumpled, groaning, red outlines on her cheeks and forehead where the goggles had been.

"I'm not like my father," Iridium whispered. "I'm better than him. You'll never catch me, Joannie."

"You...can't...do this," Jet groaned.

"Oh, I think I can. I think a pack of innocent reporters standing around will dissuade the Squadron from any hasty action," Iridium said as the alarms began to whoop.

"Iri," Jet called after her, but Iridium ignored her.

She stepped out of her cell.

This was the moment. If Jet was quick, tough, and smart like they'd tried to teach her, all she had to do was send a creeper. Iridium was exhausted and surrounded by hostile extrahumans. Jet had her chance.

The darkness never came.

Iridium turned back, once. "That's what I thought. Be seeing you, Jet."

Iridium shut the door on her former friend and walked toward the light.

CHAPTER 58

JET

Heroes must always have someone to play the villain.
Otherwise, the world would have no use for them.

Lester Bradford, statement made during
sentencing at his felony trial

On the Academy rooftop, Jet stared into the distance as the sun began its ascent. She'd been there all night, watching the stars attempt to twinkle through the haze of pollution that shrouded New Chicago. But no matter how brightly the pinpricks of light shone, they didn't make a dent in the darkness.

At night, shadows reigned supreme.

But the dawn was coming, and with it a new day . . . and with that would come the repercussions for Jet's actions. It had been her suggestion—her demand—that Iridium be sent to Blackbird instead of Therapy. It had been her weakness that had allowed Iridium to slip away from the Academy, and from justice.

For all Corp knew, Jet had arranged to have Iri escape from the moment she'd slain Paul Collins.

Snarling, Jet let fly a blast of Shadow. It curved into the nighttime sky and obliterated the few stars that had gamely tried to overcome the darkness. A flicker of white, quickly swallowed by black.

Damn her! How could she have done this to Jet? How could she have thumbed her nose at them all and just disappeared? Heroes don't do that!

But Iridium had proven she was no hero. She was rabid, like her father before her.

Jet sank to the floor, slowly, clenched her fists, and slammed them against her thighs as she knelt before the rising sun as if offering a penance to the Light, or to Jehovah, or any deity that actually cared.

How could Callie have killed that man? Jet couldn't understand; the very concept of a hero killing anyone was utterly alien. Yes, in battle there were casualties on both sides, but those were justifiable. In battle, in the war against evil and injustice, people got hurt, and sometimes, accidents happened.

But Iridium had killed him in cold blood. She could have stopped herself. *Should* have stopped herself.

From the darkness of her mind, Jet heard laughter. She frowned, adjusted the white-noise frequency in her earpiece.

How do you even think with that thing in your ear? Iri's voice was smooth and taunting, like white chocolate.

Callie, how could you murder that man?

Iri laughed. *I haven't felt one thin drop of regret for Paul Collins.*

Jet knew. And it broke her heart.

I'm not sorry about this, Iridium whispered. *At all.*

Jet shrieked her rage and her sorrow to the sky, and in her mind, the voices giggled. Eventually, her voice gave out and she broke off, panting, hearing her cry echo and fade away.

"I thought I'd find you here."

Her back stiffened, and she pointedly refused to turn around to face Night. She heard him approach, then halt just behind her, to her left.

"You should be sleeping. Tomorrow's a big day. First the tribunal for you, and then, assuming they don't expel you, you're off to graduation." Night snorted. "Little worry about expulsion, though. Not while you're the apple of Corp's eye and slated to be the Hero of New Chicago."

She said nothing as she rose to her feet. She wouldn't look at him.

Silence stretched between them as the sun rained its brilliance on the city.

"Nevertheless," Night finally said, "you're still ass deep in alligators. Both Corp and the Academy are desperate for a scapegoat, just in case their media damage control fails. I'm here to officially read you the riot act."

She lifted her chin. "I'm fully aware that if Iridium's escape ever makes the news, my career will be over. Sir."

"If she's anything like her father," Night said dryly, "escaping from lockup will be the least of her crimes. I give her three months before she starts to act outside of the law."

At that, she turned to face her mentor. "She wouldn't," Jet insisted.

"Believe me, I know the Bradford family all too well." Beneath his cowl, Night's eyes gleamed, perhaps with amusement. "Luster was already doing the things he was noted for as Arclight, even when he was still in the Squadron. Small things. Starting with disregarding procedure. Going off half-cocked. Bad-mouthing the Academy, the Squadron, even Corp. Sound like anyone you know?"

Jet flinched.

"She's as arrogant as her father ever was," Night said, walking to stand next to Jet. He, too, stared at the lightening sky. "Thinks she's above everyone and everything around her. Can't be bothered with following the rules when they're inconvenient."

"She's always had a problem with that," Jet murmured.

"Too smart for her own good," Night said, nodding at her. "Just like her father. They get bored. They act out. Iridium will follow in her father's footsteps. You can count on it."

Jet said quietly, "And me, sir? Will I follow in my father's footsteps?"

After a pause, Night said, "Blackout was a fine hero." He turned to look at the New Chicago skyline, and when he next spoke, his voice was distant, dreamlike. "One of the best. He did things with Shadow that were groundbreaking. He had no fear, and he was ready to sacrifice himself to help others."

Jet rubbed her arms, thinking about her father and how he'd looked when he'd given her mother one final squeeze. "Until the Shadow started speaking to him."

"All powers have a weakness, Joan," Night said. "Ours just happens to be more...noticeable."

She frowned as she considered his words. It had never occurred to her that other extrahumans had their own shadows to overcome. "What about Lighters? What's their weakness?"

"Pride."

Jet thought about that, then slowly nodded.

"You're in trouble, Jet. Make no mistake about that." Night's voice was full of reproach, and Jet bit her lip, hung her head low. He said, "You let your feelings get in the way of following procedure."

"I know, sir. But it was Iri."

"Iridium. No nicknames, Joan. No vestiges of friendship. That's all dead and gone now, like the man she slaughtered."

"He was a rapist," Jet said, lifting her head to see the

sun reaching higher. "She said he was hurting a woman, had hurt lots of women."

"And that gave her the right to play Jehovah?" Night snorted. "Pride, Jet. Arrogance. All Light powers stink of it. She's no different. And now, thanks to her, you may lose everything we've worked for."

Glaring at the sunrise, Jet clenched her fist. An inky stain spread over her fingers. "How do I make this right?"

"You graduate tomorrow. You've already interviewed with the Squadron recruiter, so all that's left is the waiting. Once you get assigned, your first duty will be to this city— your sponsor as well as your protectorate. You'll do what you're told. You'll save lives. You'll keep Corp happy, and will be the perfect Academy graduate. And when Iridium shows up, you'll strike."

"You're so sure she's going rabid," Jet said, nostrils flaring. "She could just go rogue, be a vigilante."

"And is that any better?"

Although her heart screamed yes, that made all the difference in the world, she said what the Academy had taught her: "No. Not at all."

Iridium whispered, *You proved that you're a lapdog who parrots the party line no matter what.*

She thinks I sold her out. Jet bared her teeth in a silent scream. *She really thought all I cared about was getting press. It never occurred to her that I'd helped her.*

"It doesn't matter," Jet said—maybe to Iridium, maybe to Night. "She's shown her true colors."

You'll never, ever be able to grow a backbone and think for yourself.

And that's where you're wrong, Jet vowed. "I'll do what I have to do."

"You'll find her, Jet."

She stared out into the dawn, the light and color playing in the sky as if in tribute to Iridium. "I will. A hero never quits."

A hero whose entire time at the Academy was spent by having everyone protect her from the things that went bump in the night. From the boogeyman in the shadows. From the voices.

From life.

She thought of Iri, that day long ago, telling Jet to stand up to Dawnlighter, and that if anyone gave Jet any shit, Iri would punch their faces in.

Jet took a deep breath, felt it fill her, cleanse her. She exhaled, shedding her worries, her fears. Her doubts.

She was done needing protection.

"However long it takes, I promise, I'll bring Iridium back home." Her eyes teared as she stared into the sun and refused to look away. "And justice will be served."

Night put his gauntleted hand on her shoulder. "It will, little Shadow. This I promise you. There will be a day of reckoning. And then, the Light will fall before the Shadow."

His words made her tremble with anticipation, and for the first time in days, Jet allowed herself to smile.

The sun rose, and a new era had begun.

NOW

CHAPTER 59

JET

*Do extrahumans have a choice in their role? Is it
destiny? A calling? Or something else, something that
drives them to put aside personal gain and dedicate
their lives to helping others?*

Lynda Kidder, "Origins: Part One,"
New Chicago Tribune, March 26, 2112

When Jet woke up, she was on the floor, on her side,
with her arms pinned behind her. It took her a moment to realize she was awake; her thoughts felt sluggish,
almost soupy, and she had to blink a few times before she
could focus. That didn't help much; all she saw was a gray
wall, very close to her face.

Floor, she thought dimly. *Why am I on the floor?*

"About time," someone said, the voice disembodied.
Floating. But not one of her Shadow voices; this one she
heard with her ears. "Thought you were going to sleep
through all the waiting."

Jet blinked again, connected the rasping voice to a
name. "Iridium?"

"Yeah."

She sat up quickly, steeling herself to fight—and then collapsed back down with a groan, squeezing her eyes shut to keep the world from spinning.

"Forgot to tell you," Iridium said. "Stun-cuffs. You want to move slow, or you'll puke all over yourself. Stink up the place in a big way."

"Go ahead," Jet grated between clenched teeth. "Gloat."

"Who, me? Sort of the pot calling the kettle black, don't you think?"

"What are you talking about?"

She heard soft laughter—a bitter sound, completely without mirth. "I'm just as much the trussed-up turkey as you are, Joannie."

Jet sat up again, much slower this time, and was relieved when she was able to hold her head up without feeling like her guts would spill out of her mouth. The wall in front of her was barren, just a long slab of gray, or maybe steel. Hard to tell in the poor lighting. She inched her way around, turning slowly until she could see the rest of the small room—a cell, really, with one door and no windows. There was just enough room for her . . . and Iridium.

Jet stared coldly at the woman across from her. And then blinked. Iri looked terrible. Sure, her posture was all arrogance: seated on the floor, she slouched against the wall like a resentful teenager. But her face told a different story. A nasty bruise, swollen to an impressive egg, discolored Iri's forehead. Her eyes, usually so sharp and almost icy blue, were out of focus, watery. Framing her ashen face, Iri's black hair stuck to her brow and cheeks in tangled clumps.

And yes, her arms were bound behind her back. Jet was able to make out the silver-and-electric gleam of the stun-cuffs.

"Yeah, I know," Iridium said, smiling thinly. "But you should see the other guy."

"He look worse than you?"

"He will when I'm done with him."

It was a good act. Jet almost believed her—that she really had been captured and thrown in here with Jet. But this was Iridium. She lied. She cheated. She hit you when you were down. Jet was too exhausted, mentally and physically, to play the game. At least there was some light in the small room; without her goggles or her comlink, the way she was feeling would have made her a punching bag for the Shadow voices.

Small favors. "What do you want, Iridium?"

"Want?" Iridium barked out a harsh laugh. "I want to get the fuck out of here and wrap my hands around Taser's neck. Christo, you think I'm junked enough to slap a pair of working cuffs onto myself, just to play you?" She shook her head. "I'm trapped here, just like you are."

Impossible, part of Jet's mind declared. *Iridium is a rabid. You can't believe anything she says.*

But that was only a small part of her mind, the part that parroted the Academy Mission Statement and insisted on duty before all else. Duty first. Always. The part that made her smile when she thought of all the good she was doing, of all the people she was helping. Of how wonderful it was to be a hero and have Corp behind her and beside her.

The rest of Jet's mind—the memory of the girl she'd used to be, the part that feared the dark because she knew it had teeth, that longed for the happily-ever-afters in her romance novels and that thought, sometimes, she didn't know who she was anymore—whispered that Iri was telling the truth.

Uneasy, Jet said, "Yeah, I just bet. Your man's the one who tagged me."

"We seem to have had a parting of company," Iridium said, "considering he's the one who flipped on me. Used my own damn neural inhibitor on me, the bastard."

"Those are illegal."

"Yeah, I'm learning the error of my ways. Crime doesn't pay. Blah, blah." Iridium paused. In the dim light, she looked tired, her face drawn and pale. "My own damn fault. It's what I get for trusting anyone again."

That stung. Jet said, "I trusted you too."

Iridium's mouth pulled into an ugly smirk. "You'd a hell of a way of showing it. How long did it take you to decide to sell me out to Corp?"

Just hearing that name set off warning bells in Jet's mind. "You can't possibly understand."

"Understand what? That you traded our friendship for herodom?"

"Iri—"

"*No.* Only my friends call me that. You don't get to do that anymore."

"Fine. Iridium. You don't understand what happened back then."

"Right, so says the high-and-mighty Jet, Lady of Shadows, the Hero of New Chicago." Iridium snorted her derision. "You're so fucking pretentious, acting like you didn't stab me in the back five years ago."

"And you're so damn self-centered," Jet said, shaking her head, feeling anger and sadness warring in her heart.

Iridium rolled her eyes. "Coming from you, that's really something."

"Damn it, Iri, I *helped* you!"

"You got my ass sentenced to Blackbird! How's that defined as help, even in the loosest sense of the word?"

"You have no idea what you're talking about," Jet growled, remembering how she'd begged Night, pleaded with him to interfere on that fateful day, and how he'd stood there and scorned her.

"Don't I?" Iridium sneered. "You were supposed to have my back, Joan! We were partners. Fuck that—we were *friends*. Remember that? How many times did I stand up for you at Academy? How much trouble did I get into, all because I had to take care of you?"

"I never asked you to take care of me!"

"But you walked away from our friendship, all because of the Academy and Corp!"

"I did what I did *because* we were friends," Jet shouted, "because someone had to intervene on your behalf. And damn it all to Darkness, Callie, it was the best I could do! It was still better than what they wanted to do to you!"

Iridium's mouth opened, a retort on her tongue, but then she seemed to really hear Jet's words, and she paused. "You're the one who got me sentenced to Blackbird," she said.

"Yes."

"And you're sitting here now, telling me that was helping me?"

Jet sighed. "Yes."

"And I'm supposed to believe that?"

"Frankly, I don't care if you believe it or not. It's true." Jet lowered her voice, said, "And when you escaped, they made my life a living nightmare. They never let me forget that you were my fault."

"Aw, poor little hero. That's what they were holding over you all this time? A little fubar like that was enough to keep you leashed and barking when they said 'dog'?"

"No." Jet closed her eyes. "What's done is done, Callie."

"Yeah, right. Done, my ass. You can't wait to bust out of here and drag me to the EC. Crow to the media about how you'd finally corrected your mistake from five years ago!"

"A week ago," Jet said softly, "you would have been right. Even earlier today, you would have been right."

Maybe Iridium heard something in her voice, because she stopped hurling accusations at Jet, barbs that cut into her and bled her soul.

Light, how long have I been their puppet?

"Jet?"

"They got into my mind," she whispered. "They did something to me, and—oh Light, they did something to my mind. I can't even say their name without thinking happy thoughts, and even as I'm saying this, I still want to serve them and be the hero and get a pat on the head!" She was shouting by then, but she couldn't stop, couldn't hold back her rage. "They brainwashed me so completely that I can't even say their name when I want to curse them all to Darkness!"

Her words echoed in the still air, and she panted, trying to regain some semblance of control.

Iridium broke the silence. "What happened, Jet?"

Not daring to open her eyes, Jet told her about Night putting her on the hunt for Lynda Kidder—about Frostbite's hostile help, about Martin Moore and what he and Everyman had done to the reporter. About how she was instructed to back up the claim that the Undergoths, with Iri's help, had tortured and murdered Kidder. About her last call with Night. About Everyman having an agreement with—

Her brain caught fire.

Jet doubled over, almost bit through her lip to keep from screaming as searing pain stole her thoughts.

Slowly, the agony faded, leaving behind a steady ache in her temples. Jet opened her eyes, blinked back tears. She was curled up on her side, and her throat hurt.

"Joannie?" Iri's voice, soft and surprisingly tender. "Can you hear me?"

"Yeah." She swallowed, winced from the rawness. She must have screamed after all.

"I think I know how they did it."

Jet whipped her head around to stare at Iri, then almost vomited from the motion. Damned stun-cuffs. She ground out, "How?"

"Your comlink."

Jet's throat tightened, and she sucked in a labored

breath. When she'd had the first...episode...in her apartment, hadn't she wanted to shove the earpiece into place? Hadn't she had a wild urge to tuck the comlink into her ear and tap it on?

"Before I took down Ops," Iridium said, "I saw hundreds of frequencies broadcasting. Not receiving. Not connected to the main network."

Jet blinked at Iridium, not wanting to understand.

"Don't you get it?" Iri said. "They *have* been brainwashing you—really brainwashing you—and the Squadron... shit, even the students at Academy. For years. Not counting those of us who never wore the damned earpiece, I guess..."

Iridium kept talking, but Jet didn't hear her.

"You missed part of the uniform," Night says that day back in Second Year. "The most important part."

Oh Light, no.

Something else gleams at the bottom of the plastic wrapping. Jet reaches into the bag and scoops up a metallic earpiece.

Had he known, back then?

"When you're old enough to go on missions, the comlink will connect you directly to Ops."

Had Night known what he was giving her? What he was sentencing her to? She'd thought he was her savior, the man who'd stopped the voices, the Shadow power who'd lived without losing his mind. Her hope for salvation.

"I was thirteen," Jet whispered.

"I understand your rage," Night says to her just earlier today, his voice quiet, and utterly terrifying. "Trust me, I understand. And a reckoning will come."

Jet's stomach lurched, and she retched in the corner of the tiny room.

"Great," she heard Iridium say over the sound of her heaving. "Trapped was bad. Trapped and stinking of puke is worse."

When Jet finished, she rose to her knees. Shaking. Tears

streaming down her face. And so much hatred in her that her heart must have shriveled and died. "When we get out of here," she hissed, "someone's going to answer for this."

"Sounds good to me. Teensy problem, though."

Jet looked at Iridium's smug mouth, her battered face. "We're still in stun-cuffs, in a closet."

"Well," Jet said, "you're the genius, and I'm the hero. We'll figure something out."

"I prefer 'evil genius.'"

"So that makes me the tortured hero."

"Kook."

"Criminal."

The words came easily, naturally. Iri grinned, and so did Jet, and there in the dimly lit room, five years of hatred began to unwind.

"So," Iri said, "a plan. We bust out of here, kill Taser, and tell all to the press."

"That's a plan?"

"The foundation of one."

"Has problems," Jet said. "The killing, for one."

"Maiming, then. He's in for a world of hurt. I'm going to make him sorry his daddy ever laid eyes on his mother."

"Hey. You took down Ops?"

"Yeah."

Jet remembered the shrilling alarm from her earpiece. "You officially get to be 'evil genius.'"

Iri grinned at her.

"Can you touch your power at all?"

"Not even enough to make the bulb overhead go up a watt. You?"

Jet reached inside, tried to touch the part of her that was one with the shadows, but it slipped through her fingers like sand. "No. Any way to get the cuffs off?"

"Sure. With the key."

"You're real helpful."

"Modesty's my best quality."

Jet opened her mouth, but that was when the door opened. A figure stood framed in the doorway, sporting tactical gear, a black stocking over his face and welding goggles over his eyes. Jet recognized the man she'd thought was Iridium's lackey, and she narrowed her eyes at him.

"Ladies," he said. "Glad to see you two getting along so famously. Aren't you glad I brought you together?"

CHAPTER 60

IRIDIUM

Betrayal of a cohort is unusual in supervillain circles. But when it comes, it is swift, deadly, and leaves broken hearts and bodies in its wake.

Lynda Kidder, "Flight of the Blackbird,"
New Chicago Tribune, July 2, 2112

Iridium looked up into Taser's face, saw her own bloody mess reflected in his goggles.

She tried to struggle up, but vertigo overcame her. "I'm going to kill you," she ground out from the floor.

"I'm just doing my job, sweetheart," Taser said, stepping back as if her glare could sear him. "You can't blame me for your mistakes."

"The only mistake I made was not dumping you head-first off that rooftop," Iridium snarled. "You planned to be there, with the Undergoths. They sent me right to you. You *used* me, is what's the worst."

Taser laughed. "You're being pretty easy on yourself, doll. You swallowed my origin story. You let me into your sanctuary, you told me your secrets, you left me with the opportunity to neutralize you, all because you *trusted* me. That's not a mistake, Iridium—that's just sloppy."

There was a note of reproach in his voice, and he didn't appear to be mocking her, which only pissed Iridium off more. "I never trusted you, Taser," she lied. "I just never thought you were a threat to me. You're *pathetic*."

He shook his head. "Now, that isn't true. You left me alone in your warehouse. You trusted me, if only a little. But it was there. Weakness."

"Trust isn't weakness," said Iridium. "Letting trust blind you is. And I was never blind, Taser."

"Oh yeah? Then how come you're trussed up in here?"

Jet looked at Iridium. "You left him *alone*? In your *house*?"

"Shut up, Joan," Iridium said wearily. "All that matters now is that we're seeing his real face." She looked back at Taser. "Treacherous, and crazy."

"Crazy?" Taser laughed softly. "You're one to talk, Iridium. I don't dress up in a wig and go visit my father every week because I can't let go. I don't think that Corp can be knocked out by a stupid spy-novel scheme."

"Not nearly as stupid as pissing me off," she snarled, feeling impotent and hating it. "You seemed pretty keen on the idea."

"I was paid to be. Just like I was paid to get close to Joan." He turned to face Jet, but he kept speaking to Iridium. "She was harder than you, Iridium. Mistrustful. Totally living in a world of her own creation. That ought to tell you something."

Jet spluttered, "What are you talking about? Until the tunnels, I'd never seen you before."

He looked at Jet, long and hard. "You so sure, honey? You need me to take off the mask? Really? Maybe tell you again about how I'd fallen for you when you saved me and the others from Crusher Jones all those years ago?"

Iridium saw the blood drain from Jet's face. Joan whispered, "Bruce?"

Taser doffed an imaginary cap. "Hi, honey. Was it good for you too?"

"You played me." Jet's voice was so low, Iridium could barely catch the words. "I let you in, trusted you. And you played me."

"Like a violin. Don't feel too bad. You couldn't help but feel a tingle every time we touched." He rubbed his fingers together, and through his gloves, sparks flew. "Perk of working with electricity."

Jet gasped, then let out her breath in a long hiss. "You *made* me feel that way?"

"Oh, don't get all high-and-mighty, honey. You sure didn't complain last night, when I made you see stars... what was it, three times? Or four? I sort of lost count."

"You *bastard*..."

Iridium stared at Jet. "You let him into your *bed*?" *Oh, Christo.* In that moment, her slip of leaving Taser to steal her neural inhibitor seemed minor. Joan would never recover from something like that. Iridium's gut knifed, thinking of what it must feel like to know the man in your bed was scheming to kill you, or worse.

Jet ignored her, said to Taser, "I trusted you."

"Lesson learned, eh, darlin'?" He shook his head. "That goes for both of you. You want to survive, you have to stop trusting. Heh, trust me on that."

"I swear," Jet whispered, her slight body trembling, "when I get out of here, I'm going to make you regret using me. I swear it."

"You're going to have to wait in line," Iridium snarled. "Let me guess, Taser—you're with Everyman?"

He snorted. "Not hardly. They hate anyone with powers, Iridium. That includes me."

"Then who?" Iridium said.

"Sorry, I'm not going to blab about who's employing me. Merc code. I do have a system I follow, you know."

"Mercenary," Jet said tightly. "I should have made you. I should have—"

"Yeah, well, you didn't," said Taser, crossing his arms. "You expected me to be strong and true, like in those damn novels you're always reading. And Iridium expected me to be cruel but pure-hearted, like her precious daddy."

"Shut up," Jet muttered. "Just shut *up*."

"Oh, ignore him," Iridium said. Taser might have worked under Jet's skin, but if her five years away from Corp had taught Iridium anything, it was adaptability. "He's just trying to upset us so we're nice and compliant when his boss shows up."

"Got me there," said Taser, shrugging.

"You are such a sanctimonious piece of crap," Iridium hissed. "How could you ever think I bought your line?"

"Didn't you tell me yourself that arrogance is death?" Taser said mildly. "I never assumed anything more than that I'd finish my job. You two were both so desperate for something that you didn't care what I really was. And you, Iridium—you never assumed I was a threat. Arrogance. And you paid."

Iridium fell silent.

"You're scum," Jet muttered.

He cocked his head. "I did my job, Jet. Nothing more, nothing less."

"Who's your boss?" Iridium snarled. "Are they going to ramble on for as long as you have?"

"He'll be here shortly," said Taser, glancing at his wristlet. "And my job goes no further than that. You've both been delivered, on time. That's all I care about."

"Delivered where? Come on," Iridium drawled, "this is the part where you reveal everything."

He cocked his head. "You really want to know? You're in the Academy, in the old meditation room. Specifically, the storage closet." He chuckled. "Want to take bets on whether a hero's going to walk through that door and save you? Oh, wait—the heroes are a little tied up, aren't they, Iridium?"

Her lip curled, but she said nothing.

"Well, ladies, I've got to go. It's been a pleasure working with you both—a real pleasure, in Joan's case."

"Bastard," Jet spat.

"And Callie," said Taser, her name sounding like a slur, "if you ever get past your daddy issues and that raging ego, we may really have something."

His comm beeped, and he tapped it. "I understand, sir. Yes. Yes, everything is in order." He turned and gave Iridium and Jet a salute. "And now I must bid you farewell. See you around, ladies."

The door behind Taser slid open before he could key it.

"Not so fast," said Night.

CHAPTER 61

JET

Eventually, the supervillain will reveal all to the superhero. Their egos won't allow for anything else.
Lynda Kidder, "Flight of the Blackbird,"
New Chicago Tribune, July 2, 2112

Jet had truly thought this day couldn't get any worse when Taser revealed himself as Bruce—her *Runner,* oh Light, her *freaking Runner,* how could she have been so stupid?

But then she heard Night's voice, and she looked past Bruce—no, Taser; Bruce was a lie—and saw her mentor looming behind the merc, larger than life, dressed as a hero in his battlesuit, the body armor gleaming blackly.

At first, her heart leapt for joy. Night had found them! He'd free them, and together they'd take down Taser.

But then he said to Taser, "Bring them in for me while I get the machine ready," and Jet's world lurched to the left.

She must have said something aloud, because Night

turned to regard her. She couldn't see his eyes beneath his cowl, but she thought she saw something gleam in the shadows of his face. "Patience, Jet. The day of reckoning is at hand."

" 'Reckoning?' " That was Iridium, all bluster and fury. "What the fuck are you talking about?"

"Such a mouth on you. Heroes have better manners." Night smiled thinly. "But you're no hero, are you, Iridium? You're a selfish Light power, same as your father."

"You shut up about my father!"

"She's got daddy issues," Taser said.

"Indeed." He glanced at Jet again, who shivered when Night's smile bloomed into a feral grin. "But don't we all?"

"Yeah, whatever. Who do I bring in first?"

"Iridium. Strap her to the base." Night's gaze remained on Jet, who couldn't move. This wasn't happening.

Light, please, this can't be happening. Not Night.

Not him.

Taser said, "Want the neural inhibitor on her?"

"That would defeat the entire purpose. But I suggest you keep the cuffs on her, unless you like it hot."

"Not in this context. Come on, darlin'," Taser said to Iridium. "On your feet."

"Blow me," Iri growled.

Taser chuckled. "I'm happy to carry you like the damsel in distress that you are. Or you can walk under your own wobbly power. Up to you."

Iridium slowly got to her feet. "I swear to high heaven, I'm going to kill you."

"Yeah, yeah. Insert idle threat here. Move it, Callie. And if you think about getting ornery, I'll prod you like cattle." Sparks jumped from his fingertips.

Iri let loose a string of curses that nearly set Jet's ears on fire, but she grudgingly walked out of the room, sparing Night a scathing look of pure hatred before she strode out of Jet's view. Taser sauntered after her, all lazy confidence.

Jet grimaced as she watched them go. Light, she'd let that man into her bed. Into her heart.

She was a thrice-damned fool.

Night looked down at her, his cape billowing around his ankles. "This is it, Jet. The moment I've been waiting for. And I'm going to let you share it with me."

The world lurched again. Damn it, nothing made sense anymore. She whispered, "Sir?"

"We're done with all the politics, with all the rules, with all of Corp and its two-faced ideals and backhanded promises." His grin stretched into something horrific. "We're done with the Squadron playing the part of lapdog, with extrahumans bending over backward to gain public trust and corporate sponsorships. Done with looking the other way when Everyman bites. This will be the dawning of a new era, Jet. The era of Shadow."

"Sir," Jet said slowly, "you're talking blasphemy." And lunacy.

He chuckled at that, a dry, raspy sound, altogether unpleasant. "Corp has preached its gospel long enough."

Her head buzzed angrily, and she said, "You can't mean that. Corp stands for justice." She heard herself say the words, and she wanted to scream.

"Ah, Joan," Night said, laughing softly. "By now you know you're just parroting the party line, don't you?"

She did. But she couldn't help it.

"It's not your fault," he said, smiling at her—a gentle smile, like one she'd never seen on his face before. "The conditioning has been working on you for years. And being what you are, you were already primed before you ever put the comlink into your ear."

"You did this to me," she spat.

"Not at all. Corp did that to you. I merely gave you a way to block out the voices. You still hear them, don't you? Not Ops. The real voices. The ones that whisper from the dark. Whisper about the dark."

She swallowed thickly, refused to answer.

"Of course you do," he said, nodding. "That you're here shows me you've been fighting them even still. I'm proud of you, Joan. Very proud of you. Even though it's all for naught."

Part of her preened to hear such praise, even knowing that Night had set her and Iri up. And Jet hated herself for it. "Iridium took out Ops. I shouldn't still be..." She couldn't bear to say "brainwashed" aloud, so she shrugged.

"Oh, the other extrahumans are free, no doubt," Night said. "And what a mess Corp will have on its hands, trying to contain *that* situation. But you, Jet, you're a special case. You're used to hearing things. You can't turn off their conditioning just because their signal has been interrupted. I'm afraid you're doomed to go quite mad."

His words chilled her to the bone. But in her soul, she wasn't truly surprised.

Everyone knows what happens to Shadow powers. Eventually.

"Either you'll be a perpetual slave to Corp," Night said, "or you'll give in to the Shadow."

Either way, she lost.

Jet sucked in a breath, held her head high. "And here I thought, all this time, you were the one Shadow who'd escaped it." Say it aloud; give voice to it. "The one who stayed sane. You'd given me hope that maybe I wouldn't go crazy like..."

"Like your father? Mmm, well, these things happen. Genetics. It's how we're programmed, on the cellular level. When he killed your mother, he did it the same way you killed Lynda Kidder."

Jet's breath caught in her throat.

"Actually, I stand corrected. Not *exactly*. He did it all of his own accord. You I manipulated, to get you down into the tunnels. But you both used Shadow to squeeze the life out of your victims." He smiled thinly. "A signature move."

Through clenched teeth, Jet hissed, "Why? Why'd you send me after Kidder?"

"Why, to kill her, of course. I had to see if you would do what you needed to do to survive." The smile bloomed into something full and rotten. "And you did. Beautifully."

Fury seared her. Trembling with rage, she stared at the man she'd trusted and admired for ten years, her vision narrowing until all she could see was his cold smile, cast in shadow.

"Don't you see, Joan? You deserve to stand by my side. Not just acting as my hand, no, but standing with me as an equal." His teeth gleamed as he grinned.

"You're insane."

"No, Jet. I'm a visionary. Picture it: Corp is out of the picture for the moment. Between a number of the Squadron being trapped in the Rat Network with no Ops to maneuver them around and coordinate them, and no ultra-high-frequency happy thoughts beaming at the extrahumans, I'd say Corp's due for a bit of a revolution." He chuckled. "Just like Everyman predicted."

"You knew all along," Jet snarled. "Not just about Everyman taking Kidder, but about the serum they've created. You know what Everyman's looking to do against the extrahumans."

"Joan, who do you think allowed Moore to get the information in the first place?"

Outside of the room, Jet heard Iri shriek.

"Ah," Night said. "Sounds like your friend isn't using good manners."

"Let her go!"

"I can't do that. I've worked too long to set events into play to let it unravel now. Had my fingers in too many pies." Beneath his cowl, Night's eyes sparkled. "I made sure that Peter Ivanoff got caught for stealing Corp funds, that certain files were just within reach for Martin Moore to hack. And that was just to lead to chaos within the Academy and the Squadron. But the real plan's been under way ever since I became your mentor."

She narrowed her eyes. "The real plan?"

"Ever since I realized the scope of your powers, I've worked toward this day."

"I cast Shadow," she said, "same as you."

"No, little Shadow. I repel light. You absorb it."

She blinked, her surprise overriding her fury. "No, I cast Shadow."

"Merely a side effect of your true ability," he said with a snort. "I've known it ever since you tried to absorb my light. My life force, if you want to get melodramatic."

"Since I *what*? I never—"

"But you did," he insisted. "You were waiting for me to speak about mentoring you, and when I saw you there on the floor in the hallway, your eyes black, your face deathly pale, I knew the Shadow had you. And I felt for you, Joan," he said softly. "Truly, I did. So young, and already tortured by the voices. So I touched you, held your shoulders, tried to offer you comfort as the Shadow held you. And then you almost sucked me dry."

She couldn't breathe. "You're lying..."

"I'm not. It was such an odd sensation. Freezing cold, so cold that it seared me. And I felt myself dying, Joan. I felt you stealing my life. And around us, the shadows bloomed. My death was giving them life. Rather beautiful."

He had to be lying.

Night smiled, shook his head ruefully. "But I'd been around far too long to let myself get snuffed out by some preteen hero-in-training. I slapped you. And that was all it took. Just that little shock woke you up, and the Shadow let you go."

Jet trembled, wanting his words not to be true...but knowing in her heart that he was telling her the truth.

"Expelling Shadow is your body's way of processing the

energy," he said. "It's a waste product, if you will. Your true strength is absorbing light. And when I realized that, everything started to fall into place. That was when I started grooming you, as well as your friend."

"My . . . ?"

"Iridium."

"Damn it, leave Iri out of this. Let her go!"

"Such a fragile bond," Night said drolly. "They tell us there's no place for friendship if you're a hero. But they're wrong. Friends keep you strong. Friends encourage you to do your best. Friends would die for each other. Yes," he said. "Friends are the ultimate leverage."

"Shut up!"

But Night kept talking. "I was all too happy to watch the two of you grow closer. And even in the face of adversity, you two prevailed. Down to you begging me to speak up for her after what she did your final year of Academy. After that, I knew it was just a matter of time." He smiled coldly. "Much as it had been for that large Earth power, back during your Third Year. What was his name again? Samwise?"

"Samson," she whispered.

"Ah. Right. Samson. You gave him your heart, and then he went and died, didn't he? Such a shame." Still smiling, he shook his head. "But then you became perfectly malleable. Anything to make the pain stop. You threw yourself into your work. Such a good little girl you were. And think of how the last of your backbone would have snapped when your best friend in the whole wide world died also."

She squeezed her eyes shut.

"Iridium would be dead, and you'd have no emotional connection to anyone but me. You'd have done everything I would have told you to do, with no hesitation." He sighed. "But Iridium, she just wouldn't die when she should have."

Jet remembered that day in Fifth Year, when Iri had fallen to the street and Jet had called it in. Jet had followed procedure because that was what heroes did—she'd called it in, and Night had told her to leave Iri and file her report directly.

Night had told Jet to abandon her friend. And Jet, oh so eager to please, had complied.

"Worse than roaches when it comes to killing her," Night said.

Jet's eyes snapped open, and she glared at the man she'd admired for so long. "Sorry she spoiled things for you."

His smile twisted into a sneer. "You have no idea. First she didn't die, then she had to go and escape. And instead of you becoming the perfect machine, you had to become the perfect hero, and fight the good fight instead of fighting *my* fight. That little bitch cost me years of planning."

"Planning what?" Jet said, her voice dripping with scorn. "What's this master vision you've been working toward?"

"Why, the end of everything." His sneer stretched into a malefic grin . . . and then with a press of his hand, he shut off the lights.

No!

They started immediately—whispers, verbal caresses, teasing laughs. They touched her, probed her . . . wrapped her in silken, black arms.

"You see," Night said, "I'm going to blacken the sun."

Oh Light, he really is insane. She took a deep breath, held it, tried to ignore the way the voices were giggling.

"Today's the big day, Jet. And you're going to help me."

help him help him hear him ramble ramble in the dark

Eyes squeezed shut, she whispered, "I don't think so."

"We'll blot out the sun," he said, as if she hadn't spoken, "and the world will succumb to Shadow."

succumb succumb to Shadow sweet Shadow crunchy sweet

He kept speaking, his voice taking on the hypnotic tones of the Shadow, his words as compelling, as enthralling, as the dark whispers. "The normals will crawl away and die in the dark."

die die down in the dark

Don't listen to them!

"And the strongest of the extrahumans will have the entire world to rule as they see fit."

Over the voices, she hissed, "With you in charge, no doubt."

"I have no ambition to rule, Jet." She could sense him shrugging, even though she was blind in the dark. "I'd let you do so, if that was your desire. For me, freeing us of the shackles of Corp and the humans is enough."

Keep talking. The voices recede when you're talking.

"People don't shackle us. We help them."

"And it never stops, does it? We help them and help them, and they never learn. They never bother to take care of themselves, because we're always the ones who save them, again and again."

"We're supposed to," Jet said tightly. "We're heroes."

"We're their slaves!" The word echoed in the dark, and she heard a quick intake of breath, then the slow hiss of an exhale. "But no more. After today, we're done with them."

done done done with them all with them squeeze them hurt them feel them crunch

"You'd sentence billions of people to death," she shouted over the Shadow, "all because you don't want to serve as a superhero anymore?"

"They're only people." His words were like silk, flowing over the whispers in the dark. "If they're not strong enough to survive, they're not worthy."

The voices agreed with him.

Panting, Jet pushed them away—but they flowed around her, held her. Desperate, she said, "You're utterly mad. You're not powerful enough to Shadow the sun."

"Of course not. I repel light. That won't help at all. But you, on the other hand, absorb it."

Jet's stomach dropped to her knees. She swooned... and the Shadow caught her.

little girl little lamb lost little lamb

"Here's what will happen, Jet." His voice warped, distorted, and she wrenched herself out of the black grip of madness to focus on his words. "You don't have to think. Just let my machine guide you, aid you as you absorb the sun's light."

suck out the sun eat the light

"It will help you drain Iridium dry. And then you'll start to cast Shadow on the sun."

wrap her hold her hear her scream

"No." A soft denial, a sound almost like a sob as she bowed her head. "I won't do this."

"But you will," Night said—so close, whispering in her ear. "My machine will force you to do it. Of course, it would be better for you if I didn't have to force you. It would be better if you do what I tell you to do. And you will, won't you? I know you, Jet. You're a Shadow, just like me. You'll listen to me. You want to listen to me."

you're Shadow you're

Jet trembled, fury and despair warring in her heart as the Shadow reached up again to embrace her. "Stop," she whispered, either to the Shadow or to Night or to herself. "Don't do this."

A hand on her cheek, cold as death. Stroking her face. Lifting her chin. In the dark, she saw his teeth flash in a grin, heard him purr, "Do this, Joan."

do this

"Do this for me."

"I..."

"Do this."

do this

The blackness held her, rocked her, and she felt herself drifting.

When Night spoke again, his voice was cold, regal, and his words were not for her. "Eavesdropping is rude, Taser."

She tried to move, to turn her head, but the Shadow kept her still.

"Came back to bring Jet inside," Taser said, his voice faint. "But you and she were having such a nice heart-to-heart, I didn't want to interrupt."

"How considerate," Night said. "Take her. Strap her to the core of the machine. She won't fight you. She's lost to the Shadow."

Me, she thought dimly, *he's talking about me . . .*

Shhhh

She shushed.

"So, boss," Taser said. "You're planning on wiping out the entire world, huh? That'll really limit my opportunities."

"If you're strong, you'll survive. You may even rule."

"The thing is, I sort of like the sun where it is."

A flash, bursting through the darkness—a bolt of electricity, surging past Jet. An afterimage of Night deflecting the bolt, as if it had struck a shield.

"Oh," Night said, and Jet *heard* the grin in his voice, felt his insanity seep out of him, staining him like a shadow, "that was an incredibly stupid thing to do."

CHAPTER 62

IRIDIUM AND JET

*I've seen heroes fight villains, both extrahuman and the
normal sort. And I admit, it's always a rush to see these
small gods wielding their powers.*

Lynda Kidder, "Origins: Conclusion,"
New Chicago Tribune, June 18, 2112

IRIDIUM

Strapped to a huge machine, all Iridium could do was
watch—it was like she was in her childhood apartment all
over again, and again. A hero from Corp came through the
door and took everything.

But Night was no hero, not anymore.

Taser stumbled backward out of the cell. Night followed
him, spreading his hands wide to send a wave of Shadow
forward. It washed over Taser like a tide, and he gasped
for air as Night drove him to his knees, then shoved him
prone.

"Bow," Night said. "Beg."

Taser fought against him, much longer than Iridium

would have been able to against the Shadow. But soon enough he shuddered, then went still.

"Hey you," she shouted, "crazy man with the Jehovah complex! You don't think you can really get away with this, do you?"

Night turned away, ignoring her to brush his body armor with his palms as he returned to the cell. A moment later, he dragged Jet forward. She walked on rigid legs, her cheeks white and her eyes unfocused. She tripped over Taser's body, and she hesitated, looking down at him.

"Bruce ..." she murmured.

"Is not going to be bothering you again," Night soothed. "Come on, Joan. I've got you."

She held her ground, her gaze riveted on Taser. "You're insane," she said, her color rising again. "You're worse than my father. Worse than Everyman."

"Gee, you think?" Iridium said, straining against her bonds. The steel bands were too tight for her even to wiggle her fingers.

"Hush," Night said to Jet, and she quieted. He looked over at Iridium, shaking his head. "Oh, Calista." He sighed. "You never could sit still." Leaving Jet in her stun-cuffs, he walked up to the machine and unstrapped Iridium's hands.

Iridium fell on him, reaching for his throat and her power at the same time.

Bright lights exploded inside her skull as Night backhanded her across the face. She sprawled on the cold floor, and her power slipped away from her, like something elusive and wild rather than the familiar heat that lived at her core.

"Having some trouble?" Night whispered in her ear.

Iridium punched him, the blow glancing off the side of his skull. Night chuckled and kicked her in the gut. She tasted blood as she choked.

"Don't be so melodramatic," Night said, not unkindly. "You're tougher than that. And I'm counting on you to keep fighting. For Jet's sake."

Iridium looked up at Night, who smiled back implacably. The end of the world, and the son of a bitch was smiling at her. "Leave Jet out of this."

"I can't, I'm afraid. She's the only one who can siphon out your power and channel it through the Shadow generator." He sighed. "I've tried to feel sorry that you won't be around to see the result of your sacrifice. But then I figured, what will the world really be missing with you gone? It will certainly be a quieter, more genteel place."

"Screw you," Iridium said, trying to get up. "Go jerk off to the sound of your own voice some more."

"Proving my point yet again." He kicked her in the back, and she lay gasping on the floor, her strength gone, her power untouchable.

"Now, Joan." From the sound of his voice, he was walking away from Iridium. She tried to move, but her limbs protested. "It's time. Help me, and you will be free from Corp forever. You want to be free, don't you?"

"Free," she repeated, her voice faint.

"Jet, no!" Iridium wheezed, lifting up her head to look at her friend. "Don't do it! He'll just fuck you over!"

"Listen to my voice, Joan," Night said. "Do this for me."

A very long pause as Iridium held her breath.

When Jet finally spoke, her voice was crisp, if soft. Heroic. "No. I'll never help you do this."

Iridium wanted to cheer.

"Fine," Night sighed. "We do it the hard way." He grabbed Jet by her hair and pulled her to the machine Iridium had been strapped to, quickly freeing her from the stun-cuffs only to strap her hands in place on the machine. Jet didn't fight him.

Sprawled on the floor, Iridium watched what Night did.

He muttered to himself, turning to the control panel of his machine. "Never easy. Never just a simple, quiet plan." The cylinders inside the thing began to hum.

Iridium stayed still, content to let Night think he'd

cowed her for the moment. Weakness wasn't lying down—
it was refusing to get back up. And she kept on watching
him, trying to fathom what sort of code he was keying in to
the generator. His fingers were moving too fast for her to
make any sense out of it. Manic, nonsensical, compulsive
as he twisted dials and keyed in codes.

From what she saw, the machine consisted of two enormous cylinders wired together with a control matrix. She
tried to spot a weak point, anything she could exploit, but
the thing was a tangle of parts and wires only Night probably understood.

Hurting everywhere, Iridium lowered her head back to
the ground. For the moment.

JET

Just before the pain hit, Jet got her mind back enough to
distinctly think that she would make Night pay. He'd betrayed her far worse than Bruce, who'd been paid to do a
job; at her core, she understood the simple professionalism
behind it. And he'd betrayed her worlds worse than
Iridium—who, at least, had been true to her nature.

Night had betrayed her even more than Corp had. Than
her father had. Night had lied to her for years. Manipulated
her. Used her.

All because she was a Shadow power, doomed to go insane.

Like him.

She struggled against her bonds, but her hands were
clamped to some sort of machine. Her back was against
cold steel. And she felt weak as a kitten. For some reason,
that made her think of Lynda Kidder.

"Don't do this," she said, pushing aside her hatred and
her fear to try to empathize with the man. "Shadowing the
sun won't do anything but kill everyone! Even the extrahumans."

"Say what now?" Iridium gasped from where she lay on the floor. "You're kidding—you think you can destroy the sun?"

"Actually," Night said, pressing a button, "I can't. But Jet can. With your help."

"You're zooming on the Crazy Train. You know that, right?"

Iridium said something else, but Jet didn't hear her. She felt something reverberating in her mind, something cold. Hungry. And so very dark.

The voices stirred again. Stretched.

And reached for her.

No, she thought feverishly, pushing them down, *no, no no—*

night night forever night forever Shadow forever

"Night," Jet shouted, desperate, "this proves nothing! There won't be anyone left on a dark planet. None would survive the death of the sun. Not you, not me, not anyone. Don't you see that? It's not a question of the strongest surviving. It's genocide on a planetary scale!"

Night paused, and for a moment, Jet thought he would listen. The voices giggled and caressed her, and she bit back a moan.

But then Night shrugged and said, "So be it. If I can't survive the Shadow, then I'm not worthy, either. The Dark swallows all of us in the end."

He slammed his fist against another control. Heat shot through Jet, seared her alive.

And she screamed.

IRIDIUM

Iridium heard Jet scream, and for a few seconds she was cold. It was like lying in the snow and feeling all of her limbs go numb.

"Do it," Night said in a hypnotic cadence. "Take her life,

Joan. Blot out everything light and harsh about this sad, sick world."

The pain started, in Iridium's blood and her bones, as if ice spikes were being driven through every inch of her skin. Shadows wrapped around her legs, and her ears rang with the sounds of the cylinders screaming as they turned faster and faster.

"Harder, Joan," Night said. "Drink all of her light down. Take her life. It's what's demanded for a world where we don't have to be afraid."

Through the pain, through the growing darkness that seemed to spread throughout the old meditation room, a great clarity came over Iridium. Her body hurt, but her mind lifted away—much as it had when the Everyman stabbed her and she lay in the rain, feeling it wash her skin. She saw Jet, blurry and slumped inside the restraints connected to the generator.

Connected by . . . nothing.

Iridium moaned as the Shadows crawled over her. The generator was connected to nothing. None of the wires made sense; the cylinders that screamed but produced no power didn't make sense. The only thing working in the room was Night's calm, convincing voice.

"Kill her, Joan. She belongs to the Dark now. Just like us."

It was the machine that was the lie.

How many years had Jet listened to Night's voice? How much time had he invested in turning her friend into the perfect, programmable weapon?

"Kill her," Night singsonged. "She's your enemy. She's all that stands between you and silence."

Ignoring the Shadow wrapping tighter around her, Iridium levered herself up on one elbow. Agony seared her, making lines of light crawl across her vision. "Joannie," she said. "Joannie, please, you have to listen to me."

"Kill her," Night said.

"Joannie, don't do this." The cold deepened, and Iridium could see her breath puffing out with every gasp. "Stop!"

"I can't," Jet whispered.

"You can!"

"The Dark wants what it wants, Callie," Jet said dully. "The Dark swallows all of us in the end. That's the way of the world."

"This isn't the end," Iridium gritted. "This is only the end if you listen to *him,* Jet."

"It's the Shadows—oh, Light, they're eating me alive!" Her voice broke into a sob.

"Joannie," Iridium cried out, "this isn't you! This is Night, telling you the same lies he's told you since the day we came to the Academy!"

"Be quiet," Night hissed at her. "No one is listening to you anymore, you filthy mistake of nature."

"Oh, *I'm* the mistake?" Iridium gritted. "Who took an innocent little girl and turned her into a robot? Who's trying to reboot humanity by using her because he's too weak to do it himself?"

"Be QUIET!" Night thundered.

"Jet," she pleaded. "Come on, Joannie. You can do this. You stop. Tune him out."

"They're the only ones who are always with me," Jet groaned, "talking to me. Whispering. Laughing. Telling me things. And now they want out..."

"Who made them come out?" Iridium shouted. "Black out *him,* not the rest of us! You know who did this to you, Joan. You know that no machine is making you kill me! Stop it, now!"

"I can't..."

Iridium hollered, "For once in your life, show some fucking backbone!"

Jet shivered, bowed her head, and said nothing.

The cold worsened.

"She's beyond hearing you," Night sneered. "You're a failure, just like your father." His face appeared down a black tunnel, his white smile the only light in Iridium's world. "I am the only one who matters to Joan. And because I decree it, she will end your life. But don't feel too special. She's going to kill most everyone, I suspect."

"Jet," Iridium said weakly. "He's going to kill me, and you, and everyone else."

"Shadows," Jet whispered.

"He's lost to the voices," Iridium said desperately, her lips frozen. "I know about them, Jet. Joannie. I know you're not gone yet. Please. Stop listening to him!"

Night snarled, "You're going to listen to a half-dead rabid bitch? She's a liar, just like the rest of her family. She spread those lies about you at the Academy." He lowered his voice, saying, "You remember, Joan? The names people called you? The whispers? She never cared about you."

"Joannie . . . he's lying . . ."

Dimly, she saw Night approach Jet, stroke her cheek. He smiled at her, and said, "I'm the only one who cares about you."

Jet's body shook, then she looked at him.

And in that moment, Iridium felt the grip of the Shadow weaken, just a fraction.

"You're wrong," Iridium said to Night. She pulled herself up and stood tall as he turned to face her. "My father was a great man who protected the weak and the helpless when Corp abandoned them, and you know what he always, *always* did? He told the truth. I'm telling the truth. I cared about Joan, and still do. And you're a crazy son of a bitch."

She balled her fist and used the last of her strength to hit Night, so hard his goggles splintered. Night staggered, and Iridium did, too, falling to her knees.

"Kill her!" Night screamed, clawing at the glass embedded in his cheek.

"Break away, Joannie," Iridium said breathlessly. "You can do it..."

"Finish it," Night growled. "Bring the Darkness."

The wail of the Shadow void continued for a long moment, then Jet let out a shuddering sigh.

"I'm...not listening." The world began to lighten again. Jet glared at Night. "Not to anybody. Not anymore."

"Finish the job!" Night screamed at her. "Make them pay! Slaughter the weak and cleanse the world!"

"No," Jet said. "You've had your run, old man. Stand aside."

"Make me."

Jet closed her eyes, nostrils and tear ducts leaking blood, but the Shadows changed course, began to wrap themselves around Night.

"You can't stop me," he hissed, repelling her creepers with his own. "You're a weak little girl."

Abruptly, Night jerked as if he were in the throes of a cardiac episode, and collapsed.

"Blah, blah, *blah,*" Taser grunted, electricity dancing along his fingertips. "You people could talk through the end of the world."

JET

She stared at Night's prone form, at the sparks dancing over him like fairy lights. In her mind, the voices laughed, delighted.

yes yes all of them all in the dark forever forever and longer

Shut. Up.

"Help me up," Iridium gasped, "so I can finish him myself! I'm going to strobe his head off his freaking body!"

"Now, now, Iri," Bruce—Taser—chided, limping to her side. "You can't go killing people. That's supervillain prerogative, not Robin Hood's." As he extended his hand to Iri, Jet closed her eyes.

forever and longer

Go away!

and longer sweet Jet sweet Joan so sweet so succulent so

Away, she pleaded.

"Ow!"

Jet opened her eyes, saw Taser rubbing his nose and Iri shaking out her fist. "You're just damn lucky I don't kill you," Iridium snarled. "Coldcocking me! Using my own neural inhibitor on me!"

"They're illegal for a reason, darlin'."

"Ah, shut it. And get Jet out of there."

"I love a woman who's demanding."

so sweet listen to him crunch

No, she thought, *no, no, no . . .*

Yes.

Yes.

Taser limped over to her, paused before he touched her bonds. "Honey? No hard feelings I hope. I had a job to do."

"Oh," Jet said lightly as the voices laughed, "I understand."

His hands worked over her cuffs. She inhaled his scent, a mix of ozone and sweat and musk.

"I still say we kill him," Iridium said, crouching over Night's body. "Trying to destroy the world. Christo, how much more textbook villain could he be?"

"Don't kill him," Jet said, her voice sounding queerly faint to her own ears. "We'll get him locked away, in solitary. In the dark."

dark the dark alone in the dark alone

"I like it," Iridium said, standing, swaying slightly. Jet saw her form burst into a thousand stars, and she smiled at her friend, smiled to see how bright she was.

How she looked good enough to eat.

"Jet?" Bruce's voice, by her ear. "Honey? You okay?"

"Oh yes," she said, shivering from his very nearness. She could smell the light inside of him, dancing with life. "I'm fine."

And hungry.

He released the last of her restraints. She punched him in the jaw, hard. Didn't feel the sting in her knuckles from the connection.

"Ow! Christo!"

"Quit your crying," Iri said. "You deserved that."

"And more," Jet said sweetly. And she reached out with Shadow and blanketed Taser, hugged him tight. "No hard feelings, Bruce."

And then she started to squeeze the light out of him.

CHAPTER 63

IRIDIUM

But when the grand battle is done, and the dust has settled and all that's left are the photo ops and the meaningless, rote threats from the defeated, I feel oddly disappointed. Gods—even the small ones—shouldn't be reduced to photo ops.

Lynda Kidder, "Origins: Conclusion,"
New Chicago Tribune, June 18, 2112

Iridium watched Taser and Jet for a moment, seeing if Jet really planned to kill him. And yup, it sure looked that way.

"Joan," she said.

"He deserves this, Iri," Jet said, her voice flat and cold.

"Joan," Iridium said again, with more force. Under the shadows, Taser groaned and writhed as ice crystals blossomed on his skin like small spidery kiss marks.

"Hear me, Joan," Iridium said. "This isn't what you want to do."

"It *is*," Jet said. "He *used* me."

"He used me too." Iridium snorted. "You think I don't want to burn him from the inside out? But you don't kill, Joan. You're not like the other Shadows."

"I killed Lynda Kidder."

"That was self-defense, for crying out loud. You got set up. And stop being such a fucking martyr. You didn't see me crying over Paul Collins."

"He deserved it."

"But Taser doesn't," Iridium said. "He's an arrogant ass, but he was operating to code, and he *did* save your life."

"Technically, both of your lives..." Taser groaned through the Shadow.

"Button it!" she snapped. "Or maybe I'll let Joan kill you!"

Jet stared at Iridium, her eyes pure black. "My name isn't Joan," she whispered, "not anymore. I'm nothing. I'm all dark inside."

"Your name is Joan," Iridium insisted. "You're a Shadow power. But you control it, Joan, not the other way around. You're not a killer. You're not this."

A tear started to work down Jet's cheek, then froze. "How do you know that?"

"I know you," Iridium said quickly, calculating that Taser didn't have much time left. He was twitching feebly on the floor, overrun by creepers. "I know you're Joan, and no one else. Those voices can't tell who you are because they aren't real."

Jet went to her knees, hands pressed over her ears. "I don't want to hear them anymore!" she screamed, and with a full-body shudder, jerked the creepers away from Taser. They flowed over to her, washed over her own flesh.

"Oh, shit," Iridium said as Jet went limp, the creepers feasting on her warmth and light.

Iridium summoned a strobe and exploded it in Jet's face. Joan cried out as sunburn blossomed across her cheekbones and the bridge of her nose. "Stop that!" Iridium ordered.

"It's the only way to make them be quiet," said Jet dully.

"I can't live this way, Iri. I'm a time bomb, just like he said. It's better this way."

"Don't, Joan." Taser pulled himself to his feet with a groan, then said, "Killing yourself is doing Night's job. That's not what you want."

Jet's eyes filled with tears. "You stay away from me."

"Come on, Joan," Iri said. "I'm your friend. Let me help you."

"You've been a lousy friend," Jet whispered.

"I know. But I'm here now. Let me help you," she said, wrapping her arms around Jet.

With a shudder, Jet collapsed against her, sobbed against the front of her unikilt.

"Joan . . ." Taser said again.

Iridium raised her free hand, a miniature sun twisting and forming on her palm. "Fuck off, Taser or Bruce or whatever the hell your real name is. We don't need your help."

He glanced at her. "You do, if you want to get out of here."

"Yeah, right."

"Fine," Taser shrugged. "Have the conquering hero there call in the cavalry. Oh, right." He snapped his fingers, making sparks fly. "Ops is out of commission and every first-string hero in this city is trapped in the Rat Network. Besides, without the Happy Thought Machine whispering in their ear, I doubt any extrahumans in the greater New Chicago precinct are going to feel much like rescuing anyone's asses but their own."

He was right, damn it.

Iridium growled, "I assume you have a grand plan."

"Might have one rattling around the old head."

"What do you suggest?"

"Call the cops," said Taser. "Nice, simple solution. No superpowers involved." He stuck a commercial comm in his ear and tapped a police frequency.

As she held Jet, Iridium realized that this was going to get press coverage. There wouldn't be any way to keep the media in the dark, not about Night. One of Corp's shining examples was about to get ousted, forcefully.

She smiled. Her father would be proud.

"I suggest you two ladies vamoose," Taser said, "unless you want to explain to New Chicago's Finest exactly how you had nothing to do with Night's insidious plot, bwaha-haha."

"Come on, hero," Iridium said to Jet. "Let's move."

"Yes," Taser was saying behind them, "I need to report a 19-37 in progress at the Corp Academy. Me? Bruce Hunter, Mercenary Worker ID 42785."

"What happens now?" Jet asked Iridium as they slowly walked through corridors blurred by emergency lights and through an evacuation door with a crowd of other injured heroes.

"I don't know about you," Iridium said as the steel sky of New Chicago rolled out before them, "but I could use a cocktail."

EPILOGUE

Sometimes, I wish I, too, could be a little extra. But mostly, I'm deeply satisfied with who I am. I wonder if the same could be said for our small gods, our extrahuman protectors. Our heroes.

Lynda Kidder, "Origins: Conclusion,"
New Chicago Tribune, June 18, 2112

IRIDIUM

Boxer put down the greasy bag of takeout at Iridium's elbow. "Two extralarge beef tacos and a cheese quesadilla. No guacamole, no pico. Just how you like it."

"Thanks," Iridium murmured. Her bandages were starting to itch. The synthesized skin around the edges pinked as it melted into her own skin. Soon it would be like all the cuts and scrapes had never happened.

Even the wound Taser's blow had caused was gone.

"Want to hear something weird?" Boxer said. "I got a call earlier from my nephew—the one you were in school with. He wants to 'talk.' He was yammering on about making amends, how you never turn your back on family. Think he's finally lost his nut?"

"No," she said, taking a taco out of the bag. "Just the opposite. You should talk to him."

Boxer lifted one shoulder in a shrug. "Never had much use for the kid, but I guess it couldn't hurt."

The door chime sounded at the front of the warehouse, and Boxer's pistol appeared in his hand. "Stay put," he ordered Iridium.

"Christo, Boxer," Iridium said, pulling her weary body to her feet. "Like that thing is going to put a dent in anyone who comes to *my* door."

The taillights of a Package Express hover pulled away as Iridium rolled the door back. A small metal box covered in shipping stamps sat at her feet.

"Think it's a bomb?" Boxer asked.

"I think that right now, we're the safest we've probably ever been," Iridium said. She looked toward downtown, where smoke and emergency hovers were still flitting through the spotlit night sky underneath the pollution layer.

She picked up the box and unlatched the lid. Boxer whistled as the small silver object inside gleamed under the streetlights. "Is that your neural inhibitor?"

Iridium felt cold, then her cheeks flushed. "That cocky bastard," she muttered, fishing out the card at the bottom.

> *Thought you might want this back. Consider it a*
> *souvenir of our time together. See you soon. —T*

"Not if I see you first," Iridium muttered, tossing the box onto her workbench, then she strode back to eat her dinner.

"So," Boxer said, following her and helping himself to half her quesadilla. "You didn't get the guy, you didn't get the cash, you didn't get Corp off your ass—what was the point of this, again?"

"Saved the world," Iridium mumbled around her taco.

"Oh. Right."

They ate in silence. It wasn't until Iridium crumpled up the paper bag and strobed it to ash that Boxer said, "So . . . is she coming after you still? Jet? You didn't tell me how things ended there."

"They didn't," Iridium said. "But no, Boxer—I don't think we have to jump at shadows." She laughed. "In fact, give it a few months, and I bet our Joannie will be walking over to the dark side."

"I don't buy it," said Boxer. "Corp had its hooks into her so deep they came out the other side."

"Oh, but that's the trick," she said. "They kept her locked down so tight because she was the most dangerous, out of all of us."

She smiled at Boxer and pushed back from the table, going over to the windows and watching the burning skyline. "Give it time, Boxer. I promise, sooner or later, Jet will be one of us."

JET

"So that's everything," Meteorite said, sipping her latte.

Jet pursed her lips as she stirred her Earl Grey. "When are you due back?"

"One more hour." Meteorite barked out a laugh. "Like that's enough time for me to catch up on any sleep."

When Jet had called her earlier that morning and asked to meet at the mall, the other woman had been harried, shell-shocked, from almost thirty straight hours of damage control. Keeping the media out of the Academy attack and the stranded Squadron members in the tunnels had been a Herculean feat, one that was still ongoing. It had been utter insanity, Meteorite told her; there'd been no time to question anything, like what in the never-ending Darkness had actually happened.

And that was all before Meteorite had fielded the vidcall from Police Commissioner Wagner, who had a stunned Night on his hands and a licensed merc's video report about how the Shadow power had tried to destroy the world. "Then," Meteorite had said, "all hell broke loose."

Jet completely understood.

Meteorite told her that she'd still be chained to her computer even now, if not for Frostbite. He'd worked his own sort of computer magic and gotten her a two-hour break. Told her to get some sleep. Instead, she'd come to see Jet. "Had to know why you'd called on a restricted line to ask for a private meeting in a public spot," she'd told Jet when she'd arrived.

So Jet had bought her a cup of coffee, and told her a story about an organization that brainwashed extrahumans into being Academy-approved heroes. She didn't— couldn't—use the organization names. But she got the gist across.

After the weight of her words had sunk in, Meteorite cursed Corp in three languages and a variety of colors.

And damn it all, Jet had cringed with every profanity, had bitten back on defending the organization that had screwed with her mind for ten years.

Then, as if to make up to Jet for all the wrongs that Corp had done to her and the others, Meteorite told her what had happened when Ops went down.

Simply put: chaos.

"After the Squadron burst out of the tunnels, half of them nearly went full-out rabid right there, and the other half acted like their thumbs were jammed up their asses. Only three of them still played the hero card without Corp's lovefest blasting in their brains." Her voice soured on the last words, understandably.

Jet stilled, absorbing Meteorite's words. Out of all the Squadron—out of hundreds of active heroes—only three had remained true.

Were the others just angry—justifiably angry—at how they'd been manipulated, brainwashed, by Corp all of their lives? Or were the extrahumans being true to a nature that they'd never had a chance to experience before?

Martin Moore whispered in her mind: *How many extrahumans would it take to rule the world? To crush humanity under its feet?*

At the time, Jet had scoffed, saying that the heroes wouldn't do that.

Moore's words, plaintive and terrifying: *But if, one day, you decided to do just that—say, that internal wiring of yours melts and leaves you more likely to, shall we say, wreak havoc—what could we humble civilians possibly do against you?*

She took a breath, held it. Wondered if Corp had been doing the right thing all along.

Jet exhaled slowly. It didn't matter. As long as some of them—even if it was only three—still fought the good fight, they had a chance to still do the right thing. To still be heroes.

"Let me guess," Jet said, sipping tea. "Steele's still a card-carrying good guy."

"Absolutely. So's Firebug."

"Makes sense." Partners tended to feel the same way about missions. About everything that mattered. Jet frowned, thought of Iridium.

"And get this: Hornblower."

Jet raised her brows—which felt so strange without her cowl pressing against them. "You're joking."

"Nope. Tyler Taft, hero at large." Meteorite shook her head. "His uncle would kill him if he did anything otherwise."

"Probably. So what's Corp planning, now that they've got the beginnings of an extrahuman revolt on their hands?"

The other woman stared glumly at her coffee. "Gearing

up for war. They've already got PR working the press." Her face paled, and she whispered, "I've heard other things, rumors. Stuff that would make you green."

"Everyman," Jet said quietly, thinking of the serum that had warped Lynda Kidder into a monster, remembering Moore shouting that they wouldn't be easy meat for the extrahumans.

Meteorite blinked. "How did you . . ."

"Doesn't matter." She blew out a sigh, pushed Lynda Kidder and Martin Moore out of her mind. "This is bad."

"Corp did it to themselves," Meteorite said, her voice a hiss. "Let Corp fix it."

They would, Jet knew. Organizations like Corp didn't take things like all-out revolution lying down. They'd contain it, control it, and dismantle it. And all the while, spin it to the media, and have the civilians eating it up with a spork.

Unless Everyman struck first.

Or any of the Squadron truly went rabid.

"When you get back on duty," Jet said, rising to her feet, "you get word to Steele. Let her know that I'll be there as soon as I can."

"You're going back," Meteorite said, horrified. "After everything they've done to you, you're going back. For the love of heaven, why?"

Part of it was because Night made all of this happen, and Jet had played a part in that. Part of it was because Night was right: Even after all this time, Jet was still weak. She had to prove to herself that she could be strong, could stand without anyone supporting her—not Night, not the Academy, or Corp.

Not Iridium.

What she said was, "I'm a hero."

She turned away and strode out of the coffee shop, then summoned a Shadow floater and sped off into the night.

ABOUT THE AUTHORS

JACKIE KESSLER used to run around in Wonder Woman Underoos and watch *Challenge of the Super Friends*. Now she watches superhero cartoons with her kids. Jackie's superpower is stamina: She survived pitching one thousand beloved comic books after a battle with a flooded basement. (Comic books, contrary to popular belief, are not waterproof.) When not writing about superheroes and the villains who beat the heroes into a bloody mess, she likes to write about demons. For more about Jackie, visit her website: www.jackiekessler.com.

CAITLIN KITTREDGE is an avid comic book reader and superhero fan, ever since she picked up a copy of *The Dark Knight Returns* at age fifteen. She once painted herself blue and went to a Halloween party as the X-Men's Mystique. She's worked as a game designer, phone psychic, and hot-dog-on-a-stick girl, and currently writes full-time near Seattle, Washington, surrounded by books, cats, and action figures. Her other novels include the popular Nocturne City and Black London series and the Iron Codex trilogy for young adults. Visit her online at www.caitlinkittredge.com.

*And don't miss the further adventures
of Iridium and Jet . . .*

New Chicago is bursting at the seams, and the violence
is starting to spread. But it's not just any violence—it's
extrahuman violence: superheroes gone mad, no
longer brainwashed slaves to Corp-Co.

And when superheroes are the cause of mayhem,
it's up to the forces of chaos to rein them back in.

*For when the answers that were once so
black and white get blurred, you get . . .*

SHADES OF GRAY

by
Jackie Kessler *and*
Caitlin Kittredge

A Spectra Trade Paperback
July 2010